Sometimes Towards Eden

Sandra Riley

RILEY HALL
Miami, Florida

ALSO BY SANDRA RILEY

The Greenbear Chronicles
Homeward Bound: A History of the Bahama Islands to 1850
The Lucayans
Sisters of the Sea: Anne Bonny and Mary Read, Pirates of the Caribbean
Stone Poems / Wotai: Help on the Way

SOMETIMES TOWARD EDEN

Library of Congress Cataloguing-in-Publication data
available upon request.

RILEY HALL PUBLISHING
6501 SW 62ND COURT
Miami FL 33143 USA
rileyhall@bellsouth.net

ISBN 0-9665310-5-1

First Edition 1986
Second Printing May 2005

Printed in the United States of America.

Acknowledgement

Her trial in Jamaica in 1720 was the last recorded event in Anne Bonny's life. Daniel DeFoe states in his *History of the Pyrates* that she was not hanged. If Anne had remained in Jamaica, she may have participated in the historical happenings which take place in this novel between the years 1730-1742. I wish to thank my friends and associates who helped me discover and shape these events: Floyd Afflick, Sharon Cleare, Captain Don Henry, Terry Herlihy, Pat and Neil Kilgore, Diane Machado, Liz Mazzie, Oscar Seigle and especially Sylvia Heller, Bonnie Hance, and Peggy Hall.

Acknowledgement

Family Genealogies

Mary Read — Tobias Sampson
Matt (10)*

Will O'Brannon — Mary

Jack Rackam — Anne Bonny — Baldwin Sommerwood

Colin (9)   William Thomas (9)   Mary Elizabeth (8)

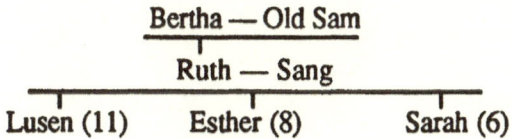

Bertha — Old Sam
Ruth — Sang

Lusen (11)   Esther (8)   Sarah (6)

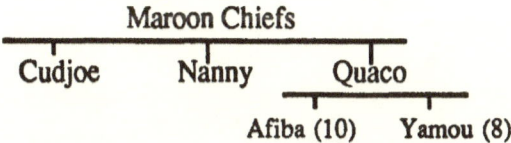

Maroon Chiefs

Cudjoe   Nanny   Quaco

Afiba (10)   Yamou (8)

*Ages of children in 1730.

Prologue

Ten years ago, pirates Anne Bonny and Mary Read were captured, along with their captain Calico Jack Rackam, in the Bay of Negril, known after that day as Bloody Bay because of the battle that ensued there. Tried and convicted of piracy, Anne and Mary were imprisoned at Spanish Town, Jamaica to await execution by hanging. Both women, pregnant at this time, were given a stay until after they were delivered. Mary died of a fever shortly after the birth of her son Matt. At the loss of her friend Anne despaired. The intensity of their relationship left an unfathomable void within Anne.

Baldwin Sommerwood, Anne's childhood friend, planter and barrister, worked to free both women. He promised Anne to raise Mary's son and her own child if his efforts failed. Shortly before Anne's confinement, the notorious pirate Black Bart anchored at Port Royal and demanded the release of his former helmsman Matt Read. Disguised as a man, Mary had shipped with him in the Caribbean before joining Rackam's crew in the Bahamas. Governor Lawes, weary of Baldwin's persistence and intimidated by the pirate's force, released Anne on the condition that she persuade Black Bart to leave the harbor.

Anne met the pirate and told him of Mary's death. Bart was saddened by the news and surprised that one of his bravest pirates had been a woman. That day, when Black Bart weighed anchor and sailed away from Jamaica, Anne sailed with Baldwin to his sugar plantation at St. Thomas-in-the-East, Jamaica. They married, had two children, and raised Mary's son Matt and Anne's son by Jack Rackam. Here, at Hill Haven, in the valley of the Blue Mountains, Anne had realized the dawning of a new Eden until one night . . . .

PART I

1730—1734

Maroon Wars

" . . . thunder
Winged with red lightning"
—*Paradise Lost I*, 174-5

CHAPTER ONE

Plantation Raid

The night seemed peaceful in the valley of the Blue Mountains. The wind had long since shifted to the west. Anne listened. The flapping of coconut palm leaves dominated the sounds coming from the variety of wood surrounding Hill Haven. Another night she might have isolated the voices of each tree—fustic, cedar, bamboo. She might have tried to catch the fragrance of each flower or to savor every herb from the garden, but not this night. An eerie quiet prevailed. The floor of the gallery gleamed white like a dead sea beneath the face of the moon. Anne left her desk and walked outside.

There was no music.

The plaintive, distant song escaping from the huts in the slave quarters which Anne had come to know as the soft texture of the Jamaican night was absent. Staring far out over the hills, Anne studied the silence.

Suddenly she felt aware of distant movement; motion which sounded like trees rustling in the wind, but was not. Anne leaned over the railing and strained to locate the danger she had sensed but could not see or hear.

If Anne could have seen far enough into the dense wood, she would have seen only what appeared to be more dense wood. Shapes without color or dimension moved slowly, winding along the narrow path, gliding down, down the mountain. No branch twisted, no twig broke, no leaf fluttered. The spongy earth embraced, then released, footfall after footfall. No owl hooted, no bird twittered, no cricket sang. Only the breeze whispered through the tall trees.

Everyone listened.

Suddenly a wall of fire leaped into the valley at the far end of the pastures. Anne hurried into her room to find the weapon concealed in the false bottom of her trunk. Only for a moment did the Spanish sword feel strange in her hand. Riotous thoughts flashed through her mind, and images of past horrors and familiar sorrows mingled with her present comfort and peace. She felt confusion, conflict, anger, but no fear. And yet her legs tingled as if she stood on a precipice looking down. Her fingers tightened on the sword hilt as she rushed into her daughter's room.

Anne shook the negro woman lying asleep on a cot between the two small girls.

"Ruth, wake up, wake up!"

Ruth's large eyes opened on the blade an instant before they shifted to Anne's face and she swallowed a gasp.

"Come."

Almost before Ruth could straighten her long, stiff body, Anne grabbed the woman's hand and whispered, "Come out to the gallery quickly."

"Why? What wrong, Miz Anne?"

The wall of fire had splintered and seemed to be moving now in the direction of the house.

"Those fires. Do they mean what I fear?"

"Maroons!" Her hand flew to her mouth. "We dead, Miz Anne!"

"Nonsense. Take the children and hide in the step-down well. I'll go to the quarters and get help."

"Dose boys no he'p you. Koromantyns be African warriors; dey run off ta da mountains. Mama say long time back . . ."

Anne was already in the boys' room. She lifted Sarah, Ruth's littlest child from between her boys. "Don't cry, little one. Ruth, fetch the girls. Colin, Matt, get up!" The boys groaned and rolled over. "Get up now!" Anne pulled the bedclothes out from under them. "Here, take Sarah, wrap these blankets around her."

Ruth hurried Mary Elizabeth and her own Esther into

the boys' room. Mary focused on the sword in her mother's hand.Her mouth opened but Ruth buried Mary's head in her bosom to stifle her scream. Esther clung to her mother.

Anne shifted her sword hand behind her back and rested her free hand against her daughter's forehead, then swept her eyes over the other children. "Ruth, where is your Lusen?"

"He in da quarters wid Bertha and Ole Sam. Dey know where ta hide."

Matt's eyes blinked wide. "Why? What's happening?"

"Please, Matt. There's trouble. Just do as I tell you. Ruth, hurry."

"Cum wid us, Missus. You can't fight by yo'se'f."

"I'm staying with you," Matt insisted with all the authority of his ten years.

"No, you will not!"

"That's mother's sword. This is no small trouble." As he snatched the hilt out of Anne's hand, the point of the heavy weapon dropped and stuck into the floor.

Stunned, Anne saw a youthful likeness of her friend Mary Read struggling to wrestle the sword out of the wood. "Look, Matt. Your mother and I could always take care of ourselves. She would want you to protect my daughter now."

"Yes, but ..." He searched Anne's face for any sign that might allow him to stay, but could see that further protests would be useless.

"Matt, go now! Hide in the well. I'll come soon. Ruth, hurry, please."

Believing she would never see her mistress alive again, Ruth bade farewell to Anne with her eyes. Matt put his arm around Mary Elizabeth and took Esther's hand.

They were gone.

In the outer reaches of the pastures brush fires blazed. Tall muscular figures drifted in and out of the flickering light, feeding their woody garments to the flames. Naked men built torches while a stately presence tented in a striped robe watched and waited. A black fist, clutching the

Maroon horn, thrust up from a wide sleeve high into the air.

"*Quememos! Quema la cana!* Kill cattle! Take our people!"

Great shouts split the air as the band dispersed, some to torch row after row of tall cane, others to ruin the muscovado stored in the three outbuildings. Flames licked then entered the raw sugar soaked in molasses like a hoary bridegroom his virgin bride. A sickening stench filled the air.

In a horse pasture, sharp cutlasses sliced delicate legs and massive bodies crashed to the ground. Gashed throats cut off high-pitched cries. In another meadow, gnarled clubs cracked skulls and incised bellies calved prematurely. Deep groans issued all around as sharp knives scalped the heads of several bulls. Laughing and shouting, some of the men tied the bloody hats to their heads with vines.

"See! See! *Toro! Toro!*"

The horned men paired off while others with torches formed a wide circle around them. A prologue of taunts and feints led to one or two dangerous passes that inspired the circle of men to chant encouragement. The black bulls pawed the ground, snorted, shot forward, locked horns, bumped and butted. Soon their actions took on the character of a savage ballet. The warriors spontaneously choreographed their powerful frenzy to the rhythm of the chant. Sweat mixed with animal blood dripped down their twisted faces. The chanters watched the gory features of the dancers change from one fierce expression to another. Unnoticed the robed leader appeared in the center of this beastly dance. The chanting ceased and all dropped to the ground, submissive to their commander.

The tall figure sounded the battle cry through the abeng, then cried, "*Atta! Atta!*"

Torch bearers and horned men gathered up their weapons. Most moved off in the direction of the slave quarters. A small party headed for the great house.

Sword in hand, Anne moved near where the wide stone

steps of the veranda spilled down to the carriage circle. The fires were in front of her; the well, refuge for Ruth and the children, far behind. The stench of burning muscovado weakened her resolve. Her mind demanded retreat but her boots riveted themselves to the wooden floor and her thoughts burst like cannonade in her head.

What bravado is this? 'Tis foolhardy. I know not the size or strength of my enemy, weapons, manner of warfare—nothing. I could be cut down where I stand. Anne retreated behind one of the stone pillars of the portico. My enemy is lurking out there somewhere. But where? Anne rubbed her cambric blouse between her breasts, drew her sleeve across her brow and stroked her sweaty palms down the legs of her riding breeches to dry them. I thought I had conquered every fear. Why must there always be one more? Her sword whistled through empty air as Anne swung around in the direction of a sound behind her. A leaf of the potted fern scratched against another leaf. Do they deliberately tax my thin patience? Fighting was simpler in my pirating days—you boarded or they boarded—no hiding behind bushes, sneaking along hedgerows, leaping out of trees. If only Mary were here, she would have a plan. Anne's clammy palm opened and closed over the hilt of Mary's sword. Be with me, Mary, she prayed. Help me save our children.

Shifting from tree to tree, bush to bush, the small band of Maroons approached the great house. Anne's eyes leaped from cotton tree to cotton tree, for to her mind they were the best hiding places in the yard. Yet she knew to expect the unexpected. Island legends say ghosts inhabit the massive trunks; the invaders would avoid those trees. Where then would they hide?

The only approach to the veranda was up the high front steps. When she turned toward the yard again, her eye caught the glint of steel in several different places—five, maybe six men, no more, not the force she had anticipated. Intent on the occasional flashes of light, Anne wondered: will they brave these steps or no? And when we meet, what then? I lack practice. Parry. Thrust. In her mind her muscles responded.

Confident that no one was about, the warriors marched up the steps. They had spaced themselves at intervals across the width of the stairs and were speaking to one another in a strange mixture of Spanish and broken English.

"*Fuego* ta de *casa*. Kill de *mujeres*."

Understanding their design, Anne thought, not this house, not this woman, you bloody bastards.

The stairs narrowed near the top; five naked men, armed with knives and cutlasses, were midway.

She inhaled the sticky night and reassured herself. Five. 'Tis not so many.

Anne sprang from behind the pillar to surprise the man on the end, ran him through, then took up his torch. Although dangerously close to the edge, Anne placed her back to the side of the staircase. Through her thick boot she could feel the low stone railing against her calf.

Recovering from his initial surprise, another man lunged at her. As Anne feinted to one side, he fell off the stairs to the ground twenty feet below. The others, insensitive to the fate of their fellows, laughed and pointed at Anne's body, then poked with their cutlasses at her privates. Her long red-gold hair tossed free of its tie, fell across her eyes. Partially blinded Anne could only deflect some of the jabs to her hips, thighs and breasts. She beat down on their weapons. Their playful thrusts nicked her body and she could feel the cambric stick to the blood at her waist.

"Dis womon fight like Nanny." Their black eyes glistened and teeth flashed through their laughter. Aroused beyond fear or care of their dead, the warriors dropped their weapons and fingered their penises.

"Huh! Womon, you like?" Each man tried to outdo the other. "Cum! Cum! We take ta mountain. Good. You see!"

Her eyes riveted to one enormous erection, Anne slashed out with her sword. The man did not realize he had been hit until he looked down at his bleeding belly. Then he dropped to his knees, clutching what was left of his penis in his fist. This action sobered the other two who scrambled for their weapons.

" 'Nuff, *mujer. Tenemos ahora.* We fix!"

It was not their savage words but the Spanish in which they were spoken that triggered Anne's fury. A maniacal energy leaped through the muscles of Anne's right arm. Her sword sliced the words of the approaching warrior. For an instant she and the other man watched the head bounce down the steps, before he sprang down the staircase past the head, and ran toward the mountains, never looking back.

The man holding his bloody parts cried out his pain and indignation and fear. "Nanny! Nanny!"

From her hiding place Ruth heard the dreadful cries and wondered if Master Baldwin had returned home to find his plantation house in flames and his woman dead. She drew the frightened children close to her bosom.

The Maroons, along with their new recruits, were already picking their way up the mountain and did not hear the cry. The plantation slaves trying to douse the fires in their huts heard it. And someone else heard it. Anne moved closer to the suffering man. She knew she would kill him if it came to that. In desperation he snatched up a cutlass and lunged.

"Debil womon!"

Missing his mark, he lost his balance and plunged down the stairs to land broken at the feet of the robed giant. Clutching the striped garment, the man whispered something which Anne could not hear, then fell back, dead. The figure stepped over the body and holding up the skirt of the robe with one hand, the abeng poised in the other, mounted the steps. Anne stumbled backwards up to the veranda. Unable to distinguish any facial feature, Anne could see only the whites of the eyes glaring out of the thick black face. The dropped sleeve exposed a muscular arm, the abeng poised to crack her skull.

Anne picked up a burning torch. When they were within sword's length of each other, Anne eyed the long scar which ran from under the right eye down to the jaw. Intent on the face before her, she almost took a blow to her left shoulder but managed to bring her torch up under the massive arm in time. Flesh burned; the arm flew back and the horn clanked down the staircase. Anne's sword only grazed the thick waist before a vise-like grip upon her wrist forced Anne to drop her weapon. Two powerful hands clamped around her neck, latched under Anne's chin, and lifted her off the ground to bring her eyes level with those black eyes fixed on her almost seven feet above the floor of the porch.

As a ship descries a sail, each saw her own womanly reflection dwarfed and distorted in the eyes of the other.

"You, womon, hab done dis ting?" said the warrior in harsh and disbelieving tones which were unmistakably female.

The pressure of the thick black thumbs against her larynx prevented Anne's speech. As the Maroon tightened her strangle hold, the giant felt her own throat constrict, and her massive chest tighten; she felt as though her brain would burst.

The next thing Anne knew was the sensation of her body hurtling through space. She landed, minutes later it seemed, several feet away.

The huge woman gulped great drafts of air. Anne could see her shoulders heave when she turned, descended the stairs and lifted the dead man into her arms, striding away into the night.

The judge's voice echoed and reechoed in the hollowness of a gigantic room. The twisted faces of the onlookers were distorted with hatred and malicious gloating as he pronounced the sentence. The room had no walls, no windows, only edges of light which expanded and contracted as the words continued.

"Witness, at this High Court of Admiralty held at the town of St. Jago de la Vega in the island of Jamaica on the twenty-eight day of November in the year of our Lord seventeen hundred and twenty, in the seventh year of the reign of our Sovereign Lord, George, by the Grace of God, of Great Britain, France, and Ireland, King, and of Jamaica, Defender of the Faith, and so forth. The sentence pronounced against Mary Read, and Anne Bonny, alias Bonn, late of the island of New Providence, spinsters, for piracies, felonies, and robberies committed by them on the High Sea, and within the jurisdiction of this court, viz.

"You, Mary Read and Anne Bonny, alias Bonn, are to go from hence to the place from whence you came and from thence to the place of execution; where you shall be severally hanged by the neck, 'till you are severally dead. . . ."

"No!"

Anne gasped and sat bolt upright. Allowing herself only a moment to recover she swung her legs out of bed. Her foot touched cold steel and she shuddered even before she looked down at the bloody sword; its significance seemed to compound the dream lingering in her pounding head. She shook her dressing gown before throwing it over her shoulders. A scorpion lurking in the folds dropped to the floor and slipped under the writing desk unnoticed. Anne stepped outside and paced the gallery in an effort to clear her troubled mind. She never remembered the whole of the nightmare, only this last part, and of that, every word. Over and over, the same flat words, the same hollow voice, the same twisted, faceless mouth loomed in her mind and shattered her sleep.

How long ago since I had this nightmare? Every night in the Spanish Town jail, after Mary died. But that was ten years ago. Never here till now. Oh, yes, the night William Thomas was born. Why then? But not since. Why now?

Anne looked out over the emerald sea and felt alone. Pirating days, days of freedom, days of adventure—did she long for them still? As the sun mounted ever higher, the breezes fresh from the east played in her hair. Anne turned to face the Blue Mountains. Her eyes swept the range with its irregular shapes, gentle slopes and rugged grades—a limited rainbow of green, green-blue, blue and blue-purple.

Always those mountains had meant beauty, given security and comfort to her and Baldwin, symbolizing a winding down of life. Now they meant fear, offered horrors and dangers, threatened her peaceful life. Her nerves felt like the hoops in an overwound watch incapable of ease until time slackened its hold.

Anne picked at the peeling paint on one of the shutters. "Hanged by the neck ..." Spared from hanging a second time. Did that giant woman spare my life only to torture me? Oh how clearly I feel the noose around my neck in my nightmare, but last night hanging from those giant hands I felt no pain, no fear. I knew she would not kill me, not then. I feel death surround me, but I cannot die now. I want to see my children grown. She kicked at the green flecks which littered the gallery. One thing is sure, we can no longer live peacefully in the shadow of this mountain. Must I bloody my sword once more to protect my family? Her hand crossed her body to her hip, but her fingers found no weapon, only the soft silk of her gown. She went inside.

Sinking down at her writing table, Anne let her glance rest on the remarkable blue and green grain of the Blue Mahoe, a special wood that echoed the blue-green of her eyes, Baldwin had said, when he presented her with the gift on their fifth anniversary. Then Anne fingered the raised letters of the portfolio--ANNE BONNY. She had been pleased with this gift made by her husband from hides manufactured on the plantation but angered that he had not put her married name on it. "The world knows you as Anne Bonny," he had said. Opening the cover, Anne's eyes fell on the letter to her father begun the day old John Sommerwood left with her son for Charles Town. Anne had intended to send the letter with her father-in-law but could not bring herself to finish it.

The words stared up at her.

"Dear Father. The world thinks I am dead and in a way 'tis true. Anne Bonny is no more, but your daughter Anne O'Brannon, now Sommerwood, lives in Jamaica and begs your forgiveness. I am sending this letter with your old friend and my young son, your namesake. William Thomas at nine is not so hard to handle as I was, I'll warrant. He keeps himself to himself, but be wary ..." Anne's hand flattened on the paper, her fingers ready to crumple the letter.

No, she thought. I have begun this letter a hundred times these past ten years; this time I must finish it. How I wish I could see him. Since last night ... I ... he must know the truth about me and my son. She scratched out everything after forgiveness. Dipping the quill in the crystal inkwell, she continued in a shaky hand.

"By now you know William Thomas. I had to send him away. I know not how to deal with him and can hardly stand the sight of him. There is evil in him which could not have come from Baldwin, only myself. Watching him makes me afraid of myself, unsure of myself, doubt my strength, even hate myself.

"There were two sweet babies in this house when he was born. Matt, Mary Read's son, and Colin, my child with Jack Rackam, only months apart in age. Baldwin loves them both and raises them as his own. William came within a year of Colin. It was November and the rainy season here. I was miserable. My dear Ruth, more friend and mother than servant, saw me through a difficult confinement. I wanted to die; moreover I wanted the child to die, but I don't know why. How can a mother say such things? I know you must think me cruel. Can you help him and help me to understand him? I was spirited, even wild, but not evil. There is evil in him, evil I sensed when he lived in my womb.

"Baldwin and I have a daughter too. She is eight. I would have sent her along for she is a gentle, caring girl, but I did not wish to burden old Mr. Sommerwood with the filly when I knew he would need both hands to handle the reins of the colt. We consider Ruth's three children part of our family, too. Esther, her middle child, was born only weeks after Mary Elizabeth. I nursed both babies 'til Ruth gained back her strength. Lusen, her oldest, is only eleven but looks after our boys and girls as well as Little Sarah, the baby of both our families.

"I had no children by James Bonny. He was every inch as worthless as you said he was. I left him and our marriage unconsummated in Nassau. Only his name I kept, a name I made infamous throughout the Caribbean, much to your displeasure and my shame.

"I don't know what you heard about my trial in Spanish Town. There is a book, written by a Captain Charles Johnson, entitled a *General History of the Robberies and Murders of the Most Notorious Pyrates with the Remarkable Actions and Adventures of the Two Female Pyrates, Mary Read and Anne Bonny*. I must say the story is somewhat true in that our adventures were remarkable; but you must believe me, Father, I never did commit wilful murder in my life and I have suffered for my deeds in ways the history books will never know.

"I do not know this Captain Johnson, but he never sailed the Caribbean waters in my day. He is an imposter and no true recorder of history if he must take the word of the rabble who witnessed our hearing in Jamaica. The court would hear no excuses for our actions. The Admiralty stepped over our good deeds as they would piles of manure. No man will ever know how I felt standing in that courtroom. Moreover, no man could ever tell the story of what followed.

"Herein is the true account of my days in prison. Both myself and Mary Read were sentenced to hang, but our deaths were to be delayed until our children were born. Mary died in prison and I managed to cheat the hangman so that I could care for Matt and Colin. This story is for your eyes alone, dear father, no other."

When Anne finished her account, she added fond endearments to her father, boldly signed the name, "Anne Bonny," and snapped shut the silver lid on the ink well.

Dressed in fresh muslin blouse and riding breeches,

Anne went out to inspect the last night's devastation. The stench of burnt muscovado lingered in the air. Descending the great stone stairs, she saw no bodies, not even a trace of blood; Ruth had seen to that. Her chestnut gelding stood next to one of the stone pillars on the edge of the carriage circle, munching a clump of grass and stamping impatiently. At the foot of the stairs Anne's eyes fell on the horn the giant woman had let drop. She picked it up to examine it closely. It was heavy and smooth to her touch. One blow in the right place she thought and shuddered. I must send that letter to father; I may not live to see him again. Anne placed the horn in her saddle bag, swung up and rode off in the direction of the negro houses.

Like other plantations in St. Thomas-in-the-East, the Sommerwood estate stretched in the valley like a small village. The sugarworks clustered below hills, some clothed in cane, others in logwood. Boiling houses, distilleries, overseer's house, even a hospital lay dwarfed amid giant cotton trees. Outbuildings used for storage and the tanning houses adjoined pastures, hog pens and guinea corn fields. The long range of negro houses bordered the river. Coconut trees surrounded gardens and neatly built stone houses with thatched roofs. Bamboo hung over the riverbed like giant plumes, making this place one of the most picturesque on the estate.

The settlement seemed deserted except for a few men cutting palm thatch for new roofs. Then Anne saw an old grandmother dousing a heap of smoldering thatch in the yard of her house and heard the laughter of children playing in a nearby coconut grove. Iron skillets and wooden water buckets beat out the rhythm of their dance. Little boys bowed and girls curtsied. The boys wore paper hats Anne recognized as the ones discarded by her own and neighbor children just days ago. For Matt's tenth birthday Anne had arranged a small party in the garden. It seemed like a century ago. Today must be—yes, today is the twentieth of December, 1730, ten years to the date of Mary's death.

Ten years.

She watched the children again, waltzing in a great circle, puffs of dust clouding up around their prancing feet. Long ribbons tied about the heads of several girls floated to the ground. Her eyes spotted a pair of blue ones bobbing around in the circle which reminded her of the way she had watched her own Mary Elizabeth dancing at Matt's celebration by following the blue ribbons of her bonnet. Musicians and dancers traded instruments and bits of costumes and the dance began again.

She jerked back on the reigns. The chestnut reared up, turned and arched its fine head in the direction of the burning outbuildings. She learned from one of the thatch cutters that none of the people had been carried off. Some had gone with the Maroons voluntarily—how many he did not know or would not say. By the look of the approaching storage buildings she suspected that most supplies had been ruined, but they could always grow more grain or buy feed if necessary.

Old Sam, Ruth's father, and several of the other field negroes busily doused fires and hauled out sacks of grain and Indian corn. Anne looked around for Caleb Foote, John Sommerwood's overlooker, but did not find him. She was anxious to get some estimate of their losses. Caleb would know. She detested him, but he was good with numbers, and Baldwin had not the authority to dismiss him.

Anne directed her question to Sam, whose small frame strained under a smouldering sack of feed. "Sam, where is Mr. Foote?"

"In da cane-piece, I 'spect, Miz Anne." Sam snatched off his straw hat, scratched his white woolly head and hitched his breeches over his rounded belly. "We lose all da muscovado and dey steal some hides, not many. Las' week de overlooker he carry a wagon full to Port Royal."

"What about the stores?"

"We suffer dere too, Missus."

"Save what you can."

"Aye, Miz Anne." Sam tightened the rope around his sagging breeches and watched Anne ride off toward the pastures. It would do no good to warn her of what she might find there. He only hoped the men were finished with their gruesome task. Shaking his head, he picked up his bucket and plodded over to a nearby water trough.

Anne was not prepared for what her eyes met in the horse pasture. In places where the men had already dragged off animals for burial, the ground was soaked with blood. Massive carcasses littered the field and in no way resembled the fine animals she had raised.

Her chestnut stamped and snorted his private anger as she surveyed the wanton devastation of her thoroughbreds. Her eyes lingered on one bloody torso after the other, a legless one, a headless one, a disemboweled one.

"Molly!"

Dismounting she ran toward the patch of white she recognized on the left flank of a black-brown mare. In only days she would have foaled. Molly's severed head was lying between her legs, her wide eyes seemed locked on the scrawny legs of the unborn colt spilling out of her split belly.

Anne leaned against the fence, retching.

A hand touched her shoulder. Mary, she thought. This happened often, first a light comforting touch, then she'd turn to find no one. But there was no comfort in this hand. It was heavy and did not go away. She turned into the square face of Caleb Foote.

Thinking to take advantage of her vulnerability, he took her other shoulder and pulled her to his thick chest.

"Take your hands off me!"

His hands fell as he watched her green eyes turn to slate. He felt Anne's riding crop slash across his face.

"How dare you touch me! How dare you!" Feeling more hatred at this moment than she had the night before against the Maroons, Anne lashed viciously with her crop striking his temple, ear and neck before Caleb could snatch the weapon out of her hand. Great welts rose up on his flabby jowls and in the heavy folds of his neck. Aroused more than hurt, his gray eyes, ringed red by dissipation, never left her. As he watched her heaving breasts his penis grew large under a belly scarcely contained by the waist band of his breeches. Transfixed by her fury he could not move.

"Where were you last night?" Anne demanded, but did not wait for him to speak because she knew the answer. "My children could have been slaughtered in their sleep while you lay abed with some tavern whore."

"The Maroons did not come to the great house."

"You think not. It would not surprise me if you knew they were coming and ran away to hide like a rat in a hole. Call yourself a man? Disgusting pig! Filthy dog!" She cursed him with every vile name she had ever heard among the pirates. Breathless, Anne struggled against faintness. "Get away from me. Go! See to your duties. And I warn you, Caleb Foote, use our people well, for if I hear another report that you have beaten . . ."

"They be slaves, Mistress!"

"They are my people! Ill use them and you will suffer, sir, I assure you. Now, fetch my horse."

Unlocking his eyes from hers, he mounted and rode across the pasture. Anne leaned back against the fence, then slid to the ground exhausted. She hooked her arms over the crosspiece and listened to her pounding head. At the sound of approaching horses, she stood. Fighting dizziness, she snatched the reins, swung up and rode off, guiding her skittish horse through the ravaged meadow.

At Mary's unmarked tomb Anne opened her arms. Orchids cascaded onto the stony lid. Unable to speak, Anne broke down in heavy sobs and allowed convulsing waves to wrack her already battered body. Maroon cutlasses were less hurtful than life's torments—a lover, a baby, a friend all snatched from her by death and now came the full realization that last night she could have lost all again.

"Your son is safe, Mary." She did not know what made her laugh at this moment, the strange sounds made by her own words or her father's saying which popped into her head. He always could stop her crying by postulating in a serious tone, "Ya know, girl, the more you cry, the less you piss. " Her laughter-ridden sobs ceased when she tried to recall if she had ever seen Mary Read cry. Her mind raced over those last miserable weeks in the Spanish Town jail.

Absently Anne moved the flowery tentacles of the octopus orchid. The patterns of her designs changed as her thoughts ranged from recent to past horrors.

"Mary, I dreamt again that we stood in the court and were sentenced to hang. I can see now why you had to leave me. You could face anything as a man but as a woman all your courage abandoned you. I felt your shame when we were shackled to each other, stripped of our clothing, and dragged back to our cell. Shame engulfed us as the white sun washed the blue sky, and I could see flowers crushed under my bare feet as a thousand eyes witnessed our nakedness and obscenities were shouted viler than any we had ever heard at sea. Of our crimes the worst was that we were women—unnatural hags, breeders of monsters, the mob said.

"I knew that day you would not live to meet the hangman. You lived as a man all your life, you never suffered such indignities. Countless times you rushed into the cannon's mouth. In battle your sword cut down twenty times the number of the crowd hurling obscenities that day in the streets of Spanish Town. Personal courage takes different shapes, I think, and you had not the courage to meet that rabble at the gallows.

"The memory of the night you died in my arms tears at my soul still. When Baldwin came to take you away to bury you in this place, I nearly went mad with fear and rage. How could he give me assurance that I would live to visit this tomb or see your son again? I cursed him bitterly.

"My child leaped in my womb the day he took you and little Matt away. After that it made no sign of life in me and I was utterly alone. If the child died, my death would come all the sooner. And I did not care.

"Remember the day we were captured at Negril? Remember how the sea looked before the rain? After you left I could see nothing else. I wasted away in despair, swallowed up by bitter loneliness.

"It rained every day in my sea dream.

"I was condemned to death in each night's dream.

"For days, nights and weeks, flat milk-white water reached toward the black horizon." A sudden pain grabbed her side, reminding her of what she really wanted to tell Mary.

"There is a woman from the hills, nay, a giant. She could have killed me last night, but chose not to. She leads those savages who attacked us and tried to incite our people to rebellion. 'Tis ironic. This very moment Baldwin is in London speaking to the Parliament of the evils of slavery. And last night his entire family could have been wiped from existence at the hands of the very people he has pledged his life to free. This cause is his obsession; he talks of nothing else and it keeps him away too much. I miss him. I need his help, his strength. I need his arms around me, his lips on mine. I love him, not just because he saved my life. No dire circumstance could twist gratitude into love for me. And I am not a girl any more, I am thirty now. I know this is not the same love I felt for Tombay. All loves are different, I think. Yes, I love Win—almost as much as I love you."

Anne lay down upon the tomb, and through the cushion of flowers, cold stone touched her cheek.

Ruth wiped the Spanish blade which she found lying on the floor next to Anne's bed. An uneasy feeling came over her as she grasped the hilt. She had never taken a machete to tall grass or sugar cane like the others. The blades she knew chopped vegetables. Never once while holding a knife had the thought of killing so much as glimmered in her mind. And yet this sword in the hand of another woman—a shudder thrilled through her body.

T'ree grown men killed by dis sword. Mebbe mo', she thought.

Ruth began to remove some of Anne's clothing from

the trunk in order to replace the sword. Men's breeches and a waistcoat of the deepest green velvet were trimmed with red-gold and silver braid. Fancy dress, she thought, like old Massa Sommerwood wear when he hab comp'ny. Miz Anne wear dese, I wonner? Ruth carefully lifted a vest out of the trunk. The cloth was so worn she was almost afraid to touch it. Dis be Miz Mary's. I see her wear it. Guinea cloth. Slabes, when dey firs' cum Jamaica wear clothes made from dis same cloth. I wonner how Miz Mary, she get dis?

Before placing the sword at the bottom of the trunk, Ruth ran her fingers over the intricately carved design near its hilt and was reminded of what Anne had told her. Dis sword belong ta Mary's doddy. He noblemon, his doddy Sponish and his mama English. Legacy, yes, dat what Miz Anne call dis blade. She gib dis ta Matt one day. Dat day Massa Baldwin and me, we cum to prison in Spanish Town, 'an we stan' outside da gate, dis sword hang at his side. He pay many gold coin to buy dis back from mon who steal it. He promise Miz Mary. Massa allus do what he promise. An' when she and Miz Anne cum out in de yard, I put da baby in his arms. Miz Mary she stare long time at da boy, den at da blade an' tears run down her face. Sun hurt her eyes too, I tink. She handsome womon. Look so sad eben when she smile at baby. Den she swoon in Miz Anne's arms.

As she repacked the trunk, an Indian tomahawk clattered to the floor. Before replacing it, Ruth studied the crude carving at the base of the handle. The much worn initials "A" and "B" were scratched inside a heart. Boy's work she thought and smiled, closing the trunk. She stood up with a groan.

Ruth was a tall woman, thin and graceful and her movements revealed an air of superiority typical of the Senegalese. Dipping her long fingers into the wash basin, she splashed water on her face. Wide forehead and intelligent eyes peered over her apron at the image of herself in the glass. Dropping the apron she examined the delicate and as yet unlined features of her face. Pulling back her headpiece revealed only a hint of gray at her temples. Not so old, yet, she pondered. Mus' be stiff from sittin' in dat well las' night.

She raised up the mosquito netting and smoothed the bedding. Then she eyed the pile of blood-stained clothing by the bed. Her fingers ran over the many rents and tears in the shirt. The cloak Anne wore when she came to fetch them out of hiding had concealed these bloody garments. As Ruth descended the stairs to the kitchen, she wondered how badly her mistress might be wounded.

The house servants were deep in conversation about the events of the preceding night. Just outside on the covered walkway which connected the main house with the cookhouse, the grass cutters were unusually silent over their breakfast. It had been their task to bury the dead Maroons.

"You boys finish wid yo' work?" Ruth asked a group of old men who were soaking up the last of their grits with a bite of cassava bread.

"Not fittin' work fo' any mon, Miz Ruth, but it be done."

The men looked at one another and shook their heads in resignation, then picked up their hoes and machetes and went off in the direction of the vegetable garden.

Ruth set her bundle outside the half door and exchanged her worried look for a smile before entering the cookhouse. With face and arms covered in flour, her Esther looked as white as Mary Elizabeth. Ruth kissed her mother, gave Mary Elizabeth and Esther a hug, and brushing the flour from her cheek picked up her bucket and went out to the well.

The other children were chasing a goat in the yard. Matt dived at the rope and was dragged for a distance. Ruth's Sarah jumped on Matt while her brother Lusen grabbed the goat's horns and brought him to a halt.

"You chil'ren be careful now. Dat old goat butt you all ta da nex' pasture. Matt, git up from dere. Sarah, git off him now. Lusen, where be Colin?"

"Down by da river, I 'speck. Fishin' mos' likely."

Little Sarah laughed and rolled in the dirt, pretending to be dragged by the goat as Matt had been.

"Sarah, git up from dere, now, you hear, I'll whip you. Matt you hab breakfas'?" shouted Ruth.

"Yes, Miss Ruth."

"Git yo'se'f clean, chil'. Won't do fo' you to roll 'round in da dirt like dat."

"Wish I had your color," Matt whispered to Lusen. "Wouldn't show dirt so much. Yesderday your mama like to rub the skin off my neck."

"Cum, Matt. Play in da barn," called Sarah who was already scampering across the yard.

"Yeh! Come on, Lusen."

They ran off, leaping like young goats.

"Matt, cum back here! I'll git a tam'rin' switch."

It was no use, she knew that. He was gone and would stay gone till lunch. Then he would run into the kitchen to grab up enough food for himself and the other children and be off again, running across the field to play near one of the many streams which ran in the hills surrounding the plantation. She had never really worried about where the children played before. Now, she would have to insist they stay in the yard. "How 'ber will I manage dat?" she wondered.

The harassed goat, now tied to a tree, looked up at the departing children. Then, with what seemed to Ruth to be a sigh of relief, went back to munching a clump of grass. Filling the water trough, Ruth shook her head and laughed. Leaving her bucket by the well, she went to one of the smokehouses to burn Anne's clothing.

High in the Blue Mountains the sun filtered through the tall trees to fall on a body clothed in vines and flowers and lying on a litter in the middle of the main road of the Maroon village. Nanny watched the changing pattern of light move on her brother's torso as the trees swayed in the gentle breeze.

She was alone.

No one in the village stirred. Every door was shut, every shutter closed. No children played in the dirt paths between the huts. No one dared venture forth until summoned and that would not happen until their commander had concluded her private obsequies.

Nanny absorbed the silence.

Belts of gold pieces, anklets of teeth and necklaces of clay and wooden beads, animal bones, and feathers adorned her otherwise naked body. An elaborate headdress, denoting her rank, brought her height to well over seven feet. She squatted next to the litter. Carefully, she removed the flowers covering her brother's genitals and anointed his mutilated parts with the fragrant bitter oils. Her voice sounded like rough wind, low and deep. No one could hear her even if they dared to listen.

"Dis Maroon work. Sponish dogs do dese kin' tings, not English planter. White witch be debil's bitch fo' sure. My people run from Sponish. Her people say she Irish, diff'rent from English dey say. Fire light up dere eye when dey say dat—'I-rish.' Hair like golden fire. Dey fear white bitch. Not Nanny, Nanny fear no ting. Witchy bitchy hab Sponish weapon."

Soothing the oils over her brother's belly with a rough hand, she droned gutterally, "Spon-ish. My great grandoddy, he Spanish slabe. He take chil'ren, run 'way. Sponish follow him, hunt *cimmaroons* wid fierce dogs. My grandoddy watch dogs tear his doddy ta pieces, eat his brains. Grandoddy dis brudder's age den—not t'irty yet. *Rancheadores* cotch him too—carry him back. Gib him two hun'red lash—whip hab claw. Granmama say she wonner how he lib. Sponish set him free when English soldier take Jamaica. Granmama she sold to English. Later he carry granmamma ta dese mountains. Steal her from plantation an' kill planter who rape her. He swear we neber be slabe ta any mon. My doddy he see ta dat, an' Nanny see ta dat. If I mus' kill eb'ry white mon, womon, an' chil' on dis island

I see ta dat too.

"White bitch hab chil'ren dey tell me. Quaco here, he little brudder, but my chil' jus' da same. His chil'ren my chil'ren. Little Afiba my daughter now. Yamou my son. He be Maroon colonel some day. Witchy bitchy she hab son, she hab daughter. Not fo' long. Son for son!" Her words reverberated in the mountains and kissing Quaco's testicles she repeated her vow, "son fo' son." The words strangled her and Nanny clasped her hand to her throat. "Not be easy. Dat womon hab powerful magic. But Nanny look hard into her mind an' challenge her, son fo' son. But now ... how I tell Cudjoe little brudder kill by white womon—soldier womon like Nanny ... I tell Cudjoe Quaco fall — hit head."

The black gash on the man's forehead stood out on his gray face. Nanny replaced the flowers as heavy drums signaled her elder brother's arrival. Nanny rose and greeted Cudjoe with the respect due him as chief of the western part of the island and commander of all Maroon tribes on Jamaica.

The great warrior leaned against his stick and bent low to study the face of his dead brother. Grief transformed his rugged face and ill-formed figure. For a moment it became impossible to distinguish the man from his staff so gnarled and twisted they both were. He had brought with him an Ashanti priest from the nearby village Cudjoe had been inspecting before his return to Accompong. As the ceremony began, the priest, clothed in bones and wooden amulets, chanted his great authority and the eerie sound, distorted by the configurations of his funeral mask, silenced the drum. His chanting ceased after a time, then he lay down his mask and put a large shell to his lips and blew. The drums started up again in a different cadence, doors opened and people came from their houses.

A grandmother, straight in spite of her great age, followed behind the dead warrior's children. Yamou, a boy of eight, and his ten-year-old sister Afiba, joined Nanny. Six men raised and lowered the litter to their heads three times as a courtesy to the Earth goddess. The procession began. Five women who were the dead man's wives led the way; the villagers followed the litter along a narrow path to the burial grounds.

When the party reached a clearing, the wailing intensified, the drums beat faster, and the warriors broke into frenetic movements. The men holding the litter moved slowly while the mourners danced around it in a circle, tossing flowers onto the body. At the priest's signal the drums stopped abruptly and everyone grew still. Shakers rustled softly as the masked figure danced around the open grave, throwing in powders and twigs. Finally the men lowered the litter into the ground and the five women pushed mounds of earth onto their husband's body. Then positioning themselves like dogs, they turned their backs to the grave and, scratching the earth between their legs, finished their task.

From a distant canefield a conch shell announced the midday meal. The fresh noon breezes fluttered through the louvers of Anne's bedroom doors, touching her nakedness. Ruth's gentle strokes caused the soothing balm to reach into the tiny nicks and cuts which covered Anne's body. Anne could feel the dull ache leave her abused muscles.

"Have the children eaten?" asked Anne drowsily.

"Dey don't stop since mornin'."

A laugh escaped with a painful groan.

"You feel better soon," Ruth said, relieved that Anne's injuries did not match those she had imagined. Still, her usually milky skin was marred by reddish cuts surrounded by areas of greenish purple bruises. Ruth looked at her own long fingers spread across Anne's broad, strong back and wondered. The muscles in Anne's shoulders and arms were firm, round and smooth but in no way did the woman's frame suggest power. Ruth dared not ask what had happened.

Anne moaned in pain.

"I sorry, Miz Anne." Ruth lightened her touch and

murmured, "T'ree."

"What?"

"T'ree Maroon warriors. You . . ."

"There were five of them. One ran off. The woman carried one away."

"Five."

"Ruth, have you ever heard of a female warrior in these mountains?"

"A womon? You sure you see womon wid da Maroons las' night?"

"Yes, a very tall and very large woman, almost a giant. A woman called Nanny. She carried the fifth man away."

Yes, 'Nanny', Ruth thought to herself. Dat da name I hear in da night, not 'Annie.' Puzzled, she answered haltingly. "Eb'ry black womon be called Nanny sometime. Mebbe you wrong."

"Ruth, I can tell by your voice that you are keeping something from me. I must know."

"I hear . . . stories, dey tell of Ashanti chief, Obeah womon, bush fighter in Blue Mountain."

"Does she have children? I had the feeling that the dead man she carried away in her arms was her son."

"No chil'ren of her own but she be mudder to all her people. Talk say she work strong magic keep dem safe."

"She is no legend, Ruth. If you had felt her hands at your throat as I did and looked into those eyes, you would soon learn that."

Anne twisted around to look at Ruth. "She left her horn, you know. I took it. What do they call that cow horn anyway?"

"Abeng. I see it dis mornin'. I 'fraid touch."

"Why?"

"I don' know why. Sound frighten me, I tink. Doddy say it African. Dey use it ta call dere people. Dey say dey can make magic sounds. If you off by yo'se'f it call yo' name. I hear horn sometimes an' sound reach someting deep inside me I no understand.

Anne murmured, "We must be wary . . . we must

watch ... we must ..." The softness of Ruth's steady stroking induced sleep. Secure in Ruth's presence Anne drifted off.

Ruth smoothed in the last of the ointment and listened to Anne's settled breathing as she would to that of one of her own sleeping children. Raising herself up slowly from the bed, she let down the netting and quietly left the room.

Pistols, muskets, cannon seemed to boom in her head, rallying Anne from sleep.

Waking did not still the sound.

Drums.

The deep steady mournful rhythm issued from the high hills. Anne dressed and went to the stable. She hastily saddled her horse and rode toward the drums. The pounding of her mount's hooves could not silence the cadence which grew ever louder and louder.

There was a place she knew—a waterfall where she often went to be alone. Anne needed to be alone now, alone with her thoughts, alone with those drums.

Lush vegetation surrounded the pool beneath the fall, moss clung to the high wet cliffs. From this height, the bright green cane looked like velvet, the sugarworks like so many villages. She reached into the saddlebag, removed the abeng and placed it in a niche in the wet wall above her. The horn glimmered like rich cream entwined in fern as green as the sea. Removing her clothing, Anne plunged into the pool and swam toward the waterfall. The coolness of the water soothed her burning face and washed away her weariness, but it could not refresh her troubled mind.

"What is the meaning of those drums?" No answer came from the deep pool or the lofty cliffs. Looking up, she thought she saw her enemy step back just out of her line of vision. The figure was naked except for ornaments—could that have been Nanny? Anne wondered. Have I stumbled on her private haunt? How long has she been watching me?

Anne stood under the fall and allowed the full force of

the water to beat down upon her body, making her head sting, her shoulders ache, and her breasts hurt. The fast-falling water drumming on her head pounded at her ugly thoughts. Thrusting her head back, Anne opened her mouth to freshen the bitter taste rising in her throat. The water dropped like tiny daggers on her tongue.

The point when pain ceases to be pain came at last. She could hear only herself—if she were to drown this very moment, she would not care.

CHAPTER TWO

Home to Hill Haven

Baldwin Sommerwood returned early in February. He had gone from London to Charles Town on a trip filled with plantation business: hides to sell, horses to trade and sugar contracts to consummate. Anxious to return to Hill Haven, it was fortunate that Baldwin's hasty deals proved unprofitable in only one or two instances. Finally booking passage on a fast sailer he accompanied his ailing father and son home to Jamaica. Anne and Matt had been out riding that afternoon and had seen the coach coming. Matt rode on to meet the carriage while Anne galloped to the plantation to alert the household. Ruth, her children, and the house servants waited eagerly with Anne, Mary Elizabeth and Colin on the steps of Hill Haven. Excitement mounted when the coach clattered onto the stone carriage circle. There was no visible sign of their earlier trouble with the Maroons. Anne would tell Baldwin about that later, much later.

Sang winked at his wife as he leaped from the coachman's bench to direct the unloading of the luggage. Their greeting would have to wait. Perhaps he might snatch a kiss from Ruth in the kitchen between dinner courses.

"Doddy, doddy," shouted little Sarah, straining to escape Ruth's hold and run to her father.

"Hush now, Yo' doddy's busy, don' you see dat."

"Lusen, cum he'p boy." Sang untied the strap anchoring the boxes to the back of the coach. "I missed yo', son," he whispered as he handed Lusen a small trunk. "Go 'long now an' carry dat up ta Massa Baldwin's room."

"Aye," Lusen replied with a grin.

William seemed taller to Anne. Especially in his traveling clothes, he was beginning to look more like his father or perhaps he was just leaner than before he went away. Since to him the outdoors meant places shaded by palms or darkened by forests, only the broad bridge of his nose showed any tinge of color. His sea-blue eyes highlighted a complexion any woman would envy. Noticing her staring at him, William Thomas walked over and gave Anne a dutiful peck on the cheek. Mary Elizabeth, locked in her father's arms, kissed his neck. "Oh, Daddy, I missed you every day."

The children flocked around William Thomas urging him to tell every detail of his travels.

"What is it like to ride in a great ship?" asked Colin above the others.

Supported by his son, John Sommerwood stepped carefully from the coach. His shrunken frame, accentuated by the black velvet of his breeches, startled Anne. The silvery garnish on his coat glinted in the sunlight as he raised his arms to greet her.

John gathered her in to his fragile arms, drew her to his bosom and pressed his soft cheek against hers. Anne's energy sparked everywhere like flint. Something dim within him leaped to catch just one of those sparks but could not.

Impatient for her grandfather, Mary Elizabeth tugged at his hand, pulling him away from her mother.

"Be careful with him, Mary." Anne's smile dimmed as she caught a look of sadness in John's eyes. When he shifted his eyes to his granddaughter, the look was gone.

Anne turned toward Baldwin and her smile returned as she threw herself into her husband's arms. Pressing her body against his and hugging him tightly, she pelted his face and neck with quick kisses until their lips met in a lingering caress.

"I brought you a surprise."

"I need no gifts. You're my gift and I mean to keep you

in bed for a week."

"Well, I brought a surprise for you anyway. One you'll like, I think."

Baldwin motioned to Sang as he kissed Anne passionately once again. Their lips parted. Anne's eyes pulled away from Baldwin's face when she caught a glimpse of the agile Koromantyn assisting an elderly gentleman from the carriage.

"Min' da step, Massa O'Brannon."

"Father!"

"Me darlin' Annie."

Throwing her arms around his thick waist, Anne remorsefully studied the deep lines of his face and wept.

Will touched her hair and kissed her forehead repeatedly. "Now, now, m'girl, no tears."

She smiled and kissed the shiny spot on the top of his head as she did in the old days. The words turned over in her mind these past years now rolled quickly off her tongue. "Oh, Father, I am so sorry for all the pain I caused thee." She had always been sorry but it seemed important to her that she could say it now when as a willful child and even more stubborn young woman she could not.

" 'Sorry', what's this, now. 'Tis a time for joy. We must put the past behind us, girl. It has been so long . . ."

"I have so much to tell you, Father. I know not where to begin." She remembered the letter and was glad now she had written it. "Did my letter reach you?"

" 'Tis why I came."

Like Anne, Will had started a hundred letters and torn up each in exasperation. During the past few years he had taken to talking to Anne when he was alone, telling her of all the humorous happenings of the day as he had when she was a child. So when his pen wrote thoughts he was sure he had already communicated to her, he'd snort and call himself a doddering old fool. He always ended these letter-writing sessions by throwing down his quill and reaching for the decanter of claret.

Tired from their journey, Will and John decided to nap

till tea. Before she took Will upstairs, Anne dragged him from one room to another, thrusting into his hands one priceless *objet d' art* after the other in her eagerness to show him all the Sommerwood treasures at once. Replacing a particularly fine Italian sculpture, she ran into the entrance hall to find her father on his hands and knees staring at the zebra wood floor. She watched as he ran his fingers across the mahogany-colored stripes of satinwood. God-given beauties of the world always gave him more pleasure than any object man could create. Joy in nature's wonders had joined their hearts—a sunset, a stallion, a flower, a pattern in the wood. Absorbed in her love, Anne almost missed seeing Will plant his cane and struggle to raise himself. Smiling at him, her eyes grew warm and moist; she brushed back his thinning white hair and kissed his forehead. "Later we'll walk in the garden and talk. I have so much to tell you."

"I too, Annie, years have piled up between us. But your old father needs rest before he can sift through all those days with you."

"We have time. Now that we are together again we have all the time we need."

Anne saw her father comfortably situated in one of the guest rooms, looked in on her father-in-law, then went down to the kitchen to arrange the supper menu with Ruth's mother.

Bertha had just set out a pan of coconut candy on the counter between the kitchen and the serving room. In spite of all her other duties, she still found time to make an occasional treat to delight the children. Anne's visits to the kitchen came invariably after the children had sailed through leaving only crumbs in their wake. Thanking the gods responsible for her good fortune, Anne took up a piece of candy and tossed it back and forth between her hands, trying to cool it.

"Bertha, plan a late supper, around nine. And fix something special, will you?"

"How 'bout black crab pepperpot?"

"Fine, that would be lovely."

"An' da chil'ren, Missus, will dey sit wid you all?"

"No, they should eat earlier. The boys are impossible at table at any hour. And should Mister Sommerwood and my father arise, serve them a substantial tea lest they grow irritable and impatient for supper."

"Yes, Missus."

Anne noticed Ruth standing at the sideboard polishing a large serving platter; her profile, at this moment, was strikingly attractive.

"Ruth, what are you doing?"

"Why, polishin' silber, Miz Anne."

"Looks polished to me."

"I likes ta keep busy, Missus."

"Well, busy yourself in the stable."

"Sang tendin' da horses, he don' need me bodderin' 'im."

"Oh, yes, he does," Anne said, smiling. Ruth threw a quick glance at the floor, somewhat embarrassed at the message in Anne's eyes."I shan't need you till I dress for supper. Your time is your own; that goes for Sang too."

"Tank you, Missus." Ruth dropped her polishing cloth and ran out through the kitchen to the barn. Bertha chuckled to herself while she dressed the lamb for the evening meal.

"And what are you laughing at, Bertha?"

"Oh, not'in', Miz Anne, jus' tinkin' 'bout Ole Sam an' me an' days gone by, das all."

"I suppose you want the afternoon off as well?"

"No'm. We too old now ta make good use of't like you young folk. I's happy in mah kitchen. You go 'long now. Berta see ta eb'ryting. Fix you all a fine supper. You hab plenty appetite." And unable to contain herself any longer she laughed heartily.

"You really are very impertinent, you know that, Bertha?" Anne ordered her face not to smile.

"I knows it, Missus," Bertha tried to choke back her laughter, "I knows it."

Impatiently Anne paced the gallery of her third floor

bedroom which spanned the entire width of the east end of the main house. Baldwin insisted that after each trip every item be put away immediately and was busy with his unpacking. As he placed his linen shirts, hose and cravats in an oak chest of drawers, he paused to run his fingers over the elaborate Elizabethan strapwork carving. Baldwin enjoyed this ritual and until it was completed he never really felt back home. Anne found the habit annoying.

Her long legs carried her swiftly along the north porch past the mountains, crisply along the east which afforded only a distant glimpse of the Windward Passage, and in spite of her humor, almost leisurely along the south gallery where she lingered to soak in the splendid view of Morant Bay and the Caribbean Sea beyond. At every other louvered door she glanced into the room to assess the progress of Baldwin's unpacking. Even though he was not quite finished, Anne entered, plopped onto the goosedown mattress and crossed her feet. The heel of one dusty boot dug deep into the daintily patterned counterpane. Rubbing her fingers across her stomach, Anne felt the linen softened by many washings. She always wore Baldwin's old shirts when riding. They were much more comfortable than her own. She untied her blouse and watched Baldwin unpack a small leather satchel.

A strand of his sandy colored hair had fallen onto his forehead. Baldwin habitually ran his fingers through the fine strands in an always futile effort to replace them. His face was pale, tanned only in places on his high forehead where his hair receded. The open shirt fell off one shoulder to uncover a mass of freckles. Anne recalled that once she had tried to kiss every one—an impossible feat but pleasant business. As his tall figure moved about the room she noticed that the muscles in his torso and arms lacked tone.

Want of exercise, she thought. This I will remedy. His white hose and wine colored breeches fitted close beneath his knee revealed his strong firm legs and thighs, which always provoked her interest in a particularly enjoyable form of exercise and she wished to commence immediately.

There would be plenty of time to talk later.

"Win, leave that for now. Sang will set everything right in the morning."

"I have something in here I want to show you."

Instead of rummaging through the bag to find the small treasure which he knew to be at the bottom, he took out his toilet articles and one by one carefully aligned them on the table next to the wash basin; then he refolded his linen undergarments before laying each piece in the drawer.

"Dear Lord, Baldwin, can't that wait?" Anne crossed and recrossed her ankles so many times that the pale yellow coverlet turned black beneath her boots.

"No, no, it can't wait."

"Can't you hurry at least?"

"It's been so long since I purchased this little item that I don't remember what the package looks like," he said in an inflection which hinted that he had found what he had been looking for. After another few seconds of searching he said, "No, that's not it."

"God, Baldwin, do you mean to drive me mad?" Anne bounded from the bed and flinging her arms around his waist pulled him away from the table.

"What's this!" Clutching his satchel to his breast, he protested. "Woman, do you mean to rape me? I'll not have it. Unhand me, saucy wench."

"Rape, indeed," she muttered as she pulled him towards the bed.

"Aye, rape 'tis now and rape 'twas then. How the girl forgets!"

"Win, what are you raving about?" She let him go. Baldwin replaced the bag on the table and continued to rummage through it, furtively.

"Oh, woman, have you forgot how you raped me by the duck pond on your father's plantation in Carolina? Callous girl to steal my virginity thus, and me a mere boy."

"Oh, that, 'twas play."

"Play, she calls it. Dear angels, do ye hear? Ah, the hardness of woman's heart!"

"Why, you bastard, do you mean to put me off now?"

"Ah hah! Yes! I mean no . . . no I don't mean to put you off, but yes, I have found it."

"Found what?"

"Here, catch." He knew better than to go near her when he could see a fury brewing in her eyes.

"What is it?" Anne turned the tiny box over in her fingers.

"Oh, a small trinket which happened to catch my eye. Open it and see." The glint in his eye betrayed his impatience to have Anne open the gift at once so she held the box next to her ear and shook it vigorously.

"Open the bloody thing, will you?"

Anne bounded from the bed, strode across the room and placed the box on her dressing table. "I think not. Perhaps after supper."

Catching his approach in the mirror Anne turned just as Baldwin snatched up the box.

"All right, m'lady, perhaps someone else will appreciate this bauble. I'll give it to Bertha. She'll thank me at least." Thrusting his jaw forward he pretended to leave the room.

"Oh, no you don't." Anne wrapped both arms about his chest. They wrestled for a few moments over the box until it was nearly crushed. Baldwin released it to her and swung Anne into his arms and carried her to the bed. Prompted by the surge of passion he experienced lifting Anne into his arms, he tore at her blouse.

"Oh, wait," Anne pleaded. "I want to see this present."

She tried to free her right hand to unwrap the paper which clung to the mangled box in her left.

"Oh, no, you don't. There's no stopping now, m'girl."

He snatched the gift and set it on the bedstand out of reach. The emerald ring, chosen because the stone matched the color of her eyes, would have to wait. Jerking off her boots, he flung them across the room. One boot after the other hit the floor with a dull thud.

Two floors below Bertha stifled a giggle.

In the guest room next to Anne's, Will O'Brannon

rolled over in his half sleep and muttered something about youth.

Baldwin ripped off Anne's clothing and most of his own. Their usual easy foreplay lapsed into fits of wrestling whenever Anne was reminded of the gift and attempted to reach for it. She stretched and wriggled, flinging her arms about and rapping her knuckles on the headboard more than once.

"That's m'girl," muttered Will. " 'Ave at 'im, Annie."

Baldwin smothered himself in Anne's large breasts, then pressing them together, bit both nipples at once, snatching her attention for the moment. Anne abandoned her efforts to reach the bedstand and the unknown jewel and instead grasped what she already knew to be a precious object. Under her manipulation he swelled.

The red-orange colors of a Jamaican sunset flashed across her forehead as Baldwin slid into her. She seemed to float for a long time. Then her body vaulted into the sky, twisting and tumbling in the intense rays of the sun until she exploded like fireworks into a thousand arcs of light and color.

Later that afternoon, the old men sat down to tea in the library. Will stuffed two small pieces of bread in his mouth at once, hoisted his portly body out of the wingback chair, shuffled over to the French doors to look out into the garden. Leaves drooped heavy with water droplets left by the sudden shower. He scratched the stubble on his cheek and wondered where the children might be. In the garden an old man stooped and plucked a sprig of mint, bent one leaf in half to release the fragrance and put it to his nose.

"This is a peaceful place, methinks."

"Aye, " said John Sommerwood without lifting his head from his book.

"Will you play at cards, John?"

"Aye, 'twould do me good. This text bores me." Shifting his withered frame in the chair, he continued. " 'Tis odd, when I was a young man I longed for the time to sit and read. Now that I have nothing but idle time, I don't feel like reading."

"I used to read to Annie when she was a girl—Shakespeare. I've lost interest now. I miss her, you know, but I'm glad she is here with you."

"Stay with us as long as you like." Will O'Brannon shuffled the cards more than was necessary, then flipped a card across the table to John Sommerwood who absently drew it closer as he did the other four. John perused his cards and suddenly chuckled.

"What is funny, John?"

"Oh, I was just thinking 'bout our children. They think they found each other, you know."

"Oh yes,"exclaimed Will in his best theatrical manner. "She was the fair maiden in distress, so to speak, snatched from the jaws of death by the tall, handsome knight."

"Something like that," John sighed. "Lord, the many times I brought that boy to your plantation and Anne would have nought to do with him. Can't blame the girl, Baldwin was such an ordinary looking boy, thin and wiry. Oh, how he loved her, smitten by Cupid's arrow the moment he set eyes on her, I think. I felt sorry for the lad and feared he'd never capture Anne's interest."

"He's a fine looking man now, that's certain. Filled out somewhat and quite handsome in the face. Remember how she'd sneak out of the house, ride off, and leave him all day sometimes."

I taught Baldwin how to remedy that. Told him to question the servants about Anne's daily activities and simply be ready when she was. One day I think they went hunting a wildcat with that Indian you used to keep on the plantation. Baldwin told me your Anne saved his life that day. She shot that cat just as she was about to leap on my boy."

"One life deserves another. I thank you too for saving my Annie. I know you had a part in that."

"What influence I could bring to bear in her behalf I'd gladly do ten times over for the sake of our long friendship."

As he reached over to touch John's knee, Will's eyes misted, but the memory of a humorous incident brought a chuckle to his throat. "Do you remember how that hunt turned into a frolic?"

"I don't think so."

"Baldwin never told you how they made a raid on the teacakes later that same day?"

"No, I'm sure I would have remembered that."

"Well, me wife was havin' a kind o' afternoon tea party. We were at Bath Town or Charles Town, I think. Yes, it was Charles Town. Anyway, Anne painted Baldwin to resemble an Indian brave and dressed herself in the head and skin of the wildcat they shot that day. Oh, my Annie could instigate mischief when she put her mind to it; I can tell you that."

"Well, go on. What happened?"

"Well, whoopin' and hollerin' like wild Indians they galloped their horses through the French doors into the parlor and frighted the ladies something dreadful."

Will laughed till his puffy eyes watered. Old John held his frail ribs which he feared might crack. As their laughter subsided, both men heard the children giggling outside the carved mahogany doors. Will signaled John to keep up his laughing, took up his cane and moved quietly to the library doors. Swinging them open, he brandished his cane and shouted, "Intruders, by God!" Sarah screamed and ran into her brother's arms. Will snatched Mary Elizabeth up under one arm and Esther under the other. Colin and Matt turned to run.

"Stand where ye be, cowards," growled Will.

"I'm no coward," Colin shouted back at him.

"Well, what do ye call it then leavin' these beauties in the clutches of a wild man."

"You'll not hurt them, will you?" cried Matt.

"Nay lad, I'm only foolin'. Come in now, all o' you." Released from her grandfather's grasp, Mary Elizabeth ran to old John and snuggled in his lap. Esther retreated and Lusen tried to leave."

"Hey, lad, come here and bring yere pretty sisters. There be enough tea here for everybody." Will took Sarah in his arms. "Did I scare ye, my pretty?"

Sarah wiped the tears from her cheek and bravely shook her head no.

" 'Tis a damned good thing, too." Will settled himself in the chair with Sarah on his lap. He saw her eyeing the teacakes on the platter beside him and handed her a particularly plump one.

"What you say, girl?" Lusen reminded.

"Tank you, sir." Sarah stuffed her mouth and wiped her fingers on her muddy dress, fresh just hours ago. Will passed the tea tray all around.

"So me lads and missies, you like that story, eh?"

"Did Mother really ride her horse into the sitting room?"

"Indeed she did," and looking into Mary's disbelieving eyes further emphasized, "and your daddy, too!"

"No!" she giggled.

"Aye, missy, and painted all over he were too, and a-whoopin' and a-hollerin' and a-rearin' up his horse grindin' cake into my Persian carpet. And yere mother a-leapin' all over the furniture, a-hissin' and a-snappin' and a-growlin' like a wildcat in heat."

John frowned. Will caught his rebuke and mended his story. "A-hissin' like a she cat."

"What did the ladies do then?" asked Mary Elizabeth.

"Swooned mostly, an' flipped their spoons and tea cups into the air, sent saucers bouncin' off the heads of some of the other guests who ran out of the room and down the road."

"Then what happened?" asked Matt.

"Well, now, those scamps filled two corn sacks with teacakes before they ran off. Now, I see that you children would never steal anything, now would ye?"

Matt halted his reach for the last piece of coconut bread.

"I thought not." Will snatched the bread and popped it into his mouth, setting all the children into fits of laughter with his lip-smacking grimaces.

Bertha bounced into the room with a tray loaded with more sweets. "I tink you gentlemon like more hot tea . . . what's dis! What you chil'ren doin' bodderin' dese old gentlemon. Out!" She set the heavy tray on the tea table. "Go on now, git!"

The children swooped like vultures onto the tray. Bertha swatted as many of the small black and white hands as she could reach. Taking advantage of the commotion Matt took a large volume off one of the higher shelves. Hiding it behind his back, he managed to scoop up three pieces of cake before Bertha chased him out of the library.

The children's shouts soon subsided and the old men gathered their scattered cards and resumed their game. Both were sad to see the children go.

"Where was young William?" Will finally said. "You'd think being so long away, he'd want to be with the other children."

Strange that Will should mention the boy, thought John. His own thoughts had drifted to William Thomas also and he was eager to talk about him but didn't know how to begin. "The boy looks like Baldwin, don't you think, Will—and he'll probably turn out to be even more handsome than his father if his baby flab ever leaves him. He doesn't sport or exercise with the other boys."

"He never does anything John, just sits and thinks — God knows what. He seems to feed on sour thoughts. His soul is flabby too. And there be more, John, I did not tell you this. One day . . . you were sick in bed, I think and I happened to be in the stable when young William brought in my mare cut and bleedin' from his whip. Then and there I laid into the boy with some leather strapping. I thrashed him good and sound. I know he hates me for it, but I could not help myself, John—to think a child could hurt a poor dumb animal that way. It makes me angry to think of it now."

John Sommerwood was suddenly afraid. Will had confirmed some of his own unspoken fears about the boy. "You know, Will, I have a wretched feeling that boy will cause his parents more serious grief than Anne ever caused you with her Indian raids or even her piratical exploits." He almost hesitated to speak further. "There is a baseness in him, and I fear someday he will do others and himself real harm."

"God trust your fears never take shape." Will turned the conversation away from sullen thoughts. "You know, those other two boys seem to be pleasant, energetic fellows. I'm quite taken with Colin's boldness, and he possesses the most ingratiating smile."

"Aye. Gets that smile from his father, Captain Jack Rackam. Anne tells me the man was quite charming."

"And Matt is a strappin' lad for his age. It looks to me he has his mind set on Mary Elizabeth already."

"Now there's my girl." A glow rushed to John's cheeks. "She's a delight to me in my old age, I can tell you that, Will, and she will have all her mother's looks."

"And much less of Anne's wild spirit, I warrant already. The girl seems temperate like her father, and a damned good thing that is too."

For a moment both men appeared to study their cards but their faces reflected the kind of warmth which springs from comfortable thoughts of family.

A sudden late afternoon shower sent the children scampering into an old canoe shed by the river landing. Colin flailed his arms, tearing webs from across the entrance.

"Look out fo' scorpions and spiders wid red spot near dere tail," warned Lusen.

The girls giggled and screamed, jumping up and down until Matt assured them that their shrieking had sent every creature flying from the place. Broken oars, fishing buckets and half-rotten canoe bodies littered the hut like dismembered stick dolls abandoned by children.

"Come on, sit in here and we'll read more 'bout the pirates," Colin said as he threw a dusty hide off one of the larger canoes. What he saw inside shook his sturdy frame.

"God's Eyes! Matt, Lusen, look here!"

The boys exclaimed together. "Lord A'mighty!" The girls crowded in to see and the boys were too startled to stop them.

Bodies of nearly a hundred parrots filled the belly of the canoe. Feathers of bright greens and yellows shrouded the heap of birds all in various stages of decomposition.

"Dey been shot," said Lusen. "Not us. We eat what we kill."

"I never eat parrot soup a'gin," whimpered Esther in Mary Elizabeth's arms. Always delighted by the flight of chattering parrots, Sarah stroked the belly of one bird before Lusen snatched her hand and slapped it hard. "What da matter wid you, girl. You want die dead?"

Sarah's lip puckered and she ran crying from the shed, flying into the arms of William Thomas. She struggled to free her arm from his grasp.

"You want to see my pretty birds?" he said trying to catch her other arm and drag her back into the shed.

"No! no! You die, deady deady!" she screamed, poking her contaminated finger at his heart. Kicking his shin released his grip and she went running to the cookhouse to bury her hot wet face in Bertha's apron.

Entering the canoe shed, William met angry stares. He smiled. "Oh, you're all here. Well, how do you like my cache?" Colin flung the hide over the carnage.

Spying the book in Colin's hand, William said. "Reading, I see. Captain Johnson's pirate history is it?"

"None of your business," retorted Colin.

"No matter. I won't bother you. I have Defoe's *Robinson Crusoe* here. He writes better stories than your Captain Johnson any day."

"We like true stories better—not characters like your Crusoe and Friday," Colin taunted.

"That book's true all right. It tells what a coward your father really was."

"Yeh! Where does it tell that?"

"Right in there—the day Matt's mother and our mother

were captured at Negril. Your father, Jack Rackam, went below and let the women fight alone."

"Mother never fought," protested Mary Elizabeth. "She's a lady!"

"A lot you know, Mary. Give me that book!" Snatching it from Colin's hand, he flipped through and finding the section for which he searched pointed to the place. "It's here in Mary Read's story, '. . . no Person amongst them was more resolute, or ready to board or undertake any Thing that was hazardous, than she,' your mother, Matt, 'and Anne Bonny'; here's the place, 'and particularly at the time they were attack'd and taken, when they came to close Quarters, none kept the Deck except Mary Read and Anne Bonny, upon which she, Mary Read, called to those under Deck, to come up and fight like Men, and finding they did not stir, fired her Arms down the Hold amongst them, killing one, and wounding others.' "

"That's not true. Mother wouldn't do that," shouted Matt, grabbing the book. "Look here, later it says, 'This was Part of the Evidence against her, which she denied' see, I knew it. Besides it goes on to say 'whether true or no, this much is certain, that she did not want Bravery. . . .' "

" 'Tis not Mary Read's bravery in question here but Rackam's cowardice," said William.

"Captain Johnson doesn't name my father as one of those in the hold," Colin replied in defense.

"He was Captain of their vessel. Where was he then? And look here at mother's story. Let me read you what she said to him the day Rackam was hanged." Taking the book from Matt, William found the place and read. " 'The Day that Rackam was executed, by special Favour, he was admitted to see her; but all the comfort she gave him was to say, "that she was sorry to see him there, but if he had fought like a Man he need not have been hang'd like a Dog." ' "

"Let me see that," Colin stared at the words a long time then snapping the book shut threw it to the ground. "I don't believe it!"

"Well, you're the one who likes true stories. Coward's son."

"Why, you bastard!"

"No, Colin, you're the bastard, not me — a coward's cowardly bastard."

Colin jumped William and pounded both fists into his face before William was able to push him off. He tried to run but Colin caught him around the knees, bringing him crashing to the dirt floor.

"Colin, don't hurt him," cried Mary Elizabeth. She jumped on top of Colin and pounded on his back until Matt lifted her aside. Then both Matt and Lusen tried to separate the boys but caught only flying fists for their trouble.

"Run, get Anne," sputtered Matt, fending off blows.

Mary raced toward the great house. A cluster of bamboo bent low by a sudden wind crashed against the roof of the shed. Esther flung her arms up to save them from the giant fist of God threatening to punish them all.

Arm in arm, Anne strolled with her father along the bamboo walk. From one end of the garden to the other, coconut trees lined their path like pillars supporting the feathery bamboo. The catalogue of every lovely and tragic detail of her life brought tears to Will's eyes. Again and again she begged his forgiveness and, kissing his wet cheeks, she smiled. "Ye know, Father, the more ye cry . . ."

"I know, girl," and they finished the saying in unison. "Oh, 'tis a comfort to my old age to hold you in my arms again, Annie. 'My Cordelia, come . . .' " He hadn't recited lines from *King Lear* since he held her on his knee back in Ireland. Somehow they seemed more fitting now. " 'We two will sing like birds i' th' cage. When thou dost ask me blessing, I'll kneel down and ask of thee forgiveness.' "

Will's recitation triggered words Anne believed had been buried in her child mind. " ' Wipe thine eyes. The good years shall devour them, flesh and fell, Ere they shall make us weep!' "

Mary Elizabeth came running down the path to her. "Mother, Mother, come quick. Colin and William are fighting."

Anne caught the child up in her arms. "Where are they?"

"In the old canoe shed down by the river."

"Take your grandfather's hand and show him back to the house."

"Can't I come with you?"

"See to your grandfather first. It's getting dark. And wake your father. Tell him where we are."

"Yes, Mother. Come, Grandfather."

Anne pulled the boys apart by their hair. All four had bloodied themselves in the fray yet Anne added one solid slap to the already bruised cheeks of Colin and William. She turned to Matt and Lusen, hand poised to strike.

"Wait," Matt panted, "Lusen and I only tried to break them up."

"You weren't much good at that, I see."

Coming to their rescue, Colin struggled for words. "It's true, Mother. Matt had no part in this. It was between William and me."

Anne removed her scarf and handed it to Colin. "Here, wipe your nose. I fear I did that. Now, tell me what happened here. Why were you fighting?"

"William called Rackam a coward. Tell him, Mother. Tell him it's not true," Colin begged.

"Hanged like the cowardly dog he was," Colin reached to strangle William's words and the fight was on again.

"Stop it, you two!" This time Anne's voice was enough to break them apart.

William scrambled for the book. "Isn't it true, Mother, what Captain Johnson says that Rackam went below, leaving you and Mary Read to fight off the governor's men?"

Anne hesitated. "Yes, that's true."

"See, coward's son. I told you."

"That's enough, William. Now hear me out. Colin,

your father was not himself at the end. He was ill and
. . ."

"You didn't hate him like they said, did you, Mother?"

Anne pulled Colin to her breast. "No, son. I could never
hate Jack Rackam, handsome as he was and kind. Here, put
your head back in my lap; that will stop the bleeding. You
know Rackam put Charles Vane out because he mistreated
our prisoners."

"That's mutiny, isn't it?" said Matt.

"Aye, boy. Your mother and I voted with Jack. Vane
was a cruel man; he believed killing was a necessary part of
piracy. We did not. That man was a true coward, only
cowards hurt other people for no good reason." William
became sullen and fell to brooding. "You know, Colin,
when your father was captain we took a slaver and a hell
ship and freed all aboard. That's the kind of man Jack
Rackam was."

"What's a hell ship?" Colin asked sleepily.

"Vessels bringing criminals from England to America to
be indentured as servants. Captains treated their prisoners
worse than those on slave ships."

"Was my mother as brave as they say?" asked Matt.

"Yes, indeed. She was a soldier and fought for the Queen
in Flanders. She saved your father's life once by dueling
with a man who would have killed him."

"How did my father die?"

"Tortured to death because he would not confess to
piracy. They could not take him to trial until he would say
he was guilty or not guilty. They laid great stones on him
but still he would not say aye or nay. He was a brave man,
but he was not a pirate.

"Why did they not believe him?"

"I don't know, Matt. We needed a skilled carpenter, so
we took him from another vessel. Rackam told the court he
had impressed him but the judge would not believe him.
And your mother never told the court he was your father.
She was afraid that would implicate him in piracy."

"A carpenter?"

"Aye, as good a carpenter as your mother was a sailor. She was taught by the best, Bartholomew Roberts, the most feared pirate in all the Caribbean Sea. He rescued your mother from a Dutch slaver and me from prison at Spanish Town."

"I thought Baldwin rescued you," protested Matt.

"He did. Baldwin convinced the governor to let me out to talk to Captain Roberts, for you see Roberts had learned that your mother, Matt Read, he knew her as, was in the jail and he threatened to blast the island out of the water. He did not know your mother was dead, you see. If I could convince him to leave the harbor, the governor promised to give me a pardon. I did and Baldwin held him to it. I was never so frightened as that day we sailed out to meet his vessel the *Royal Fortune*. Lusen and Esther, your mother and father were with us, too. Your daddy served Captain Roberts' tea without spilling a drop. I couldn't have done that, I tell you."

"Tea! I thought pirates drank rum," said Colin rallying.

"Not Black Bart, he always drank tea."

"He couldn't be much, then."

"You think not. He was a terror, I tell you. He was a tall man with black hair and black black eyes. He was not afraid to be seen in a sea fight, either. He always wore a red damask waistcoat and breeches and stood right on the quarterdeck. The day I saw him he wore a red feather in his hat and a big gold cross studded with diamonds. He was always a fair man but brutal in battle."

"Well, looks like the war is over." Baldwin ducked under the low roof and sat down, pulling Mary Elizabeth onto his lap.

"Mother was just telling us how you rescued her from prison in Spanish Town."

"That was mainly Black Bart's doin', Colin. I wish I could take more credit."

Even though she had heard the story before, Mary Elizabeth wanted more details concerning their romance.

"Tell how Mother knew you when you first came to the

jail. You hadn't seen each other since you were children. Well, go on."

"Yes ... well, your mother probably doesn't remember this," he said winking at Anne, "but I came to her cell and showed her a tomahawk she had given me on one of my visits to Carolina. I had carved something on the handle and ..."

"Oh, I know, I know,' screamed Mary Elizabeth "It was a heart and inside the the heart you carved the first initials of your first names—'A' and 'B'."

"That's right. What a clever girl you are." Hugging his daughter, Baldwin looked at his wife and could not help being drawn into the green sea of her eyes.

The stable door was shut against any intrusion. The rain which had crescendoed with their lovemaking ceased now and Ruth and Sang rested in each other's arms, listening to the occasional stamp of horses beneath them, the scratch of a dead branch moving across the eave, and the spatters of rain hitting the roof whenever a breeze shook the overhanging tree.

Sang had missed the feel of Ruth's long thin legs wrapped around his powerful calves and thighs, her sinewy arms locked over his wide shoulders, the touch of her soft hands on his broad chest. He had longed for a chance to reflect in the luster of her eyes and to study her high cheek bone, smooth forehead, valleys of her face, full lips, and the graceful curve of her neck. He ran over this inventory again in his mind.

This quiet time opened Ruth's troubled mind. She hesitated to break their tranquil mood but could think of no other peaceful time to tell her husband about the Maroon raid.

"Sang," Ruth said softly, "we hab trubble here some months ago."

"Trubble, what kin' o' trubble?"

"Maroons cum burn cane, kill cattle. Miz Anne send me hide wid da chil'ren."

Sang opened his lips to speak, but Ruth pressed her finger across them. "Miz Anne ... she fight. We bury t'ree men nex' day."

"What?" Sang lifted himself on one elbow to look into her eyes.

"I hab say."

"Do our people know she do dis?"

"Dey 'speck. I fine bloody sword nex' mornin' by her bed. I never speak a word to anyone, not eben mama."

"Dat be best. Miz Anne she tell da massa what hoppen. I wait 'n' see if he say anyting to me."

A dreadful pounding at the door shook them. The pounding became more urgent.

Sang reached for his breeches. "Dat bloody overlooker wantin' to put up his horse, I 'spect. Stay here. You no cum from dis place."

When the door was unlatched, Caleb Foote pushed his way into stable. "Blast ye. Why must you bar the door? Got your gold stashed in 'ere or one of your black whores, more likely."

Sang's bare shoulder muscles rippled but he held his tongue.

"Oh, piqued is ye. Come, provoke me. I would have cause to beat thee. Come on, house nigger, master's bugger boy, me mistress' lap dog ..."

"I be nuttin' to da missus but good serbant an' you know dat."

"No, I do not bloody well know dat. But I know one thing dat be the last time you'll use your tongue on me, boy."

In one motion Caleb snatched the whip from his saddle, catching Sang across the chest with stinging accuracy. Feeling the hurt as though her own, Ruth pressed both hands against her breasts.

"That's just a taste, boy." Throwing the reins of his horse in Sang's face he quit the stable.

Ruth dressed quickly in spite of the pain which barely allowed her to take more than short breaths. Sang closed the door and led Caleb's horse to its stall. Ruth came to him.

"Sang, you hurt?"

"Not my body."

"I fetch some salve," Ruth said, staring at the welt on her husband's chest.

"What kin' o' salve hab you, womon, fo' my min'?" Sang took up a jar of horse liniment from the shelf. "Here, use dis. It be good 'nuff fo' horses. It suit me. I nuttin' but animal ta dem." He globbed on some of the liniment. His eyes absorbed the blackness of his skin until he saw Ruth's golden hand touch him, gently smoothing the strong smelling ointment over the affected area.

She thought of Anne and the day after the Maroon raid. Ruth did not take notice of Sang's dark skin, only the image of the whiteness of Anne's flesh spread before her now and she did not know why.

One March morning before dawn Baldwin rode out to Fort Morant—a pitiful outpost with a few scattered tents, a platform, and cannon. It was his third visit since Anne told him about the raid on their plantation. His mind raged with thoughts of revenge so unlike himself that he wondered at his anger.

My own guilt is at the root of this, he finally concluded. This is Jamaica, not Grey's Inn. Talk is useless here. The situation wants action. Knowing Anne, she probably made light of the matter. I have the truth of it from Sang, and Caleb Foote's inventory bears out the extent of our loss. My father spent a lifetime building a plantation and almost lost it in one night to fire and pillage.

And what of me? 'Tis mine now and will be my son's one day. Baldwin dug his spurs into the flank of his horse. Thoughts of William Thomas made his blood seethe. Worthless sot, I can see it already. My two wards, both sons of pirates, have more mettle than he. A perverseness lies fallow in him—he already proves less than a man.

The sun broke through the fog just as Baldwin entered the encampment. Through the haze he saw Caleb Foote kneeling, poking a small fire. As he came nearer, Baldwin watched as Caleb's efforts to stoke the dying fire with one hand caused coffee to slosh out of the stained cup in the other. What does he do here? The atmosphere turned sour. Baldwin no longer wanted to be in this fort on this mission, but his presence had been noticed.

"Why, Master Baldwin, what brings you here?"

"Well may I ask the same of you, Mister Foote."

"See there, sir. 'Tis been a busy night." Caleb pointed to a black woman tied to a crosslike stake several yards away. She had been whipped. No sound had passed her lips then, none now. Sensing she had been addressed, she glared in hate with eyes that could pierce any fog. Baldwin felt his blood chill; he turned his eyes toward the fire.

"Hot coffee, sir?"

"Eh?"

"I said, will you take coffee, sir?"

"Yes, thank you." Baldwin thought that there must be some truth to the rumors that nights Caleb Foote was not whoring, he scavenged the hills looking for bounty. "Is Captain Stoddart about?" Baldwin asked, staring at Caleb as though he were the face of doom.

"Aye." Caleb handed Baldwin the thick brew. "You have business with him?"

Baldwin's eyes narrowed. "I would like to speak with him, aye."

"I'll fetch him then." Baldwin's cold response stirred Caleb's curiosity.

Captain Stoddart, a lank gentleman whose stiff strands of light brown hair poked from under his cap, marched over to Baldwin who was now sitting on an overturned wooden bucket. The taut white shirt rippled over the muscles of his shoulders and chest as the captain tucked its tail into his breeches. By the time he reached Baldwin, he had one long arm in the sleeve of his jacket, he reached out with the other to shake hands. Caleb Foote sauntered a few steps behind.

Baldwin shook hands with the captain before addressing his overseer. "Caleb, you have business at the plantation, have you not?"

"Aye . . . ah . . ." his eyes stared at the captain's polished boots.

Stoddart stuffed his hand into his breast pocket and pulled out a wad of pound notes and counted out several bills into Caleb's dirty hand.

Licking his fingers, Caleb counted the money again.

"Stay behind that wench, Cap'n, or she'll bite your nose off. Hah . . . ah . . . I'll take my leave then."

When Caleb had gone, the captain remarked. "A good man that. Crude, but the kind of man I want next to me in those hills."

"Do you plan an attack, then, Captain?"

"Aye. Very soon now. On Nanny Town, behind the ridge up there deep in the Blue Mountains. I'm waiting only for reinforcements and some small cannon from Port Antonio."

"You are certain it was those men who raided our plantation?"

"I have no doubt of it. They are fierce, even the women. A woman is their commander—one Nanny. A giant, so they say. We'll take her town and that will be the end of it. The Windward Maroons will trouble you no more, sir."

Glancing at the woman who now seemed to be staring straight at the sun, Baldwin asked,"Is she one of them?"

"No. She is one of Mr. Winter's runaway slaves, always rebellious, that lot. Well, can we count on your people, Mr. Sommerwood?"

Baldwin nodded, swung onto the saddle and disappeared into the lingering haze. He wondered how Captain Stoddart could possibly think that only one action against the Maroons could put an end to the trouble or that the British would be prepared to attack Nanny Town soon. "Very soon, indeed." Nothing done by the British was ever done in good time.

CHAPTER THREE

Nanny Town Besieged

Baldwin propped his feet on the gallery railing, looked out over the rim of his coffee cup and sucked in the sultry air of St. Thomas. Peter Manwaring concentrated on his coffee, made from the first beans of what he hoped would be his best crop. This morning Peter had ground the beans himself and hovered over Bertha while she brewed the coffee. Now he waited for his boyhood friend to speak. The tasting of new coffee had been a ritual. For decades, the first beans from his coffee plantation westward of Port Morant on the southern slopes of the Blue Mountains in St. Andrew's had always been brought to old John Sommerwood at Hill Haven. His opinion had always been respected by Peter's father and now Peter depended on Baldwin's appraisal.

John Sommerwood had died a little over a year ago. Peter had been to Hill Haven only once since the time he came to comfort his friend during the final days of John's illness. He had watched Anne rock Mary Elizabeth through that lingering summer night. The child had cried for days, anticipating her grandfather's death. The night he died was like the opening of a floodgate: Peter had never seen a child cry so hard or so long. But even in her motherly concern Anne had motioned to Peter to see to Baldwin who had stepped out onto the gallery and that only minutes after John Sommerwood had spoken his last words to his son.

Peter looked now at the very spot where Baldwin had stood that night. He remembered the rise and fall of Baldwin's shoulder under his own hand as his friend, without even raising his hands to his face, sobbed quietly, limply. It had been the longest night of his life. Baldwin seemed to echo his thoughts through his tears. "The dawn will never come again." Peter, who had lost his own father some five years earlier, assured him that dawn would come in time. Time. Time had worked its magic on this family. Sorrow had made Mary Elizabeth more womanly in some ways, though he'd like her to remain a little girl at least for a while longer. Colin and Matt, manly in their grief, had become more solicitous toward Anne and Baldwin. William Thomas remained a dark mystery. Peter always felt most uncomfortable in his presence.

Turning his eyes from the black pool of his thoughts, Peter could see on Baldwin's profile that indeed the dawn had come and it was as glorious as this September morning.

"Well?" said Peter, unable to wait a second longer for Baldwin's opinion of his coffee. "What do you think?"

"Wonderful!"

"Aah, not the day, the coffee. What do you think of the coffee?"

Baldwin took another sip, letting the liquid slosh against his palate and roll around his tongue.

"Well?"

"It's cold."

"Bloody 'ell!"

Peter let his saucer slam on the tile side table and reached for his hat.

"No, I jest. Don't go. It's good, Peter, really, very good."

" 'Good.' Is that all, just good? Six months ago you sent Sang to fetch me in the middle of the night to come and taste your rum. You hardly let me swallow it down when you jerked me rudely by the collar, demanding an opinion. What would you have done if I said, 'good, very good'?"

"Well . . ."

"You'd throttle me 'till I gave a proper answer. You

bloody well know you would. And here I come bringing my first beans, as a bridegroom to his virgin bride and, at a decent hour I might add, and what do you say 'good, Peter, very good.' You weren't even paying attention. Inhaling the morning, that's what you were doing. Admit it."

"I admit it. The fragrant autumn mingled with the aroma of your splendid coffee so that I could scarcely tell the difference. Your Blue Mountain blend is as fresh as a Jamaican morning."

"Oh, my, listen to this, then. I must write that down to use in my next advertisement in the *London Gazette*. Rhetoric like that befits the coffeehouse in St. Michael's Alley. You are a bloody clever fellow, Win Sommerwood." Peter was satisfied.

"Listen, do you hear that?"

Their eyes flew up the hills, past rocks and woods to the purple part of the mountain from which the sound of the abeng emanated.

Peter sank back into his chair. "That bloody cow horn, you mean?"

"Aye. What are they up to? The call of that horn positively rattles my bones."

"Any news from Stoddart?"

"Nay. He waits like an old grandmother. It has been nearly two years since he promised an attack—and still he waits, waits for swivel guns from Port Antonio, waits for Indians from the Mosquito Coast, waits for the rains to cease. He waits. And we must live in fear. Peter, this cannot go on."

"The last slave revolt was 1690, I think. Jamaica has not experienced one the like of it since—three hundred slaves rebelled. Do you think we are headed for something like that?"

"Not if we stop those Maroons."

"They increase and grow more troublesome. Nanny rules Portland, St. Thomas will be next, methinks."

"Not without a fight," murmured Baldwin grimly.

"You speak about the Maroons as if they be a foreign

power. They are Jamaican, as Jamaican as you or I."

"But they are at war with us, Peter. They might as well be French or Spanish, for they are not our people, black or white."

"I never heard you talk this way before, Baldwin."

"I never had a family before. A man never knows real fear till then. 'Tis like swimming out too far. There are things inside a man that will come out only when he be tested."

"You have much to lose, that's certain. I did not mean to make light of your family, this plantation, your slaves."

Baldwin's blue eyes flashed. Peter knew he had struck a nerve."

"I like not the sound of that word—slaves. My people are not slaves! Baldwin roared.

"What do you mean—of course they are slaves. What are you talking about?"

"I can't wait for Parliament. 'Tis like waiting for the West India Regiment to move against the Maroons." As much as Baldwin had hoped for the destruction of the Windward Maroons to allay his fears, he had also prayed and lobbied for the abolition of slavery. He had long ago convinced himself that the Maroons had nothing to do with plantation slaves. "Abolition must come!" he would shout at the dinner table no matter who or how many guests he entertained. Anne had said quietly on one occasion, "Maybe in a hundred years."

"I couldn't wait a hundred years, Peter."

"What are you talking about? Wait a hundred years for what?"

"Peter, I have manumitted them."

"No, you couldn't have. What of the rest of us? I can't do it, and I doubt another planter in the valley would even entertain such a thought."

"I have freed every blessed soul. I am no longer a proprietor of slaves. I am no longer a solicitor. I am a planter, and these people work for me."

"Did your father know you felt this way?"

"We never spoke of it, but he knew. As a boy I read a novel, *Oroonoko*. It impressed me then. The author, an English woman, was sympathetic to the negro and critical of the slave trade. I can't remember her name, 'twas an odd one, but that woman made the suffering of negro slaves so real for me I have never forgotten them or her. I found the book in Father's library. He must have purchased it although we never talked of it. John taught me everything I both know and feel. Before he died he asked only that I safeguard his fortune for the sake of his grandchildren. I promised I would."

"I can't believe what you are saying. You pay wages, then?"

"Aye. I give them a roof over their heads, their food, their clothes, educate them, and pay for their labor besides."

"When did this happen?"

"The day my father was buried."

"You mean if Sang decided to go to Trinidad and take his family, he has papers and your leave to do so?"

"Yes, he has papers. He is legally a free man. They are all free, every man, woman and child, all one hundred and thirty-nine of them."

"Have any left your service?"

"Not since I fired that Caleb Foote, Father's overlooker."

"My God, over a hundred. How do you maintain so many? Surely you did not heed your father's instruction. How can you keep your father's fortune and pay one hundred sl . . . workers?"

"My fortune is already two times greater than my father's, thanks to Anne."

"I had no idea she had inherited. When did her father die?"

"He did not die. Old Will was alive and hearty when he left here just two days ago. My fortune comes from spirits."

"Eh?"

"Rum. We make the best rum in all Jamaica. You

know, you've tasted it."

"Yes, 'Tis uncommonly good but I never dreamed your were producing on such a grand scale."

" 'Twas Anne's idea. She had the recipe from the pirate Calico Jack Rackam, Colin's father. He developed the formula in Haiti some years ago and Anne remembered the recipe. We have been working on its improvement for several years now. We export to England, America, Bahamas, Barbados, and other Windward Islands, even South America."

Peter sat with his mouth open for a moment before he spoke. "I had no idea. You have a bloody empire here."

"You must visit more often, my friend. Just this afternoon in two hours or so, we are having a horse race—my finest against the regimental horses."

"May I enter? Look down there. My man is bringing around my filly, now. I've been itching to try her against Anne's gray. Would Colin like to ride her?"

"Colin has gone to Carolina with his grandfather."

"Oh, and how does Anne feel about that?"

"She misses him. That boy saved her life, kept her from the hangman's noose. That makes a special bond I think. 'Twas like sending a part of herself home with her old father. They are great friends."

"And Colin?"

"He really took to the old man. Loved to listen to his stories and their friendship grew into love. Anne insisted Will settle his fortune on the boy if he proved interested in the life of a planter."

"Colin has pirate in him; he may long for the life of the sea."

"We'll see. Who knows what destiny awaits him. Come, let's take a look at your filly. She looks small to me."

"Well, we're three floors up. Wait till you see her up close. She's a beauty."

As he took the stairs two at a time, Baldwin's mind leaped back to last night's walk with Anne. Neither could speak of their emptiness. After a while they separated, he to the family cemetery and she to the secluded spot where Mary was buried, each to engage in private conversations with friends gone before.

"Peter, Peter!" cried Mary Elizabeth as she flew into the arms of the handsome man who always laughed at her greeting.

"One Peter is never enough for you, eh, girl."

"William, come see Peter, Peter is here!"

William Thomas reluctantly left his swing on the veranda to join his sister. He had no interest in Peter Man - waring whose conversation consisted mainly of stupid ques - tions such as "How old are ye now, boy?" or inane remarks such as "Why you're grown into a fine strappin' lad, now haven't ye." He was nearing eleven and was bored by most people except his sister. Much as he enjoyed his own com - pany, he found himself missing hers. Yet there was some - thing wicked in his attachment which he didn't understand.

Setting Mary Elizabeth down but holding her by two hands at arm's length, Peter said. "Let me have a look at ye, girl. My, how tall! How old are ye, now?"

"Ten. Well almost." She smiled and her face radiated the innocence and freshness of youthful beauty.

"Ye look more like your mother every day." Peter seemed lost in the porcelain luster of Mary Elizabeth's face. The sun caught the reddish hints of her gleaming hair. "Splendid. Really splendid." He was so transfixed he hardly noticed William take one of Mary Elizabeth's hands from his own and hold it jealously. William fixed a stare to wrench Peter's eyes from his sister's sparkling blue eyes, drawing them into the dull blue of his own.

"Why, William Thomas."

"How are you, sir?"

"Fine, lad, fine. Do you ride today?"

"No, Mother thinks I should wait a year to race."

"Wise, no doubt."

"Matt rides Mother's gray," said Mary Elizabeth proudly.

William's eyes darkened and he let go of his sister's hand.

"Oh? Well now, I can see your mother means to win this race. I am surprised she does not ride herself."

"Who is that?" Mary Elizabeth stepped closer to her brother and pointed to the near naked man with straight black hair who was leading Peter's filly toward them.

They descended the front steps, walked across the cobbled carriage drive onto the lawn. When Mary saw Anne come out on the veranda, she ran to her and took her hand to hasten her pace. "Mother, come see Peter's horse."

"Peter, you slept well, I hope. Lovely afternoon," she remarked. Peter hastily kissed her hand as Mary dragged her past him.

"Lovely . . ."

Anne followed the tugging. Mary, afraid yet curious about the strange man, wanted to see him at close range, protected of course by the indomitable presence of her mother.

"A fine filly you have here, Peter. She's sleek and spirited, I see."

The small man had some trouble controlling the animal as the group came closer. The Indian jerked sharply at the horse's bridle as she snorted greetings to everyone.

The man's naked torso, compact and muscular, shone like the filly's coat which he stroked now to calm her. When he finally turned his attention from the horse to the group, Anne noticed his flattened forehead.

"Is this your rider?" Anne asked.

"Aye. His name is Kai."

"Arawak?"

"How should I know? He wandered down out of the mountains one day."

"Arawak?" Anne directed her question to Kai this time.

"He doesn't speak. He can ride, and he has planted a small tobacco crop; what kind of Indian he is does not interest me."

"It does me. His family probably escaped from the

Spanish centuries ago. I knew an old man of his tribe once long ago, very long ago. His name was Cuffee."

Kai nodded in recognition of the Arawak name.

Anne looked at him and escaped into her private thoughts. Columbus's San Salvador. Cuffee's island. Somehow Cuffee's family escaped the Spanish—the ones after Columbus who came not to learn from the gentle Arawak but to destroy the heathen whose knowledge was not the same as their own. San Salvador was a paradise for me, too, before Spanish invaders butchered my family, and Cuffee. I left the old Arawak's head fixed on a Spanish spear, a silent sentinel to guard my dead. I left the island but could not leave behind my memories.

Anne looked into Kai's bronzed face as if the Indian's features held the answer to some half-forgotten mystery. The bustle of arriving guests gathering at the pasture fence blocked the question and the answer. Her concentration was finally broken by Mary Elizabeth who had her arms around her waist, nearly squeezing the breath out of Anne when the Indian smiled at her.

Colonel Hargrave dipped into the punch bowl. His girth strained every seam of his lacy coat fashionably buttoned at his waist. Ruth and her army of helpers set up tables in the small grove of coconut palms. Bertha seasoned the pig; sometimes slapping at the men with her basting brush for turning the spit too swiftly.

Creole women dressed in their finest moved in and out of the crowd of people. Big loop earrings danced from ears half covered with bright cloths as servants fussed about their mistresses whose bodies bent double over hooped whalebone skirts in an effort to reach a listening ear. Ragged children pushed palm fronds to fan the sultry air about the milk-white faces and sweaty bosoms of these gossips who, in spite of their tight-laced discomfort, were already busy in conversation with one another.

Eyeing Anne from time to time the ladies smiled and nodded when she walked by, but as soon as she passed hid behind their fans, whispering their disapproval.

"Means she to ride today, think you? Look at her. Doeskin breeches. Lord of the manor house. High boots and crop. What kind of example is that for her daughter? And she's such a pretty thing. So dainty, so delicate. Look at her over there with my sweet Ella, my lovely Susan, my pretty Nancy."

"Mary Elizabeth, is your mama riding in the race today?" Nancy twisted her sash saucily.

"I don't think so," replied Mary, somewhat suspicious of the question.

"I've never seen Mistress Sommerwood in a dress, have you, Ella?"

Susan's sarcastic tone irked Mary and she rebutted. "She wears them . . . sometimes . . . at the dinner table."

Ella rocked back and forth on her heels. "I guess that's why I've never seen her. I've never been to dinner at Hill Haven, have you, Susan?"

"Why no. Do you eat at table, Mary? You mama loves the horses so much methinks she eats in the stable or in the pen with the pigs."

"She does . . ." Mary, on the verge of whimpering, could not continue.

"Does what? Eat at a pig trough?" Stepping dangerously close to Mary Elizabeth, Ella taunted. "Do you eat in the stable with your boy mama and nigger friends . . . well, do you?"

"She does . . . wear dresses . . ." The girls laughed viciously at her confusion. "And . . . pretty ones too, not rags like I see on those fat ladies squatting under the trees over there." Mary pushed Ella, and she fell into the other two. Sprawled on the ground they struggled to right themselves. As Mary walked away, she heard them sputtering and fussing about the grass stains on their pretty frocks. Turning back she shouted, "That's what you get for wearing your only pretty dress to a horse race."

As she watched her daughter pirouette and dance over to Ruth and Esther, Anne could not help thinking how much prettier than the other girls Mary was. Did all mothers think that? Yet she was lovely. Pleated front and back and tied with satin ribbon, her lavender gown flowed bell-like from her slender shoulders. It shifted as she ran, revealing the dainty lace trim of her calico underskirt.

Reluctantly, Anne shifted her attention to the officers from Port Morant, who, trying not to spill the punch from the cups they were carrying, marched toward several young girls who whispered and giggled behind thatch fans. The ladies thanked their uniformed admirers and used their punch cups as an excuse to shift their glances to the muscular half-naked black men readying the horses for the race.

Anne smiled, walked up and spoke to Matt who was sitting on the fence twisting his crop impatiently.

"The captain's chestnut is too heavy in the rump. The coat of the colonel's sorrel is too dull. Peter's filly is game, but she'll run herself out before the last dip in the hill up there. That's when you make your move."

"Not till then?"

"Don't be so impatient, Matt."

"You always say that."

"I don't always know that. I had to learn patience. I still do. You can either heed my advice or learn for yourself, after you lose this race. Now which is it to be?"

Matt threw his head back like a spirited stallion and laughed. A sudden wave of sadness swamped her. She put her hand to her mouth to stop a rising sob and turned away. She did not understand why she was so vulnerable today. She had cried earlier when she had recalled with forboding Will's and Colin's departure. Matt always laughed that way and when he did Anne always saw his mother. She was almost angry that she could not control her feelings whenever Mary's presence touched her. She took a deep breath.

"What's the matter?"

"Nothing. Just . . . after the dip . . . let him go after the dip in the hill."

She wanted to hold him in her arms and cry with abandon, but she couldn't very well do that now, here, in front of all these people.

Ruth came to her and handed her a glass of punch as Anne stood by a coconut tree mopping her brow.

"You sick, Miz Anne?"

"Just out of sorts today—melancholic. I don't know why. Perhaps I near my time o' the month."

"Mebbe so, Missus."

"Do you need help here? I should busy myself. I begin to be anxious about the race."

Ruth handed her a pile of serviettes and watched as Anne's shaking hands made triangles out of the brightly patterned squares.

More than once these past two days Ruth had caught her mistress in a similar mood, and was at a loss to know what to say or do. Ruth thought it must be difficult for a woman so wise and so capable to deal with moments when she is just a woman.

Baldwin placed one arm around Lusen's shoulder. Their heads inclined together in secret consultation as the two strolled toward the pasture where Sang was holding Baldwin's bay. Ruth watched her husband grinning proudly at his son. She took Anne's hand. "They begin, Missus, cum."

Lusen and Matt clasped hands and swung into their saddles. They walked their mounts to a bamboo clump far up the slope—the designated starting point.

Baldwin kissed Anne when she reached him and whispered in her ear. "My bay shall beat your gray."

Biting his ear playfully, she replied. "I wouldn't bet on that, my love."

"Don't do that, the old nags will see."

"The horses don't mind." She laughed.

Baldwin looked around and smiled at his guests who pretended not to see their exchange of intimacies.

Mary Elizabeth sat on Peter's shoulders. William Thomas leaned sullenly against the pasture fence post. Esther and Sarah, each pulling on one of Bertha's arms, dragged her closer to the finish line.

When the horses were lined up to his satisfaction, Old Sam fired a pistol. The horses leaped down the slope, momentarily disappeared in one valley, reappeared on the next hilltop only to disappear again.

Anne's gray was easiest to spot. Mary Elizabeth bounced up and down on Peter's shoulders shouting, "There's Matt. Come on, Matt!"

Colonel Hargrave's horse stumbled. A cry went up. The jockey rolled away to safety. The sorrel got up and went over to a clump of grass and grazed.

"Drat!" was the colonel's only comment before he went in search of the punch bowl.

At the last dip before the level grass, Anne and Baldwin shouted simultaneously. "Let 'im go!" Both laughed.

"Where's my filly?" shouted Peter, unable to see anything because Mary's skirt had dropped over his head.

"Run out," said Anne.

"Oh, blast!"

"Too bad, old friend," replied Baldwin.

"Come on Matt!" shouted Anne.

The gray and the bay were neck and neck and coming on strong. Baldwin was so excited he jumped up and down, the veins of his neck straining as he shouted words of encouragement at the top of his voice first to Lusen, then to his bay.

Anne quietly urged Matt to let her horse take his own stride. "Let him take you, boy. That's it. Let 'im stretch out." Then she shouted, "Hah! Nosed him out!"

"He did not!" Baldwin was furious.

"He did. He nosed 'im out."

Baldwin was so disgusted that he sputtered and fumed and tossed his cocked hat to the ground.

Anne laughed when she saw Matt raise his hand in victory, turn and bring the gray back to the group. Mary Elizabeth dragged Matt from the saddle and smothered him with kisses. Money passed between the men.

Baldwin reached for his purse.

"How much did you lose?" Anne queried.

"Enough. Serves me proper. I should know better than to bet against you. You win at cards, at the gaming table . . ."

"I win at love, too, " she retorted.

"Yes," he laughed. "At love, most of all, at love."

Anne had to embrace both Mary Elizabeth and Matt in order to congratulate the rider.

Lusen grabbed his friend's only free hand. "Nex' time, nex' time I cotch you."

"Maybe, maybe not," Matt shouted over the excited well-wishers.

Anne turned away and saw William Thomas glaring at the scene with hatred in his eyes. She had been aware of William's jealousy of Matt, especially where Mary Elizabeth was concerned, but thought it only childish envy. Seeing his look now called up dire dread.

Suddenly a pain struck full force at the base of her brain. After it released her, Anne opened her eyes to see Colonel Hargrave lift a silver punch cup to his lips with both hands. The sound of pounding hooves drummed in her head and once again she closed her eyes against the noise and pain. But the pounding only grew louder until she envisioned a coach and four racing along a wooded road, the drivers ducking low under flying branches. Then what appeared to be giant squirrels dropped down on them. Horses reared as coachmen grappling squirrelmen were caught in motion. The figures of a man and a boy were frozen like a picture in her mind.

The image vanished with the pain and Anne opened her eyes to witness her guests in high excitement. Children perched in cotton trees shouted and clapped as the thoroughbreds trotted toward the stables.

Colonel Hargrave counted doubloons into one of Peter's open palms. Baldwin put a small sack of gold coins into his other hand. "How a man can bet against his own horse is beyond me."

"You told me yourself, Win, my filly was too small to compete with the others. I wanted to bet, so I did. I made the right choice. Sorry, old friend." He patted Baldwin on the shoulder and walked off with Colonel Hargrave, giving him a few words of unsolicited consolation.

Captain Stoddart, dusting out his now empty purse, walked over to Baldwin. "How did she do it?"

"Strategy, Captain, strategy."

"I could use some now. We attack the Maroons in two days' time."

"At last! How many men do you need?"

"As many able-bodied men as you can muster, Mr. Sommerwood."

"Your plan is firm?"

"Not as yet."

"Speak to Anne. These Maroons don't fight like British Regulars. They are bush fighters. This is your first command, is it not?"

"Aye, but . . ."

"Well, you'll need strategy. Anne will show you how to approach their haunt and how to position your men to advantage. I tell you true, Captain, I'll not accompany you unless she direct the operation. Anything else would be foolhardy."

"You would listen to a woman over a soldier in these matters? I am surprised Mr. Sommerwood. What does your wife know about such things?"

"Never mind how. She knows, that's what's important."

"Will she fight too?" Stoddart laughed out derisively.

"If she chooses, she will, aye."

"I can't believe it. You jest, sir."

"You know me better than that, sir." Baldwin turned to walk away.

"Wait. If you are in earnest . . . I will speak to the lady."

Colonel Hargrave thought it a most delightful coincidence that Anne should have lived in Bath Town, North Carolina. The colonel, not a proper colonel, but a

magistrate, was a stocky, unattractive man, quite bald but
not without a certain charm. His intake of rum seemed
inexhaustible, his appetite enormous, and his conversation
endless.

"Annie, you must visit my little village of Bath on the
Plantain Garden River," he slurred and attacked his third
dish of fried yams. "Up in my mountain a hot spring
bubbles. I make a punch of the mineral water—awful
tasting stuff but quite good for you. You look a trifle
peaked, Mistress. You really should try my mineral
spring."

"Yes, sometime, Colonel."

"Yes, do, do. I'll lay out a feast—roasted peacock, ring-
tailed pigeon, mountain mullet. You look a bit scrawny
too, except for . . ." he unlocked his eyes from her breasts.
"Well, umm . . . at any rate I can entertain you in fine
style. I've come into a fortune lately."

"Really, Colonel."

"Quite right. I had a modest share in Lord Muskerry's
treasure salvage expedition—oh 'long about two autumns
ago. He brought 220,000 pieces of eight. Muskerry sails
again soon. Would you like to invest in his next
expedition?"

"I think not, Colonel Hargrave. I have all the treasure I
need in my daughter and sons."

"Quite right. Well, 'tis an exciting business at any rate.
This last wreck, for instance, stood very near this island."

"Was it deep?"

"No, not at all. A Spanish man-o-war she was, lying on
the shoals of Ponto Pedro—due south of Negril, I think."

"Negril."

Night came at last to wed the void. Dark thought
without form invaded even the deepest part of Anne's sleep.
She woke at every hour, walked to the gallery, looked out
but heard nothing except the creaking of the bamboo and
the distant roll of the sea.

Daylight broke still, stiller than any other day.

"Baldwin, wake up."

"Huh . . . what is it?"

"Wake up. Come downstairs with me. I am uneasy."

"What time is it?"

"Daylight."

"Are you all right? Did you hear something? You've been acting strangely ever since your father and Colin left us. Shall I fetch the doctor?"

"No. Come down with me now."

"Shaking her robe in response to a habitual fear of scorpions, Anne left the room, dressing as she went. After much grumbling and struggling with his boots, Baldwin followed her.

When he came out onto the porch, Baldwin saw Anne staring at something on the ground at the foot of the veranda steps. The sight held her frozen. A sudden gust whipped her dressing gown from her body. Or did she rip it away? He was not certain. Her fingers tearing through her hair reminded him of Orestes' Furies. He stepped back into the doorway and continued his backward motion until her world-piercing screams brought him to her side.

Mangled bowels of man and boy arrested his attention at first, then shifting his eyes to their faces, he beheld first Will's gray in death, then Colin's; Baldwin's eyes locked wide in horror at the sight of the boy's own penis stuffed in his mouth.

He took Anne into his arms, stifling her screams in his chest. Matt and William Thomas ran down the stairs. Instantly recoiling from the scene, Matt ran. Only intermittent retching stalled his pursuit of the river path. Transfixed, William twisted his lips in and out of smirking grimaces.

"Your sister is coming. Hurry, stop her. William, for God's sake, don't let her see this. Move, will you . . . you . . . bloody bastard."

William began to laugh hysterically and point to Colin's face." Not me. There. There's the bloody bastard."

Releasing Anne, Baldwin snatched up Mary Elizabeth

before she reached the bottom of the stairs and carried her into the house. He put her in Ruth's arms. "Get Sang to fetch a cart. Keep everyone away from the carriage circle, especially the children." Baldwin went into the drawing room and pulled one of the heavy tapestries from the wall.

"Mary, go ta Berta. Tell her fine Sang, tell him cum."

Ruth descended the veranda steps and drew her eyes away from the gruesome sight just as Anne flew at William's throat to stop his uncontrollable laughter. Racing back into the house, Ruth called, "Massa Baldwin, cum quick. Miz Anne, she kill da boy."

William was no match for his mother's strength, fired now by frenzied grief. Baldwin came back in time to stop her from killing him. Disoriented and gasping for air, William crawled off into a hedge clustered with red licorice beads. Baldwin spat his disdain, then flung the curtain over the bodies.

Anne staggered up the steps and sent every movable piece of porch furniture within her reach hurtling across the veranda. Ruth followed her to the library and closed the doors softly.

Anne took up a decanter of brandy and with determined hand poured a glass, drank it, then lifting the crystal goblet into the morning light, watched it flash colors about the room. Decanter, glass, tray and table crashed through one of the French doors. The statue of Diana with her bow hurled through the other. Books pulled from the shelves littered the carpet like headless birds. No object was safe from her wrath and no amount of destruction would gratify it. Unable to tear apart one particular volume, she shot an angry glance at its binding. The word "Shakespeare" glared like the sun back at her. Clutching the book to her breast she fell to the floor and gave way to exhausted sobs.

Sunset streaked the sky. At Fort Morant Bay, the army made ready for their march up the mountain—the steepest part but the least expected avenue, and in the dead of night. The captain shook his head bewildered as he stuffed powder and shot into his pack. If only he had more time. He had sent dispatches to England but had received no word as yet. Rainy season or no, action must be taken now. He had delayed a week already and could delay no longer.

Anne's plan confounded every detail of military strategy he had ever studied in books. A letter from Whitehall would surely contradict her, but what did those bewigged secretaries know of Maroon warfare? Nothing. His own narrow experience reminded him that it was only by some quirk of fate that he was still alive.

His captain had marched boldly into a Maroon village in broad daylight as if he were Marlborough on the plains in Flanders. The dark warriors dropped on the British like hailstones just as the captain gave the order to attack. They came from every direction except from the front. How the Maroons got behind an entire company troubled Stoddart's sleep to this day. It was wholesale slaughter. He was among the few to escape.

Yes, Anne Sommerwood was right. Surprise them at night. It was the only way to survive.

Since the ambush of her son and father, Anne's grief had been swallowed up by vengeance. She meant to flush out all the Maroons in the East and kill each one single-handed if necessary. Her army was marching tonight at midnight, with or without Captain Stoddart and his West India Regiment.

Anne had determined that if Peter's Arawak had found his way down the mountain at night, he could find his way back up. Kai understood her plan. He took a stick and indicated the entrance to the mountain path. It was very near the Sommerwood sugar boiling house. His stick scratched a twisting, curving, tortuous route into the crusty earth.

Captain Stoddart arrived at the boiling house with his army of twenty men, three swivel cannon and fifteen Mosquito Indians, expert in smelling out Maroon haunts. Peter brought ten good men. Baldwin mustered thirty of his strongest negroes.

Everyone was dressed in dark clothes, even the soldiers. The captain felt naked, helpless almost, out of uniform; and he could not understand the nature of his fear. Was it the woman or the night? What was he without his uniform? James Stoddart, face blackened by charcoal and mud. Who was he? He wondered, peering into his battalion of black faces. Was it the black faces that frightened him? Who was he to follow a woman into battle? Who was he not to?"

Baldwin tapped his arm. "Let's go. The cannon are tied together. My men will drag them up, carry them up the mountain, if they must."

Sang issued arms from the platform at the east end of the sugar boiling house. Anne went to him.

"Protect our children in our absence."

"Wid my life, Miz Anne."

"After this night, not one Maroon will live to threaten us again. I promise you." She stuck a pistol in her belt, signaled Baldwin and followed the Indian out of the boiling house, across the cane field to the path.

Falling rock.

Cooking fires dwindled outside the huts in the mountain village and plantation settlement. Maroon children slumbered on grassy beds, negro babies on straw mats. Pipes smoldered.

Dance and song and story.

Falling rock.

Exhausted, drenched to the bone by wet leaves, scratched by thorny vines, bruised about the ankles by stumps and rocks, the little army struggled up the mountain.

The cozy lights of the plantation below receded as Anne clawed her way from tree to tree, wrenching her neck by the constant looking up, and back, and up again. Finally, she grasped Baldwin's outstretched hand and allowed him to pull her up the last few yards to the provision fields outside the Maroon village.

Clothed in soot and night, their muffled exertions brought the army to the brink of dawn. Carefully stepping over rows of yams, gently pushing aside stalks of corn, they spread out and positioned themselves as planned to wait for dawn.

Dawn broke.

The warning cries of the Maroon sentries gurgled in sliced throats. Cannon shot blew huts into the air. The sound of alarm was deafening in its terror and anger, but it was too late. Victory belonged to the English. In moments, village streets were strewn with bits and pieces of bodies that, blasted by the cannon, writhed and jerked and squirmed in the rubble of the houses.

Hand-to-hand combat had been relatively brief. Anne fought like a maniacal harbinger of doom. In her hand, Mary Read's sword became a death machine, slicing, cutting down her enemies.

The annihilation dealt by his wife's hand disturbed Baldwin more than the devastation wrought by his army. He watched, for as long as he dared, from a safe place just as he had done that night on the veranda of Hill Haven. Colin's corpse assaulted his eyes, then, and now he could not turn his head anywhere to avoid the mangled bodies of Maroon dead. Baldwin looked up into the trees to freshen his mind but the stench of blood filled his nostrils fouling his thoughts once again. This is vengeance. "Blood will have blood." I can taste it even. This soldier. This woman, nay more than soldier, more than woman, or less? This is how the she cat fights to protect her cubs. We are not men and women up here, but animals. Baldwin hacked his way toward Anne and reached her in time to catch his wounded wife in his arms.

When Anne had sighted Nanny, she hesitated for an instant before firing. The mother-soldier took careful aim to

avoid hitting any of the children crowding around the
Maroon chief. There was a blink of recognition from
Nanny as she stopped Anne's bullet with her hand. At that
same moment a musket ball entered Anne's thigh. Before
she fainted, Anne thought she saw Nanny catch more
bullets with her bare hands. Then, it seemed the giant took
up a queenlike girl of William's age in one arm, and a boy
about Mary Elizabeth's age in the other. Ascending into the
sky, the swarm of children clinging to Nanny's robe looked
to Anne like a throng of angels about the feet of Raphael's
madonna. Later she would convince herself that, seized by
the pain of her wound, she had only imagined that. But
what last assailed her blurring eyes she could neither deny
or erase. Hand in hand, line after line of Maroon women
leaped from a precipice. Seemingly without a thought and
certainly without a cry or moan, dozens chose death over
slavery.

She had heard of this and thought of it often during her
long months of recuperation. The old Arawak on San
Salvador had told her that his people jumped into sinkholes
when the Spanish came to take them off the island. Mary
Read had told her that on the Dutch slaver she had seen the
captives leap overboard and drag their chained partners to
watery graves. Baldwin had told of striking field slaves who
committed mass suicide by taking poison. She remembered
nothing more. As the smoke of cannon and guns had
cleared, Baldwin carried her through the misty morning,
down the mountain, back to Hill Haven.

The bullet lodged deep in Anne's left thigh. Ruth
assisted in the surgery and through her gentle care Anne's
leg healed. Pain she could bear, but the chaos in her mind
she could not. Weeks and months passed slowly. Grief and
shame tormented her days and fantastical dreams her nights.
Baldwin often sat with her during the interminable evening
hours."Where are the children?"

"Ruth is reading to them from the Bible."

"William Thomas, does he listen?"

"He listens. He is curious why Esther is so intent and

watches her. But he listens."

"You know, Win, I look at him and see myself."

"Come now, Annie."

"It's true. If I had not one drop of human compassion in me, I'd be like him even now."

"Do you hate him, Annie?"

"No, not anymore. I can't."

"I hate him. My own flesh and blood and I hate him. He knows it and keeps his distance. He has no interest in the plantation. Matt never leaves my side, the whole day he works with me. He is more my son than William Thomas."

"I feel neglected. Mary Elizabeth sits with me all day sometimes. She brings William Thomas with her and he stays for a while, even acts civil towards me. But I never see Matt until after dinner and then I wonder if he comes on his own or just to be with Mary Elizabeth."

"What do you mean?"

"Don't you see the way he looks at her?"

"I'll kill him. If he touches her, I'll kill him."

"Baldwin, what's the matter with you tonight? Come here. Lie beside me."

Baldwin put his head on her breast. His face was hot and steamy like a child's when it cries. Anne brushed his hair from his eyes and felt tears.

"I don't hate him, Annie. Damn! I come in here to woo you from your melancholy and look what happens. I'm blubbering like a silly girl. I feel I have lost my son . . . "

"I have lost him too: he is lost to me as well, for I cannot understand the boy."

"See what I mean? How many sons is that for you, Annie? 'Tis not the pain in your leg which brings those dark looks I see in your face each night. It is the hurt in your heart caused by the loss of so many loved ones."

"I try to tell myself that we have Matt and Mary Elizabeth. They will bring joy to our old age, give us grandchildren, carry on here after us. I am trying to convince myself that that is enough. That is all I need.

"Can you be certain they will love each other?"

"I'm certain, but Matt won't touch her, you needn't fear."

"I know that. I don't know why I said it."

"You're frightened."

"Frightened. Frightened of what?"

"Frightened of Matt, William Thomas, the Maroons, frightened of yourself mainly."

"The Maroons are gone."

"Are they? Win, I never told you, but I have dreams."

"What kind of dreams?"

"Strange dreams, hideous and macabre and she . . . that woman is always present, fixing me with her black eyes. I'm caught in those eyes and changed somehow. I don't know, bewitched maybe, in a way. I see such horrible visions and feel myself engulfed in fire as if I'm standing in the bottom of a burning pit on red hot logs. And when I wake I reek of smoke."

"Smell of smoke, you say? So that's what . . ."

"Ask Ruth, she'll tell you. She has smelled it sometimes. The Maroons are up there, Win, I know it and I'm frightened. This is not a game. Playing at piracy, that was a game. This be deadly serious."

"I hope you are wrong, Annie. God help us, I hope you are wrong."

CHAPTER FOUR

Muscovado

Ruth knew she would never forget her. Taller than any woman Ruth had ever seen, she towered over patrons haggling with her over the few baubles she had for sale in the crowded Kingston market. Her ebony skin enhanced the gold bracelets which covered both arms. Dozens of gold chains fell in neat rows onto her glistening bosom. One bejeweled hand wiped a colored napkin across her brow and dragged into the valley of her breasts while long thin fingers reached into the basket on her head to draw out more trinkets.

As the vendor walked along the wharf, Ruth thought of Nanny. Perhaps it was only because this woman resembled a Queen Mother walking among her subjects as she leaned forward to show a string of glass beads to a prospective buyer or stooped to pat the head of a child.

Absently Ruth fingered a bolt of coarse linen. Why think of Nanny? It had been over a year since the raid on Nanny Town; and rumors had circulated that the Ashanti priestess was dead, poisoned by her brother Cudjoe who was said to be jealous of her skills in warfare. That was only one of the many stories rumored in the East. Depending on the imagination of the inhabitants of each plantation, the woman had been shot, knifed, hanged or beaten to death. Ruth doubted that there was one shred of truth in any of the rumors surrounding Nanny's demise. But this woman was not Nanny; she was too frail. Then who?

Their great plantain walk had suffered no destruction, so the survivors of the massacre at Nanny Town in 1732 did not have to leave; they would not starve. That had been her only fear. Nanny had wasted no time assessing the extent of their damages. Yamou helped the men who were instructed to salvage what lumber they could from the smoldering huts. Women picked up their machetes and followed Nanny into the fields. Afiba, shaken by the noise of the guns, refused to leave Nanny's side. Nanny dug up a handful of dirt and ran her thumb through it, then spread her fingers allowing the dirt to fall back to the ground. A few yams had been trampled under the wheels of the cannon, otherwise her provision field was intact. She gave directions on how to save every plant molested by the English soldiers. If the British had destroyed their fields, victory would have been complete and unconditional. Her people would have perished. She silenced the abeng and the drums. The rhythm of life slowed, but only till the Maroons of the East grew strong again.

Taking Afiba's hand, Nanny smiled and started toward the village. She stopped along the way at a banyan tree to gather the girl into her powerful arms and kiss the tears away from Afiba's shining face. There would be no loss to compare with this girl. The bullets caught by her magic had been aimed at Afiba, her princess. She had hurled them back with such force that she had killed the soldier who fired them. He stood defenseless, bewildered at what he had just witnessed. Then scooping Yamou and Afiba into her arms, Nanny's eyes pierced the clouds and finding the moon lifted the children to safety.

Nanny could always rebuild her village as long as her world was safe in her arms. She heard the running of the river stream and looking up saw that the giant banyan, clutching the side of the mountain, had dropped thick roots protectively around them. Somewhere near here they would rebuild Nanny Town—on a finger of the Rio Grande River high in the John Crow mountains.

Nanny ran her fingers down Afiba's arms. "Skin like moonlight."

"Nanny, me 'fraid."

"No, no 'fraid. No ting harm Afiba."

"I bleed." She held her hand between her legs. "I bleed here."

"'Bout time you bleed dere."

"Den, I no die?"

"No, chil'. Dot hoppen all womon. You womon now."

"I no like. I mess myse'f—no like. Nanny make stop. "

"No stop. Dat how womon gibe life, make baby, make grannie for Nanny."

"I 'fraid make baby."

"Not now." Nanny took the weeping child to her breast. "You princess. Someday you Queen, Queen Mudder. You want be Queen Mudder someday?"

"I tink so."

"Tink so? No tink so. Be so. Time soon cum. Now . . . now you bleed."

It was time. Two acres of cane were ripe. Baldwin had watched his crop turn from grass green to popinjay. While he watched, he planned. After sixteen long months of study, he was prepared for this moment. The cane must be harvested, milled, boiled, and sent to the curing house all in the space of a few hours. The processing of muscovado required stamina and skill, but he had both at his disposal. Many workers made up for the stamina of a few; and he had trained not one or two but teams of feeders and boilers.

Everything which could be made ready before was ready now. The huge copper boiling pots had been cleaned, platforms and pipes repaired, and firewood gathered. The cooper built barrels for the rum and hogsheads for the cured sugar. Anne checked the giant cisterns and distillery.The rum-making part of their enterprise was her domain.

Matt took a hand in every phase of the operation. This particular two acres he even helped plant. Alongside Baldwin, who was also stripped to the waist, he dug the trenches. Mary Elizabeth laid cuttings of old cane end to end in the furrows, and Esther followed, lightly covering the plants with soil.

Later, when Baldwin called them out to the field, the girls screeched with delight to see the first sprouts shooting from each joint of cane.

"Matt, get more cuttings. I see a few here and there with no shoots."

Matt was off like lightning. Mary hoed around the dead pieces of cane and Esther pulled them up.

"Save those pieces, Esther," cried Baldwin. "You and Mary toss them on the pile with the other cane trash. Later, we'll mix it all together with manure and make enough fertilizer to spread over this whole field."

The girls were not enthralled with the idea of manure but entertained themselves by chasing each other back and forth from ditch to trash pile. Now, sixteen months later, Mary Elizabeth, nearly twelve, had become much too grown up to play in the cane-piece.

Every night after supper Anne and the children sat around Baldwin, listening to his endless instructions concerning sugar processing which he liberally spiced with colorful stories his father had told him about earlier sugar days. Curiously, William Thomas, who would not take part in any of the work, seemed to take an interest in these sessions.

Anne did not see Matt smile at Mary Elizabeth and take her hand lovingly. Their eyes locked momentarily before Mary would shy away confused, not by Matt's actions, but by her own feelings. William Thomas saw this happen more than once, and more than once had dropped down on the floor between them. Matt, not one to tolerate this kind of intrusion, punched him secretly and slipped around to Mary's other side. William held back his blow only because his sister had moved into the way of it.

Apart from competition for Mary Elizabeth's affection William paid little attention to Matt, but often embittered thoughts filled his mind. Let him work himself to death in the bloody hot boiling house, what do I care? I will inherit here, not him, now that Colin is gone. So during these meetings, William never bothered to disguise his boredom, and for this reason Baldwin's eyes seemed to rivet on the boy's face. Frustrated by his son's lack of interest, Baldwin wished William would act downright rude so he could slap him, just once. Baldwin launched into a story in order to grab the boy's attention.

"Once, as a boy, I had begged the worker at the water mill . . . you know the one up on the hill."

"The one by the great cisterns?" asked Matt.

"Aye, lad, the very one. Well, this day . . ."

"How old were you then?" asked Mary Elizabeth.

"Oh, 'bout twelve, your brother's age, I guess."

"I'm nearly fourteen," protested William.

"Well, twelve or thirteen, I don't remember. Anyway, I had persuaded the worker, Gloster I think his name was—no, March—his name was March. I persuaded March to let me feed the cane into the roller. And I was doing it, too, when your granddaddy came in. Old John he came up behind me so carefully and quietly that I didn't notice him. Just as I finished feeding one stalk and went to reach for another, he picked me up and swung me away from the roller."

"What happened next?" asked William, his interest piqued by the prospect of more violence.

"Well, he slapped me roundly. I remember that part very well. Then he ordered the driver to whip March."

"Grandfather would never do that!" cried Mary Elizabeth defensively.

"Well, he did it, I tell you. He was so angry his face was beet red. You see, March shouldn't have . . ."

"No!"

Anne was about to interrupt. Baldwin threw her a forbidding glance. "And what's more, girl, while the driver was whippin' March, Old John put me over a barrel and beat me with a tamarind switch."

"No!" Mary ran to Anne, sat on the floor and buried her face in her mother's lap, crying. Anne glared at Baldwin as she stroked Mary's hair. She would not question his authority, especially in these matters or in front of the children. These stories were meant for their instruction. Her only objection was that he took too long to get his point across. By the time he delivered the thrust of the story, the entire household had turned into bedlam. Anne doubted the children understood him at all.

"That's not all, lads!"

Anne knew too well that her husband was cranking up for a splendid finish. He drew up his body, flashed his eyes and began waving his arms about. Even though she had not been directly addressed, Mary Elizabeth stopped crying and listened.

"Your grandfather dragged me out of the mill, put me in a dung cart, and drove me to Fowler's plantation. He took me straight to one of Mr. Fowler's animal mills."

"Why?" William Thomas usually knew where his father's stories were aimed, but this time he was baffled.

Matt leaned back on his elbows, looked and caught Anne's eye, then shifted his glance to Mary Elizabeth and sat up, content that she was still in the same room with him.

"He took me there to watch."

"Watch what?" asked Matt, afraid he had missed something.

"To watch the feeder feed the cane into the rollers."

William started to get up and leave the room.

"Sit down, boy, I'm not finished. Now, that particular man had been standin' feeding cane into that roller for ten hours. John had been there that very morning and saw him at it then. Ten hours mind you, standin' in one spot juicin' cane. So we watched him, your grandfather and me, for six more hours. I was miserable, my legs ached and my backside, and I had to relieve myself something terrible. Any time I shut my eyes and leaned my head back, Old John 'ud poke me."

"Oh, I get it, " shouted Matt. "He wanted you to realize what it was like for that slave to stand for such a long time at a boring job."

"Aye, Matt. And more."

"What more?" shouted William. "You'd learned your lesson, I should think."

"Well, Old John didn't think so. We stayed an hour, maybe two more. I was wet and wretched by now, I can tell you that. Two more hours watchin' cane go in the roller, juice squeeze out. Cane in. Juice out. Over and over. Cane in. Juice out." Anne coughed. Baldwin paused. "Then it happened."

"What?"

"The man's finger, just his finger mind you . . . caught!"

Mary gasped.

Baldwin continued slowly, drawing out each word. "The man's whole body was dragged into the mill and was crushed to death."

Esther, who had been listening at the door, screamed in fright. Her screams started Sarah weeping. Their cries brought Ruth rushing down the hall, drying her wet hands on her apron as she came. William was fascinated, begging his father for more details. Anne stood up and exclaimed, "Enough!" Matt came to Mary Elizabeth and held her in his arms, but this time she was too horrified to cry. The lesson was lost in the confusion. Baldwin would have to explain to them another day the importance of training several men to do one job and rotating workers every few hours as the best prevention against accident.

The next day Matt accompanied him to the boiling house, giving Baldwin an opportunity to implant another caution in the boy's mind. "Boiling sugar is a hazardous job, just as dangerous as juicin' cane. You see, lad, if the bubbling sugar should splash out of the kettle it will stick to the boiler's skin like tar, and nothing can stop the sizzlin' glob from burning right through the man's hand."

Matt watched while the boiler skimmed off the residue and ladled the juice into smaller and smaller coppers which boiled over hotter and hotter fires. Hovering over the smallest pot, the boiler waits for the precise point where the sugar crystalizes. Then, as a hunter lets go his spear,

the marksman pulls his trigger, or the fisher jerks his line,
the boiler strikes. He dampens the fire and ladles the sugar
into the cooling cistern.

Once the sugar hung in the curing house drying into a
rich brown cone called muscovado, the Sommerwood
plantation fell back into its usual easy routine. Anne
distilled the molasses into rum. Baldwin planted another
field of cane. It was May, 1734.

His body was hard and tanned. Anne delighted in the
feeling of him on those long rainy afternoons they spent
together. The children, occupied by their tutor, would not
bother them for an hour or two at least. They would glory
in each other's bodies, finding new ways to excite and
satisfy.

"Aah."

"Oh, I've hurt your leg." Baldwin swung over to Anne's
right side. Fondling her breasts, he kissed her forehead and
eyes before drawing from her lips all distress. Breathing in
tranquillity, he continued kissing her even though he knew
she had fallen asleep.

Anne felt as though she were falling, sliding down a
gently sloping waterfall. Reaching the bottom, hours later
it seemed, she saw herself floating face down in the water.
Dead? A tall woman came rushing though the milky water
towards her. Her muslin blouse clung to her slightly
rounded belly. Mary Read! Surging forward Anne seemed to
be pulled back up into the sky as if plucked up by a giant
bird. Why does she not hear me? Why can't I go to her?
Locked in space hovering above the figures Anne could not
move. She thinks I'm dead. I'm not dead, Mary! Mary drew
Anne's body into her arms and blew into her mouth. Then
rocking the lifeless body in her arms, Mary kissed Anne's
forehead and eyes and mouth. Dark clouds hovered about
her, obstructing Anne's view of the scene below. Vision
clearing at last, Anne saw her body sail towards the black
horizon.

A rapturous pain aroused her. Baldwin's full weight had

settled into every curve and valley of her body, and she could feel the fullness of his testicles pressing moist against her thighs. Drawing his hips to her face she took him into her mouth where he swelled to bursting, shooting warm semen into her throat.

The fires in the center aisle of the curing house drew the moisture from the sugar packed into hundreds of earthenware pots. Each one was stoppered for forty-eight hours to allow a quantity of molasses to collect at the bottom. Uncorked, the thick juice shot into the pans. The initial release accomplished, each cone-shaped vessel relaxed into an uneven dribble of molasses which splashed into the wide dripping pan below.

Despite the wet season Nanny Town had been rebuilt. Some of the new huts in the Maroon village were now shingled. Caleb Foote had been foolish enough to wander too near Nanny's community but had been smart enough to save his neck and even turn a profit providing tools and building materials. Nanny gave him gold and gemstones but with certain stipulations. If he betrayed them, he would die.

"You go far, no far 'nuff. Nanny's eye fine you. You one dead mon."

"I understand."

"House here."

"Thank you, Nanny."

"See dat mon. You look out him."

Caleb saw a man limp by on a wooden leg carved out of a branch. "Just point out his wife, Nanny. I won't bother her."

"No care, womon. See dat guava tree nex' hut you. Dat belong him. You take fruit, he kill."

"You take womon, any womon dat hab you. You see girl dere." Nanny pointed to Afiba who was crushing spices in a wooden bowl polished smooth by centuries of use.

"Oh, a rare beauty, to be sure."

Nanny lifted him under his armpits and hoisted the squat thick man off the ground as easily as she would a small boy. Nose to nose he might understand her better. "You no touch. You touch, I snap ting like dry twig. I tear out balls by der roots."

"Caleb no touch. I hear you Nanny. No touch."

Nanny tossed Foote aside as she would a peel of orange. He landed in a bush of flowering gardenias and the dead white waxy blossoms sprinkled all over him. Caleb was afraid to move for fear he might discover broken bones. Instead he allowed his weight to sink into the branches and watched the children play at bushman. Helmets of grass draped over their heads and curls of long thick brownish grass fell into their faces as they darted behind trees and jumped from high branches. Someone kicked his foot. He struggled to his feet and looked up into the dark, scarred face.

"Nex' time Foote bring guns. Nanny need musket. Soldiers take."

"Guns. Yes, Nanny. I bring guns."

As she walked away from him Nanny stopped to touch the belly of a pregnant woman. The loss of so many women angered her — women were providers not only of food but of children. Gently smoothing her hand over the woman's rounded belly, Nanny remembered the day she carried nine children into a valley on the back of the Rio Grande. She had planted a mahoe on the spot where she buried them, to grow large and spread its protective arms over them.

In October of 1734, a wild boar had been reported in the neighborhood of St. Thomas East. The excitement of the hunt stirred in Anne when she heard that it was the largest boar ever seen on the island. Boar hunting had been a weekly activity on New Providence. But now as easily as the urge to hunt swelled within her, she resisted it.

Baldwin had gone to Kingston with Sang. Before going off to check the distilleries, Anne warned Mary Elizabeth to stay close to the main house and sent a crew out on horseback to patrol the provisional fields.

Matt accompanied Anne to the distillery and watched her mix up a blend of molasses, cane juice, and skimmings from the boiling coppers. The mixture of just the right amounts of the ingredients made the difference between inferior and superior rum. He was beginning to taste the difference between his brew and Anne's. Not yet fourteen, he was allowed only a taste. Neither Anne nor Baldwin drank very much so he never really thought about rum. He had, however, seen William at the jugs more than once. He wondered if Anne or Baldwin were aware of William's drinking.

Anne took several sips from Matt's most recent mixture. "Good, very good."

He smiled, pleased that she would say it, even if it wasn't true. "Still too sweet, don't you think?"

"A little, yes, but decidedly an improvement over your last. So much so, in fact, I shall be able to retire soon."

"I hardly think so."

Anne watched him stir the vat. He was handsome like his mother, and gentle mannered like his father. He was already as tall as she and growing every day. His broad shoulders strained, pulling taut his shirt. Thin, soft hair the color of her chestnut gelding fluffed in the slightest breeze and fell across his forehead. Looking at him now, Anne was reminded of a young colt leaping about the pasture, not quite ready but itching to race.

Matt wanted to talk to Anne. Somehow he felt she would understand the strange feelings which stirred within him of late. On several occasions he had started to tell Baldwin; words formed in his mind but the conversation turned to something else before he could speak his thoughts. Every day, more and more, he felt like a man trapped in a boy's body.

"Anne?"

"Yes."

"Oh . . . nothing."

"Nothing? Something troubles your mind, has been for some weeks now."

"It's not my mind. My body torments me."

"Oh." So that's it, she thought. Anne had forgotten that he was still a boy. He does a man's work, thinks man's thought, talks like a man. Now that she thought about it he was never a boy, really. "And what does your body tell you?"

"It yearns."

"For the touch of a woman?"

"Aye. Things happen to my body. Like now I . . . you . . . she . . . Oh, God!" He swelled, he knew it, but was afraid to look down.

Dear Lord, what now? she thought. 'Tis my turn to speak. Give me the right words, Mary Read. This is your charge after all. Well, what do you say, woman? Your son needs help. You see what has happened, don't you. It makes no sense he should suffer so. And yet, he will suffer, for he is like you, my friend. He will burst before he will touch either myself or Mary Elizabeth.

"You know, Matt, I am reminded of a boar hunt."

"Boar, what boar?" Matt was puzzled yet relieved in a way that Anne had changed the subject.

"Well, not the one who harrasses these plantations of late. I was thinking of the one that almost killed your mother."

"God! When did that happen?"

"Years ago, too many years now—on the island of New Providence in the Bahamas. We used to hunt boar there for sport."

"Sport!"

"Aye. Well, one day your mother stabbed a particularly obnoxious beast but in doing so fell against her spear handle striking her left shoulder near an old wound."

"How was she wounded? In the Flanders wars?"

"Aye. She saw dangerous action there, lad. Well, I lured the animal away from her, then finished the kill. Later she would not let anyone tend her wound. Rather, she stole away to her hut alone. You see, Matt, she did not want to betray her sex. At the time everyone knew her as a man."

"Even you, you never suspected?"

"No. In fact I fancied myself in love with Matt Read. I even went to your mother's hut that night to make love to her. The salve I brought for her shoulder was only a pretext."

"God! What did she do?"

"Put me off, in a gracious way, mind you, but she sent me away all the same."

There was some message in Anne's story. Matt turned it over in his mind. "Are you telling me . . . not to love you?"

"I'm not saying that at all. We never really choose whom we love, it just happens sometimes. I loved your mother with the same intensity after I found out she was a woman as I did when I thought her a man."

"Mary Elizabeth is two years younger than I."

"You see that as a wide chasm now, but 'twill not always be so. Can you wait?"

"I can wait."

Of course he can, Anne thought to herself. But I must speak to Mary Elizabeth, she approaches the age. Now she is a delicate flower, but blossoms have a way of transforming themselves into fruit: they ripen and ache to be picked in season.

Lusen was running towards them. "Miz Anne! Miz Anne!"

Alarmed, Matt dropped his ladle into the vat.

"Miz Anne . . . Mama say . . ." Lusen was so out of breath he could barely speak.

"Lusen, slow down. Breathe." She wiped his sweaty face with her handkerchief. "Now, what has happened?"

"Mama say mabbe . . . Miz Mary and Massa William gone from da yard. Mama . . . Mama, she be worried."

"Dear God! I told them to stay close to the house today. Where would they go? Do you have any idea?"

"No'm."

"Anne, I think I know." Matt wiped his sticky hands on his breeches. "Mary has been begging me to take her up the mountain to see the ginger plants in bloom. There is a patch of bushes up the slope beyond the boiling house. I didn't think William Thomas would take her, he so hates the stench of boiling sugar, but maybe now, that the boiling process is finished . . . Oh God, I don't know. Shall I go back for guns?"

"No, there are cutlasses and spears in the boiling house. Let's go. Lusen, are any horses missing? Perhaps they are riding."

"No'm, all be in. I was in da stable when Mama cum ta fetch me. When Massa Baldwin and doddy cum home?"

"They won't be back till past dark."

"Mama she try sen' some mon out ta look for dem, but dey cum back soon. Dey 'fraid to meet wil' boar."

"Lusen, go back and tell your mother not to worry. We'll find them."

"Yes'm."

At the boiling house Anne grabbed a cutlass and as many spears as she could carry and followed Matt, who worked his way carefully through the dense growth. From time to time they stopped to listen.

Matt could not hear for thinking. William brought Mary up here. I know it. She pressed him. Probably told him that I would not take her. That would do it. William is so jealous of me. He'd do anything to discredit me and lift himself up in her eyes. But why? Why does William hate me so? Matt could not recall a time when he had done William a single wrong and though he saw the envy, Matt did not see the depravity in William's nature.

Mary Elizabeth was transfixed with delight. The blossoms were even lovelier than she had dreamed. She had known it was time even before she had pestered Bertha into telling her when the ginger would bloom. Reluctant at first, William smiled, a smile for her alone, then followed his sister into the mountains to the place where the ginger bloomed. The unusual flowers grew all along the green stalks and were colored a waxy ivory on the outside petals while inside glowed burgundy speckled with flecks of pink and gold.

"Oh, William, aren't they beautiful!"

He picked one of the flowers and his fingers played over its ruffled petals.

Mary spun around and around, delighting her senses with the colors, textures and fragrance of the blossoms. William delighted his in the sight of her. Fondling the flower, William's voice found a tone softer than it had ever produced. "Do you love me?"

"Of course, I do."

"Why?"

"You're my brother, silly."

"Is that why?" Struggling to maintain the gentle tone, he crushed the flower in his hand. "Do you love Matt as a brother too?"

"Sometimes."

"And other times?" He came closer to her now.

"I don't know. I can't explain it. I . . ."

"I can." William took Mary by the shoulders and drew her to him. Her tiny breasts burned like hot coals, searing his chest. "It feels like this, doesn't it. How do you feel right now, Mary? What sensations stir your stomach, burn in your breast?"

"William?" His voice was so soft, so soothing that Mary did not realize that her delicate arms ached in his strong hands.

Anne took Matt's arm. "Listen." He stopped. "Do you hear voices?"

"There they are, over there."

The voices had stopped. Not far from where Mary and William were standing another sound captured their attention. The boar snorted his annoyance at the invasion of his territory, bent his head and charged. Mary Elizabeth screamed. William pushed Mary out of the boar's path but tripped. One of the lower tusks hooked his right arm, ripping William's shoulder out of its socket.

Anne reached the ginger grove in time to see what happened but not in time to prevent it. Matt ran toward Mary Elizabeth before Anne could stop him. "Come on, Anne, the boar's run off."

She hesitated and turned slowly in a complete circle. "Not for long. He'll be back. Get them to a safe place."

Mary struggled, reaching for William as Matt hoisted her into a tree. As gently as he could, he dragged William behind a dead stump for protection.

Anne listened as she turned again in the direction of the boar's departure. He would make a wide circle, she thought, and attack from the rear. "Matt, get up in that tree," she whispered. Just then a bush rustled behind her and the boar thundered toward her..

Dropping the cutlass, Anne hurled one spear. It hit a vital spot; black blood spurted out. Tearing her shirt away to free her throwing arm, Anne maneuvered and struck again, and again, until a fourth spear, well aimed, brought the massive animal to its knees.

The excruciating pain from the torn muscles and nerves in his shoulder rendered William unconscious. Mary Elizabeth was hysterical.

"Matt, give me your shirt."

Anne applied pressure to William's shoulder, trying to stop the bleeding. Unsuccessful, she placed the bulk of the material on his wound and secured it with vines, then she tied William's arm to his body so that she could move him. There was so much blood, she couldn't be sure his arm was still attached.

"Slap her, for God's sake!"

"I can't."

"Slap her! Do as I tell you. Do you want the entire Maroon tribe down on us?"

Matt slapped Mary until her screams turned into sobs, then he muffled the sound of her crying by burying her face in his chest.

Anne looked up at them. "Matt, I'll need your help to

carry him." Anne took Mary firmly by the hand. "Mary, you run ahead of us. Have Ruth gather plenty of clean rags and send a litter to meet us. Mary, do you hear me? You can cry later. If we don't stop this bleeding, your brother will die. Now stop this, you hear!"

The girl's face bobbed up and down. Anne sent her off down the mountain slope. "Hurry!"

"Matt, take him up now. She'll be all right. I'm not so sure about William here."

Ashamed of his preoccupation, Matt gently lifted William's torso. Anne took his legs and backed down the hill.

In the middle of the cane-piece, they were met by four men who put William Thomas on a litter of plaited palm thatch and carried him to the great house.

Once his shirt was cut away and blood cleared, Anne could see the extent of his injury. Blood was pouring from the tear in the boy's right shoulder where the boar's tusk had penetrated and ripped through muscles. It looked as if his right arm had been wrenched nearly off his body.

Ruth and Anne took turns applying pressure to the wound and were able to control the bleeding until the doctor came. He first closed the wound as best he could and bandaged it. Even with William dulled by laudanum, the process of putting his arm back in place was a painful one. The boy's screams sent Mary Elizabeth into her mother's arms. Just as no drug could kill his pain, no word could bring comfort to the girl. It was all her fault. She had asked him to take her, begged him to go. And he had been hurt saving her life. Nothing Anne could say would change that.

Anne released Mary into Matt's arms in order to have a final word with the doctor. He told her the boy would probably have excruciating pain for several days and left medicines behind that would help. It was inevitable that the wound would fester but with constant care amputation could be prevented. He would return before the week was out. Then, with difficulty, he told her that William would never have the use of his arm again.

Baldwin came home to find the household in turmoil. He was greeted first with the news that the pesky boar had been killed by his wife, then by the fact that William Thomas had been gored. Anne was exhausted, but she refused to go to bed. All night she and Baldwin sat by William's bed. Sarah held the basin while Esther washed William's arm and hand. She scraped what appeared to be white or red flower petals from under his fingernails and wondered how they had gotten there. Ruth and Bertha brought their own brand of medicine. There were leaves to bind the wound, others to soothe pain, and reduce fever. Everything that could be done to save William's arm was done. And it was saved, but he would never move it again.

Days passed in agony. Weeks later, frustrated and angry, William insisted that he felt pain in his shoulder. The doctor had neither the heart nor the strength to deny him the laudanum even though he knew it was William's mind not his body's pain that craved the drug.

Through months of lingering numbness, William never left his room. Mary spent her days there. The shutters were always closed against the light. The smell of the doctor's medicines mingled with the herbs and gave a fetid odor to the room.

Mary lifted one of the louvers on the gallery door and a shaft of sunlight streaked across William's body. He seemed, at times, to take a morbid pleasure in watching his once strong right arm shrivel by his side. At other times one glance at it would set him into raging despair. Mary shrank from the twisted smile on his face as he studied every detail of his sagging arm and she shut the louver.

"No, leave it. Come sit. You see this useless thing here. 'Tis now half the size of my other arm. How far will it shrink, think you, 'till dead skin covers dried bone?"

"Stop it, William, please!"

"I'm sorry. I didn't mean to make you cry. But, tell me, Mary, how shall I live with this arm, with these useless fingers?"

"Oh, William. Can you ever forgive me? I'll be your

arms, your hands. Just tell me what you need."

"Only your company. It's lonely here without you."

"I'm here. I'll always be here for you, William."

He shifted slowly.

"Are you in pain?"

"Not much."

"Oh, God! How could I do this to you? How could I be so selfish, so stupid?"

"Please, Mary, please don't cry. Don't blame yourself. It's not your fault."

"But it is, it is!"

William reached over and wiped the tears away from her face. "I wish I could hold you, comfort you." He squeezed her arm. "But you see, I can't."

Mary stiffened at his touch and did not know why. The bruise on her left arm had taken weeks to disappear. She had convinced herself that it had happened when William pushed her out of the path of the boar. She wanted to run out of the room, but suddenly his hand left her arm and clutched his right shoulder. Mary fell across his chest and held him close as he writhed in pain. It was a long time, it seemed to her, before the pain passed.

There was a knock at the door and Baldwin peeked in, offering a handful of books. "Thought you might like something new to read. How are you feeling today, son? Much improved, I hope."

"Not much, Father."

"Sorry to hear it."

"I'll take the books, but I can't turn the pages very well. And Esther, well, she won't read anything but the Bible to me."

Mary got up from the bed. "I'll read to you later, William. Now I must go help Bertha with lunch."

Suddenly anxious, he seized her hand. "Must you leave? She has Esther and Sarah to help, doesn't she?"

"Yes, but there are certain things I do—my specialties."

He released her and fell back despondent and bitter. "What do we have today, not parrot soup again, I hope."

Baldwin puzzled at the boy's remark. "We've never had parrot soup ... Mary, have you . . ." She was gone. "Well, would you like me to read to you awhile?"

"Not now, Father."

Baldwin pulled up a cane chair and sat. He felt awkward, uncomfortable in his son's company. He never knew how to begin a conversation. "Would you like a drink of water?"

"No, thank you."

Baldwin watched as William twisted the bedclothes around his finger. Something on the ceiling held William's attention. Baldwin studied the boy's shriveled arm and useless hand—white against the sheet, almost whiter than the sheet. Baldwin had noticed hatred growing in the boy like leaf mold. He looked so vulnerable at this moment, was not whole anymore; how would he protect himself? Holding down a surge of pity, Baldwin opened one of the books. "Here's a book by Swift, *Gulliver's Travels Part I*. Looks interesting enough."

"I've read it."

"Oh." Baldwin shut and book and, fingering the bindings of the others, pushed them aside. "What interests you up there?"

"A spider's web."

Baldwin looked up and saw nothing.

"It's silver."

"What is?"

"Is that what a man becomes when he dies—a silver spider web?"

"I don't know, William. I never thought about it." Did William really long for death? Why his morbid fascination with it. Had the boy given up? No one could protect him from himself, but as his father, he must try. "Do you sometimes think that maybe a living man might be a silver spider web?"

Baldwin indulged the boy's every wish. It pained him to watch his son grow more bitter with each passing day.

Although she pitied the boy, Anne grieved that he

should become more and more dependent on the family. He would do nothing for himself and had the entire household at his beck and call. He would never do for himself if they catered to his every whim this way, she thought.

"Sang, there is nothing wrong with his legs. He is too big for you to be lifting him like that. Ruth, put down that tray; we must stop this." When individual reprimands failed to work Anne gathered the household staff and the family together.

"No one is to enter William Thomas's room for any reason for the next three days. That includes you, Mary Elizabeth."

The girl's eyes filled immediately. She shot a look of pure hatred at her mother.

"Oh, Mary, please understand. You don't want to see your brother grow old up there, now do you?"

"No . . . but can't we go on caring for him a bit longer? He has such pain, Mother, he tries to hide it, but I know it."

"The doctor told me that William probably has little or no feeling at all in his arm now. He is using your sympathy to get anything he wants. It is not good for him. He must learn to compensate. One arm must serve for two so that he can get on with his life. And we must get on with ours. This is a large household and it has been turned upside down since the accident. Can't you see that lying up there day after day is hurting him?"

As much as Mary Elizabeth hated to admit that her mother was right, she had to. The past few weeks had been unbearable for her; even she had dreaded seeing her brother, and had gone to his side out of guilt and fear, not love.

She promised Anne she would stay out of William's room as she requested. Preoccupied with her own thoughts, Mary Elizabeth left the room, brushing past Matt as if he had been a post. He couldn't help thinking that her sorrow had made her even more beautiful, if that were possible.

Anne repeated her instructions to the staff in stronger language now that her daughter had left the room. "William is too fastidious to lie in his own filth. He will get out of bed to use the chamber pot. He has plenty of water and sooner or later, hunger, if nothing else, will bring him downstairs. Now, is that clear?"

When they had left, Baldwin, who had come in on Anne's final remarks, spoke. "He's not a fox to be flushed out of the woods, Anne."

"Perhaps not, but we must treat him as one or a perfectly healthy boy will be an invalid the rest of his life. That's not what you want for your son, I know it."

"Damn it, woman, why must you always be right!" Sputtering and fuming, he stormed out of the house. When he reached the barn, Baldwin sat down next to Old Sam who was puffing thoughtfully on his pipe. Baldwin lit a fat Cuban cigar.

"Fo' hun'red an' t'irty-two pound," Sam muttered.

"What do you say?"

"Fo' hun'red an' t'irty-two pound. Dat what da boar he weigh—fo' hun'red an' t'irty-two pound."

"That's right." Baldwin had heard some of the boys talking about it only this morning.

"Dis one o' da tusks." Baldwin looked down to see what Sam was carving. Crude pictures of a rabbit and a parrot had already appeared on it.

"Seben foot, leben inch long, snout ta tail, fo' foot nine inch, backbone to groun'. Tusks, nine inch. Fo' hun'red and t'irty-two pound—'magine dat."

The excitement generated by William Thomas's wound had caused nearly everyone on the Sommerwood plantation to forget the great kill, but in the eyes of the neighboring planters Anne was a hero. She had saved many of their crops from almost certain destruction. Mostly, they had been happy that now their slaves would go back into the fields to work.

For three days William Thomas rang his bell incessantly and shouted. Two nights the family sat to dinner, picked over their food and listened to the sounds of rage hurtling from the upstairs room. Glass smashed, furniture shattered. A thud.

"He's fallen!" Baldwin rose from his chair and threw his serviette into the middle of his plate. Anne placed her hand on his arm. He sat down again, tried to retrieve the cloth from the gravy, gave that up, and reached instead for his wine glass. Mary Elizabeth ate nothing. Her eyes were swollen, her face drawn.

Except for an occasional crash, the upstairs room had been relatively quiet tonight, this the third of their siege. The silence frightened Anne. She arrived at the point where she was almost ready to admit defeat. Just as she was about to leave the table to go up to him, William appeared in the dining room. His walk was unsteady; he looked pale and disheveled. His shirt remained unfastened and was stuck at odd angles into his breeches. He sat down at his usual place beside his sister, took up his fork in his left hand and stabbed a piece of meat on the platter, bringing it to his own empty plate. He tried for a while to cut it with the edge of his fork, before tearing at the meat with his teeth.

No one spoke. All waited for Anne to do or say something. She smiled.

"Sang, Ruth, serve up William a proper plate of food, will you please."

Mary put a serviette in William's shirt. Sang handed Ruth a plate of freshly sliced, bite-sized pieces of beef. She heaped it high with sweet potatoes and corn. William continued to tear at the meat until Ruth exchanged the plates. Sarah set down a saucer of bread and Esther filled his wine glass. Everyone watched William eat before attacking their own plates with relish. When William stopped to take a sip of wine, everyone reached for theirs and, laughing at their spontaneous gesture, raised their glasses and drank them dry.

CHAPTER FIVE

Fire from the Mountain

Festivals brightened the Sommerwood plantation several times during the year, but preparations for the Christmas celebrations to close out 1734 stirred everyone into a flurry of activity. John Canoe costumes showed imagination and spirit. Anne saw in them an odd mixture of colorful symbols: the cow head of fertility, the top hat of the gentleman, the red mask of wealth, the fan of office, the horn of leadership, the whip of power.

Feathers composed some part of every costume. Anne and her children learned what they represented. Red feathers symbolized danger; the blue feather, war; and porcupine quills prevented injuries from thunder and lightning. Propped against trees in the yard, huge birds extended supernatural powers through their expansive wings.

Music brought everything to life in the moonlight of the crisp night. Fiddlers played on verandas and in the gardens while visiting planters danced the Scottish reel, set to the beat of the goombay. The dancers twisted in and out of line as the violin melody fought its way through the rhythm of spoons, graters and drums. Anne wore out a series of dancing partners—Baldwin, Peter Manwaring, then practically every other planter in the valley.

William worked up a prodigious thirst dancing with Mary Elizabeth. The quantity of rum punch he drank in no way quenched his thirst but did force him to relinquish his lovely partner to Matt. He glared at them, watching their blurry images spin and sway in and out of the long line of dancers.

Draining his cup, William staggered back to the punch table and pushing aside the half-filled goblet Esther offered him, dipped his cup into the bowl. Overfull, the brew dripped down his chin to stain his cravat. Sang, who always seemed to catch William in some disgusting business, dared not reproach the boy himself. He looked around for Baldwin but found him engaged in serious conversation with two neighboring planters and did not wish to interrupt him.

Anne had no qualms about snatching Baldwin away from his guests; she took him by the arm and spun him into the whirl of dancing partners. "Do you like this mazurka?"

"I like holding you in my arms. Did I tell you how ravishing you look tonight?"

"Oh, you're just grateful I wore a dress and not breeches."

He bent low and kissed her breasts which were spilling creamy white over the taut bodice of her silk gown. "Come outside with me, you ravishing wench, and I'll show you more advantages gowns have over breeches."

"Dost mean to ravish me, sir, in the garden!"

"Aye, wench, most thoroughly."

"Well, to protect my virtue I will return you to your boring company."

"Oh God, not that!" It was too late. Baldwin found himself standing dizzily between Robert Winter and Colonel Hargrave.

Once again, William dipped into the rum punch. By this time Sang had lost count. He threw his eyes heavenward and thanked God his own son never caused him a moment's grief. Another thought struck him as swift as his prayer. Mebbe we blin' to our own an' can see da debil only in udder people's chil'ren. Can dis be true? Cum ta tink, where my boy? Just as Sang looked around again, he noticed Lusen walking down the breezeway with Anne. They were headed toward the nearest outbuilding where the festival ornaments were stored. He laughed to himself, I tink dat boy take 'bout everybody to see his John Canoe by now.

Anne welcomed the cool breeze. She had been sitting in the garden for only a moment when Lusen handed her a glass of palm wine. He sat down beside her, eager to talk about tomorrow's festival and, above all, his costume—had she seen it, could she suggest any improvement?

"I must admit, Lusen, I must be the only person in the house who hasn't had the honor of a preview of your costume."

"Cum, I show you now." He snatched up a torch, took her hand to pull her weary body up from the bench. Her legs tingled, and momentarily resisted motion. Walking was an effort but she went along. The layers of blue print silk answered the crackling of the torch. The sounds seemed more vivid now that the music had faded.

Old Sam leaned against one of the posts at the end of the breezeway. Children sat all about him. He sucked his pipe and told them stories of the duppies, troublesome little spirits who lived in cottonwood trees and fed on bamboo roots.

Hailing them as they went by, Sam offered Anne a dram of his rum. Happy with the delicate taste of the palm wine, she refused but lingered a while inhaling the fragrance of a nearby trumpet bush and listening to the old man spin his stories.

In a moment, the island stories took Anne back to the brief, yet tragic period she had spent in the Bahama Out Islands. On other tranquil nights such as this one, her family would sit around the fire and listen to Cuffee, the ancient Arawak, entertain the children with tales of his people and the evil Caribs who came to eat them. The Arawak culture lived in these stories and was passed on in the same way that Sam gave Africa to his children.

Anne observed the children, some sleeping, others looking up into Sam's glowing face. Sensing Lusen's impatience, she bid Sam good night. The sweet smells of rum, pipe tobacco and trumpet flowers mingled, then faded.

The storage building contained three tall narrow rooms or bins. Sacks of grain were piled high in one bin and bales of hay in another. Lusen opened the heavy door of the third room where many of the John Canoe costumes were stored.

Before he could place the torch in the wall, Lusen was seized from behind. The flame sailed from his hand; the paper and feathers caught fire immediately. In his flailing movements he saw that Anne had been captured in a similar way. Neither dared move now except in the direction they were guided. Hooked knives, used for cutting cane, encircled their throats.

Anne hoped the fire would somehow deliver the warning she could not give. Her hope was extinguished when the heavy door was shut against the flames.

Lost in the spell of his own words, Sam was alerted to danger by the smell of smoke. When he opened the door of the outbuilding, little flames shot up here and there. Blinded by the heavy smoke, he feared what he could not see. His age demanded that he believe the worst. He kicked at the ashy remnants of headgear, masks, wings, and body pieces. Only the bones of the garments remained, bits of wooden supports, charred but not completely eaten by the blaze. Groping around on hands and knees, he called their names several times into the darkness. Red hot sparks blistered his fingers, his clothes smoldered in several places, smoke filled his lungs and brought tears to his eyes. He crawled out of the building and coughed until he retched, before losing consciousness on the damp earth.

The moon, high and full, stared down at him. At length, he awakened and wondered what he was doing sleeping outside. He raked one tattered sleeve over his sooty face, tasted burnt cloth, inhaled the smoky air, and remembered.

His eyes burning, Sam groped his way back to the main house. He was in the garden when Sang spotted the old man staggering toward him.

"Ruth, take dis tray. Doddy drunk 'gain. I'll fetch 'm home."

"Dear Lord, not 'gain! Mama brain 'im. Dis be da t'ird time dis week."

"Mebbe he sleep it off 'fo' she cum ta bed."

Sang reached Sam and hoisted him to his feet. "Cum, ole mon, let me fetch yo' ta home." Sang had so anticipated the smell of rum that when the stench of burnt cloth touched his nostrils, the odor took a moment to register in his brain. "Sam, what hoppen? Cum, ole mon, talk wid me!"

Sam could hardly breathe, let alone speak. The few words he uttered were pieced together by Sang in a way which made further discourse unnecessary.

"Ruth, fetch Massa Baldwin. Tell him to bring torches and water buckets and meet me at da outbuildin' wes' o' here. Da one where de John Canoe be kep' an' he'p Ole Sam. He hurt."

The urgency in his voice choked her questions. She dropped the tray, ran toward the house, found Baldwin, but from old habits she hesitated to interrupt his conversation. Luckily his eyes caught the look of panic on her face, and he drew her aside.

"Ruth, what is it?"

"I don't know." Her expression twisted into one of fear mixed with horror. "Where's Missus . . . Miz Anne?"

"In the garden the last I saw her. Why, what has happened?" The look on Ruth's face frightened him and it was so unlike her to stammer so.

"Sang say to meet him at da wes' outbuildin', bring torch and buckets—da John Canoe . . . fire I tink."

"Peter, come—something terrible has happened. Quickly! Have some of the men bring water buckets!"

Baldwin grabbed a torch and ran along the west breezeway. Surely there was more to this, he thought. Ruth would not become hysterical over a few ruined John Canoe costumes. I should have pressed her for more information.

Sang met him and demanded the torch. "Stay here!"

"What do you mean?" The storage building had burned—he could see that. Torch still in hand, Baldwin started into the room. Sang gave Baldwin a shove which knocked him to the ground and sent the torch flying. Sang scrambled for the light, seized it and rushed back into the smoldering building.

Stunned by the fall, Baldwin shook his head. What is wrong with everyone? This is crazy. He got up just as Sang came out of the room and pushed the heavy door closed. Torch lights bobbed across the lawns toward him.

"Sen' dem 'way, Massa Baldwin."

The grotesque shadows which danced across Sang's face alarmed Baldwin. Meeting the men half way, Baldwin sent them back to the party. "False alarm. The fire is out. Go back to the music. I'll join you soon."

In no way did his words stay their panic. More men gathered.

"A fire! Did he say fire?"

"Maroon attack, think you?"

"God, no."

"Did he say Maroon attack?"

"Let's get to our houses. Try not to alarm the women and children."

Lights splintered in every direction. Hooves clattered and wheels grated on the carriage circle. In less than half an hour all the guests had left. From the valley road Peter Manwaring looked back on Hill Haven still aglow with a hundred candles; then he rapped with his cane on the wall of the coach to hasten his driver.

Taking a platter from Bertha's hands, Ruth said, "Go home ta ole Sam, Mama. I'll finish up here."

"Oh Lordy, I know dat old mon fine trubble. Eb'ry John Canoe he fine trubble."

The children swarmed around Ruth.

"Where's Lusen, Mama?"

"Where's Mama, Ruth?"

"Wid yo' daddy, I 'spect. I don't know chil'ren. Bes'

ting we do here is douse dese lights and go ta bed. Daylight tell da tale."

"Something has happened to Anne and Lusen." Matt wet his thumb and forefinger and snuffed a flame.

"How do you know that?" cried Mary Elizabeth, suddenly panicked.

"He don' know dat." Ruth dumped a handful of dirty punch cups on the table. "Use a snuffter, boy. I'm in no mood ta fool wid burns tonight. Dey all right, I tell you."

"You always say that, Ruth," William slurred, "especially when it's not true."

"Go ta bed, boy. Take yo' drunken se'f ta bed. You should be 'shamed. Matt, he'p him upstairs."

"No, no, I don't need help." He tripped over a large gourd. Water sloshed out and William sprawled in it.

"You're disgusting, William." Mary Elizabeth stepped over his prone figure. "Esther, come upstairs and help me with the candles. Ruth, can Esther sleep in my room tonight?"

"Me too?" asked Sarah.

"Me too!" said Matt.

She had not meant to do it, but Ruth sent a stinging slap to Matt's cheek. He was more startled than hurt.

"Ruth!" Mary Elizabeth protested.

"I sorry, Matt. But yo' mus' watch yo' mouf, boy. 'Pologize ta Mary. Rum loosen yo' tongue too much, I tink."

"I only had a little." Matt brushed his red cheek against his shoulder. "I'm sorry, Mary. I was only joking, really."

"Drunk, by God!" William was singing now. "Drunk as a pirate! 'Now if I be drunk, I'll be drunk with those that have the fear of God and not with drunken knaves.' "

"Esther, come along." Mary started toward the stairs. As Esther passed him, William swung his good arm over her shoulder. She gasped in fright. "Esther will help me upstairs, won't you, Esther?" She helped him along but kept her eyes on the floor. "You have the fear o' God afore yere eyes, now don't you, girl. I know you fear God,

Esther. Tell me, Esther, what does the Bible say about drunkards."

Esther hesitated a moment, then spoke almost inaudibly. "Woe ta dem dat rise up early in da mornin', an' follow strong drink dat continue 'til night, till wine inflame dem."

"Huh . . . inflamed in the night."

Matt stared out into the night wondering if Anne had been taken from him forever. Glimmering specks of green light danced before his eyes. "Look Ruth, fireflies. What does Lusen call them?"

"Em'rald drop. Dey bring good luck." She stopped clanking dishes and held a wish in her mind.

Baldwin's smile turned to a look of anger as he stood facing Sang at the entrance of the storage bin. Sang stared back, saying nothing. He had not seen any pieces of cloth or charred bone and could not be sure Anne's and Lusen's bodies had been burned there. It was best to keep the matter to himself and not alarm Baldwin with his unwarranted fears.

Baldwin spoke through his teeth. "You will tell me what you found in there. You will tell me now, or I'll break you in half."

"I no fine anyting," Sang replied miserably. "Go back now."

"Jesus God, man!" Baldwin took Sang by the throat, pitched him to the ground, leaped on top of him, and smashed at the man's twisted face with both fists.

Sang locked his arms around Baldwin, pinning him to his own body and rendering his arms useless. Baldwin tried to twist himself out of the man's powerful hold. "Let me loose, damn you!"

Baldwin felt the man shudder beneath him. Sobs wracked Sang's body, spasms shook him, still Baldwin could not break his hold. Gripping Baldwin to his chest, Sang answered the man's demands with strange groans and cries. Finally, words came out, words he'd rather have not had to tell his friend. Baldwin stopped struggling and listened to Sang whisper in his ear.

"My son . . . your . . ."

"In there? Anne?" he groaned. "God, no! It can't be. How can you be sure?"

"I can't. We mus' wait . . . till mornin'." Sang released Baldwin, who rolled away.

Part of the night, Baldwin pounded the earth. Part of the night he cursed. He cried. He sighed and cursed and cried again. A short distance away from him, Sang lay huddled in quiet dread.

Not a scrap of cloth or remnant of any sort lay visible in the ash-littered room to confirm that Anne and Lusen had been consumed in the fire. Relieved, the two men began to search the grounds but their scuffling had obliterated any other footprints in the immediate vicinity of the building. Sang went back to the house to organize a search party. Baldwin started off in the direction of the mountains.

Ruth stared bewildered at her husband who appeared almost happy to tell her that her son and mistress were missing.

"How's Sam?" he asked.

"Oh, fine," she answered coldly.

"Did he tell you anyting 'bout what hoppen las' night?"

"He tell me no mo' den you."

"Later, womon. Dis be no time fo' cold looks. Our boy be gone, God know where. Let's be 'bout findin' 'im."

Matt and Mary Elizabeth assaulted Ruth with a barrage of questions for which she had no answers. She followed the search party back to the outbuilding. Sang instructed them all to fan out in every direction from the building and to keep a sharp eye.

"Matt, shall we wake William?" Mary Elizabeth spoke hesitatingly.

"No, leave him. Are you coming?"

"Wait, Matt. I must get my shoes."

"Well, hurry then," he called up the staircase in a voice filled with anxious concern.

It was Mary Elizabeth who found the piece of blue silk hooked in a twig on the slope of the hill. Matt ran to find Baldwin, instructing Mary not to budge an inch from the spot. Sang, Ruth, and Baldwin followed Matt up what seemed an imperceptible path. Several times the small party became entangled in the dense growth and had to backtrack and try another way.

When they got close to where Matt thought Mary should be, he called to her. By following in the direction of her voice they picked their way through the bush to reach her.

Baldwin led the way. Something glimmered on the path partially hidden under a new fallen leaf. It was Anne's emerald bracelet. Without comment he pressed on. Then Anne's ring looked up at him from the path. It was the one he brought her from London a few years ago. She insisted on wearing it even though it fit too snugly. He couldn't recall ever having seen her without it. How did she get this off, he wondered.

Further up the path Ruth picked up what looked like a piece of root but knew it to be the tiny bird her father had carved for Lusen when he was just a baby. He always carried it.

"He see what Miz Anne do and copy her by droppin' someting o' his own," Sang whispered.

"Thank God, they're alive." Baldwin breathed deeply, squeezing the gemstones in his palm.

"What do we do now?" asked Matt impatiently.

"We go back." Baldwin tore off his shirt and, ripping off pieces of it, tied them in bushes to mark the path. At the bottom of the slope he looked around for a landmark.

Sang piled loose stones in a heap by the entrance to the

path. "Do you know dis place?"

Baldwin ran his fingers through his hair and squinted up the slope.

"The path we took to Nanny Town was over there." He pointed east. "About a hundred yards from here, I'd say. You don't suppose . . . they must have rebuilt their village near the old one. Anne had thought so. But why would they do that, I wonder?" He did not voice the thoughts now racing through his mind. Did they take Anne for revenge? How long had they been watching us? Here we sat smugly thinking we had been rid of them. Two years now and the Maroons up there smiling and watching our every move. First anger, then pain flashed across his face. Oh, I hope they do not harm them. Dear God. I hope not.

"What will you do now?" Sang asked, eager for some action to be taken.

"As soon as I put on fresh clothes, I'll ride to the fort. This time we'll blast them out of their mountain haunt once and for all."

Anne and Lusen sat back to back, their arms bound together around a pole planted in the middle of a wide circular clearing. Anne woke, shivering in her scant clothing. The events of last night raced through her mind. If I had to be captured, why couldn't it have been when I was riding and wearing a warm blouse, breeches and boots? If I had been riding . . . Anne saw her escape in another series of pictures. I'd not be here tied like a goat to a stake. Would I have known to be wary? The soldiers tell of pregnant women and women with children banging at their breasts luring the men into the mountains. And of Maroons lurking in secret like tigers in the jungles of Africa—their only object murder. Why am I alive? It can only be that Nanny has some horrible death planned for me. Where is she now? Anne tried to wipe the picture of Colin's dead body from her mind. Fear rumbled her bowels and an acrid taste rose to her throat and stopped there.

The pressure of the ropes cut across her bare chest and the hemp dug deep into her arms and wrists; Lusen must have fallen forward in his sleep. Terror had kept them both awake most of the night. She did not want to wake him now even though his comfort made it more difficult for her to breathe and intensified the pain in her shoulders and neck.

Twisting about, she found some relief, but only because this new position was slightly different from her old one. She could hear the rushing water of a nearby mountain stream but could not see it. The feel of dense wood hung all about her. Through the morning mist the jagged outlines of tiny huts began to appear along the muddy avenue stretching long before her. Tall figures drifted about the hazy street and small ones darted back and forth from hut to hut. Children. Their screeches sounded like the birds flying in the trees above her now. How do these children grow up to be such monsters? Oh Father . . . Colin. Anne wrenched her focus from her memories to the birds flitting from branch to branch, diving at each other. One small bird would chase another off a coveted limb. Senseless waste of energy, she thought. There were, after all, hundreds of branches, one every bit like another. There were thousands of branches in hundreds of trees and bushes, yet the pecking, biting, diving, and screaming went on. And Jamaica, it too was large enough for all kinds of people to live on, yet. . . . Suddenly the noise of the birds ceased. Anne turned her head but could see no one, instead she heard a dull thudding sound.

Lusen, awakened by the pounding of a stick against his chest, looked at the mammoth figure of a woman standing over him. His gasp mingled fright and pain.

"Don't hurt him. God damn you, don't hurt him!" Anne sensed the attacker was Nanny. She wanted to confront her but the Maroon remained behind her.

The woman dropped to her knees straddling Lusen's lap. Robed arms swung around him, locking the ebony stick across Anne's throat, mangling her words.

"Kill me, go ahead, kill me now!"

Lusen screamed and struggled, smothered in the woman's giant breasts.

Anne heard the faraway sound of a young girl calling "Nanny. Nanny!" The giant released her hold and rose. Through dimming eyes Anne watched her hem dust the earth behind her as her long strides carried Nanny along the road. Dozens of children appeared from inside huts to flock around her. Her wide sleeves seemed to swallow them up. Turning at the end of the long thoroughfare, the Queen Mother and her brood disappeared in the direction of the calls. Then blackness absorbed all sound, sight and feeling as Anne collapsed into unconsciousness.

Curious as the villagers were, they stayed away from Nanny's prisoners. They obeyed her orders but wondered what sort of death she planned for her captives.

"Dey be mine an' die when Nanny say. We wait till time be right. You stay 'way or Nanny's eye fine you too. Magic make you suffer."

It was some time before Lusen could breathe quietly. When he did, he called out to Anne but she did not answer. The weight of her body pulled the ropes tight against him and he was gripped in deadly terror.

"Yes, it must be Nanny. I am certain of it." Dreams of Anne's plight had troubled the few hours of sleep Baldwin had managed to seize during the night.

"Mr. Sommerwood, I . . ." Captain Stoddart scratched his head, tipping his tricorn hat to one side. "How can you be certain?"

"I just told you. Look, Captain. I'd not like to try this again without your help, but I am prepared to go up there myself if I must. Well . . . are you with me or no?"

"I'm with you, but I think you're wrong. We annihilated them; you saw for yourself."

"She's up there, I tell you. They have my wife up there and I mean to get her back."

"How can you be sure she's still alive?"

Stoddart looked at the man and saw his thoughts. Although he had not seen the bodies of Anne's father and her son, he had heard about the shameful enormities performed on their dead bodies. The Maroons rarely took captives, but when they did they were especially cruel. Both women and children were raped in the most horrible fashion, men killed and their bodies mutilated beyond recognition.

"All right, tomorrow."

"No, tonight." Baldwin countered. "And bring those Indians of yours, and the dogs as well. We'll need both to sniff them out."

"Aye. We just received a detail of Indians from the Mosquito Coast last week. Once they hit upon a track they are better than any dogs at smelling out a Maroon haunt."

"They had better be keen tonight."

"Tonight then. Aye."

The sun lifted high over the Maroon village before Anne regained her senses. Lusen, weak from thirst, hunger and despair slumped forward, jerking her into consciousness. She moaned.

"Miz Anne! Miz Anne, you no dead!"

"I'm alive, I think. Are you all right? She didn't hurt you, did she?"

"No, but I so 'fraid I wet myself."

"I pray God that's the worst that happens to you."

"You know dat womon?"

"Nanny."

"I hear girl call name. Whoever she be, she sabe yo' life, I tink. Nanny go when she call. It pas' noon now. Nobody cum since she go 'way."

"Thank God for that. We're lucky to be so ignored."

"I t'irsty."

"I too, but more scared than thirsty right this minute."

Women carrying machetes entered the village street.

They were followed by other women carrying crude hoes and water buckets. When Anne realized that they were coming back from the provision fields, she felt somewhat relieved. Others with high stalks of plantain balanced on their heads seemed to glide across the paths of the field workers. Two tall men, naked except for bits of cloth covering their genitals, carried a wild boar, fresh from the kill. Another man scraped a rough thumb across the edge of his cane knife, testing its sharpness, and once again Anne cringed in fear.

The boar dropped to the ground no more than twenty feet away from her. The man with the knife slit its belly in a single stroke and dragged out the animal's entrails for the inspection of one old man. For a moment both men perked up their ears as a dog does when it hears an almost inaudible sound. Once the sound had been identified, they bent low over their task again. The stench from the animal's split belly did not seem to bother the men. Anne turned her eyes away and held her breath against the odor that nauseated her even at this distance. Finally the beast was dragged away to be dressed. The old man came nearer to her and gazing up at the sun, squatted; loosening the strings of the leathern sack hanging about his neck, he poured out its contents in a semi-circle in front of him. Children bent over him for a moment or two, then as if they knew that it might be hours before the man spoke his message, hurried away to play at mock fighting.

Anne watched the activities in the hut nearest to her. Several women, it seemed, lived in that hut with one robust man. His noon-day meal finished, he moved on to more lusty amusements. First, the two women who had been laboring in the field went in to him. After an hour or so they came out and wearily attended to the household tasks while another went in, and then another. In turn, outside, fires were stoked, plantain mashed, small brown babies given the breast, and older children taken to the stream for bathing.

Three hours of this routine bored her; Anne concentrated

her energies on escape. There was no one guarding them, at least no one in sight. A man could be hiding in a nearby tree for all she knew. If they could get a chance to break away, they could slip down the mountain by following the stream.

Their bonds seemed tighter somehow. It would be impossible to squirm out of them even with the utmost cooperation between them, but they continued to try.

"It be no use, Missus. We no get loose. We die soon, I know it."

"Stop that talk. Baldwin will find us in time. He and your father are looking for us right now."

"You tink so? If only I reach knife."

"You have a knife? Where?"

"I tie it ta my leg. I feel it dere now. Dey no take."

Anne twisted about and groaned. Lusen moved with her, trying in vain to weaken a section of the rope. He gave up and watched Anne's shadow bounce and jump on the ground. A young boy appeared at the edge of her shadow. In one hand Lusen thought he saw a rectangular container, in the other hand its cover.

"No! No! Go 'way from here. Go 'way, boy. Keep movin', Miz Anne, fight hard. Go eb'ry which way. Move fast, Missus. You, boy, go 'way. I fix you, boy! You hear, I fix you!" Hysterical with fear, Lusen threw his body this way and that within the limits of his bounds. In the midst of their struggles, a cloud passed over the sun obliterating their shadows. A clap of thunder sent the boy scurrying down the mud road.

"Stop now, Missus. He gone. Scare' by tunder."

"Who was that?"

"Boy 'bout Esther's age wid small coffin.'

"What?"

"Boy hab coffin fo' ta cotch shadow in."

"What are you talking about?"

"Obeah. Ole Sam, he tell me. You cotch shadow an' keep in coffin, bury it in grabe or nail it ta cottonwood tree—all da same. Person die widout dere shadow, Missus.

But boy no take. I sure . . . I sure."

Hours later, a new sound at the stream woke him and Lusen opened his eyes on the loveliest girl he had ever seen. Afiba stooped to fill two water buckets. Her skin was slightly darker than the richest copper. Her limbs were smooth and slender as the figure of the goddess with the bow he had seen in the Hill Haven library. Her small round face beamed at her reflection in the stream. She scooped up two handfuls of water and brought them to her face, then splashed water up her arms and basked for a moment, her neck arched into the setting sun. Lusen was almost refreshed watching the girl by the stream as she drank from her hands. He had not seen the direction from which she had approached the stream but hoped her return would bring her closer to him.

Their eyes met and lingered until she looked away across the stream and into the woods beyond. Quickly, she gathered up the two buckets, her delicate arms straining from the weight as she walked toward the street, her eyes intent on her bare feet.

Lusen prayed she would stop and speak to him.

Leaving one of her buckets on the road, Afiba brought the other to where Lusen was tied. She dipped her cloth headpiece into the water and wiped the sweat from his face. Filling the ladle with water, she held it to his lips. He drank the water, watching his reflection in the luster of her eyes.

"Tank you," he whispered. She smiled. "Please, Missus drink too." Afiba's face darkened. She snatched up the bucket. It grieved him that he should anger her.

At the call of her name, the girl bolted toward the village. Lusen caught another look at her when she ran back to fetch the second bucket she had left on the road.

"Afiba." The word formed on his lips as he watched her.

"Nanny!" she shouted while looking straight at Lusen. "I cum."

The sound of Nanny's name called out so close to her ear brought Anne back to the nightmare of her thoughts.

She caught the smell of smoked hog meat. The strong odor of spices, potent peppers, and scallions sickened her.

Lusen felt Anne's head fall against his own. "You feel bad, Miz Anne?"

"I will be fine, Lusen. Baldwin will come and we will all feast together tomorrow night. I promise you."

"I sorry girl no gib you water."

"What girl?"

"Pretty girl, Afiba. She gib me water."

"Is this the one, coming this way now? She brings food I think. If she unties you, look for an opportunity to slip me your knife. Lusen, did you hear me? Slip me the knife!"

"Aye, Missus." Lusen could feel his heart beating faster. but before Afiba reached them, Lusen gave out a sharp cry. It was a cry not of fear, rather of pain. Anne wrenched herself around.

"What is it? Lusen? Who is there?" Then she heard a bawdy laugh which sounded vaguely familiar—familiar enough to set her own heart pounding. "Caleb Foote, what are you doing here?" A part of her hoped he'd been sent by the army to infiltrate this haunt, another part told her there was no hope of that.

Caleb laughed and swung around the pole in front of her. "I live here, Mis-tress." Spray squirted from his mouth and rained on Anne's face. Weeks of grime stiffened his clothes and he smelt like burnt charcoal drenched in hog fat. Afiba had reached Lusen. Anne heard her give out a little cry. The boy was hurt and Afiba had discovered it.

"What have you done to the boy?"

Caleb drew out a long knife and placed it at Anne's throat. "Oh, I jerked him under the chin like this." Anne felt a prick but no more. Caleb held a small vessel up under her chin. "Nanny wants a special ingredient in her rum. We're having a festival here tonight." After placing the vessels aside, Caleb held one hand across Anne's mouth while the other searched under her petticoats, rooting in her private place. "You see, Mistress Anne, Nanny gets what she asks for, Caleb Foote gets what he takes."

Anne tightened herself against his intrusion.

"Nanny has big doin's planned for tonight. A lively party, you might say, lively, that is, for everyone except you. Nanny has promised me ten minutes with your dead body. Thought I'd warm you up a bit afore hand."

Afiba saw Lusen listening to what was happening behind him. "Fu fu. Fu fu." She poked the wooden spoon full of the whitish mess into his mouth. "Yam, good. You eat, boy. No listen, you eat."

"Make him stop."

Afiba shook her head and crouched close to him in fear. He hoped she did not smell the urine on him.

Anne finally succeeded in kicking Caleb Foote away. "You . . . you bastard! You'll not live to see me dead."

"Oh no? Smell that pork, Mistress; hear those drums, see these strong lads. They get to have at you first." He grabbed a muscular looking man by the arm and brought him over to her. "This is Banafou. You'll be his tonight. Look at those arms and shoulders. I am jealous. See the muscles in these legs?" Caleb turned the man around for her inspection and snatched off his loin cloth. "What a buttock. Fine, eh? And look at this," he said, turning the man around to face her. "Eight inches at least. You will die happy, Mistress. You will die a very happy woman."

Caleb laughed and Banafou laughed with him. "Oh, I forget, he is also intelligent. Smart like your husband. Banafou is Mandingo. He can read and write. Maybe we send a message to your husband an' tell him what a lusty woman you are."

Banafou smiled. "Me write."

"Yes, we know Banafou write. Not proper English writing. Banafou writes Arabic like all Mandingo. But I am sure he can scratch characters to describe the wonders of your body, Mistress. Oh, Nanny sent me to give you some of her best rum." Opening his flask, he poured a quantity of the raw liquor down her throat. Able to prevent herself from swallowing all of it, Anne spewed the rest directly in his face. Caleb laughed, but Afiba, terrified by her action, ran away. Caleb pushed the Mandingo aside, picked up the two small vessels filled with blood, shook them at her and laughed. Then he turned and walked down the long avenue away from her.

"Depraved. Body and soul depraved." She coughed up more of the bitter-tasting drink but was able to force it back down again. It burned her throat but warmed her stomach. "Why did the girl run like that, Lusen?"

"Obeah. She tink you know strong magic. Obeah womon sometime spit white rum in corners of da room before ceremony."

"Long ago I was told Obeah was a power given by God to man to protect and heal himself. I have never feared it. Why should she?"

"She hab seen de power do ebil things, not good tings. I 'spect tonight we see much ebil magic, but we not lib ta tell."

"That's what they want you to believe. Magic can't hurt you, Lusen, unless you believe it can."

"I know, Ole Sam, he say dat too, but I 'fraid, Missus. I 'fraid to die. I no lib yet. I no love yet."

"You will," she whispered. "They will come," she murmured. "They must come."

Hundreds of armed men pulled their way up the mountain. The Mosquito Indians had caught the scent. Spanish dogs sniffed and pulled the soldiers onward. Gravel crunched under heavy boots and slipped down the slopes. The sound of labored breathing was the only steady sound in the night.

Unable to make headway without slipping back, Baldwin gripped his fingers around his musket and dropped to his knees. Matt crawled up next to him.

"Go back home, right now! Go on."

"No, I won't. How can I? I love her too, you know. Lusen is my friend, too."

"Matt, you're just a boy. 'Tis too dangerous. Anne

would never forgive me if anything happened to you. Besides, I promised your mother."

"What? What did you promise my mother? My mother would walk through fire to save Anne Bonny and you know it. She'd expect no less from her only son. That I know."

"All right. I have no defense against such arguments."

"Some solicitor you are."

"Just never mind. And stay behind me for God's sake!"

Fires shot up all around. Fingers struck drums hollowed out of trees with green goat skins stretched taut across one end and pinioned. To Anne the fingers moving with such speed appeared almost motionless.

Agile men in hideous costumes danced and leaped around her. Depraved, foul and debased, she thought. What manner of men were these to put their heads inside the decaying heads of ox, horse and hog? Cow tails dangled grotesquely from their backsides, giving the men a macabre aspect. Bones rattled at their wrists and ankles: feathers floated on their necks. But at moments when fear loosened its grip on her, Anne could not help admiring the strength and beauty of their bodies and the agility and grace of their movement; then terror seized her again.

A man clothed entirely in croton leaves seemed to fly out of nowhere, landing right in front of Lusen. The colorful dancer so attracted his attention that the boy hardly noticed the frenzy mounting all around him. Horns blew, drums pounded, fires shot with rum hissed and danced.

Anne was untied and stripped naked, her extended arms and open legs tied to short stakes in the ground. Lusen looked away from Anne straight into the eyes of his father who was concealed in the bush by the river. Quickly he looked back at Anne who was straining to free herself from the ropes.

Tall men danced around her. Nanny sat on a short stool away from the scene. Fixing Anne's naked form in her eye, Nanny took up her cup and drank. Her action seemed to be a kind of signal to the others. More men and women gathered in a circle about Anne. Swilling white rum, they laughed and shouted, their obscene gestures encouraging the dancers on to more vulgar activity.

The rhythm of the drums and rattles seemed to beat a frenzy into the group, bringing them closer to madness. The sounds were deafening; the rhythms inescapable.

The group circled around Anne had their backs to Lusen. He could no longer see her and he was afraid to look over toward the river. Someone might be watching him. He could not risk betraying his father's presence. Anne was right. They did come, but when would they strike? He shut his eyes against the riot before him and only imagined he heard Anne scream.

Afiba crept up behind him, cut his ropes and quickly disappeared into a group of observers.

Slowly Lusen reached under his trousers to pull out his knife, then put his hands behind his back again. He was grateful now that he had not looked back at his father. Not every eye had been on Anne. Afiba had been watching for an opportunity to release him. He prayed his father and the others would attack soon. The girl would wonder why he did not run away, but he could not abandon Anne.

With difficulty Baldwin held his position until he was sure the frenzied mob was surrounded by soldiers. He suspected that Anne might be the center of their attention, but he could not see her. Nor did he see the razor-sharp point of the cane knife draw a thin line of blood down the inside of both her thighs.

Her screams had been swallowed up in the din. She screamed because she did not want to lose consciousness, but fear mixed with pain brought her to the brink of a blackout. The curses she hurled in the face of the giant Mandingo pumping on top of her went unheard; the agonizing violation was rendered even more insufferable because she was totally powerless to prevent it.

Suddenly Anne felt the ropes at her wrists being cut away. Groans and screams issued all around. Gunfire had silenced the drums but she had not heard it. Nothing had disturbed the man on top of her.

A knife was placed in her right hand. Her instincts urged her to plunge it into the Mandingo, but her hand would not thrust up into his heaving belly. Suddenly the man arched and groaned, then slumped on top of her. Anne struggled vainly to slip out from under his sweat-soaked body. His odor of scorched wet leaves threatened to suffocate her. Dead weight lifted. The night air rushed against her face.

Matt had pushed the man off her. He cut away the ropes binding her feet and pulled a robe off a dead Maroon woman to wrap around her. Once on her feet, Anne's head cleared. Seeing a machete on the ground, she stooped to pick it up, then flung both arms out, knocking Matt aside. With furious determination she tried to slash her way through the crowd of black faces but could not move. Powerless though she was, no one dared to approach her, terrified by her dreadful energy.

Anne sank to the ground and pulled her hands, still clutching cutlass and knife underneath her, then drew up her knees to her breast. As Matt covered her with the robe, he was reminded of a child embracing a pillow in peaceful sleep. He managed to fight off all attackers until Baldwin saw him and came to help him carry Anne away from the action.

The battle lasted over an hour. Bodies of the dead Maroon warriors littered the clearing. Captain Stoddart ordered the village to be burnt to the ground. "Burn the fields! Pitch their bodies over the cliff. Search the area and leave no survivors, but bring Nanny to me alive!"

Lusen heard his father calling. After he had placed his knife in Anne's hand, he had found Afiba and dragged her to safety behind a boulder at the edge of the stream. "Wait here, Afiba. You cum wid us. No one hurt you. I promise. Wait here."

Lusen ran to embrace his father, then dragged him back to where he had left Afiba. His beaming face clouded when he found her gone. He heard musket fire and ran toward it.

Sang followed.

"No! Dey no kill her. She sabe my life. Tell dem stop. No more killing!" Lusen turned over the body of a young girl just shot by a soldier. It was not Afiba. He saw another soldier raise his musket to his shoulder and knocked him to the ground.

Finally, all the guns were quiet. Lusen, distraught and heavy-hearted, followed his father down the narrow path.

PART II

1735—1737

Darkness Visible

" . . . without thorn the rose"
—*Paradise Lost IV*, 256

". . .the garland wreathed for Eve
Down dropped and all the faded roses shed."
—*Paradise Lost IX*, 892-3

CHAPTER SIX

Flight

It took both Matt and Baldwin to wrench the machete from Anne's hand.

"Ruth, fetch warm blankets."

"Where's Lusen?"

"He's safe with Sang. Hurry with those blankets, please."

Anne lay shivering on the bed. Baldwin looked at her, stroked her hand and smoothed her hair. His hand came to rest on her shoulder and he noticed the striped robe for the first time. "What is this garment? Where are her clothes? How did she . . . why is she wearing this robe! Matt, answer me."

Matt pried open Anne's hand and fumbled with Lusen's knife. "I . . . put it around her."

"Where in the name of God did you get the thing?" he shouted.

Stepping away from Baldwin's wrath and towards the door, he said, "I took it off a dead Maroon."

"Why?"

"Anne, well, she was . . . naked."

"Naked! Why in God's name?"

"I don't know! I . . . she was tied to stakes . . . her legs far apart. There was a black man . . . on top of her . . . he was . . . Anne had this knife and was stabbing him, I think. I drove my bayonet into him."

Both hands clutched the handle of Lusen's knife and Matt stabbed the air like a bird its prey.

Baldwin took his hand from Anne's shoulder.

Matt dropped his hands and the knife clanked to the floor; then he turned toward Anne with raging compassion. "I had to kill him . . . the black bastard was . . ."

Baldwin stared at the sobbing boy. When Ruth came in to cover Anne, he turned his cold eyes upon her.

"You want me send Sang fetch doctor?"

"No." She saw his eyes dart in confusion. When he brought them to rest, they were once again glaring at her as if she were a criminal. "No. See to her yourself."

"Where is she hurt?"

Without looking at Anne, Baldwin left the room. At the doorway he paused, then ordered, "And burn that garment."

Matt stood as if his boots were nailed to the floor and watched Anne's face contort with fear and pain.

"Well, you goin' jus' stan' dere, boy? Mebbe you tell Ruth where she be hurt?"

A flash of hot embarrassment reddened his face and suddenly finding his legs, Matt ran from the room.

Ruth placed a damp cloth on Anne's forehead. "Dese men folk no he'p. Good for nuttin' sometimes. Where you hurt, chil'? Tell Ole Ruth. You shake so I hate ta take dese clothes off a' you."

Having no other choice Ruth removed the robe and checked over Anne's chest and stomach. When she thought to see if her thigh wound had been reinjured, she saw dried blood smeared between Anne's legs. Removing the cloth from Anne's forehead she wiped away most of the blood.

"Lordy Lord! Some big mon fairly tear you 'part. I see now why dese men act so peculiar."

"Ruth?" Anne's voice was so weak and broken that Ruth was slow to respond.

"Yes, Miz Anne, Ruth here. You no worry."

"Ruth . . . Baldwin?"

Ruth could see tears welling up in Anne's eyes. "I sen' dat mon out da room, Miz Anne. He be right outside. Soon I finish here he cum right back in. You res' now."

Finishing her ministrations, Ruth cradled Anne in her arms until she fell into a deep sleep. When Ruth came out,

Baldwin lifted himself from the chair he had placed by the door.

"Is she all right?"

"She be all right in two, mebbe t'ree day, I tink. She sleep now. Bes' ting."

Drawing his eyes away from the bloody water in the basin, he said, "Go to Lusen now, and tomorrow burn that bloody robe." His whisper fell like a shout on Ruth's ears.

Baldwin quietly entered the room and lit a candle. Holding it near Anne's face he watched the light play over her delicate features. With her eyes closed she appeared vulnerable to him; he had never thought about her vulnerability before. He leaned over to kiss her lips, but something stopped him. Baldwin backed away, sat down and stared into the flame of the candle and talked as he would to someone else, not himself. You are a stupid foolish man; well, maybe not foolish or stupid, just not . . . as perfect as you think you are. Why are you acting this way? It's not her fault, you know. If you were defending a criminal, you'd treat him better. God's Breath! How would you like it? He studied that thought for a moment, running it one way through his mind then another. I tell you one thing, Baldwin Sommerwood, you had better get right with this business before the night be out, else by morning you had better find that dark whirlpool in the mountains and drown yourself in it. Blowing out the candle, his mind gave the order to his arm to reach over and lay his hand on top of Anne's, but in the darkness he felt nothing. Then he realized that his hand had not moved at all. He dropped into the chair and sat in the darkness.

The next morning Mary Elizabeth and Esther overheard Ruth and Bertha talking about Anne's condition. The word "rape" stuck in the girls' minds like a fly in a barrel of molasses.

"Do you suppose that's why Ruth wouldn't let me into Mama's room this morning?"

"I no sure what rape is?"

"Well, like the cats. William showed me when our cats mated. The boy cat seizes the fur at the back of the girl cat's neck . . ."

"What dat do?"

"Well, she can't move, can't get away from him. Then the boy cat, well, he rapes her."

"Ting in ting."

"What?"

"Boy cat, he put his ting in her ting." Esther placed her hand first on her crotch then pointed to Mary Elizabeth's. "People too, ting in ting make baby. But I 'fraid. What you tink, Mis Mary, you tink dat hurt?"

"How would I know."

"I tink rape, dat hurt."

Matt didn't know how, but William Thomas managed to get from him all the details concerning the raid on Nanny Town, including Anne's rape.

"Rape! God, I wish I'd been there. Did you watch?"

"Why, you heartless bastard, Anne's your mother."

"Wish you had been the one to do it, don't you?"

Matt wiped the smile from William's face with a sweeping blow. Then wrestling him to the ground pummeled him into silence.

Baldwin did not drown himself in the waterfall but held Anne's hand clasped in both of his until she awoke. Her body healed quickly but weeks passed and Anne refused to leave her bed. Mary Elizabeth pleaded with her to come down to listen to her play the spinet and every morning Matt rapped on her door and asked her to ride with him. One day, Baldwin installed himself in her bed and conducted plantation business from there, thinking she would tire of the constant intrusions of Sang, the overseer and the bookkeeper. But rather, she absently took his hand, managing to hold and turn the pages of her book with the other hand. Realizing that this arrangement worked against his design, he contemplated a new plan to drag Anne out of her depression.

"Anne, come to London with me."

"What?"

"London. Would you like to sail to London with me?"

"London, in the middle of February? It's too cold for me."

"Not with the proper wardrobe. We'll buy you all new clothes once we arrive."

"That's a waste of good money. I have no need for heavy clothing here."

"Think of the plays we could see and the dress balls we would attend."

"The theatre would be nice but the parties ... God, Win, I couldn't take that—all those inane people and their idle conversation. You go alone. It's been four or five years for you, hasn't it?"

"Annie, you can't stay in this bed forever."

"I know. I just . . . I can't seem to separate my thoughts and feelings—they seem to stick to one another like drippings on a candle—all very neat and pretty, but useless really. I need more time to myself. By the time you get back I'll be my old self again, you'll see."

"I hate to leave you like this."

"But you must. George II and his Parliament may be plotting the ruination of the colonial planter."

"Sarcasm?" Baldwin assumed an attitude and lectured. "Face it, Anne, you well know our sugar exports were nearly wrecked by the increased production and lower prices in the Dutch and French West Indies before Parliament enacted the Molasses Act."

"Yes, I know, I know." She could stifle a laugh but not a smile. "You need London, Baldwin. Political intrigue stimulates you. Right now, I need quiet friends and peaceful days with nothing of real importance demanding my attention."

"All right, I see you won't be satisfied until you're rid of me, woman." She made no response, so he raved on. "Well, I'll go then. I can see that I'm not needed or wanted around here."

"Win, shut up and come here." Anne drew him down on top of her, placing her hands against his chest to allow her arms to give way to his descent. She lay still as if pinned under a great iron door. Her pelvis burned beneath his icy loins. She stretched her arms to warm him but confined as they were she could not reach him. It seemed that as she thrust, the weight intensified as did the heat and the cold.

Baldwin slid away from her hands and kissed her breasts, drinking first from the right then from the left to suck out a spark that would enflame him.

Hours passed. Stray thoughts intruded. The far pasture fence needs fixing. The distillery wants adjusting. Black tar. There is something I must do with tar. What? Maybe her loins will warm me. I'll try that. He could smell the delicate spices hanging in the air and hear the distant cows mooing in the pastures but he could not feel the passion that would lift him.

Before he left for London, Baldwin arranged for a small detachment from Fort Morant to quarter themselves on the estate. Peter Manwaring promised to visit often. Matt, able and willing to take on more of the plantation responsibilities, assured Baldwin that he would look after everything and everybody.

Baldwin felt an inexplicable sadness at his departure. He needed to go. He wanted to go. And although guilt accompanied his thought of Anne's staying behind, he was relieved that she was not going with him. Am I jealous? Is that it? I have no real cause. Who? No one person. I must be envious of everyone who has touched her. No, I am not jealous. Then why? He pushed at his penis as if it were a stubborn child who refused to obey commands.

About a week after Baldwin's departure Anne grew restless. It was not the old restlessness when she yearned for adventure on the high seas. It was the frenzied restlessness that came with searching for something that was lost, a loss so intimate. . . . She was angry and bitter that somehow she had been made to feel culpable for her own decay, made to feel like a rotten place in a piece of fruit.

When one morning she did not find Anne in her bed, Ruth looked all about the house and grounds before she found Anne sitting on the stone bench by Mary's tomb and weeping.

"Miz Anne, tank God I fine you." Ruth wrapped a long cloak around Anne's shoulders. "You want Ruth go?"

"No, sit with us a while."

Ruth brushed the few plum blossoms from the bench and sat. The bright pink flowers carpeted the ground at their feet.

"You didn't know, but I loved a black man once, long ago—an African named Tombay. His love was as special and delicate as a wild orchid. And when he died I saw his face in every leaf, in every flower." Anne picked up one of the plum blossoms and looked deep into its petals. "But now when I look into a flower I see only the Mandingo who . . . and Baldwin, he . . ."

Ruth put her arms around Anne and patted her shoulder softly. "Dere now."

"The sight of these mountains sickens me, Ruth. I know it won't always be this way, but now . . ."

"Mebbe, Massa Baldwin, he right. Trip do you good."

Anne stood up and laid both hands on Mary's tomb and remained that way for a long time as if drawing energy enough to speak but moreover to act. "Ruth, I think maybe a trip would do me good."

"Will you go ta London, Missus?"

"No. Charles Town. Father's estate hasn't been settled. His solicitors have sent several letters. Perhaps I'm strong enough for that business now. And on the way I'll stop in the Bahamas. I've a friend at New Providence. Yes, a sea voyage is sure to freshen my mind and give me some answers." And with the first smile Ruth had seen in over a month, Anne took her hands. "Come, let's pack my trunk."

The next morning the smoke from smouldering huts mingled with the mountain mist as Nanny surveyed the destruction wrought by the English during the ceremony to Accompong—creator and preserver of mankind. Bodies littered the avenues of her village. Afiba and her little brother Yamou stood beside her. Taking up their hands, Nanny vowed that the English would never again destroy her village.

"Me almos' kill white boy, Nanny—boy who kill Banafou. Spear me jus' miss 'em. I kill he nex' time Nanny, you see."

"When you cum mon, den you kill many English, like Nanny."

"How many English you kill las' night, Nanny?" the boy asked.

"Mo' den t'irty. Still mo' English den Maroon. Someday we hab more soldier—soldier wid strong heart like Yamou. Day cum soon when Afiba Queen Mudder. You fight fo' her." Afiba slid her hand out of Nanny's grasp. The Queen Mother did not notice; she was watching one of her warriors drag a dead English soldier to the precipice. "Leave him!" she ordered. "Cut he teeth out firs'. Take teeth all English soldier. We wear an' we remember."

Nanny took up Afiba's hand again while issuing more instructions. "Bury own dead—one grabe. We hab little food—mus' keep strong."

"What Nanny do now?" asked Afiba.

"We go join great commander in West. Go ta Cudjoe in Cockpit Country."

"But why so far 'way, dere be fiel's near here."

"We go!"

"Yes, Nanny."

Afiba thought of the boy with the bright face and gentle eyes. There was sorrow in her heart now to think of being separated from him—so far, the west country. It take months ta reach dere, she thought. Mebbe never cum back Windward shore, neber see dat boy face and dose gentle eyes 'gain. Tears streamed down Afiba's face. Why? Why mus' dere always be war? Why love not be stronger dan hate? What will happ'n when I be Queen Mudder, the girl wondered.

Why had she not gone with him last night? Did she fear Nanny would in turn destroy the plantation village as the planter destroyed theirs, for the love of his woman? Why so much fuss over one woman? Yet Afiba knew Nanny would destroy the entire island to protect her. Will she eber let me go my way? she thought. I not want to be Queen Mudder and rule Windward Maroons. I want only ta love dat boy wid da soft eyes at the foot o' Blue Mountain.

Nanny gave orders to gather up all the food which was edible. Baskets of Indian corn, plantain and yam were crowded under the bamboo by the river. The goat sacrificed in last night's ceremony was salted and every part of the uneaten pork was wrapped in leaves.

Clothing taken from the bodies of the dead soldiers was piled in one place, weapons in another. Small mounds of food, clothing and weapons grew up along the bank of the stream.

Teeth were cut from vicious dogs. Last night watching these animals rip the throats of her brave warriors, Nanny had been so enraged that she fixed the dogs in her eyes until they turned ripping and tearing at each other—even eating their own entrails until every one was killed.

Besides the dog teeth, beads taken from the dead Indians, small sacks of grave dirt, eggshells, fish bones, parrots' feathers, snakes' teeth, toads' feet filled small gourds and sat on the rocks by the glistening stream.The dead animals tossed into the river would soon pollute the water supply which reached the plantations below.

They were ready to leave. Nanny's troops numbered only thirty. They had searched the dense forest and could find no more survivors. Caleb Foote had run away. This Nanny had expected, but she needed him now. Nanny was concerned that their meager provisions would not sustain them on their long march to the West.

Thirty. Ten were small children, fifteen women and only five men. The trek to the Cockpit Country along the backbone of the island was a dangerous undertaking. Could her obeah imbue the necessary stamina to carry thirty people across the densely forested, craggy mountain ridge? Could her strong magic warm them in the long cold nights, keep them sure of foot through the morning fog, multiply the dwindling food supply? This would be the greatest test of their love for her, and the ultimate test of Nanny's powers.

On the first of April, Anne stood on the deck of the *Pison*. Captain Morewell and his first mate Joseph Evelyn sang out the orders for getting underweigh. From time to time the crew answered them with a hearty, "Yea! Yea!" When Port Royal lay far astern the captain issued his final request for every man to say his private prayer for *bon voyage* and the song was ended.

Fred Canfield, the helmsman, muttered something foul under his breath. Anne could not be certain if it was in response to the captain's entreaty or the sea's answer to his helm, for he was bearing down hard upon it. Having inquired about this sullen man, the captain told Anne that he had killed his brother in Bristol, then ran away to sea.

"Keep to yere course, Mister Canfield. We must run half way to Bahia Honda afore we can turn her into the wind."

"Aye, sir."

"Abram, look to those lines, man. You see Mister Halsey is busy there in the rigging, see to those hogsheads. And mind you, Mr. Isaacs, see they are safely stowed."

The *Pison* bore away hard on its long tack. Like other vessels of its kind, the two masted thirty-eight foot sloop did not go windward very well. It would take almost two months for the vessel to reach Nassau with its cargo of sixty-five hogsheads of molasses processed on the Sommerwood estate.

The corpulent Adam Morewell had been many years at sea. His hair and beard were white and cropped close to his head and face. The sleeves of his shirt had been cut out exposing heavily tatooed arms. One picture fascinated Anne. She studied it as the captain explained the voyage to her. The tatoo was a serpent endeavoring to swallow its tail.

Since he had given over his cabin to Anne, Captain Morewell moved in to share the cabin with his first mate Joseph Evelyn. It was here that he and Anne sat sipping claret and studying the chart of the Caribbean sea.

"So, explain to me, Captain, why are we heading south?"

"Going north by way of the Win'ard Passage is tedious—it bein' 'gainst the trades. Sometimes it takes six to seven weeks to sail from Port Royal to Morant Point where you live."

"That long?"

"Aye. So this first week we must beat southeast half way to South America before we can make our turn and beat back nor'ward. That second week 'tis a hard beat, for we must ride high up on the wind and heel sharply; we'll take in the most water then, I fear, but we will get into the Win'ard Passage. We must navigate 'round Navassa Island in the daylight for she be hazardous at night." The captain ran his hand across his scalp and stroked his beard several times.

"So by the third week we're back to Jamaica where we started from."

" 'Fraid so, Mistress. Navassa be off Port Antonio as you can see. Once we pass Cape Dona Maria we must tack to Cuba then back to Haiti two, maybe three times. You see, Anne, we gain only three leagues each time we do it."

"A bloody tedious design this."

"And the winds blow wet and cold in that passage late at night. Once we pass Cape Mayse, you see it here on the nor'east tip o' Cuba, we can take to the east and make Heneagu in the fourth week.

"That's in the Bahamas, is it not, captain?"

"Aye. We pass the west end of Heneagu in the fifth

week and should be able to fall off just enough to set a straight course for the Mira Por Vos. This passage right here." He ran a fat finger up to the southwest tip of Acklin Key. "It means 'look out for yourself.' "

"Indeed."

"Then with the luck of the wind, the sixth week we can sail along the east side of Long Island. At Cape Santa Maria at the north end we should be in a reach through Exuma Sound. We make a little turn here in the seventh week, and once again with the luck o' the wind we can make a run for Providence." The captain's hand circled his belly. "Must be nearly dinner time. Mister Evelyn has a private stash of apples in here someplace. Oh, here 'tis. Will you share one with me, Anne?"

"I'd love to, Captain. How did he get apples?"

"Evelyn sailed in from Virginia just two days ago. You see, Mistress, coming back to Jamaica is an easy run; it take only a week to ten days."

Warm suns.
Cool moons.
Wet mornings.
Windy evenings.
Long days.
Cold nights.

In the seventh week, The *Pison* reached, then ran into Nassau Harbour.

Nanny's trek westward took over a month. No one counted the steps or thought of the distance or the burdens they carried. The women balanced baskets of food and cooking utensils on their heads. Even the children hauled bundles of clothing. The men made a litter and piled it high with weapons, strapped down with vines. Guns. Nanny would bring guns to Cudjoe. They would win the war with Nanny's guns. The British would leave the island and Jamaica would once more belong to the Maroons. Some women, infants strapped to their breasts, could think only of warm huts and cooking fires. The older children, tugging on bits of jerked pork, sometimes jumped from rock to rock across the river streams.

From the top of the tallest tree, the terrain looked like small green rabbit holes. Down below, the country was wild. Marching behind Nanny the Maroon band had to cut their way along the backbone of the cockpit. Her huge frame tented in striped robe, with staff in one hand and abeng in the other, led them over hundreds of craggy, densely wooded hills and valleys and across hundreds of noisy streams rushing away from steep waterfalls.

Afiba walked in the path made by Nanny's majestic strides. The princess carried no burden except that of Nanny's stool, the symbol of her authority as Queen Mother—the shrine of her soul. This could not have been left behind, and only a princess was allowed to touch it. Her legs ached, but she was careful of her bearing. Afiba proudly carried her round head high, for it was a sign of her heritage and beauty. She must always be an example to the others; Nanny had instructed her. The stones cut her feet. Perhaps tomorrow she would wear the leather coverings Caleb Foote had given her long ago. Her pace quickened. To rid Jamaica of men like Caleb Foote, she would walk to Africa.

From the time they put out their fires in the morning until Nanny chose the place for the night's repose they never stopped to rest. Often times after climbing a steep hillside the tangle of growth forced them back down again to find a new path. As the days wore into weeks, the children tired. Women carried the younger ones most of the day now. Nanny carried a three-year-old girl in one arm and a boy of two in the other.

Nights the tribe would huddle together, for their small fires and the red coats of the British Regulars could not protect them against the freezing temperature. Whatever small birds the hunters managed to catch along the way were spitted over a fire and served as dinner for everyone. No adult touched a bite of food from dawn to nightfall.

Even the food gatherers brought back every morsel caught, speared, shot or picked. Not one berry passed their lips until the evening repast. Some nights edible roots were all that sustained them. Other nights a few pieces of fresh fruit finished off their meal and there was always an abundance of fresh water.

Each night, Nanny distributed the food. The portions always seemed meager, but once consumed were strangely satisfying. After the meal there was no Komina drumming or dancing as there had been in their lovely village—Nanny's town. They spread their charms from bags and gourds onto the cold ground and chanted softly.

Many nights Yamou begged for a story. He was curious about the wonders of the heavens and the earth and had puzzled long over the problem of how the first man came to be on the earth. "Nanny, can you tell Yamou 'bout de firs' mon? How get he here?"

" 'Firs' mon, he cum up from holes in de groun'. On a Monday night a worm he tunnel up thru de earth an' seben mon, seben womon, a dog, an' a leopard cum up thru de passage. Now on Tuesday dey all 'fraid, so de leader he put his han' on each one o' dem and dey get down ta work on Wednesday."

"Dat Doddy name day, Quaco."

"Das right. So on Wednesday dey build dere houses. On T'ursday, dog, he bring fire back to dem. Dey cook de food, but dey smart, dey try de food on de dog firs'."

"Dat all, Nanny? Eb'ryting dey do dey finish on T'ursday?"

"Yes, Yamou, T'ursday."

"What hoppen odder t'ree day, den?"

"Well, de God o' creation trable 'roun' de earth makin' dis ting and dat ting. By Sunday he finish makin' eb'ryting. It time ta sleep, boy. Nanny tell you nudder story tomorrow night. Sleep now." Nanny placed her hand on his head and restful sleep came to him. Nanny herself always slept with a small child in the crook of each arm.

In this way the Windward army struggled up and down

the hump of Jamaica deeper into the Cockpit Country, the place which whispered to all white inhabitants of the island this warning: "Me no ask, you no cum." This warning called out especially to the British marauders, camped at the foot of treacherous paths which they believed would lead them to Maroon haunts.

Cudjoe would welcome his sister Nanny. She knew he would although she had not seen him since the day of the burial of their younger brother Quaco some five years ago. For both of them, it was fighting which had filled those years. How could she have known that Cudjoe was beginning to tire of combat. His spirit was leaden and since he had moved farther into this wild country, she had had little communication with him. Drums, even the largest, were sometimes muffled by the trees. Sounds were swallowed up in the thick bush. Distance had created an estrangement, silence a void.

Charloner Jackson, collector of customs at Nassau, detained everyone aboard the *Pison* until he made a thorough investigation. Nauseated by the stench of Nassau Harbour and anxious to find her friend, Anne paced the deck. Finally the crew unloaded the sixty-five hogsheads of molasses into the hands of Messrs. Sweeting and Thompson, proprietors of a general store on the bay.

"Will you take a cup o' rum with me later at the tavern, Mistress Anne?"

"Aye, Captain, 'twould be my pleasure. What do they call the inn now? I remember it as the King's Head."

" 'Tis called the Crown and Anchor."

"Can I hire a horse there, think you?"

"Aye. Do you want one of my boys to accompany you?"

"No, thank you, Captain, I remember the way."

Anne trekked up the hill, turning back from time to time to look out over the harbor to the reef beyond. Once out of smelling distance the bay took on a picturesque quality with many island sloops clustered about the few imposing square-rigged vessels riding at anchor. The breeze, although warm, refreshed her. At least the air was moving, not like the dead calm of the harbor. Looking about, Anne felt a confidence grow within her. No mountain looked down on her to intimidate or threaten her well-being. A church steeple caught her eye; she had not remembered that. Anne's pace quickened when she saw the tavern path bordered with conch shells, their coral fans fading to white in the sun. The bowsprit figures decorating the yard differed from the ones she had known, otherwise the tavern looked the same.

A tall muscular man wrestled with one of the shutters which was hanging by one hinge from the top of the tavern window. When he leaned over, a roll of flesh spilled over the waist of his breeches. He took off his straw hat, wiped his head, face and neck with a napkin, then draped the napkin over his head and jammed his hat down on top of it.

"I beg your pardon, can you direct me to the owner here?"

"Yes, Miz." He removed his hat, but left the napkin. "I'm Marmaduke Darvill, proprietor of this establishment, innkeeper, tavern keeper, cook and carpenter, as you can see. Will you be needin' a room, Miz . . ."

"Sommerwood, Anne Sommerwood—not if a friend of mine still lives on New Providence—Henri Duplaissez."

"Oh, yes, Enree, 'e's on the island and been 'ere since I can remember."

"Good, then I'll need a horse."

"I can take you to 'is 'ouse in my carriage if you would like, Missus?"

"No, I'll be here for some time and would like my own horse. If you can spare one, that is?"

"Aye, Missus. Benjamin!" A boy of ten with floppy hair and wearing nothing but a pair of breeches cut off above the knees appeared in the tavern doorway.

Anne was startled by the boy's appearance—he was so much like Colin. Her throat constricted, but she resolutely put her son out of her mind and looked for peace across the tranquil bay. She had to replace past sorrows with pleasant thoughts or she would never build enough strength to return to Jamaica.

"Benjamin, fetch the brown mare for the missus."

"Aye, sir."

"She's a love, that mare. Nice 'orse for a woman—gentle, you know, Missus. An' Benjamin Saunders 'ere 'e takes good care o' 'er."

"I appreciate that, sir, but I'm used to riding all manner of horses. I am a breeder of horses in Jamaica and have in my stables a good many of all kinds."

"Jamaica, is it? Lovely place, Jamaica. I visited there often in my sea-faring days." Darvill suddenly realized the napkin was still draped over his head and snatched it off. He looked longingly at the sea for a moment, then abruptly took Anne by the arm. "Forgive me, Miz Anne, for keepin' you standin' in the sun. Come sit under this almond tree."

"Who is governor here, Mister Darvill?" Anne watched the sand cloud her boots as she walked."

"A vinegar-pisser, forgive me, Missus, name's Fitzwilliam. God's Eyes, 'e's a mean bastard—a bloody tyrant. 'E drove off all the hard workin' people of this island—them German—Palatines Woodes Rogers called 'em. Them Palatines brought us pineapple and taught us how to grow it too. Would you like to taste one?"

"Not just now, Mister Darvill, perhaps another time. I guess Woodes Rogers went back to England."

" 'E died, Missus, three year ago."

"Oh, I hadn't heard."

"Was 'e a friend o' yours, Miz Anne?"

"I knew him."

"Sorry, Missus. 'Ere's Benjamin with your 'orse. The reason 'e looks sad is she's 'is favorite. 'E takes 'er out after supper every night. Don't say anything. 'E thinks I don't know it; but I figure the boy and the 'orse, well, they both need friends." As the horse approached Anne noticed she had a white spot on her rump, just like her mare butchered in the Maroon raid.

"She's a fine looking animal. What's her name, Benjamin?"

"I calls her Miz Molly."

Anne's stomach sank, and her foot missed the stirrup when she tried to mount.

"You all right, Missus? It takes a while to get your sea legs suited to the land. Let me help you up."

Anne put her foot in Darvill's hand and as he lifted she swung into the saddle.

"She's real gentle, Missus—only needs a little nudgin'." Benjamin handed Anne the reins.

Anne wanted to invite Benjamin to come and ride Molly but choked on her words when her hand touched his as she took the reins.

"Oh, what about your trunk, Missus? Want I should send it up to the 'ouse?"

"Yes," she said, finding her voice. "That would be most considerate and what is the cost for this fine animal?"

"Oh, a shilling a day, Missus, that will do."

"Here's five pounds on account."

"Thank you, Missus. You know the way?"

"Aye, Mister Darvill, like going home."

Henri looked up from his sewing to see Anne riding up the hill and dropping everything he ran to meet her.

"Cherie!" He pulled her from the saddle and swung her around until she was breathless and dizzy. Allowing Anne's feet to touch the ground, he smothered her face with kisses. *"Ma petite*—too long, since I see you, too long."

"At least fifteen years, *mon cher.*"

"Zat long. *Mon Dieu.* Come to ze house. I fix coffee and you tell Henri everysing."

"Can we swim instead, Henri?"

"But of course, *cherie.* A swim will refresh you from ze, how you say, fatigue of ze sea."

A mulatto, Michael Fox, came to take Anne's horse. After the man had gone, Anne asked, "Is he your lover?"

"No, *cherie.* Michael keeps ze house, cooks ze meals.

Henri get so lazy in his old age. And instead of play I read in ze bed at night. Zere are no young men for me zese days."

"Why, Henri, there's scarcely a gray hair on your head."

"If I were not blond, you'd see plenty, *cherie*."

The man smiled down on her. The flesh at his jowls hung loosely and his figure was more Lydian than Anne had remembered but the energy was the same. His gray eyes examined every part of her form as if she were a banquet and he could not decide what delicacy to taste first.

"Will you swim with me?"

"Of course. You sink Henri let you out of his sight? You may run away again. How long you stay, *cherie*—two year, three year . . ."

"Perhaps a year, we'll see. I have a family, you know. I cannot leave them for too long— my husband is in London. But come, let's go down to the lagoon. We can talk there. My, your gardens are lovely," she said, rushing to catch up with his strides.

"Zis is ze work of Michael Fox. Nosing zat man can't make grow in ze ground. I have every fruit tree in the whole Caribbean, I sink. Ze lime, sour orange, sugar apple, guava . . ."

Henri kept up his horticultural litany until they reached a secluded lagoon hung all over with wild vines and fern and shaded in part by sea grape and coconut palms. Laying their clothes over a branch of sea grape, they dipped into the cool water.

"Let's swim out to where ze sun is warming ze water. Zis is much too cold for me."

"It's nearly June and beastly hot here, Henri."

"I know, *cherie*, but the blood she get thin. When you get old like me, you see."

"I'm not too far from forty and I know you are not much older."

"Oh, *cherie*, you are kind. Henri is fifty-two."

"No. I can't believe it. You're so slim and handsome, more handsome than I remember."

"And you, *cherie*, are more ravishing, if zat is *possible*." He squeezed her biceps. "And as strong as ever too. Enough, tell me about your husband is he handsome and your children are they pretty like zere mozzer?" Anne recounted everything that had happened to her since the night he had helped to rescue her from Woodes Rogers jail in 1718. He cried with her as she told him about Mary Read's death. The story of her tragic experiences in Jamaica were liberally punctuated by his cries of *"Quelle horreur!"* and his compassionate kisses. Her tears seemed cleansing rather than embittered. Maybe it was the water which sparkled clear down to her feet that gave her calm or the subtle current swirling around her ankles caused by the multicolored fishes that almost made her smile. But Anne decided that peace really came from her friend. This honest, open-hearted man never hesitated to pour his generous love upon her.

Henri disappeared under the water and bit her ankle before he burst to the surface. *"Mon Dieu!* Did you see zat fish?"

"He bit me I think, but I'm not afraid of him; he's harmless."

"Is zat so." Henri wiped the water from his eyes but there was more. He tried to think of something to make her laugh so that he could stop crying. "Ze boy, Matt, is he handsome like his mozzer?"

"Oh yes." Anne laughed, "How she fooled you, *mon cher*."

"Henri was so in love wiz zat man." Henri laughed with her. "Zen you tell me he is a woman. *Sacre Bleu*—how devastating. I cried for a week."

"Remember that vest you repaired for her."

"Mon Dieu! How can I forget. Ze cloth, she is so old, I put ze braid, I put ze leazzer to cover ze holes. I beg her to let me make her a new one. But no, she wear only zat one."

"I found out why. One day in prison she told me. Remember how she was rescued from a slaver by Bartholomew Roberts?"

"Oh, yes. Zat was before she take us wiz Rackam and Vane, no?"

"Yes. Well, the captain of that slaver had ordered Mary whipped because she refused to murder some slaves who had gone blind."

"*Incroyable!*"

"Mary's shirt had been stripped from her body and one of the slave girls gave her her only garment."

"Now I see. What happened to zat girl? Do you know?"

"Bart ordered the ship burned, slaves and all. When Mary could not stop him, she tried to rush into the hold to save the girl. But in her weakened condition she blacked out and the pirates carried her to their vessel."

"*Quelle horreur!* Oh, *cherie*, please no more sad stories. Henri's heart will crack."

"I am sorry, dear friend. I don't mean to distress you. No more. Now you tell of your life. What has happened here since Woodes Rogers rid the Bahamas of pirates?"

"Zey still here—smugglers, pirates, same sing I sink. Zey call zemselves wreckers and live off the salvage of misfortunate vessels. We also have whalers and turtlers like before. Henri take you to ze Crown and Anchor tonight. Zen you see for yourself."

"And your governor . . ."

"Oh, zat man, he's a monster. *Vraiment.* He comes here last year and ze first sing he makes a census. Rogers he just make a census in 1731, but no, Fitzwilliam, he must make anozzer. What's more, he threaten everybody wiz ze whip if zey refuse to make return."

"My God!"

"Last month a black man cutting braziletto in ze woods, he shoot and wound, only slightly, his overseer, who mistreat him and his friend working wiz him. Well, zis governor hang him and his friend."

"But the other man was innocent, wasn't he?"

"But of course, Fitzwilliam say he hang him to keep ze ozzer one company. Can you believe zat? Ze military, zey unhappy, too little pay, zey say. Last week ze governor hang one of ze soldiers for stabbing his sergeant. Men say ze man have cause."

"God's Teeth! He hasn't bothered you, has he?"

"Not any more. He try once. Send his man, Archibald, to beat me for not attending special church service honoring ze governor. I send zat man back to him one bloody mess. Zat night at ze tavern I wear my belt, you know ze one wiz a dozen knives in it and I put on a *demonstration*. He never bozzer me after zat." The blow of a conch shell sounded dinner.

"Is that call for us?"

"Yes, Michael Fox doesn't like to serve cold food, besides ze sun is down. Did you see it, *cherie?*"

"Yes. It was behind you and as magnificent as always." A commotion in the leaves and a tall pink bird took off across the lagoon, its black wings beating against the purple sky. "A flamingo. It's as tall as you, Henri—six feet at least. What's she doing here, so far from her flock?"

"Son of a whore! I don't know what he is doing here, but if he comes back tomorrow I'll send Michael to shoot him and we have a fine dinner."

"Oh, no. I could never let you hurt such a beautiful creature."

"But zey make excellent eating, *cherie.*"

"Think of me as that bird. Now what do you say?"

"Zat is not fair."

"Who said life was fair, Henri?"

"C'est la vie, ma cherie. C'est la vie."

Anne's appearance at the Crown and Anchor captured every eye. Her muslin breeches of deep green dipped at her knee into high boots of cordovan leather of the richest brown. The sleeves of her linen shirt were trimmed in falls of Mechlin lace at her wrists. She wore no baldric or sword but a brilliant blue silken sash circled her waist. Henri had offered her one of his own swords but she had refused to wear it. Not trusting the manners of the crude sort that frequented the tavern, he wore a brace of pistols and his belt of many knives in addition to his sword.

"Henri, you look like a bloody arsenal. You frighten me. I hope this evening will be interesting but not too exciting."

"You are on my island and I am responsible for you."

"Tombay said that to me when he took me to his home at San Salvador."

"Oh, I sorry, *cherie*. I did not mean to bring you a painful memory."

"It's forgotten. Now let's find a place to sit down."

"Zis one is best." After seating Anne, Henri clattered into his chair. The table in the corner gave them the advantage of the entire room. Anne looked up into the eyes of practically every patron.

"Ze only sing to do is to introduce you. Do you mind? Zen maybe zey will stop staring at you."

"No, I don't mind. Just don't introduce me as a famous pirate, that's all."

"Gentlemen, zis is Anne Sommerwood from Cork, Ireland, ze Carolinas, and lately from Jamaica."

Before Henri sat down, a red-faced young Irish sailor stood up in the midst of his fellows and raised his tankard. "To Ireland and the most beautiful blue-green eyes that ere sailed from Cork!"

"To Ireland!" The Irish sailors shouted and drank. Unable to unlock his eyes from Anne's, the boy had to be pulled back down into his chair by his mates.

"Oh, *cherie,* you have captured zat boy's heart. Henri wish he could still do zat."

After the eyes left Anne, Henri pointed out some of the more colorful, as well as the somewhat prominent people present. A grimy little man sitting with the well-dressed Messrs. Thompson and Sweeting was John Petty—a wrecker and one of the wealthiest men in the town. Anne looked at the shirtless, shoeless man dubiously as ale spilled from his mouth and Mr. Petty rubbed it into his hairy chest. The Lowe brothers sat together. Mathew, Gideon, John and Benjamin were whaling men from Bermuda. Read Elding, an elderly, smartly dressed malatto had been Lt. Governor of the Bahamas in 1699. He was sitting with James Irving, a surgeon from Charleston. Like many of the Jamaican planters neither man wore stockings.

"Who's that?" Anne's eyes were drawn to the nearly naked Indian wearing an elaborate headdress of all sorts of feathers intermixed with down. His olive skin glistened as he downed tankards of rum almost as fast as Marmaduke Darvill could bring them to him.

"Oh, ze Indian—a chief, Cherokee, I sink."

An odd assortment of loud blustery men grouped about the room: soldiers, turtlers, wreckers, logwood cutters, shark fishers. Bahamian whaling men rarely sat with New Englanders; however, Bermudian and Eleutheran wreckers clanked tankards at every round. Anne knew she would never keep the old islanders' names straight in her head. There were too many and all the same. Of the Curtises, there were three Henrys, of the Sweetings—two Johns and two Benjamins, of the Robertses—three Johns in Nassau and three more Johns at Harbour Island. There were two William Thompsons there also, and perhaps a half dozen John Currys. Anne laughed to herself. She never believed Henri; he probably had forgotten their first names and created this absurdity for her enjoyment.

Dr. Irving came over and bored them with talk of his flourishing rice and indigo plantations in Charles Town and bewailed the fact that he could not make anything grow in these Bahamian rock fields. He left when the Reverend Mister Smith approached. Well fortified with two cups of rum, he asked if she would teach at the school during her stay. She respectfully declined and William Smith went away crestfallen. Read Elding was charming and reminded her of Black Robin who had sailed with Rackam for a time. Anne turned cold when Elding asked if she had known any pirates. Henri rose from his chair, and reached for his sword. Elding apologized to Anne and quickly went away. Just then one of the soldiers from the Independent Company was shoved by his companions towards Anne.

"Please sit down, Lieutenant . . ."

"Harkness, John Harkness." He sniffed and ran his hand under his nose. "My men were wonderin', Mistress Sommerwood, if you know any soldiers in Jamaica?"

"Yes, I know some."

"Well, we . . . they were wonderin' if those men received any additional pay. Before we left England we understood we would get supplemental pay for duty in the American colonies. That's why we came here."

"Why yes, Lieutenant, I believe they do. I remember my husband speaking about that very thing with a captain of our West India regiment."

Satisfied, John Harkness stood up and pulling down his coat in a determined way, saluted and rejoined his fellow men. They fell immediately to whispering; Anne shifted her attention from them when the Widow Albury came to their table with two tankards of rum punch. A woman in her middle years with peppery hair and plumpish figure, she greeted Anne with a bright smile, then went about to the other tables. She brought her tray down hard on one or two fellows who had the impertinence to slap her bottom.

"Don't tell zat woman anysing, *cherie*. She has a long tongue."

"A long tongue, eh, well I'll watch mine then." Anne drank and surveyed the patrons of the Crown and Anchor. Not much different from pirate days, she thought. More straw hats than plumed ones, but the manners have not changed. The men still keep their hats on at table and slap at anything that walks by.

"Look up zere, *cherie*." Henri pointed to an ensign hanging from the rafter. The white design was so covered with grease that it was almost as black as the field. "Ze flag I make for Jack Rackam—don't you recognize it?" Now she could see it. The death's head cradled in crossed cutlasses glared ominously at her. It gave her an eerie feeling to think the pirate flag under which she sailed had presided over the gatherings in this tavern for the past sixteen years. The din of a thousand conversations assailed her ears and the smell of greasy food from a thousand meals turned her stomach. Anne excused herself to Henri and went outside.

The whine of mosquitoes and soft song of the night birds punctuated by the intermittent crashing of waves against the moonlit reef refreshed her. The noise of laughing men slapping their knees faded into the background as she inhaled the sweet fragrances of the Nassau night.

A distant drum beat and Anne's eyes swung away from the sea high where the mountains should be, but she saw only the sky cloaked in stars. Realizing at last that the drums came from the negro settlement, she sighed deeply. The brisk beat of the goombay was a familiar one–both gay and grave. Anne listened and watched as her mind's eye placed the dancing figures on the moonlit reef–the woman all languishing and easy in her motions, the man all fire and action. When the couple disappeared Anne went back to Henri.

Looking up again at Rackam's flag, Anne laughed.

"What is funny, *cherie?*"

"Remember our pirate adventures in *La Petite Mort?*"

"*Mon Deiu*, how can I forget. Zat actor, what was his name?"

"Alfred Butler."

"Yes, Alfred. All zat stage makeup—tatoos, frightful hair, fierce eyes, your beautiful body covered wiz charcoal and pig's blood.

"God, what a sight we must have been. 'Once more into the breach!' "

"Zat crazy actor and zose Dutchmen we capture. We scare zem so bad zey shit dere pants. Oh my, zat was fun. You know Anne, I sew ten years on ze fabric and lace we steal from zat merchantman."

"What about your friends Cuthbert and Nelson. Do you ever see them?"

"No, zey leave ze island long ago. Zose crazy bastards."

"Remember when we boarded the merchantman they thought they were giving the enemy a brave assault. When they opened their eyes they found out they were fighting with each other."

"Zose crazy bastards. Stupid idiots." Henri's head nearly fell to the table. *"Merde!* Speaking of idiots, here is our governor wiz his whore."

The soldiers grew quiet as the governor sauntered past them. Archibald, his scurvy companion, held out a chair and lifted the tail of the governor's coat, situating it so that Fitzwilliam would not crush the lace as he sat. Richard Fitzwilliam wore a small wig with an enormous queue, a linen shirt with mounds of ruffled lace at his bosom, black velvet breeches, gold-clocked stockings, and red-heeled shoes.

"My, he is well scented; I can smell him from here. Oh, here's my captain come to join us." Captain Morewell settled his girth into the chair next to Anne and signalled Mr. Darvill to bring him two tankards of rum. "Henri, this is Captain Adam Morewell."

The captain shook Henri's hand. "Pleased to make your acquaintance, sir."

"Henri Duplaissez, *a votre service."*

A loud conversation erupted amongst the Eleutheran and Nantucket whalers at the two adjoining tables. A Nantucketer, one Captain Philip Rawlings, banged a hairy fist on the table and stood up. "Have you never been to sea in your lives! I tell you I saw the bloody thing."

Nathaniel Bethel shouted back."There be no sea beast like that anywhere in the world. Sit down."

"Bridle your tongues over there," shouted one of the soldiers.

Rawlings' voice fell into a harsh whisper as he leaned his rugged body on his hands and spit the description of the sea monster at the unbelieving Eleutherans. "I tell you it were a strange creature—his head like a lion with very large teeth, ears hangin' down, a long beard and curled hair on its head. His body were sixteen feet long and its buttock round with a short yellow-colored tail and it beckoned us to follow it in our boat."

All the sailing men were silent now, some even enthralled by his story. "And did you follow it?" asked one Eleutheran.

"Aye, a fine brisk chase we gave him, lads. But he were fierce and gnarled his teeth with great rage when we attacked him. We shot him three times and wounded though he was, he still rose up out of the water to brave us—gnashing his teeth and growlin' in our faces. Harpooners struck at him but could not hold him. For five hours we chased that beast far out into the open sea. Then he tired of our games and slipped into the deep and never came up in our sight again."

For a long while a reverent silence prevailed.

Nathaniel Bethel spoke at last. "I don't believe it. There's no such grisly beast as that in the ocean sea." He grabbed Philip's sleeve. "Come on, sit down and 'ave another drink."

One whack at his chest and Nathaniel crashed to the floor, chair and all. A scuffle ensued among the whalers. Leathern fists pounded leathery faces.

"Why doesn't the governor stop this?"

"*Cherie*, you see him zere, stuffing his face. He does not involve himself in private quarrels. If you ask him, zat is what he will say."

"Jesus God, look at this, now the Irish sailors are into it."

Anne and Henri worked their way out of the tavern in the wake of Captain Morewell who parted the sea of whalers by sending men flying to the right and left of him. Once outside, the captain kissed Anne's hand and bid them both good night. On his way home, Henri continued his tirade against the governor. "One time two planters came to him with some complaint against each ozzer. 'Fight it out amongst yourselves,' he said 'and if one of you gets killed, I'll hang ze ozzer one.' Zat's what he said, *cherie*."

""Has anyone reported his conduct to England?"

"Yes, a few men. Henri knows that he will be recalled someday. I wait. Zis is my home; I will never leave it. I wait. Woodes Rogers, he left."

"But he came back again."
"And he went away again."
"That's true. It seems we have no remedy but patience."

High in the western mountains of Jamaica at Accompong Town, the Maroon huts either clung precariously to the side of the cockpit or squatted complacently by the side of the muddy road. Cudjoe greeted his sister and took her to a large thatched hut on the road but somewhat removed from the other houses. He was grateful for her guns, her people, but most of all her heartening presence. His army was formidable, but the British had begun to show their power. Cudjoe told Nanny what he dared not even whisper to his colonels.

"If you had kill one white mon wid eb'ry step you take to get here dat no be 'nuff to stop English. Dey grow stronger eb'ry day. Forts dey build on paths ta our towns. Dey hab Indian know Maroon habit and fierce dogs."

Nanny tramped about the dirt floor already packed hard by the feet of other warriors. "I hab see dese Indians and dere dogs. No frighten Nanny. Wid soldiers Nanny fight. Soon all Jamaica—no English."

Newly fired by Nanny's determination Cudjoe agreed to attack the fort at Carlisle Bay. "Tonight we hab festival. Tomorrow we make war plan."

The air in the damp Cockpit grew thick. From the window of their hut Yamou and Afiba looked out over the ravine. The sky turned black and a crash of thunder breaking between the two mountains sent Yamou running into his sister's arms. The instant that Nanny took them both into her arms the rains came. Snug against her invincible bosom, they watched the gray sheets of rain pour down. The wind ripped the palm leaves and bent the slender young coconut trees almost double while tearing green fruit from the old ones. The ravine was a waving mass of broad leaves and in the bottoms the wind beat the sugar cane to the ground. Lightning streaked the sky, followed by great cracks of thunder. Yamou buried his face in the valley of Nanny's breasts.

The rain stopped as suddenly as it came.

Nanny took Yamou and Afiba down the winding rocky road through the muddy avenue to her own spacious hut where she prepared a bath for them. An oval basin carved from a cedar tree glowed black with a high patina. Spicy odors rose from the wild pigs roasting on pits of hot stones outside and mingled in the hut with the sweet smell of the coconut oil Nanny rubbed on the bathing children. Once dry, Yamou and Afiba sat with Nanny on the floor mat of woven banana trash. Afiba rubbed her arms, inhaling their scent. Yamou ran his fingers through his thick wavy hair. The copper brown of his slender, solid body glistened in the afternoon light. Since the rainstorm Yamou had been puzzling over the question of thunder and lightning and, unable to come up with an answer regarding their origin, he decided to ask Nanny, who was expert in all these matters.

"What is tunder, Nanny?"

"Why, de thunderbolt, dat be God's axe. Yamou, no 'fraid tunder, now."

"Not now. Nanny here wid Yamou now. Nanny no 'fraid anyting."

"Not so. Nanny 'fraid darkness. You know boy dey a time when dere be no darkness. When God firs' make de worl' de sun shine all de day long."

"Did sun shine at night too?"

"Dat what I cum to now. At night de moon gib off light so bright dat mon see eb'ryting clear as day. Den one day God put he lips to de abeng an' call de Bat. When Bat cum God gib him basket ta take ta de Moon, but he no say what Moon do wid dat. On de way Bat he git tired an' set down de basket while he go off ta fine food. While he gone some udder creatures day see de basket and tink dey fine food. Jus' when dey take de cober off, Bat cum back but too late, darkness already 'scape."

"What hoppen den? Did Bat try to fetch de darkness back?"

"Eber since dat time de Bat he sleep in de day, but when de dark cum he wake up and chase 'roun an' try to cotch de darkness ta put back in de basket ta take to Moon like God he order him ta do. But he neber can cotch de darkness and when day cum, Bat, he hab ta sleep 'gain."

"Where God, Nanny?"

"Eb'rywhere, Yamou—in da trees, in de flowers, in da . . ."

"All same time?"

"Yes, he eb'rywhere, in Yamou even, Afiba too. Nanny carry God inside." And she pointed to her own heart.

It was twilight in the cockpits and the flopping, squeaking mouse bats enticed Yamou outside to investigate their furry webbed wings and white mouse teeth. Afiba napped fitfully. Nanny dipped her fingers into a gourd of coconut milk and smoothed them across the girl's forehead to clear her mind and bring peaceful sleep.

The abeng called all Maroons to the parade. Men and women, some robed and some naked, gathered under the open pavilion. Warriors adorned their splendid bodies with the prizes of war consisting predominantly of toothy necklaces of both animal and human origin. The women wore trophies taken in plantation raids. Jeweled earrings dangled from noses, rings circled toes, lavalieres hung at navels and dozen of brooches decorated colorful head scarves.

Seated on their stools, Nanny and her brother presided over the festival from a raised dais with the Maroon colonels and captains beside them but at ground level and sitting on mats of river rushes. Afiba and Yamou took their places on the ground just below Cudjoe and Nanny. Raising his abeng to his mouth, Cudjoe announced the commencement of the meal. Nanny studied Cudjoe's horn; it was made from deer rather than cow's horn and had belonged to Juan de Bolas, the first chief of the Maroons. He had received it from some Arawak or Spanish ancestor. The tall earthenware jars containing fresh spring water also belonged to that early period.

As Nanny cast her eyes about the assembly she found that the most familiar faces belonged to her own people, the most unfamiliar to a tribe of jet black men and women whose language sounded different from her own. Shorter and more delicate of figure, these blacks had features which more clearly resembled the European and their hair was loose and soft textured like the mulatto. Nanny leaned into Cudjoe and asked him who they were. "Madagascars" was his only reply, as though that were enough to answer any questions in her mind.

The meal ended. Music, dancing and story telling followed. Gourd rattles accompanied the melody of the bamboo flute and the rhythm of the goombay. Athletic-looking men walked around in a great circle, stretching their muscles in preparation for the jumping dances. His body already gleaming with sweat, the drummer stopped to pour rum on the new skin of his goombay, then taking in a long drink, commenced his beating.

Pace quickened, shouts boomed. Maintaining their wide circle, the dancers crouched, attacked, feinted, swerved and leaped in every attitude of bush fighting. Two men broke from the circle and jumping to the center squatted, flapping their arms and bobbing their heads in a pantomime of cocks fighting. The rhythm changed and a man and woman came together. The steady rolling motion of her hips excited him to a frenzy. His whole body twisted and writhed; his limbs shook. The assembly began chanting softly, "Kus kus. Kus kus."

Nanny whispered to Afiba. "Dose de words of de python. Soon he spray riber water ober her belly an' she hab baby."

When the chanting reached a crescendo, the man squatted before the woman, thrusting his arms wide and setting his hands to trembling. Eye level with her pelvis, he began an undulating motion of his own. When the chant fell to a whisper and the goombay softened, the dancers drifted apart and out of the circle.

The Koromantyn flute served as background for the Anansi stories and its plaintive sounds followed the Maroons down the road to their houses. Nanny led Yamou and Afiba to their hut. Delighted by the stories of the clever spider, Yamou would not go to sleep until Nanny confirmed the story his father had told him about how Anansi became a spider.

"Anansi hab fine fiel' o' corn, but one day de King's ram cum an' trample de plants an' eat de young corn shoots. So Anansi he kill de ram. He try to blame de deed on anudder mon but King he fine dis out an' kick Anansi into a t'ousand pieces. Dat why Anansi smaller now an' you fine him in eb'ry corner o' de house like spider broke into many pieces." The boy slumbered in Nanny's lap. Gently she laid Yamou on a mat of marsh weeds. The bright Jamaica moon poured a silver flood through the shutters onto the sleeping figure of the boy.

CHAPTER SEVEN

Return

In the final days of 1736 the westward Maroons concluded their period of rigorous training. Cudjoe instructed his soldiers in the use of the musket and machete; Nanny taught them the art of spear throwing, a skill at which the Madagascars were particularly adept. Ironhanded discipline prevailed in the army as it did in the family unit. In a Maroon village every household was a little government where, like the colonel's, the mother's word was law.

Yamou perfected his skills in the arts of war and begged Nanny to allow him to fight in the attack on the British fort at Carlisle Bay. "I fo'teen dis winter Nanny; I ready. Make trial fo' Yamou." Nanny took the matter to her brother and Cudjoe decided that it was indeed time Quaco's son became a man. Accompanied by two Madagascars, Yamou would hunt a wild boar. The boy must make the kill himself and bring back the boar in three days' time.

The sun had barely risen on the first day when Yamou, followed by the spear carriers, left the village to wind their way down the north side of the mountain into a densely wooded bottom interlaced with shrub and vine. Yamou led the way, looking for tracks along the twisted road. That night they camped by a mountain spring and the next day pressed down deeper into the tangled cockpit. The sun was high, but only thin streams of light reached this place. Stopping to rest, Yamou motioned for silence. His fingers clawed the rough fibre of the lacebark tree. Deep in the hollow of the bottom he heard snorting, grunting sounds;

reaching for two spears, he crouched and waited.

The boar sensed the intrusion of man and came crashing through the bush toward them. Yamou stepped from behind the lacebark to face it, hurling both spears too soon. One missed, but the second struck deep, angering the beast. Yamou snatched two fistfuls of spears and worked his way around behind the animal. As the boar circled to find the hunter, the spear in its shoulder struck a tree and snapped. It was moments before the confused boar sighted its target again. Head down, it charged. Two more spears hit their mark but did not halt the boar's advance. Yamou's foot caught in a vine. He fell into a sharp tree stump and ripped his leg from knee to groin. He tugged and pulled but could not twist out of the boar's path and the animal closed in on him. The Madagascars drew the animal away from the boy with their shouts and Yamou cut the ensnaring vines with the sharp edge of his spear. Painfully struggling to his feet, he called to the boar. It turned and came slowly toward him. Two more spears brought the animal to its knees. Yamou dragged himself closer to the boar who looked smaller now as it writhed in the throes of death. Looking into the eye of the beast, Yamou summoned all his strength and plunged his last spear into the boar's neck.

One of the Madagascars strapped broad leaves around Yamou's leg with vines while the other cut the boy a walking stick. By late afternoon of the third day the hunting party, led by Yamou limping on his staff, returned to the village. His pain was forgotten in the excitement as Nanny and Cudjoe inspected his kill. Yamou's face beamed with pride when Cudjoe gave the order to prepare his boar for the eve of battle feast. In two days the Maroon army would march to Carlisle Bay.

Removing the blood-soaked leaves binding Yamou's leg, Nanny learned that his cut was not as deep as she had anticipated. With Afiba's good care he would heal in a matter of weeks, but not soon enough to enable him to join the army at Carlisle Bay.

"Nanny make magic. Yamou mon now. Me want

fight."

"Wound mend in own time. Eb'rymon make his own magic fo' dat. Yamou heal se'f now, time for fighting soon cum."

The Maroon army marched for days to windward along the treacherous passes of the vast stretch of mountain and cockpit. Taking the west bend of the Minoa River, they crept into the Clarendon Precinct. Just before dawn on the tenth day of their expedition, the Maroons surrounded the encampment of British Regulars sleeping in the crotch of the river. In a matter of moments the victims of the silent massacre began to float down the river toward Carlisle Bay. The army moved swiftly through the pasture lands along the Minoa. Nearing the fort, the Maroon warriors paused under a tall guango tree to dress their gleaming copper bodies in branches. The moist ground cooled their feet as the wide spreading branches spit a juicy rain down upon them. The crunch of dried curled pods beneath their feet spoke the only warning of their presence. A moving forest advanced on the crumbling fort at Carlisle Bay.

Cannon fired. One of the Maroon's greatest warriors, Colonel Bucknor, caught a cannonball in his hands and returned it to the enemy with even greater force. Cudjoe's small square goombay beat out the rhythm of the slaughter. Soon more British soldiers were added to the carnage disgorged from the mouth of the Minoa into the bay of Carlisle. Surveying the scene of British defeat served only to increase Nanny's appetite for revenge. To Cudjoe this victory followed many earlier triumphs; he had lost his taste for war.

Riding, sailing and swimming had done much to repair Anne's body and Henri's gentle wisdom and dignity restored her mind. From him, she had relearned contemplation and patience. Their nightly conversations rejuvenated her spirits and in the company of his warm good humor she had forgotten the meaning of violation and fear. How she would fare when put to any real test Anne did not know. She did know that she longed to be with her family again, especially since her return from the Carolinas.

Too many memories there. How Colin would have loved Bath Town, she thought. She could see him riding in meadows and forests, sailing on the winding river, growing up strong and healthy as she had on her father's plantation.

Father. Will O'Brannon was everywhere, in every room, especially the library. She could feel her body barely fill the spaces his form had occupied in the old leather chair where she sat on his lap for hours listening to him read aloud. Anne touched the bindings of his books. It was like touching him—smooth in places, rough in others, but Will O'Brannon every inch of him. She took a few of his books with her to Charles Town where she stayed during the six months it took to sell the plantation. There was nothing else she wanted to take from there. She did not want to leave. She had to leave.

Walking for days in those rooms, she could almost feel her blood blast up and down her body. She was too aware, painfully so, of Will's part in her. Her legs throbbed, ankles swelled, knees buckled. Rest gave no ease and she could not sleep. When Anne left her childhood home the pains vanished.

He is myself, she decided, Will invaded my body. Why? Surely I am safer here in the Carolinas than in Jamaica. He drove me out of his home. Why, father? Vengeance? I can't believe you can still be angry with me for abandoning you those many years ago. No. What then? Nanny. The name popped into her mind like a bubble in a lake. I would happily forget her. There are soldiers. There are other planters plagued by the Maroons, why must I fight her alone? How will I build the strength to fight her alone? But that was not what tormented Anne's mind. Rather, when confronted, would she have the courage to fight or would terror immobilize her.

I must return to Jamaica. Fear has kept me here too long. She looked at Henri. And this man too, she thought, I could easily spend a lifetime in his company. But I miss my children. And since I have lost as many as I have now, I want to be near them. Letters are not enough.

Mary Elizabeth had written every day; intermittently, Anne had received bundles tied with blue ribbon carefully ordered by date and filled with news of everyone on the plantation. Baldwin's letters were enclosed in these packets. Vessels sailed from England to Jamaica more often than to the Bahamas. His stay in London, he was happy to inform her, was coming to a close. He hoped to be home by the coming John Canoe 1737. He prayed that Anne could find an opportunity to return around the same time. Although sprinkled with political news, Baldwin's letters expressed a concern for her well-being that touched Anne. She put down her letter to address her feelings to her friend.

"You know, Henri, I have come to realize that to be loved by someone so genuinely and so completely is a rare thing."

"Yes, *cherie*, zis does not happen to everyone. You have known zat kind of love two, three times, I sink—ze African, Mary Read and now your husband. You are most fortunate in love, *Cherie*."

"His letters are so tender, Henri. I wonder if . . ."

"If he can make love to you now?"

"Yes."

"I don't know. Perhaps time has healed him. Ze important sing is how you will respond to whatever happens. Are you ready?"

"I think so. How can I be sure? I want to go home. I have stayed much too long."

"Yes, I know. I have been waiting everyday since your return from Charles Town for you to tell me 'Henri, my business, she is finish. I must go.'I know. I know. But Henri, he will cry when you leave."

"Oh, my dear friend, I cannot bear to see you cry."

"Zat cannot be helped. You must go and Henri must cry. But first you must answer ze governor's invitation or life for me on zis island after you leave will be *impossible*."

"Tell him we will dine with him tomorrow night. Today Lieutenant Harkness gives me a tour of the fort. I have put him off too long already and *mon cher*, can you inquire what vessels might be sailing for Jamaica?"

"Of course, *cherie*. March is still ze whaling season. Perhaps zere is a vessel going to Abaco or Harbour Island. From zere many vessels go to Jamaica and ze Leeward Islands."

The ruinous condition of Fort Nassau was one subject Anne intended to bring before the governor. Lieutenant Harkness had showed her barracks ready to topple down. What guns were operable stood on rotten carriages, others rammed full of stones were stuck in the sand. Broken carriage trucks and shot littered the beach. She watched as inhabitants gathered rusting cannonballs to use as ballast for their boats. The entire situation along with the meager pay had made the soldiers an unhappy lot on the verge of doing something desperate to remedy their situation.

Henri had made Anne several new gowns and she had decided to wear one of them to the governor's house that evening. Henri hand-painted his fabric using island subjects but executed his designs in such a subtle way that a close look was required to recognize the parrots and flamingoes among the island trees in the variable greens of the print she wore. Anne was certain the governor would never notice; his eyes no doubt would be fixed upon her bosom rising from her tight bodice. Besides Henri and herself, there were Captain Walker and a Colonel Howel. Colonel Howel had been surgeon to a band of pirates but had gained respectability in the government by purchasing a lieutenancy in the Independent Company. He also joined the local militia for the sake of the title.

"I hear you leave us tomorrow, Mistress Sommerwood, and I scarce did get to know you." With great difficulty Governor Fitzwilliam brought his eyes out of Anne's bosom into her face. She returned his lewd expression with a wry smile which he tried unsuccessfully to imitate.

"Why, Your Excellency, I do believe you heard the news before I did."

"Yes, well, do you go straight for Jamaica?"

"Abaco first, I think, with Captain Lowe. Is that right, Henri?"

"Yes, *cherie*. Gideon Lowe sails to Abaco to inspect zere trying-houses. Zen he take you to Harbour Island where he will arrange passage for you to Jamaica."

The colonel interrupted. "I understand they built a fort at Eleuthera. Do you know anything of that, Captain Walker?"

"A small one, yes. And they built a larger one at Harbour Island."

"Yes, the plantations there become more considerable," said the governor.

Anne took her opportunity. "What about Fort Nassau, it is in some need of repair, don't you agree?"

"Well, Mistress, I brought an engineer with me when I came here—Thomas Moore, I believe his name was, but he died one day while working on the fortifications. I petitioned Whitehall concerning a replacement, but I never heard from England. I think they have forgot me here."

Archibald served the dinner of turtle steak. Tired of fish and turtle, the sole diet among these islanders, Anne had threatened more than once to go out and kill a wild boar, but she could find no one to hunt with her.

"Where is your husband, Mistress Sommerwood?" inquired the Governor.

"England, sir, at the Parliament. Besides being a planter, he is a solicitor."

"Ambitious fellow." For a long time only the clinking of forks and scraping of knives could be heard.

Searching for conversation that might prove interesting to the governor, Anne finally spoke. "My husband writes that General Oglethorpe who settled Georgia plans to attack the Spanish at St. Augustine. May that prove a problem to you here?"

"I'm happy someone has heard news from England."

Colonel Howel and Captain Walker laughed with the governor. "Really, Mistress, I have heard nothing of the Spanish at Florida."

"Do the Spanish trouble you much here at Nassau?"

Captain Walker answered. "Aye, Mistress, their *guardas costas* lurk about Hole in the Rock, Abaco and intercept English vessels bound for home and confiscate our brasiletto wood."

Fitzwilliam left off eyeing Anne lewdly to enter the conversation. "Yes, the Spanish say, insist in fact, that brasiletto grows only on their islands."

"Absurd," responded the colonel.

More than she wished she could escape from the lecherous glances of the governor, Anne hoped she would not encounter the Spanish on her voyage to Abaco.

Suddenly their meal was interrupted by one of the sentinels from the fort who was so out of breath from running up the hill that it was several minutes before he could speak. "We were surprised, Your Excellency; some of the soldiers, sir, have taken the garrison."

"What! Archibald, call my guard!" Fitzwilliam snatched up his sword. "Are you with me, gentlemen?" Captain Walker wiped his mouth and threw his serviette in his plate. Colonel Howel was trying to get up but his sword caught in the rungs of his chair. "Monsieur Duplaissez?"

"No, Your Excellency, I am so stuffed wiz your wonderful supper I cannot move."

"And you, Mistress Sommerwood? Colonel Howel here tells me of your skill with the rapier." The colonel flushed with embarrassment, finally stood up and straightened his coat. Obviously he knew Anne from an earlier time but she could not remember him. "Well, Mistress, will you help me put down this mutiny?"

"I am sorry, Your Excellency, but I have no stomach to fight British soldiers."

"Very well, then. Archibald, rouse the inhabitants; use force if you must. Guards, gentlemen, follow me." Brandishing his sword high over his head, Governor

Fitzwilliam ran down the hill to the fort.

"What a riduculous man." Anne frowned at her last bite of turtle steak, then asked. "Henri, how on earth did Howel learn of my swordsmanship?"

"Remember zat night at za tavern in ze pirate days . . . Charles Vane's mistress, zat Haitian devil Nicole, she attack you. Well, ze colonel, he was present zat night."

"No! Are you sure?"

"I sink so, *cherie.*"

""Dear God, I remember that hell cat ripped my tunic off my body, then snapped my sword in half with her cutlass. Mary had to toss me her rapier."

"Zat was some battle."

"How would you know? You fainted."

"Not right away. When zat she devil draw blood on your beautiful breast, zen I faint. Did she leave a scar? Let me see."

Anne playfully slapped his hand away from her bosom. Blasts from a volley of musketry reached their ears and Anne jumped into Henri's arms.

"Dear God, I thought I had conquered every fear. I thought myself whole again and ready to face life in Jamaica."

"It is natural to fear. Zat does not mean you lack courage to act in ze face of zat fear. I see ze change in you, ze confidence, ze calm. Not like ze old days when you rush at ze cannon. Zat is not courage, zat is bravado. You have real courage now. Ze kind zat comes wiz knowledge of self. Ze test will come, zen you will see. Henri is right."

The next day, Henri returned from town full of news. The deserters had stolen a slocp but had not gotten very far when Captain Walker captured them at daybreak. Fitzwilliam had convicted them all and by noon the governor had hanged twelve of the more notorious mutineers at the fort including Lieutenant Harkness.

"Poor bastard. Twelve you say? My God."

"Come, *cherie.* Let me help you down to your boat.

You sail at sunset."

Theirs was a tearful goodbye. Anne removed her napkin from her eyes to see Henri's brightly colored scarf waving long after his face faded into a silhouette. Anne recalled the last time she had to leave Henri behind. Woodes Rogers' man-o-war rode in the harbor. With Mary and Rackam, she had escaped in Vane's sloop sailing out behind a flaming merchant vessel, blasting their guns at the governor's ships as they went. Bravado. That's what Henri called it. Did she wish he was with her now once again aboard *La Petite Mort* embarking on some pirating adventure? No. How absurd, she thought. That life is behind us both now. He will spend the rest of his days sitting by the silent lagoon. And me. Well, I may wish for quiet days, but will I have them? She pondered this as *The Carpenter's Revenge* cleared Nassau Harbour and headed on a northwesterly course toward the Berry Islands.

Anne learned that their trip would take a week. Their sloop would have to tack hard back and forth between the Berry Islands and the northern tip of Eleuthera before they could turn and beat northward along the southeast coast of Abaco. The danger of encountering the Spanish in the Northeast Providence Channel kept the crew on strict watch.

Gideon Lowe, a capable seaman kept the helm; his brother Mathew and Nathaniel Bethel manned the lines. The enterprises of the Lowe brothers at Nassau, Abaco and Harbour Island were many and diversified. Besides whaling, they engaged in turtling, sharkfishing, wood cutting and the perennial occupation of all Bahamians–wrecking. Mathew, a thin man of average height, was well into his middle years and reserved in his outward behavior. Gideon, about ten years younger, was as tall as his brother, somewhat thicker, and livelier. Nathaniel Bethel, often recipient of their aid in hard times, could attest to the kindness and generosity of these brothers. Mathew and Gideon lived on Harbour Island and worked between there and Abaco while their younger brothers Benjamin and John maintained the New Providence branch of their businesses.

On the third day of the voyage *The Carpenter's Revenge* sighted a Spanish vessel, but fortunately they were on the easier northwesterly tack and could outrun the *guarda costa*. When the sloop beat back toward Spanish Wells, they were well upwind and out of reach. Their only cargo was supplies Mathew was carrying to the try-works at Great Guana Cay; nonetheless, Gideon wanted nothing to do with the Spanish and Anne was grateful and relieved to avoid a confrontation. On the sixth day *The Carpenter's Revenge* entered the Abaco cays at Little Harbour and reached for Little Guana Cay, anchoring in a pleasant commodious harbor at its north end.

Nathaniel Bethel invited Anne to stay at his encampment while Gideon and Mathew went off to Great Guana Cay and she accepted. Since he spent most of the eight months of the whaling season at Little Guana Cay, he had built a two room thatched hut on the narrow rise of land between the harbor and the sea. It commanded a spectacular view of the sun rising over the ocean and setting over the whaling sloops in the harbor.

Nathaniel Bethel had sandy colored hair and beard, bright blue eyes and a gentle disposition unless provoked. He wore a scar over his right eye which he had earned during Anne's first night in the Crown and Anchor in the disagreement with the Nantucket whaler over the sea beast. Anne had never seen the man in a pair of shoes. She had taken hers off now to walk on the beach with him.

"Look 'ere, Missus." He picked up a gray lump of something that looked like solidified sponge. "Smell this."

"It has a musky odor. What is it?"

"The sperm whale. You see, 'e gets indigestion, I guess, and these lumps build inside 'im and if 'e can't expel them, 'e will die."

"How awful."

"Awful for the whale, good for the whaler who strikes a whale with this inside 'im. We don't find much of it on the beach though."

"Are there whales near here now?"

"Why yes, Missus. Come with me. I 'ave my dinghy in the 'arbor. I'll take you over to Marsh Sound. Whales come in there to wean their young. It's near the end of their time 'ere but there may be a few left still."

Nathaniel's dinghy glided over the variant blues of the Bahama shoal waters. Hues of cerulean to milky white sparkled in the sun. The scrub along the bank fluttered with every shade of green. When they neared Marsh Sound, Nathaniel shouted and pointed to what Anne thought was a small cay. "There's a whale. See over there, Miz Anne."

"That's an island."

"No, watch. You'll see 'er move."

"I don't believe it, but it is moving now."

"You see, sometimes a whale collects so much dust on 'er back that weeds and grasses grow on it."

"How many sailors in their cups have looked up to see a cay swimming past. Look there! What's going on with those two? Are they playing or is she bathing her young one?"

"Neither. The baby whale is beached on that shoal there and the only way the mother can get 'im off is by spouting water over 'im. Whales cherish their young, Missus. I've seen the mother swallow the baby to protect 'im in a storm then spit 'im back out when the storm has passed."

As black clouds closed in the mother whale remained undaunted at her task. Although occupied in finding shelter for Anne, Nathaniel noticed her concern for the whales. "The sea'll 'elp 'er. Soon a wave'll wash 'im off the shoal. We'll scull over to that whaler. I know the captain."

When Nathaniel and Anne boarded, the crew was hustling about making fast barrels of whale oil. The *Juniper*, out of Nantucket, proposed to set sail for Nassau and New England as soon as the weather lightened. Large drops of rain fell slowly. A filthy, shirtless man tied to the grate of the hold opened his mouth to drink the rain. In spite of the grime covering his breeches, Anne noticed that they were calico.

Captain Slocum escorted Nathaniel and Anne down to his cabin. "I 'ave nothin' but grog to offer you, Mistress."

"That will be fine, Captain."

"I know Nat 'ere relishes our New England grog."

"Indeed I do, Cap'n."

"We've 'ad an adventure 'ere, Nat—captured a slaver turned pirate vessel just yesterday."

"Pirates, God's Eyes!"

"Not proper pirates, mutineers. Their leader, a stupid fellow 'ad not wit enough to pilot into the 'arbor. Rowed up 'long side the *Juniper* and demanded at gunpoint that I come pilot 'im. I took the pistol out of 'is 'and afore he knew what 'appened. Stupid fellow that."

"Where will you take him now?" asked Anne.

"To Nassau."

"Fitzwilliam will sun dry him surely."

"Aye, Mistress. You know what the fool told me when I asked 'im why 'e 'ad turned pirate? 'E said piracy seemed a thrifty and promising business."

"Promising indeed. It promises a thrifty end, that's sure."

When they bid goodbye to Captain Slocum, Anne looked again at the would-be pirate. The sight of him saddened her in an eerie way.

Once aboard the dinghy, Nathaniel was the first to speak. "Poor wretch. 'E'll dance a jig in the air tomorrow."

"Pirating be no business for half-wits and drunkards."

"And women?"

"Not any one, full-witted or no."

Weeks in the cockpit passed quietly now. Yamou's leg healed and he spent his days climbing to the tops of tall coconut trees to gather fruit. Afiba could not lose the sadness she brought with her to Accompong. She longed to return Windward to the boy she had captured but could not keep. Nanny watched the girl, a woman of seventeen now, and felt her sadness, but knew it was something her magic could not touch. One March afternoon Nanny and Afiba walked to a grove of cool silverthatch palms.

"Nanny, how long we stay Accompong?"

"Why you ask? Where you want go?"

"Home to East."

"We hab no town dere, or yo' fo'get dat?"

"We build new town. We do dat befo'."

"Not easy ting do. Nanny tink on dat."

"Oh, Nanny, tink hard!"

"I say I tink on dat!" She did not mean to raise her voice but Afiba's behavior had disturbed her for some time. Cudjoe had arranged a marriage for the girl and Nanny did not know how to approach Afiba with the offer. "Afiba, tell Nanny someting. Why you no lay wid mon whole time we Accompong?" Afiba did not answer. "In Nanny Town, when you girl you sleep wid many boy. Before you bleed, you lie wid boy."

"I fine no joy in dat now."

"You womon now. Time you marry, make baby. Cudjoe make match soon."

"No, I no marry Cockpit, I marry East."

"No one ta marry back dere. You stop dis foolishness, girl. Afiba hab pick o' Maroon colonel in Cockpit. You want be Bucknor wife five, Juba wife t'ree, Montague James wife fo'?"

"No! Afiba be wife one or no marry. Why Nanny no marry?"

"Nanny Maroon warrior, commander, no wife."

"Den I be soldier too!"

Nanny looked at the slender beauty Afiba had become and could hardly believe the determination in her words. She did not understand Afiba's stubbornness. "If we go East. I mus' leave you here. An' you marry mon Cudjoe say you marry."

"No stay. I go wid Nanny or cut throat wid cane knife!"

The words fell like thunder on her ears, and Nanny had only to look in the girl's eyes for an instant to know that Afiba meant what she said.

Anne stood next to Gideon Lowe at the helm and felt the surge of *The Carpenter's Revenge* now in a broad reach westerly between the main of Abaco and its northern cays. Mathew had stayed behind at the Lowe Try-works on Great Guana Cay and Gideon made for Green Turtle. He pointed out Whale Cay on their starboard, then his sharp blue eyes saw almost dead ahead a single fountain of water shoot into the sky and hover like a misty cloud over the hump in the water.

"She blows! See there, Missus, a sperm whale."

Anne turned in time to see its flukes disappear into the water under the cloud mist.

"She dives now, Missus. The sperm whale be a deep diver. I know. I went with 'er once. Like a fool I 'eld the drag of the 'arpoon I struck 'er with. 'Twas strange. When I passed under the water I thought I 'eard a 'undred whales answer 'er distress many waters away." After a moment Gideon's voice swelled as though his helm had turned pulpit. He raised one hand above his bowed head and recited. "Then 'the waters encompassed me about, even to the soul: the depth closed me round about, the weeds were wrapped about my 'ead.' " Then he concluded in a thunderous voice. "And 'when my soul fainted within me I remembered the Lord.' " A dramatic pause held Anne spellbound for over a minute. His hand came back to the helm and he spoke again. "Next thing, Missus, I was back in the boat coughin' up water."

"The sea spit you back, eh, Gideon?"

"Yes, Missus. God ordered 'er to, I guess."

"Will the whale surface again, think you?"

"Maybe she'll breech, but not for a long while. I hope she does, for 'tis a sight to behold."

"I can see that whaling men have two adversaries, the whale and the sea."

"And both be treacherous. These waters especially. You're likely to go crashing against a reef in a chase. Every day I pray to God to go with me."

"Why not carry him inside you, Gideon. I do."

"Not inside this foul flesh. 'Twould pollute the Lord to enter it."

"Maybe God doesn't mind that?"

"Oh, mighty Leviathan. Look there, she breeches!"

Far out ahead, the whale leaped high into the air and landed with a shock that resounded for miles.

"'Tis an odd looking animal, but I could not define it at this distance."

" 'Er 'ead be a third of 'er body with 'er jaw runnin' the length of it. Sometimes the 'ead will give a ton of spermaceti. Oh, 'tis a sight to behold, Missus, when she comes close and turns 'er small cold eye upon you—a look to shrivel your soul. Then she opens 'er jaw and aims to crush your boat in 'er teeth, the size of a man's fist. And when she dies in 'er flurry spouting scarlet the sea is red for a mile."

March was the clearing season. Maroons worked in the fields everyday and the council house stood empty. Not since before the assault on the British at Carlisle Bay had Cudjoe summoned Nanny there to make war plans. It was not in Nanny's destiny to watch her days slip idly past. She approached Cudjoe with a plan to raid the plantations in the St. Ann's Precinct.

"We no fight now. When British cum ask Maroon make peace, Cudjoe make peace. Stay wid us, sister; join us in peace."

"No. Nanny neber stop fighting. Eben from tunnel grabe Nanny fight."

"No fight Accompong. No fight Cockpit. Where Nanny go fight?"

"Nanny go back—to East and fight. Take people home."

"Do dey want go home?"

Even though their trek westward loomed fresh in their minds, Nanny's people did not desert her. Cudjoe allowed them to take their new wives and husbands with them. The two Madagascars who had played a role in Yamou's manhood hunt decided to make their home with him.

Nanny's army was small but her men and women had courage and stamina. Tears filled Nanny's eyes when she embraced her brother. Something deep within told her she would never see him again. The time spent with him at Accompong had washed her soul and she was prepared for destiny to offer its final challenge.

Afiba led their way to Windward. Nanny began to realize that the girl was not running away from her recent proposals in the Cockpit but flying to something or someone: what or who it was the Ashanti woman could not imagine.

The up and down of their days wore on. Four strong bearers heavily laden with supplies dragged behind. Cudjoe had provided Nanny's people with every essential tool needed for rebuilding their town and enough food to last until they could plant their fields and lay new plantain walks. The Madagascars slashed at the bush with machetes sharpened on both edges making short work of cutting paths. Still, their journey would take months. Every afternoon dark clouds hovered over them and cast black across the face of the sun.

Lightning flashed, thunder crashed, limbs cracked and fell across their path. Nanny could protect her people from falling trees, but not from their personal fears. A thunderous crack caused Afiba to drop the water vessel she was carrying. She felt certain one of God's thunderbolts would strike her. She should have never left the boy with the gentle eyes, for now she doubted she would ever see him again. Moments later the rain stopped and a rainbow appeared over a dazzling waterfall. Once again with hopeful heart Afiba and the Maroon band trekked onward.

At night by the crackling fires Nanny sat on her stool with Afiba on her right side. Yamou squatted to her left on the flat white stone Cudjoe had given him when he had been envious of Nanny's stool. Fourteen women, ten men and seven children huddled around them.

On one of these nights when the shivering cold had silenced their singing, Yamou questioned Nanny about death.

"Can a mon die from de cold?"

"I tink mebbe he can. Nanny keep Yamou warm, he no die o' de cold."

"Where mon go when he die, Nanny?"

"Ta de worl' above."

"How he get dere?"

"Some story say he hab ta clumb tree. Story say one day young girl go out ta cut grass an' fine a place where de grass grow tall and t'ick. But when she put her foot down, she sink in de mud. She sink deeper and deeper 'til she disappear."

"What hoppen to her, Nanny?" asked Afiba. "Did she die?"

"I tink so. As she sink she cry out dat ghosts drag her down. On de spot where she sink a tree grow. It grow taller and taller 'til it reach de sky. In de heat o' de day, boys bring dere cattle ta res' unner dat tree. One day a boy climb dat tree. He shout back dat he climbin' ta de worl' above."

"Did he eber get dere?"

"I tink so, Yamou. One ting certain, he neber cum back down."

After everyone had fallen asleep Nanny stared into the fire. For hours she kindled the dwindling coals with the blaze of her eyes. This she would do every night. One night a vision appeared in the fire—the features of a man took shape on the face of a red moon. The face was fluid and changing. It was not a face Nanny could recognize until the movement stopped. Then she saw, not a man's, but a woman's face—a woman forgotten at Accompong. Nanny had failed to kill her twice before but she would not fail again. Until then she would send her enemy troubled dreams. Slowly and deliberately Nanny's eye traced the outline of the deadly scorpion upon the woman's face.

At the southern end of Green Turtle Cay the bay fingers into a narrow sound. It was here that the Lowe brothers maintained try-works and a log cutting camp. Gideon intended to remain only long enough to load the mastic and ironwood recently cut by his Harbour Island crew. James Cash, William Sawyer, John Roberts and Samuel Saunders, all hefty and able men, made short shrift of the work. No black men were employed at logwood cutting, but Anne was startled by the presence of a tall fleshy black woman sweating over the brick ovens of the try-works, boiling whale oil out of blubber. Looking at the woman's back and neck momentarily arched toward the sky Anne was reminded of Nanny, but when she turned around to greet her, Anne noticed that her round pleasing face bore no resemblence to her enemy. The mulatto woman wiped her brow and hands on her apron and curtsied when Gideon introduced Anne.

"This is Rhoda Kemp but we call 'er Mama Rhodie. And don't let that sweet face fool you, Missus, she runs this camp with an iron 'and."

"Pleased to make your acquaintance, Mama Rhodie."

"Likewise, Mistress Anne."

Gideon went off to inspect the loading and Mama Rhodie returned to her boiling pots, leaving Anne to her own devices. Thatched huts lined the hill top but provided no view except that of the forest of tall trees, thick scrub and every imaginable variety of fruit tree. The Bahamian dogwood shed their pink blossoms over the path of red-yellow leaves. Wild orchids bloomed clinging to the rough bark of the buttonwood and the golden berry of the mastic gleamed in the hints of sunlight.

Anne discovered a kind of lookout platform and climbed up to it. Looking out over the ocean she could see the palms arching on a nearby cay. The waters of the bay on the lee side displayed a myriad of greens glistening in the late afternoon sun. Down on the beach at Green Turtle Bay, Calico Jack Rackam once careened his pirate vessel and it was here long ago that he and his pirate crew decided to sail to Nassau and accept the King's peace.

After their meal of grouper and cassava cakes, Mama

Rhodie passed around a basket of plums which looked like black olives. Anne was surprised to find them sweet-tasting, yet moments later it seemed they turned sour in her stomach. Anne stared into the fire while Gideon discussed future plans with Mama Rhodie and her crew. So intent on her thoughts, Anne did not notice when the men drifted off to their huts. She was tired but much too restless to sleep, a condition she attributed to the excitement of returning home to her family. Snatches of old nightmares played about in her mind. Then a scorpion crawled out of the fire towards her right hand. She backed away from it. Not recalling that she had ever seen one out in the open before, Anne thought to herself, "But why was it not consumed by the fire?"

At Harbour Island Anne met Mathew's wife Sarah and Gideon's wife Martha. Their houses sat side by side in the town situated on the teeming harbor and populated by the oldest inhabitants of the Bahamas, those who originally came from England and Bermuda in the mid-seventeenth century. Gideon had arranged for Anne to sail in the morning with the four John Currys bound for Curacao with a cargo of wild cinnamon. They would sail first to Jamaica to load supplies for their return voyage because they preferred English to Dutch goods.

The Curry cousins came from Scotland perhaps by way of England or Ireland, Anne was not sure. She found their dialect difficult to understand at first. The elder John and captain of their vessel was a muscular man with snow white hair. The next John, more portly than the elder, blazed with red face and hair. The third was a well-proportioned man with thick wavy black hair and the last and youngest was painfully thin with silken hair and pallid complexion. All four men looked upon Anne with piercing blue eyes except the black-haired John, whose right eye glazed gray in blindness.

With the morning star still visible in the sky, Adam Greenleaf, the fifth member of the crew, weighed the anchor and except for the screeching of three gulls flapping overhead the *Alpha and Omega* slipped silently out of the harbor.

The vessel tacked out about fifty miles and turned to beat down along the windward side of Eleuthera and Cat Island. A little past sunset on the day they sailed near San Salvador and between Conception and Rum Islands, a thunder storm hit. The air seemed charged with an inexplicable energy which held Anne to the deck. The wind whipped her hair across her wet face. Holding tight to the mizzenmast Anne looked up the mainmast where she saw silver sparks arc off the tops like blue spider webs rapidly changing patterns. More sparks crackled and snapped along the wet lines. Adam Greenleaf called this compelling sight St. Elmo's Fire. Alert during the storm, the Currys did not sleep that night and neither did Anne. The *Alpha and Omega*, full of eyes, reached for Mira Por Vos. The evening they passed Heneagu Anne looked out over a sea of glass to witness a green flash at sunset—a rare but memorable sight in the Bahamas.

On the tenth and final day of their journey the vessel ran down the Windward Passage like riding a great road. The four Johns, dressed in white, stood in a line at intervals level with the foremast. Anne stood next to Adam at the helm aft.

"We're about to pass Navassa, Mistress. The seas funnel there and will give us a stirring ride. Back 'ere it may seem like the sea will swamp us but it won't. Hold tight to the 'elm with me."

The *Alpha and Omega* was running large before the wind now.

The sea billowed up behind lifting the sloop high into the pounding wind carrying it along the sky only to drop it down again almost to the floor of the ocean. Anne's whole being surged, exhilarated when the following seas came up under the stern, picked up the vessel, bearing it aloft and delivering, as it were, herself and her four pilots to heaven's door.

PART III

1737-1742

Black Horizon

" . . . a long day's dying."
—*Paradise Lost X*, 964

"the world was all before them."
—*Paradise Lost XII*, 646

CHAPTER EIGHT

"Children Far From Safety"
— *Job 5:4*

Several months before Anne's return in late March of 1737, a situation developed on the Sommerwood estate that neither Sang nor Ruth could control. Asserting his independence at fifteen, William Thomas had been seen too often in the company of the soldiers at their encampment at the river. What Ruth did not know was that Sarah, nearing her thirteenth year, secretly visited their tents after her parents were asleep. If her pretty face, sparkling black eyes, slender arms and full hips were not enticement enough, her ripening breasts of the richest cocoa color provided the soldiers yet another lure. When she felt inclined, Sarah could leave behind her childlike manner and put on an attitude to suit her maturing figure. William Thomas took notice but never approached her. His indifference intrigued Sarah.

More and more William looked like his father. Nearly six feet, his handsome face had a dissipated cast which suited his withered right arm causing him to look, in features and form, slightly unbalanced. Every night he drank a goodly portion of a soldier's bottle. The men had thought to teach the boy to gamble, get him in his cups and take his money. Their scheme snapped whiplike in their faces. More than one soldier had had to resort to stealing laudanum from the medical supplies in order to settle a debt with William and his capacity for liquor seemed insatiable. Learning their games easily, he won adroitly and even learned to shuffle and deal the cards with one hand. As William's fortune grew, it drew the attention of Caleb Foote who would sneak into the camp late at night. On several occasions he had taken William to the tavern in the village of Port Morant where he introduced him to his personal aggregate of whores. William paid his women well, but Caleb got the healthiest share of the money.

The tent reeked of rum, sweat and Cuban cigars. Although swarming thick outside, all but a few mosquitoes had abandoned the tent. Lieutenant Birdson and Private Robert Cosins sat at a campaign table with William Thomas. The men puffed heavily on their cigars and William clicked a stack of gold crowns as they waited for the return of John Church who had left the tent ten minutes ago to relieve himself.

"That man pisses more an' he drinks," puffed the lieutenant. Cosins rendered his own theory as he filled his tankard from a bottle of the Sommerwood's finest rum. "I'll wager he's found a tail to hit on."

"Aye, that Sarah maybe," laughed Lieutenant Birdson. "She's a short heeled wench."

William drained his tankard and wiped his mouth with the sleeve of his shirt. 'We need a fourth."

"Where's that cock bawd, Caleb Foote? He's usually here by now." The lieutenant stacked his meager stash of coins.

"Smokin' some bloody fen in the town, no doubt," responded Cosins.

The men made for their muskets when they heard a man scream and what sounded like a wildcat hissing outside the tent. But no one made another move to investigate the disturbance. The scuffling, screaming and growling stopped and John Church staggered into the tent, cussing and wiping blood from his eyes. His face was streaked red with bright gashes. "Black slut!"

The two men put aside their rifles and laughed, flinging ribald remarks his way.

"It's your own fault, Church."

"Sarah fixed you proper this time, did she?"

"That's your reward for tryin' to bull a tigress. You're lucky to get out o' that with your tools intact."

"Damn her eyes!" Private Church poured rum on his napkin and dabbed at his face gingerly, wincing and cursing. Downing the last of his tankard he scooped up his few coins and nearly knocked down Caleb Foote who was entering the tent.

"Had ta shit through 'is teeth, did 'e?"

"No, Caleb, Mr. Church is not sick, he went to lick his wounds. He tried to frig a wildcat."

"Wish I'd a known he were so desperate, I could've found him a more willing partner than Sarah. I'd not touch her. Yet one look at her fetches my prick to a pretty stand, I tell you that."

"Sit and play, Caleb." William Thomas pulled his right arm into his lap and shuffled the cards.

"Looks like you took the table again tonight, William." Caleb lowered himself into the chair vacated by Church. "I'll sit one hand. Little good it'll do me."

As William dealt the cards, Sarah slipped into the tent and circled the table. She ran her fingers along the back of Cosins' neck and tipped the lieutenant's hat forward. Rocking on her heels, she smiled coyly at Caleb Foote, causing him to push hard on his penis. William Thomas was so involved in the game, it was a moment or two before he noticed Sarah stroking his shriveled arm. He slammed down his cards and grabbed her delicate wrist viselike in his hand. "Don't ever do that to me! Do you hear?"

Sarah cried out in a childish whimper. "I hears. I hears. Don' hurt me, Massa William."

"Leave the girl alone, William," said the lieutenant absently.

Releasing her arm, William sat down, took a long gulp of rum, picked up his cards and studied his hand. Sarah stood behind him rubbing her wrist and smiling enigmatically.

Ruth heard Sarah creep into the house late in the night and gently nudged Sang who moaned, turned towards her, and opened one eye.

"It Sarah," Ruth whispered.

"Good, she back. Now go ta sleep, old womon."

"Sang, you tink she lie wid soldier?"

"What!"

"Ole Sam say he see her cum from camp las' night. Dat girl worry me, way she carry on, and William Thomas too."

"I speak wid her wid a switch if I need ta, but I can't learn dat boy better. We mus' wait for Massa and Missus to cum home take care o' dat."

"Dese chill'ren so diff'rent. Esther so quiet and Lusen . . . you tink he still love dat Maroon girl?"

"Mebbe. He no look at any girl here. He work hard all day, read at night. Neber talk 'bout womon way odder boys do."

"He mus' fo'get dat girl."

"What you want, womon? You want Sang beat her face out his min'? I do dat de minute I finish wid Sarah. Now," he said reaching for her, "lie back down and go ta sleep."

"I can't. It be a long time Sang, ober two year now. Time 'nuff dat boy fo'get."

'I neber fo'get you. Remember, your mama, she fo'bid you marry rough Koromantyn fiel' slabe."

"An' I obey her. You house slabe when I marry you."

They laughed and held each other close, caressing until they finally fell asleep in each other's arms.

Nanny settled her band to the east of her old village. New Nanny Town grew up on both sides of the ravine situated in the John Crow Mountains and was surrounded by patches of lands suitable for planting. The village rested against the Negro River which provided an excellent view downstream for about six or seven miles. The location provided access to the torturous paths which twisted their way through thick forest and fought down to the coast of eastern Portland.

With men and women trained to fight with cunning, Nanny made several successful raids in Portland and St. Ann's. Many Koromantyn warriors seeking freedom from the rigors of field work and the brutality of the drivers, populated her town and impregnated her women.

Like a chronic disease, Caleb Foote reappeared in November of 1737 and brought with him a handsome young man with a withered arm. Nanny's first thought was to execute both of them on the spot, but the ironmongery and weapons that only they could provide would make her houses strong and her army invincible. Besides, the boy was obviously a planter's son and could furnish information about the neighbor estates which would help her to plan raids. A sinister pleasure came with the thought that this lad was betraying the whites in a way that would soon prove fatal.

She saw Yamou creep around behind the two men and wondered what wickedness he had in mind to do. He had no weapon and would not dare to kill them without an order from her. He dropped something from a little sack onto the boy's shoulder. From this distance she could not see the scorpion begin to crawl down the left sleeve of William's coat.

William gasped when he saw the deadly creature but did not move. The scorpion slithered closer to his hand. He thought his right hand had moved to brush it off but when William saw the scorpion still on his left sleeve he knew he hadn't, couldn't do that. Great beads of sweat broke out on his forehead and dripped into his eyes. "Caleb, help me!"

"What is it now?"

"Get it off. The scorpion on my arm, knock it off, will you!"

"Do it yourself."

"I can't, you friggin' bastard. You know I can't!"

Caleb swatted the creature to the ground and William crushed it under the heel of his boot. Caleb went back to his figuring—"Two barrels o' nails, twenty hinges . . ."

William reached into his pocket and drank from a small vial, then pulled out a napkin and wiped his brow. When his eyes cleared they saw Afiba talking with a young man who bore a long scar on his left thigh. William rubbed his right shoulder and observed her naked breasts lifting high and round as she spoke. His eyes stroked her coppery arms, ran down over her slender hips and dipped into the golden honey of her thighs.

"Fifteen saws, axes . . . how many axe heads did Nanny say she wanted? Eh, William." Caleb looked in the direction of William's lustful glances then swung the boy around, replacing Afiba's pretty face with his own grizzly features. "Eh, William, you see that monster of a woman there, Nanny, you see her, lad?"

"Aye."

"Well, let her catch you eye that girl and she'll fry you where you stand."

"That old woman doesn't frighten me."

"Foolish boy. She can wither your other arm and any other part she chooses and leave ye wonderin' what became of your former self."

"Come now."

Caleb grabbed William's freshly laundered shirt, soiling the flowing collar with his grimy fingers. "Listen to me . . . you spoiled bastard. While you're up here with me, you keep yere pisser inside yere breeches. I don't aim to meet the devil just yet, and I don't fancy being shipped hence by the likes of a snivelin' whelp like you."

"You take my money quick enough."

"That don't mean I like your company. Besides, if the return on your money don't suit you, find other employment." Caleb walked away.

William Thomas took his arm. "Wait, for God's sake. You can't leave me here. I'll never find my way back. Look, you can't leave me here!"

Caleb spat on the ground very near William's shiny boot.

"All right. No women, I promise. Strictly business."

"Good. Now, if Nanny should offer you a plump black wench, don't be shy, lad."

Both men laughed the bawdy laugh customary among men who are comrades in whoring.

Anne had dismissed the soldiers even before Baldwin's return. It was Ruth's account of Sarah's crimes that prompted her to do it. But she, Baldwin or Mary Elizabeth could do nothing to stop William's drinking or his nightly escapades in Port Morant. In spite of the worry caused by William, the plantation and the family had fallen back into its pleasant and easy routine.

Baldwin brought back from furniture craftsmen Chippendale, Adams and Hepplewhite contracts to export to England mahogany cut on the Sommerwood estate. Besides bringing more wealth to the family, this new logcutting project had toned Baldwin's muscles and developed Matt into a healthy, strapping man. He was ready to leap to the altar, but Mary had not bestowed the favor of even one kiss upon him.

Snuffing the candle, Baldwin crawled into bed and slipping one arm under Anne's shoulders drew her to him. "Are you happy with me?"

"You know I am."

"Were you afraid my first night back that I wouldn't be able to make love to you?"

"A little, yes. Can you tell me now what the problem was?"

"I don't really know for certain. I think it was the image of that Mandingo violating you. For a long time I denied it, but in truth I think that was the reason."

"Because he was a black man."

"Yes, partly."

"I told you about Tombay."

"You see, that's it. You permitted Tombay to love you and so in my confused mind I thought, if you allowed

Tombay to make love to you, then you allowed the Mandingo. I knew this wasn't so, but I couldn't help how I felt and only after a long time could I admit my prejudice."

"Do you think a woman wants to be raped? Many men think that, you know."

"No, God in heaven. Look, Anne, before I left for England I wasn't thinking at all. I was feeling, feeling betrayed by you, by Tombay, by Rackam, the Mandingo—everybody. You see, that night by your bed I thought I had straightened out my thinking, but I hadn't—not really. When I tried to love you, nothing happened because my feelings got in the way."

"Did you think me soiled in some way?"

"Must I answer that?"

"You don't have to, of course, but I would like your honest answer."

"Yes, I did. Then in London, I disputed the matter with myself. I paced my rooms at night and argued in much the same way I would defending a case. Of course, you didn't want to be raped. And who was I to judge you anyway? Or myself for that matter. I did, you know. I punished myself for a long time for feeling I was so clean that I would defile myself by entering you. In truth I was jealous and I had to hurt you back somehow. I hurt myself as well. You had every right to go away and never come back. For a long time I thought you might never return."

"I'm glad I did."

"Not as happy as I am. You know I feel such joy with you tonight that . . ."

"Win, let's not talk anymore. Let's . . ."

Anticipating her remarks Baldwin's lips covered hers.

Near dawn two birds were bickering on the gallery but it was Baldwin's muttering which woke Anne.

"Win." Anne shook him gently at first, but when he did not awaken, she became more persistent. "Win, wake up!"

"Huh? What is it?"

"You were talking in your sleep."

"Oh, what was I saying? I didn't say anything

incriminating, did I?"

"Oh, interesting. Are you sure you told me everything about your London trip? You didn't leave out any juicy escapade by any chance."

"Anne, really, you know me better. I would never. Come now, tell me what I was saying in my sleep."

"Something about Matt and Mary Elizabeth. I couldn't tell what."

"Oh, I knew I had something important to tell you last night, remember? Yesterday I asked Matt when he planned to wed Mary Elizabeth and do you know what he said? 'Tomorrow if she'll have me.' Have you asked her yet, I said. 'No,' he said."

"I had this very same conversation with him a week ago."

"Well then, you tell me why he won't ask her!"

"He's afraid she'll say no."

"Well, will she?"

"She might."

"What's the matter with the girl?"

"She tells me that she wants to be certain that he really loves her. She is such a romantic. Love must be total and everlasting, just the way it is in the children's story books."

"So, she thinks Matt will fall short of her fantasy lover?"

"Partly. But more than that she fears his ardor will wane."

"Did you tell her about what happened to me before I left?"

"No, that would only intensify her fears. I think she sensed something was wrong between us."

"Except for that brief time our marriage has been wholesome. You know Anne, every time I make love to you, I feel the same excitement I felt on our wedding night. I will have to talk to that girl."

"She may be right for all we know, Win. Some men fall out of love with the woman the minute the vows are spoken. The excitement of the hunt was all that sparked an interest."

"Is that so! Well, in that case, I'll get up then." He swung both feet to the floor.

"Bloody 'ell, you will!"

Flailing legs and arms poked and punched the mosquito meshing. After a few moments, the billowing net settled, undisturbed now by the lovers resting in each other's arms.

In 1738 Edward Trelawny took over the government of Jamaica and imposed a tax on imports from non-English islands. Baldwin gave up smoking the Cuban cigars of which he was inordinately fond. Sam carved him a handsome pipe out of hickory. Peter made a particularly fine blend of tobacco from Kai's crop. Anne was pleased with any change which replaced the offensive cigar smell.

"Want to try this?" Baldwin offered Anne his pipe one afternoon as they relaxed in the garden house he had recently built under a giant banyan at the end of the bamboo walk. "It has a bit of an orange flavor. Go on, try it."

Anne took the pipe from him and was at once taken by the smoothness of the bowl. She took in two short puffs but held the pipe longer to enjoy the feel of it in her hand.

"Well, what do you think?"

"The pipe is wonderful. The vessel is so smooth to the touch."

"What about Peter's new blend?"

"Nice. It's the aftertaste I don't like. Nothing can be done about that, I suppose."

"I suppose not." Baldwin took back his pipe, stuck it between his teeth, and took up the *London Gazette*. From behind his spectacles, he squinted at the print through the smoke.

A soft breeze fluttered through the open lattice work which was small enough for privacy but large enough to allow refreshing breezes to wander in. The octagonal garden retreat was covered with thatch and furnished with wicker lounges and chairs covered with brightly colored cushions, patterned in green, yellow and blue flowers and leaves. Plants of every variety, flowering and otherwise rested on tables and shelves. Anne and Ruth had taken particular pride in the cultivation of the delicate and colorful orchids which hung everywhere.

Bored with her reading, Anne looked about, soaking in the restful atmosphere of this quiet place; then she leaned her head back and closed her eyes.

"Tired?"

"Tired of reading. Right this minute I am interested in love, not in love poetry. What do you say to setting aside our reading and falling into each other's arms?"

"Hum."

"Win, you aren't listening."

"Yes, I am. You said you were interested in love poetry. Shakespeare's sonnets, is it?" He took off his spectacles and rubbed his eyes. "You know what I would love right now?"

"I can't imagine."

"A big fat Cuban cigar."

"Baldwin, that's positively obscene."

"Obscene to you maybe, but not to me. To me, it is paradise."

"Why not pay the bloody tax then and enjoy your cigars."

"It's the principle. You know what's next, don't you? They'll tax English goods next. Mark my words. How would you like to give up your tea?"

"To ask an Englishman, or an Irish woman for that matter, to forego afternoon tea is like asking them to stop breathing. It's absurd."

Baldwin tapped his index finger on the paper. "Says here, we are at war with Spain."

"Again. That's not news. A tax on tea would be news."

"At any rate, we're at war. The War of Jenkins' Ear, they're calling it."

"And how, pray, did the *Gazette* arrive at that clever

title?"

"Seems this English captain, Robert Jenkins, was seized in Havana where a Spaniard lopped off one of his ears. Well, Cap'n Jenkins literally took his bloody ear and presented it to the King, and so now we're at war."

"Oh, come now, Baldwin. His Majesty wouldn't go to war over somebody's ear. That's ridiculous."

"There's more to it of course." He put on his spectacles and glanced at the paper again. "Says something here about problems issuing from merchant trade."

"Now, that's more like it. England will go to war over money. I can see that, but not somebody's bloody ear. Jenkins' ear, indeed. Where did you get the *Gazette* anyway?"

"Peter brought it. He's just returned from England, yesterday."

"Wonderful, I hope he brought the books I asked for. I'm dying here from lack of intellectual stimulation." Anne got up and went over to Baldwin and playfully ran her fingers through his hair, fluffing the gray at his temples where it was thickest. Removing his spectacles, she placed them on the table. "God knows, I don't get much from you. Our communication has degenerated horribly."

"Oh?" he said, pulling her down on top of him, sandwiching the *Gazette* between them. "So it's intellectual stimulation you want, old woman." Pressing his lips to hers in a lingering kiss, he drew away briefly before kissing her again. His hands rubbed her back sensuously. The thin pages of the *Gazette* crackled. Anne broke the kiss and raised herself up to look into his bright blue eyes. "Is this what you call intellectual stimulation, making love on top of the *London Gazette?*"

"Why not. It's a highly respectable publication."

Anne opened his breeches and massaged his stomach and thighs until he was ready for her. She descended upon him like a vessel of cooling water. He twisted inside her, swimming in her juices mingled with his own, then floated out over a tranquil bay.

When he opened his eyes he saw Anne bespectacled and leaning on his chest reading the newspaper. He laughed, joyful in her unfailing sense of humor, the pleasure she always gave him, and the wonder of each day of life with her.

In 1739, the British made peace with the Maroons. A Doctor Russell, representative of the British army traded hats with Cudjoe and the drums celebrated peace from village to village in the Cockpit Country.

On a blistering June afternoon, a young British Regular from Fort Morant brought the news of the peace to Nanny. Placing his hat under his arm, he carefully unfolded the parchment and read the terms of the treaty. Cudjoe had been appointed commander for life. He went on, but Nanny had stopped listening to his directives concerning the division of lands. She took up a machete and the droning stopped. Picking up the dripping head by the hair Nanny carried it to the brow of the John Crow Mountain, flinging it and her vow down the ridge over the eastern valley into the Caribbean Sea.

"I swear by dese eyes in my head I will neber live in peace wid de English."

All that day drums beat out her defiance for all Windward Maroons to hear. Working far out in the pasture lands Lusen heard the drums, tied his horse to a bastard cedar and walked into the mountains. He climbed higher and higher determined to reach those sounds, for somewhere near those drums Afiba waited.

He was a man now, nearly twenty, and had taken no wife. Had she taken a husband, he wondered. The very thought of another man looking into her eyes, touching her soft skin angered him. Perspiration dripped into his eyes. His legs ached from the steep climb, his muscular arms strained as he pulled himself from rock to rock, climbing towards the drums.

After four years of silence, the drums called to him. If he were caught, there would be no hope of rescue this time.

He would be killed in some horrible way. That did not matter. He had lived long enough, since life without her was agony.

A huge boiling cauldron loomed up before him, spattering its bubbling mixture out in every direction. The pot had no fire under it, not even one spark. Wisdom dictated that it was best not even to wonder about such things.

Hearing the river, he made his way to it. He was careful not to disturb a stone which might start a landslide or break a branch and warn a sentry. Exhausted, he leaned his back against a large river rock to catch his breath. It was then, in the quiet of the wilderness, that he heard singing. Accompanied by forest birds and river creatures, a woman chanted in a high delicate voice.

He was almost afraid to look. The sound came closer. Lusen turned slowly and looked around the boulder. It was Afiba and she was alone. Afiba stepped out of her robe, laid it casually aside and walked into the river.

Lusen, spellbound by the beauty of her naked body, could only gape until she disappeared under the water. When she emerged, the sun caught droplets of water in her shiny black hair and on her skin the color of cocoa in places most often touched by the sun. He would speak to her now. Crawling through the tall grass to the water's edge, he called her name.

"Who calls Afiba?"

"Lusen." He pulled off his boots, breeches and shirt and slipped into the water.

"You?"

"Lusen is my name."

"Lusen," she repeated. It was not the name she had made up for him. That did not matter now. "Lusen."

"I heard you singin'."

"You cum up mountain to fine me?"

"Yes."

"You dead mon. My people fine you, you dead mon, you know dat?"

"I no care now dat I see you 'gain."

"Why you cum?"

"I love you. Since dat day I love you."

She had to make him say what had been in her mind these past four years. "You be foolish mon."

"I know dat."

"Go behin' dat rock. No look. Afiba dress. You no look."

"I no look."

She watched him pull his muscular body out of the water. Lusen quickly picked up his clothes and hid behind the rock. He pulled up his breeches but did not dress further. After a second thought he stuffed his wet feet into his boots. If he had to run there would be no time to put on boots. A stab of fear struck him. He shot up to look around for warriors. Maybe she had betrayed him. He had poured out his feelings for her but she had not offered him one word of kindness let alone love. "Foolish mon," that's what she called him.

"Foolish dead mon," he said to himself.

She pushed him down behind the rock. "I tell you no look."

"I . . . t'ought . . . ."

"Cum." She took his hand and led him through the bush to a grove of tall trees, sat him down on a carpet of moss and looked at him. "Soft Eyes."

"What?"

"Soft Eyes. My name you—Soft Eyes."

He smiled.

"What you call se'f? Tell Afiba 'gain."

"Lusen."

"Lusen," she repeated, determined to remember this time.

"You beautiful, Afiba."

"Wife on plantation love Lu-sen?"

"No wife. I wait fo' Afiba."

She liked the way he spoke her name. Maybe she would get used to his. "Mo' handsome den before. Meat on bones now."

He giggled as she poked him about the ribs. Impulsively he took her in his arms and kissed her full ripe lips.

Lusen was embarassed. He had never kissed a woman full on the mouth before, except his sister Sarah, and she did it only to tease him. This was different. It was a pleasurable experience. He longed to repeat it. "Does Afiba belong to warrior in village?"

"No. Afiba Ashanti Princess. Mus' marry colonel. No colonel here now."

"Is Afiba sorry?"

"No, not sorry. Lonely sometimes."

Lusen gathered her in his arms and held her tight. There on the mossy bed he took her in an instant. One instant of passion was all there was because he was young and inexperienced in love-making and had waited so long.

Unable to express their feelings in words, their fingers studied every part of each other's bodies and acted as instruments to communicate their long-denied emotions. Their lips touched and quivered no more than a puddle visited by a raindrop. Then desire flamed into passion as he entered her again. This time Lusen had a sense of Afiba's participation in their love-making. He rode long and hard and felt her glide with him. She knew this time he would not go off into some private ecstasy leaving her behind. And he did not.

In the cool freshness of the Jamaica morning, Matt and Mary Elizabeth rode the blue slopes. It was the only time during the day he had her all to himself.

Since Mary did not share her mother's athletic inclination, they would walk their horses most of the time. Once or twice they'd break into a canter but never a gallop. Every morning Matt would admire the loveliness of this woman with whom he had had the privilege to grow up.

Except that Anne began to show a hint of grey in her reddish hair, and her face, though unlined, exhibited the mature settled look of her forty years, there was little to distinguish mother and daughter by appearance. Both captured the admiration of the planters in St. Thomas, with their wide dark-lashed eyes and flawless complexions.

Taller and somewhat thinner than her mother, at seventeen Mary was perhaps the most sought after young woman in the East. Matt was hopelessly in love with her, so much so that he could not take his eyes from her even when they rode. His gawking proved a hazard this morning. He paid little attention to where his horse was taking him and a low hanging limb hit against the side of his head knocking him from the saddle.

"Matt!" Quickly Mary dismounted and tied up both horses. She fell to the ground beside him. "Matt! Can you hear me? Oh, please wake up!"

Matt was stunned but not unconscious. Since the opportunity had presented itself, he would indulge himself in her attentions a while longer. God only knew when he would ever get another chance like this one.

She fussed over him, slapped him gently and wiped his face with a fragrant handkerchief. The intoxicating scent almost induced him to swoon. He moaned deliriously.

"Oh, thank God," escaped her lips.

Unable to stop himself, he drew her down on top of him and kissed her lips, prolonging the dream and the kiss as long as he had breath. Mary did not struggle to break his hold, but when he finally released her, she slapped him hard.

Matt pretended to come to life. "Oh," he said moaning and shaking his head like a young colt. He ran his fingers through his chestnut hair and winced when it struck the bump on the side of his head. He blinked his eyes open and looked up at her scowling face. "What happened?"

"You fell," she spoke coldly.

"Oh, now I remember—that branch."

"Why weren't you watching where you were going? You could have been hurt. In fact, I thought you were hurt. Now I'm beginning to wonder."

"What do you mean?" Matt sprang to his feet. "I was knocked senseless by my fall. I have a bump the size of an egg on my head." He touched the spot again. "Oooh! See here?" He bent his head for her inspection.

"I can't see anything."

"Please look again. It hurts—I can tell you that."

"Don't you remember anything?"

"Let's see ... the branch struck me. Swack! I hit the ground. Crash! Then the next thing I felt a stinging sensation in my cheek. A slap, you slapped me!"

"I should have knocked you truly senseless."

"Why? What did I do?"

"You kissed me; that's what you did."

"No! I must have been delirious. I would never have been so ... so ...."

"Forward."

"Aye."

"Rude."

"Nay. Forward, yes. Rude, no. Bold, maybe. I would never have been so bold as to take advantage of a situation to show ...." He knew he had better bridle his mouth. He had already said too much. She didn't believe a word of it. Her eyes pierced him. Unless he wanted to see the full bent of her anger discharged on him, he had better keep still.

Oh, now he could see it. Right now, she was every inch her mother—those cold flashing green eyes, arms locked across an iron bosom, hidden claws itching to strike. What a magnificent woman, even in her anger she is a most splendid woman.

"Well, go on. Show, show what?"

"Oh, nothing."

"Why you miserable ..."

Now it comes, the fury of a thousand devils, the torrent of the great deluge.

"You ... you despicable wretch!" She looked around for something to throw at him or knock him senseless with.

"You kissed me, you wretch, and now you say it was nothing!" She went for her horse, but in lieu of mounting she grabbed her riding crop and came for him.

Matt ducked once, and took one stinging blow to his arm before he could seize her wrist.

"How could you!" she sputtered, "How could you do such a thing, then say such a thing?"

"I was dreaming. Believe me. I was in a dream. Every night, I dream of kissing you. How do you expect me to know which is the real kiss and which is the dream?"

She continued to struggle. How he loved her anger. His strong arms overpowered her and he drew her to him and kissed her passionately. It was a kiss to equal a thousand dreams.

"Now," he said releasing her. "Now I know the difference."

Breathless, Mary Elizabeth had no strength to retaliate. She was not even sure that she wanted to.

It seemed to Matt that Mary was ready to fling her arms around his neck and kiss him again. He was sure he had not dreamed that. But just then William Thomas rode up behind him and she dropped her arms to her side.

"Well, out for our morning ride, I see. Mary Elizabeth, why didn't you wake me? I asked you to last night, did I not?"

"You were drunk last night; I didn't think you meant it."

"You look distressed, Mary, what has he done to you?"

William Thomas dismounted and took her arm in a manner which to Matt showed more than just a brotherly concern. Perhaps it was just the awkwardness of his other arm dangling useless by his side which gave that impression, but he didn't really think so.

"He did nothing to me," said Mary Elizabeth recoiling from her brother's touch. "Matt fell off his horse. I was concerned, that's all."

William began to shake with laughter. "What's this? Can't e'en sit a horse proper these days, eh, Matt?"

Even though she knew this would embarass Matt, Mary had to turn the conversation away from the real issue. She found it difficult to lie to her brother whose cruel and vindictive behavior toward others frightened her as much as his charming and manipulative way with her confused her. She did not want to provoke him, and she most assuredly would never tell him what really happened here.

"I have duties, excuse me." Matt swung into the saddle. "William, will you see Mary home?"

"I had better, hadn't I. God knows you're not man enough to do it." He took her hand in his.

It took all Matt's will to keep himself in his saddle. What he wanted most to do was jump on William and beat him to death. Withered arm or no, if Mary had not been there he would have done just that. Instead he dug his spur so deep into the flank of his horse that it reared back several times. Matt struggled for control. William's laughter frightened the horse even more. Matt finally calmed the animal and took off at a gallop towards Hill Haven.

William was still laughing when Mary jerked her hand out of his. Throwing her brother a disgusted look she said, "Why do you treat him that way?"

He took her arm roughly and shook the look from her face. "Stay away from him, you hear me?"

"William! You're hurting me." He had never shown violence toward her before and the wild look in his eyes frightened her now. His face was contorted.

"He's no good. He's the son of a despicable pirate. He's not for you, Mary. Don't waste your time on him."

She had regained her composure enough to retort.

"That's a stupid argument and you know it. Our mother was a pirate, too, or have you forgotten? She's strong and brave and treats us with respect and love, which is more than you return to her."

Not expecting such a spirited response, William finally remarked, "Listen . . ."

"No, you listen. I am a woman now, William Thomas. You can't treat me like a child anymore."

His left hand went to his right shoulder. Sometimes he did this out of habit; at other times, like now, he felt real pain. Impossible though it seemed to him, his shoulder throbbed. Either way, the action never failed to wring sympathy from his sister.

Her resolve gone now, she rushed to him. "Oh, William, don't hurt, please. Come let me rub your arm with the new oils I bought."

His wince turned into a smile as he put his arm around her and pulled her to him. The soft flesh of her breasts pressing against his chest thrilled him in a way no other woman's had.

Mary stiffened but endured his embrace until the whinny of her horse summoned her and she had an excuse to extricate herself from his grasp.

Esther lay in the comfort of John Sommerwood's bed unable to stir. She inhaled the fresh morning air and watched the curtains snap about the gallery doors. With both hands clasped around one of the cherrywood posts, Mary Elizabeth swayed her body from side to side until a memory clouded her high spirits.

Mary's interrupted motion caught Esther's attention. "Why are you sad?"

Just thinking about grandfather. It felt strange to sleep in here last night but I'm glad we decided to. You know, I used to swing on this post when I was a girl. I miss him."

"He was a good mon, like da king in da book o' Esther in da Bible. Dat mon 'low no harm cum ta Esther's people. Ole John, he like dat."

"I wonder what grandmama was like?"

"Mama say she look like a queen, act like one too."

"They slept together in this very bed from the night they were married. Daddy was born in it. Can you imagine? Esther, what will it be like that first night, think you?"

"I neber tink 'bout dat much."

"When you do, what do you think?"

"Mama, she say, make love first time no feel good, but

if mon be gentle soon cum time woman enjoy dat."

"I guess so. It scares me a little. Tell me, Esther, if you could have any man for your lover, who would you choose?"

"Well, member dat story you tell me 'bout da white knight who cum save da princess. Dat da mon I want love me. He be tall an brave and gentle. An' he love me mo' dan . . . mo' dan his horse."

Mary Elizabeth laughed and bounced onto the bed. "A white knight, eh?"

"An' you, what 'bout you?"

"Well, you'll laugh but the black knight interests me. Mysterious. A man it would take a lifetime to get to know. And clever and witty and he would meet each day with wonder as I do. And together we would find joy in our bodies, in this house, in this island. Yes, the black knight must be my life's companion. I leave the white knight to you."

"Is Matt yo' black knight?"

"I think so."

"Funny, I neber tink o' black knight dat way. I tink ebil, like what I see in yo' brudder."

"Does William frighten you, Esther?"

"Mos' times. Dat look in his eye make me shake all ober."

"He frightens me at times, too. He hates Matt bitterly."

"He jealous. Matt hab you, an not he."

"Esther, really. That's an awful thing to say."

"Be da truth. I 'fraid he rape you."

Mary Elizabeth stared into Esther's black eyes for a long time and was frightened. What she saw there was a small patterned cloth of many colors buried under a mound of dirt. What did it mean, she wondered?

Ruth always knew where to find her daughters in the late afternoon. The garden house was only a short walk from the cookhouse, under a long arbor hung all over with bougainvillaea of every imaginable hue and down through the bamboo walk.

The girls stopped giggling when Ruth entered. Mary Elizabeth had been teaching Esther and Sarah to crochet. Sarah was getting quite good at it. Ruth knew better than to ask what they were giggling about. The three lovely faces beamed up at her.

Surely Hill Haven was blessed with beauties. Esther, seventeen and stately like her mother, turned the heads of every worker on the plantation. Although two years her junior, Sarah was much prettier in the face. Ruth feared she had long since compromised her virginity. Esther would wear her virginity to her wedding or like a shroud to her grave; but Sarah flaunted herself shamelessly. Ruth was certain the girls were laughing about one of Sarah's latest conquests. Was it Barnaby or Rufus she had met behind the stable today? Ruth shuddered.

"Mama, look what I made!" shrieked Sarah.

"My, it bery t'ick." Ruth commented as she fingered the piece work. It was open patterned, of an eggshell color and about the size of a pie.

"Yes, I use heaby cotton, ta keep hot dishes from burnin' da table."

"Ruth, see here what Esther is doing." Mary Elizabeth pointed to the delicate multicolored doily Esther was making.

"I make dis fo' yo' dressin' table, Mama, da one Miz Anne gibe you. You can set yo' brushes an' tings on it."

"My, you girls bein' so t'oughtful and nice. Now don' tink yo' can sweet-talk Ole Ruth out o' yo' evenin' chores. Dere's work need doin'. Berta gettin' too old ta do up supper all by herse'f. An' straighten up in here fo' yo' cum. Mary, yo' mama an' me, we allus habe some foolishness ta pick up in da mornin' fo' we 'gin da gardenin'."

"Yessum," all three responded in unison as they began to gather together the remnants of the afternoon's entertainment. Crochet hooks, orange peels, mango pits, cups and trays, balls of yarn were scattered about the garden house.

"Mary, look up yonder on dat she'f, ain't dat one o' yo' crochet hooks?" Ruth asked.

"Oh, yes, that's the very one you needed for this fine work, Esther. Wish we'd seen this before."

"Well, bring dose tings back to da house, dey jus' rus' out here in da damp."

"Yessum."

"I'm goin' ta he'p Berta. You girls don' be long now."

"Yessum."

Ruth took up the tray of glasses and left the garden house.

"Mama sure is cranky dese days," Esther said as she rolled a stray line onto a ball of yarn.

"She change life," commented Sarah in a sophisticated way.

Mary Elizabeth laughed. "What do you mean 'change life'?"

"Oh, all da ole womon, dey do dat."

"What do you mean? Who told you?"

"Berta say dat." Sarah had to bring an authority into the discussion. She felt she was losing ground. "Odder mornin' Mama she yell at Old Berta fo' sompin'. Ole Berta jus' shake her head an' say ta herse'f, 'Ruth, she jus' change life. Dat what da motter is. No fret yerse'f. She change life das all.' An' den Berta go 'bout her business."

Still expecting a definition which didn't come, Esther asked again. "Well, what do it mean?"

"What?" responded Sarah.

"Change life! What do dat mean?"

"I dunno."

Mary Elizabeth joined Esther. "Well, Silly, didn't you ask Bertha what it meant?"

Esther and Mary Elizabeth shot hot looks at Sarah. "Well? What did she say?"

Sarah raised her nose in the air and said, "I not tell."

Mary and Esther exchanged glances. It was clear what had to be done. They had been through this kind of futile repartee before. Slowly they separated and moved menacingly toward the girl.

"No, no, don' touch me."

"Get her!" The two girls chased Sarah round the wicker table and finally trapped her behind one of the lounge chairs. Esther held one arm and Mary Elizabeth the other.

"No, no, don'. I tell. I tell," she shrieked.

"Tell then," Mary demanded.

"What change life is? What Berta say?" Esther threatened raising one finger before Sarah's wide eyes.

"She say . . . she say she . . . tell me later, when I older."

"Oh you devil, you are infuriating, you know that."

"Oh, please, don' tickle, please don'. I pee myse'f."

"Baby. Go 'head pee yo'se'f."

"Please no . . ." Sarah had not been touched, yet she fell to the ground screaming, rolling, and twisting hysterically.

Anne burst through the door. Both girls jumped away from Sarah who was writhing on the ground screeching in anticipation.

"What in heaven's name is going on in here? The girl sounds as if she is being murdered."

"We no touch her, Miz Anne. I promise."

"Mary Elizabeth?"

"True, Mama. We didn't lay a finger on her."

"Well, you must have done something." Anne knelt down beside Sarah. Mary Elizabeth and Esther backed away, snatched up a handful of crochet needles and bolted out of the garden house.

Still out of control, Sarah screamed when Anne rested her hand on the girl's shoulder.

"Hush, it's Anne. The girls are gone. Hush now, they won't hurt you." Anne smoothed her cool hand across Sarah's burning forehead. "Now tell me why is it they torment you so?"

Deliberately falling into a childish whine Sarah answered. "I dunno, Missus. Dey allus pick on me since I little."

Anne was not fooled. She knew full well the older girls weren't entirely to blame. Sarah provoked them. Esther and Mary had been close since early childhood. Little Sarah, always the third wheel tagging behind, had to find devious ways to get their attention.

Anne cradled the girl in her arms. "Oh, there now, my poor little innocent."

After indulging herself for a while in the warmth and comfort of Anne's arms, Sarah sniffled and whined. "Dey make me pee myse'f."

Because the girl sounded so miserable, Anne fought hard to suppress a giggle.

Baldwin returned home from Fort Morant with startling news. Their friend Captain Stoddart was ill and had been for the past month. Anxious to get the details regarding the Maroon peace, Baldwin had ridden out there this morning.

"Does the doctor know the cause?" Anne asked.

"No. He is baffled. Anne, you wouldn't recognize him. He is half his former size. He's wasting away."

"The flux will do that."

"That's what I thought at first but that's not it. He has good appetite. He feels fine, so he says. Yet every day he drops weight."

"Does he have pain?"

"No physical pain. His mind is tormented not knowing what is happening to his body. He shakes with the fear of death. Do you think someone is trying to poison him, with ground glass maybe?"

"Well, there must be some explanation. A man just doesn't waste away from nothing unless . . ." Anne looked as though she had been struck by a terrible thought.

"Anne, what is it?"

"Obeah?"

"No. Who?"

Anne walked out on to the terrace and looked toward the Blue Mountains. Baldwin followed her.

"Nanny? Do you think she . . ."

"Why not? Twice he has destroyed her village."

"But there is peace now."

"Perhaps Nanny has not heard of the peace or she has no intention of honoring it. She's up there somewhere. I know it." Anne tried but could not conceal the fear in her voice.

"I heard the drums, Anne, but thought I only dreamed that. Then I thought if she is back, the drums mean she has accepted the peace. I tried to give it no more thought."

Both retreated to the library. Anne spoke hesitantly. "Since the peace my dreams are more frequent. Horrible battles rage in them, sometimes in the sky, sometimes in the sea. Always she stares at me, victory shining in her eyes and William Thomas is there brandishing a bloody sword and laughing at my defeat."

"Oh, Annie, Annie." Baldwin took her into his arms.

"There's more and this is not a dream. I thought I saw William in Morant Bay Village in the company of that despicable Caleb Foote."

"Maybe we should have kept the soldiers here, Annie. Their leaving has not improved William's behavior. Every night he stumbles in here drunk, muttering to himself, and pulling himself up the staircase with his one good arm. I can't talk to him. Where does he get his money, that's what I'd like to know. Not from you, I hope?"

"You know better."

Baldwin poured two brandies. Anne took a quick gulp and set her glass on the marble mantlepiece and forgot about it.

"Win, did you ever find out what William did with the five thousand pounds he received from grandfather John's trust when he turned sixteen?"

"Not really. At first he told me he'd pissed it away. That's what he said to me, his very words, 'pissed it away.' Gambling I thought at first, then later . . . remember when Mary Elizabeth showed us the ruby necklace he'd given her? Well, I confronted him."

"What did he say to that?"

"Tossed his head and laughed. Said he could buy ten just

like it, if he chose to."

"Did he say how he got the money?"

"He muttered something about making a profitable investment. 'You make safe ones,' he said to me. 'I don't make wise investments, just profitable ones.' He called me a stupid old fool not to enjoy all the pleasures I could right here, right now. That one day all this would go up in smoke before my eyes and blow away."

"He was drunk, of course."

"Stone sober. That's what scares me, Anne. Something is eating away at him and it's not just his useless arm. What's happening to the captain's body has been happening to William's soul. We all have a dark side, but his dark side has taken over. Our son is pissing his life away, Annie." Baldwin grasped the mantlepiece with one hand and seemed to hang there, staring down at some mysterious speck near his foot.

Anne finally broke the silence. "I think I'd rather take on an army of ten thousand Maroons then endure ten minutes' conversation with my own son."

"He can kill himself for all I care. I just hope to God, he doesn't hurt anybody else. I don't think I could bear that, Annie."

"Perhaps I didn't love him enough. Perhaps I loved Colin more, or Matt...he is so jealous of Matt."

"Oh, come, Anne, you're grasping at straws. Colin has been gone for years and well...Matt...Matt is easy to love."

Baldwin put his arm around Anne's shoulders and walked out to the terrace to scan the sky looking for an answer to their trouble. "The constellation Scorpius is clear tonight."

Anne glanced heavenward. When recognition of its shape struck her mind, she dropped her head and stared into the black Jamaican night.

For a long while Baldwin studied the constellation's largest star Antares and was disturbed by the recollection that it had been so named because like Mars it is red in color.

CHAPTER NINE

"Boast Not of Tomorrow"
—*Prov. 27:1*

Lusen met Afiba from time to time. The tiny bamboo forest by the river became their home. The wind as it played in the tall arches of the stalks creaking and groaning over the lovers tendered protection and music.

Touching her rounded belly, he followed the activities of their child. Moments when the singing trees hung silent he would listen to the melody in her womb, the faint heartbeat—a life, which in cooperation with some larger, mysterious force, they had created.

One afternoon like this almost nine months ago, it had happened. The event had gone unnoticed as did the fluttering leaf which came to rest on the moss at that very same moment. The day she told him he wanted to shout. Instead he leaped upon the bamboo and climbed so high that it arched almost to the ground. Kicking for joy, he dropped to the earth, sending the reed crashing against the others. Lusen's announcement reverberated in the hills. Now her time was nearing. She told Lusen she would not come again for a while, a week perhaps or two. A feeling of helplessness came over him.

"Cum wid me home, Afiba. be my princess. No prince treat you better."

"I no can cum, Lusen. Afiba too much danger ta yo' people."

"But de fightin' be ober now. Cudjoe sign peace."

"Nanny will neber sign peace. War ober in West, not ober in Windward. Take care below, Lusen. Tell yo' people watch. Nanny promise vengeance on you all."

"Den dere be danger fo' me in dis place."

"No, Afiba no cum here, meet you, if she tink dere danger. Maroon 'fraid cum dis place. Tink duppy here."

"No, don' tell me dat. I 'fraid ghost too."

"Dis duppy no hurt Lusen. Ghost Nanny's sister. She buried here, dat bump dere. Nanny no let Maroon cum here. Nanny no cum here."

"God, all dis time, we . . ."

"No 'fraid. She good womon—die young, hab baby an' die."

"An' you . . . you hab baby. I 'fraid fo' you now."

"No 'fraid. Afiba no die." She took his right hand, kissed it, then placed it on her belly in benediction. "Nex' time I cum, I bring baby."

"But when? How I know? Will dere be drums?"

"Mebbe. Listen ta yo'se'f. Inside, you will know."

When she reached the village Nanny grabbed Afiba's wrist and dragged her to the river's edge.

"Nanny no wait minute mo'. You tell me now, who de fadder dis baby?" Nanny pulled the girl into the water. "Plantation boy? De one we capture?"

"No, Maroon boy, nudder village."

"You lie."

"Afiba no lie ta Nanny."

"Den why you no gibe me he name?"

"Boy . . . a cripple . . . no whole."

"Afiba no hab strong warrior dis belly? I kill both, now." Nanny held the girl under the water. Afiba did not struggle; she knew Nanny would not kill her. After a minute Nanny pulled her up by the hair and spit her final threat into Afiba's face. "Dat baby drop out twisted I kill he." The long scar on Nanny's face throbbed and Afiba knew the Queen Mother would carry out her threat.

The still March night breathed heat. The moon, full and bright, sizzled in the sky. The cattle snorted their discomfort as mosquitoes buzzed about their heads by the hundreds. The plantation people sweltered in their tiny huts, shutters closed against the insects. A few people sat by fires encouraging the smoke to cover their bodies with a natural insect repellent. Anne and Baldwin, naked under the bed netting, had been lying still since midnight, silently cursing the irritating night for being too hot—much too hot to touch one another.

Esther left the closed hut, chased by bugs, fire, heat and smoke and wandered the grounds trying to walk herself into a state of exhaustion. After a time her feet strayed from a circuitous path and took her to the garden house.

She did not remember falling asleep. When she heard the crashes it took her a few moments for the sounds to register and somehow provide a clue to her whereabouts. The dull sound of clay flower pots cracking as they hit the ground was unmistakable. A man stumbling about and mumbling in the dark suddenly fell onto the delicate wicker table smashing it to bits.

"God's Death!"

Perhaps if she lay quiet he would go away, she thought.

Finally the man found what he was searching for. Match and candle came together spreading a faint light over the entire room.

Esther darted for the door. She ran too near the man's left side; his arm shot out and grabbed her wrist. Because the man made no attempt to hold her with his other arm, she knew who it was.

"Massa William!"

"Who's this, now?" Swinging her into the candlelight he slurred at her. "Why Esther, lovely Esther. Come to have a wee drink with me, did ye?"

"No, Massa William."

"No. Well, you won't mind if I indulge myself. Slabe girl don' mine pourin' fo' da massa, now do she?" He gave her arm a hard twist. "Do she?"

"Lemme go!"

"Look here nigger wench. You'll do as I say. Reach into

my pocket and put that bottle to my lips or I'll break your skinny black arm. Tip it up, damn you." The liquor spilled down his throat, some fell out of the corners of his mouth down his shirt. Draining it dry, he shook his head, knocking the bottle out of her hand onto the ground.

William threw her onto the lounge and flung his entire bulk on top of her. With his good hand he tore away her white shift and ripped open his breeches. At this, he was expert. William struck her several times to stop her screams. She struggled beneath him but could not free herself either from him or the unknown terror of his impending violation. The more she fought, the more excited he became. Aroused to hardness, he tore into her. Esther's cry, no louder than that of a night bird, went unnoticed. His brutal assault continued for a short while, but for Esther the agony of those few moments would burn forever in her memory.

William stumbled out of the garden house.

Finding it too painful to move, Esther lay on the lounge where he left her. Her hands absently rearranged the bloody fragments of her shift in a futile effort to cover herself. The candle went out as a final spill of wax hit the ground.

Tasting the tears falling into her mouth, Esther cried out softly, "Mama."

"Nanny! Nanny!" Afiba's desperate cries brought the woman running to her side. With two fingers, Nanny felt inside the girl.

"Too soon. I call Nanny too soon?"

"Yes, I tink too soon. Baby cum him own time."

Nanny alternated wiping the perspiration from Afiba's face and gently massaging her abdomen with coconut oil to ease her through the pains. She puffed steadily and heavily on her pipe. The smoke acting as a narcotic seemed to calm the girl.

Nanny's cursory examination hinted at something which did not please her. "You rest, Afiba. Nanny go. Cum back soon."

"No, stay. Afiba need Nanny now."

"Nanny need he'p bring dis baby. You lie quiet, girl."

Nanny had sent for the Kingston woman two days ago. Ryna was young but an expert midwife and an Ashanti. Nanny did not fear to bring her into the village. Yet she insisted Ryna swear to secrecy and had watched as the tall woman with rings of gold encircling both arms bent low to kiss the earth at Nanny's feet.

Ryna put her basket in the corner of Afiba's hut. She tucked the cloth around her own sleeping baby girl, then opened a sack containing jars and boxes of special powders and ointments. Fresh water was brought in by a young girl who quickly withdrew, glancing only briefly at the naked distorted figure lying on the mat.

Afiba cried out. "It cums; I feel him."

Nanny soothed Afiba with soft words. Then she placed her large hands and fixing her eyes on the girl's abdomen mumbled something in her native language.

Removing the rings from her small slender hands, Ryna dipped into a jar and greased her hands heavily before anointing the area in preparation for birth. Reaching inside the girl, she turned the baby and slid it out of the womb. She cut the cord and laying it and the afterbirth aside, she bathed the healthy boy in cold water and rum before placing him into Nanny's outstretched hands.

Old Sam had chosen an African name for Lusen's child, without realizing that that was what he was doing, for Lusen gave his grandfather no reason for his questions. No one know Lusen was about to become a father, or that he met Afiba in secret. Her name never passed his lips. She filled his thoughts so entirely, it was surprising even to himself that her name never slipped out.

"Quant" was Sam's favorite, because he had had an uncle by that name. He liked the name "Bina" for a woman. He was not sure if Bina was an African name, he just liked it.

I tink I need boy's name. I tink it cum, he here, now. His whole body burned with excitement.

Ruth and Sang approached the fire outside their hut and broke his ecstasy.

"Son, you see Esther walkin' 'bout?"

"No, Doddy. How long she been gone?"

"Two hour or mo'," said Ruth unable to keep the worried tone out of her voice.

"I'll look fo' her, Mama."

"Suppose she's asleep at the big house wid Mary 'Lizbeth," she said to her husband.

"Well, go see woman, if you tink she dare. I'll look in da barn. Lusen, see mebbe she wid Ole Sam and Berta."

Ruth hurried to the great house. Esther would be there. The girls often slept together. But Esther usually told her where she'd be. She was not like Sarah; Ruth rarely knew where Sarah was these days, and Lusen . . . Lusen was a man now; she didn't think it right to question his comings and goings. But Esther . . . it was not like Esther to disappear without a word. Mary Elizabeth was alone in her bed. When Ruth adjusted the mosquito netting, Mary groaned. "That you, Esther?"

"No, it Ruth. Jus' cum ta see yo' net keepin' da bugs 'way, is all. Go back ta sleep now."

Ruth closed the door quietly, turned and met Anne. "Oh Miz Anne . . ." She couldn't hold back her tears. "We can't fine Esther."

"Wait here. I'll get Baldwin."

"Oh, don' wake da massa. Mosquitoes so bad dis March, he mos' likely ain't got no proper sleep yet. He be angry."

"He will not. He'd be angry if something happened to your Esther when he could have prevented it."

Anne, Baldwin, and Ruth left the house by way of the back stairs and met Sang and Lusen running toward them carrying torches. As if guided by something they did not understand, they all looked down the long arbor at the same time and hurried off toward the garden house.

Esther, huddled behind the plants in one of the corners of the room, would not have been noticed if Lusen had not heard her soft cries. He bent down to help her up, but she yelled out so fiercely that he backed away.

"Don' touch me!" She picked up a pointed gardening shovel and thrust it at him. "Don' touch me! I kill . . . kill!" Lusen jumped back in time.

Sang moved in closer with the torch. Ruth knelt beside her daughter. "Esther? It's Mama. Esther, gibe dat ta Mama."

"Esther. Now stop dis. No one here goin' hurt yo'." Ruth succeeded in wrenching the tool out of Esther's grasp. Now, tell Mama what hoppen. You hurt? Show Mama."

Esther pushed both her fists into her lap and rocked forward. When the girl rocked back moaning, Ruth saw. "Oh, Lord no!"

Baldwin knelt beside her. "Ruth, what is it? Where is she hurt?"

Esther pulled back further when she heard his voice and Baldwin saw the blood in her lap.

"Jesus God! Who could have done . . ."

A chilling glare was followed by a growling sound more animal than human as Esther lunged for Baldwin's throat. There was a tremendous power in her arms and it took both Sang and Anne to pull the girl away from Baldwin. Finally Esther sank into her mother's arms sobbing.

At once, all recognized Esther's violator. Baldwin's physical resemblence to his son was close enough to elicit a violent reaction from the hysterical girl. Anne was so horrified she sank to her knees unable to look at either Ruth or Sang. William's loathsome deed stirred memories of her own violation; she could not keep back the bitter taste rising in her throat.

Baldwin struggled to his feet. His face beet-red moments before, now drained of all color.

The garden house spoke a stillness now. Even Esther's sobs were barely audible. Baldwin listened to the sound of his own breathing. For a long time he listened.

Sang finally spoke what everyone was thinking. "Where William Thomas now?"

"I fine 'im!" shouted Lusen. "An' . . ." Sang grabbed the boy's arm and pulled him back with such force that Lusen fell into the splintered table on the ground.

"You stay right dere, boy." Sang gave Baldwin a hard look.

Baldwin, forcing back tears, swallowed hard and spoke. "I'm not sure where he is, but I'll find him. He's my son, my responsibility. I'll find him."

Anne pulled herself to her feet. "Baldwin, I'll go with you."

"No, you might kill him. I won't kill him. But when I'm finished with him, he'll wish I had."

Baldwin knew where it was kept. The whip hung in a cluttered corner of the stable, unused now for upwards of forty years. His steps were determined, even though the idea of using it filled him with disgust. On neighboring plantations, he had seen enough abuse administered by the cat to cane cutters, men and women alike. Just last week, in Portland, he had seen a pregnant woman prone on the floor, a special place hollowed out to receive her swollen stomach. Her beating was a horror so compelling he had had to wrench his eyes away. He left that plantation without concluding his business.

Standing in the stable holding the cat, Baldwin could see that this instrument of torture was useless. Six of the knotted leathern tails had rotted, the other three were cracked. Searching further he found a whip made of lashbark. Used in a certain manner, it could flay layers of skin off a man; he had seen it. This would serve.

The moon illuminated the road to Morant Bay Village. Whip in hand, Baldwin mounted the tavern stairs; he opened every door. Finally amid shouts of indignation, and curses of the bedded couples he had interrupted, he found the room William Thomas occupied. Fully clothed, his son lay stretched across the bed on his stomach.

One stroke of the whip roused him. The next brought him to his feet, and the next face to face with his father.

"You scum, you filthy animal!" Baldwin struck wildly at William Thomas, who received blows, which in spite of the pain, failed to remove the execrable smile on his face.

"Poor father," he spat through his teeth. "Never really learned how to curse, did you?"

"Why you . . . Devil!" Baldwin lashed out with all the power of his right arm. If words were inadequate, perhaps stripes would teach him. The whip lashed around William's body flinging his useless arm about as easily as if it belonged to a rag doll. The boy's efforts to catch the whip with his left hand were futile. The lashbark tore the shirt from his body, leaving heavy rents in his shoulder, back and chest. Finally, William cried out in pain, pleading with his father to stop. Baldwin did not stop until a tightening in his own chest and a piercing pain in his right arm forced him to drop the whip. Struggling for breath, he flung one last warning. "You are not . . . to return to Hill Haven . . . ever!"

"Does this mean . . . I am out, Father?"

Baldwin's words came out in gasps. He felt a choking rising in his throat. "Disinherited . . . disowned . . . I never want to see your face again. Set foot on the plantation and you will be shot."

"You may not live to change your will, old man."

Baldwin's face turned white as he stared in disbelief into his son's face which was contorted with laughter. Somehow he managed to leave the room and nearly tumbled down the steps of the tavern.

Once mounted, he fell unconscious over the neck of his bay who took him home.

Sang helped Baldwin up to his room. The doctor who had been fetched earlier for Esther was still there when Baldwin arrived home. The heart attack was a mild one but he was to have complete rest. To insure at least initial sleep, the doctor gave him a sedative.

Anne pulled the wicker lounge closer to the bed and listened for any changes in Baldwin's breathing. She thought back to the time of the early months of her pregnancy with William. Her mind had been filled with foreboding then as it was now. She looked at her husband, and reached under the netting to hold his hand. Anne felt the warmth of life. Would he leave her now? He had left for London before he knew she was pregnant with William. Perhaps that was why she had been filled with such dread. With each day her illness worsened; Ruth concocted a vile herbal mixture which stopped her retching but long after, her body ached as if angered that its means of expelling the intruder had been blocked. Sleepless from fiendish nightmares, Anne procured a potion from an obeah woman. She had been warned that it would kill the baby but might kill her also. For days she paced the gallery trying to make the decision, but one day Ruth found the mixture and disposed of it. Anne sighed. Baldwin moaned as if he sensed her agonizing thoughts. She answered by stroking his hand. This fitful dialogue went on the rest of the night.

Ruth did not want to disturb Anne, but by mid-morning she could no longer contend with Mary Elizabeth's incessant questions. "Where was Esther? Why couldn't she see her? What happened to Father? Why couldn't she see him? Had William come home last night?"

Ruth encouraged Mary to ride with Matt who waited with the horses downstairs, thinking if the girl would leave the house, she could get on with her nursing duties. Mary Elizabeth, sick to death of Ruth's shushing, told her so. She refused to leave the house until somebody told her what was going on.

It was a tearful session. Anne told her daughter as delicately as possible what her brother had done. Matt paced back and forth outside the sitting room. Anne's efforts to stress the importance of not upsetting Esther or exciting her father just now were lost in the whirlwind of Mary's emotions.

"How could he do it, Mother? How could he?"

"Your brother is evil, Mary, truly depraved."

"Rape, my God, I almost can't believe it. His drunkenness does not excuse him this time. He's gone too far. Poor Esther. How can she ever forgive me?"

"It's not you she needs to forgive."

"What can I say to her? How will I ever know what to say to her?" Mary buried her face in Anne's shoulder and sobbed. "Oh, I hate him. I don't care if he is my brother, I hate him. He's hurt father, too. I hope he burns in hell an eternity. Oh Esther. How can I look in her face?"

Mary Elizabeth ran out of the room and out of the house. Anne stopped Matt from going after her. "Leave her alone a while, Matt. 'Tis best."

"Will somebody please tell me what is going on here? The pall over this house is maddening."

Matt studied the figures on an oriental vase while Anne told him the sordid events of the last evening. When she finished he picked up the vase and hurled it against the hearth. "That bastard, that filthy bastard. I hope I never see him."

"It's not likely any of us will see him again." The crash of the porcelain shattered Anne's already brittle nerves. Matt heard the strain in her voice and took Anne into his arms. Anne relaxed in his grasp. She needed this moment of comfort. She needed his help and confidence. Energy flowed back into her. He was the source of her strength now as his mother had once been. And unlike Mary Read, he would stay.

Matt knew he would find Mary Elizabeth in the bamboo walk. Not wanting to startle her he kept at a distance and placing his hands on the smooth yellow-green bark absorbed its coolness. He had hoped she would seek the comfort of his arms, but she did not.

"Mother told you what happened?"

"Aye. It could as easily have been you, not Esther. You

know that, Mary."

"I know it. It's my fault it happened."

Unable to stay away from her any longer, Matt took her shoulders and turned her toward him. "How can you say that?"

"Because it's the truth. I saw it happen in her eyes one day, but I didn't pay any notice. I didn't warn her. I didn't protect her. She warned me. Can you believe it?"

"You can't blame yourself. It's his fault, his evil, his perversity."

"He's my brother. The same blood runs in my veins. It is the same as if I have violated her."

"Mary, that's crazy. Maybe depravity has nothing to do with blood. You are no more like him than that lizard like a butterfly."

"I don't know. I tried not to believe that what William felt for me went beyond . . . Maybe I wanted him to love me that way. Perhaps I am as perverse as he. I don't know."

"Mary . . ."

"Don't touch me." Unsure of everything else, Mary was absolutely sure she did not want to be touched by any man at this moment.

"Mary, please, listen to me. He's gone. Don't let him come between us anymore. I want to marry you, raise our children to enjoy all this. Look around you, Mary, can't you see?"

"No, not now . . ."

Matt watched her run toward the garden house and dropped his head in misery. It seemed so right, loving her, working this plantation, living on this island. At times it seemed within his grasp and . . . Was it meant to be? he asked himself.

Nearby, a clump of bamboo flowered.

Baldwin stared at the walls which blurred through the gauze of the mosquito netting. Where was he now, he wondered? Had he died? He looked at his hands, his clean white nightshirt and tried to remember. His eyes fell on one familiar object after another in the room and he remembered. He wished he had died. Then he recalled the last words spoken to him by his son and knew why he had not died. He had kept himself alive for a very important reason. He called out for Anne.

Hearing his faint cries Ruth hurried down to find her mistress, who, somehow sensing his call, was already mounting the stairs to answer him.

"Win, you're awake." She raised the netting. "What can I get you?"

"Sang. Send him to bring the colonel here."

"Look Baldwin, you really must rest. The doctor said . . ."

"I don't care what the doctor said. Colonel Hargrave must come here now, today. Once you've dispatched Sang, you must bring pen and paper up here."

It would upset him to argue so Anne did as he requested.

Anne wrote as Baldwin dictated his last will and testament. She did not like the task. His words rang cold and distant. It was the solicitor talking, not her husband, not the man she loved so desperately. Anne caught a tear before it could fall on the paper.

"You're sure you want to do this?"

"I'm sure. Now please make a copy before the colonel arrives. You don't want the old windbag to stay the afternoon waiting for it, now do you?"

Cheered by his humor, Anne sat at her Blue Mahoe writing table and applied herself to her task silently. She wanted him to rest. It was clear he wanted to talk.

"Matt will marry our daughter."

"Baldwin, you don't know that."

"I do. She loves him."

"He loves her, you mean."

"She loves him, mark my words. You know the last wedding here was our own." In spite of the misery William Thomas caused them, his love for Anne and thoughts of his wedding day and night brought warm feelings to fill his heart. Anne was squeezing Baldwin's hand when the colonel burst into the room without knocking.

"What's this? Down, are ye? Here Anne, put some o' this in his tea and he'll be fine in no time." Colonel Hargrave placed the bottle of clear liquid on the night stand, pushing aside the other medicines as though his spring water was the only cure for every ailment.

"Now, of what further service can I be?"

"Please to witness my will, Colonel."

"I see."

Anne handed the original to the colonel to read while she dusted the copy.

He cleared his throat once or twice; otherwise the colonel said nothing. The plantation and all the Sommerwood holdings fell to Anne. In the event of her remarriage or death, the estate would pass to Mary Elizabeth and Matt. Under no circumstances was William Thomas to receive a penny. Land and other monetary considerations were bequeathed to Sang. There was enough for him and Ruth and their family to live out their days in comfort. The last part concerned the revocation of all other and former wills. The document was dated 16 March, 1740.

Since his duty as magistrate was to witness wills, not question them, the colonel did not ask about the deliberate exclusion of William Thomas from the bequests. Baldwin signed both copies in a shaky but recognizable hand. Colonel Hargrave and Anne witnessed his signature on both copies. The colonel folded the copy and stuffed it in his pocket, instructed Anne to put the original in a safe place, and bade them both good health and good day.

"I'd like to come to your mineral spring, when I'm feeling up to it, if I may, Colonel?"

"By all means, Mr. Sommerwood. 'Twill do you good. Yes indeed. Do come and honor me by bringing your lovely wife." He kissed Anne's hand and left so brusquely she had to shout their thanks after him.

As soon as he was sure his sister would be all right,

Lusen climbed up to his mountain home. Just as Afiba had told him, he had known the very night that his baby had been born. It had been two weeks but he had been afraid to leave Esther. Resting her back against a log, Afiba was giving her breast to her baby. Entirely absorbed in her blissful task, she neither saw nor heard Lusen approach. Concealed in the bush, he watched her.

Soon satisfied, the baby fell asleep with Afiba's nipple still in his mouth. When she drew him away, his eyes opened. He was deciding whether or not to cry when she spoke to him.

"No cry. Seem like, yo' only tiny boy wid no doddy. But dat not so. Doddy cum soon. Mama promise."

Lusen could hardly believe what he was seeing and hearing. He had fathered a son. His only wish was that he could have been there. Now for this moment at least they were all his. Here among the bamboo and dense bush, his family would grow in love and knowledge of one another.

"See boy . . . your doddy here now."

Lusen approached and kissed Afiba, thanking her for their fine boy baby. He studied the tiny naked body for a long time. The baby grabbed one of his fingers. Such tiny fingers and toes. Such a lot of hair. No less than a miracle.

When the warm spray shot up and struck his face, Lusen laughed. Afiba cleaned him off and covered the baby with a loin cloth to prevent any further mishaps. Lusen was sure the baby smiled up at him.

"He's bad. You know dat. Look how he laugh at what he do. What do we call him, Afiba? Hab yo' t'ought 'bout dat? I hab name, if you not already gibe him one."

"Nanny name him. She proud fine boy Afiba make."

"Oh." Lusen could not hide his disappointment. He had conveniently forgotten about Nanny. Alone here in the woods, in his world there were no other people. He carried their private world inside himself when he left her. It only now dawned on him that Afiba could hardly have kept her pregnancy a secret as he had kept their relationship a secret from his family. She could not have had the baby in a dark corner, like a cat.

"Him named after Nanny's brudder Quaco, my doddy."

"Quaco." It sounded very much like the name Old Sam had picked.

"We mus' do someting now." Afiba brought out a gourd from behind a bush.

"What dat?"

"In dis gourd is baby's cord. We mus' plant dis and put small tree on top." Afiba picked the spot where they made love for the first time and Lusen dug up a tiny bamboo shoot with his knife and planted the gourd and the shoot together.

"Now, baby Quaco hab he tree."

"What yo' doddy, Quaco, tink o' his grannie?"

"Quaco dead. He killed in battle. It great honor boy named fo' him. Quaco Maroon colonel."

"I hope he not killed time soldiers cum rescue Miz Anne and me?"

"No, Quaco kill ten winters pas'."

Ten winters struck at some almost forgotten memory. "How killed? Where?"

"You not hab to know more den dat, Lusen."

"Tell me, Afiba. My chil' name' after mon. I want know mo' 'bout him."

She hesitated. "He killed in plantation raid."

A cold damp chill thrilled through his body as the memory of that night flashed through his mind. On the night of terror which he spent hiding in the bush with Old Sam and Bertha, Afiba's father had been killed. He could almost smell the slave huts burning and the stench of scorched muscovado.

Lusen vowed he would keep his family safe from horrors like those. He would find a place, his own place, in the mountains away from the Maroons and the hideous atrocities they committed, away from the plantation and men like William Thomas who could so brutally, carelessly ruin women like his sister.

Lusen didn't realize how desperately he clutched Afiba

and their baby to his breast, until a flock of screeching parrots broke through his thoughts.

At the sound of Mary Elizabeth's screams, Anne bolted from her bed. When she reached the hallway, Matt was pounding on her daughter's bedroom door.

"It's locked. She won't open it."

"What is it?" Baldwin tied the sash of his dressing down and ran his fingers through his hair. "Why is she screaming like that?"

Anne went for her weapon. Matt rammed his hefty shoulders against the door again and again until it finally gave way.

Mary was standing by her bed, staring down at Esther and screaming. Matt moved her away from the bed. Secure in his arms, Mary was at last able to tear her eyes away from the ghastly sight and her screams subsided.

Baldwin lit a candle and held it over the bed as Anne rushed into the room, sword in hand. As Anne came to his side, Baldwin leaned over Esther's still figure. "Dear God. She's killed herself," he gasped. "Slit her throat."

Esther's eyes were open, and she was lying on her side. There was a gaping slash in the girl's neck under her jawbone. A small knife lay in the midst of a great circle of blood.

"Baldwin, stay here, I'll fetch Ruth." Anne took her weapon back to her room, grateful its use could go untested, then hurried to the settlement.

Placing two fingers on Esther's eyelids, Baldwin gently drew them closed. He put the candle on the nightstand, and lit others in the room. He looked at his daughter, clutching Matt's shoulders, her body shaking with the violence of her sobs. Matt's soft voice stammered words of comfort.

There is no comfort here, thought Baldwin. Not for any of us. The evil of one vile deed reverberates throughout this house and touches all of us.

Ruth rushed to the side of the bed, Sang followed behind. In shocked silence they stared at the gaping wound.

Sang reached to touch Esther's arm but suddenly drew back his hand as he would from a burning log. Ruth turned Esther onto her back, straightened her legs, placed the girl's arms at her side and brushed a stray curl from her forehead.

Baldwin brought Ruth a chair and she sat by the bed where he knew she would spend the rest of the night. Sang stood at her side. Anne took a clean towel and laid it over the pool of blood. Then she put her arms around Ruth, kissed her cheek and laid her head against hers. Ruth's gaze never left her daughter's ashy face, but she reached up to place her hand over Anne's.

Esther had not been herself since the incident in the garden house. She hardly spoke to anyone, even Mary Elizabeth. There had been no recurrence of the violent outburst which took place that night. The girl just wandered about the plantation, never returning anyone's friendly greeting. As quietly as she had passed her days, Esther had ended her life.

A European visitor thought the plantation was having a festival but was informed by his host that it was a funeral. Ruth dressed Esther in an indigo dress which had a wide green stripe about the hem and was trimmed in white lace at the collar and sleeves. Her favorite, it had been a birthday present from Mary Elizabeth.

Anne, Mary Elizabeth and Matt were present in Ruth's small hut when they laid Esther in the coffin Old Sam had made. Bertha cried into her clean white apron and Sarah wept on Lusen's shoulder. Music celebrating a better life filled the valley. Outside a crowd of people sang praises to the Lord who both gives and takes life. Baldwin had been weeping all morning. Anne explained to Ruth and Sang that for this reason she had asked him to stay at Hill Haven. She did not feel that so soon after his heart attack he had strength enough to endure the emotional ordeal of Esther's funeral.

Ruth nodded. Sang took a last look at his daughter. Massa Baldwin griebe as if she his own chil', he thought as he touched Esther's hand. I 'spect she was. Dese chil'ren allus one fambly, dey play and eat togedder. They had planned a party for next week when they moved into the new house he had built for Ruth on the ten acres of woodland Baldwin had given him. Dat house too big already, he thought. Sarah gone ta work fo' seamstress in da village, now Esther gone too.

Sang placed a white rose in Esther's hand before he and Sam nailed the coffin shut. On its lid Mary Elizabeth laid garlands of pink frangipani which she and Matt had strung together.

The sad party followed the musicians and singing mourners to the cemetery at the foot of Blue Mountain.

CHAPTER TEN

"All the Trees of Eden"
—*Ezek. 31:9*

Matt and Mary Elizabeth were not married until January, 1741. A small quiet ceremony at Hill Haven celebrated the event. Matt, handsome in his morning suit, watched his bride walk with her father towards him. He was only twenty-one, she nearly nineteen, but it seemed to him that he had waited for her an eternity. He recalled their young days, morning rides, and sad times, but moreover the intimacy of the past few months came to mind. This was the time when they had grown to be friends. With the absence of William Thomas's disruptive presence, they had had time to talk, to share fears and to dream and plan for a happier future.

Mary Elizabeth looked at the flowering trees all around her, inhaled their fragrance and absorbed their energy. "This is what Matt had felt that day there in the bamboo walk when he said he wanted to share all this with me, but I was not listening. I could hear only the sounds of William's assault on Esther." Her eyes glimpsed the garden house and she quickly swung them into the radiant face of her husband, burying all thoughts of her brother. But she could not drive out of her mind the wish that her friend could share in her joy today.

Ruth stood next to Sang. They too were thinking of Esther. Her hand reached over and took Sang's. Lusen stood beside them. Sarah had not come. The family saw very little of her these past months.

I all the fambly left, Lusen thought, I wish I could tell

dem I hab a wife and dey a grannie, den mebbe dey not look so sad. Someday ... someday dey know an' all da pain wash 'way. He stared at Matt and Mary Elizabeth kneeling before the minister and imagined Afiba and himself in their places. Pride swelled his bosom.

Sang looked at his son wondering what caused the audible sigh that escaped the boy. What dat boy tinking? His t'oughts so loud dey knock at my ears. Dat woman prob'ly. Sang did not like to think about this possibility and Lusen was so quiet—always dreaming. Sang wished he could see a corner of his son's fantasy.

Baldwin took the purple tentacles of the orchid Anne was holding and entwined their clasped hands. To him this marriage meant hope, hope for Hill Haven and hope even for himself. He squeezed Anne's hand and inhaled the fresh morning air with all its promise for a happier future, then expelled the past with the stale air from his body and mind.

Anne returned Baldwin's smile, but unlike her husband her thoughts locked on the past. She watched as Mary placed the ring on Matt's finger. How handsome he is, she thought. Other than being slightly taller and more muscular, Matt looked exactly like his mother. Anne could see now why her lover Jack Rackam, not knowing Matt Read was a woman, had erupted into fits of jealous rage whenever he saw Anne too much in the company of her dearest friend. Now the union of their children would be the physical representation of the mental and emotional bond between herself and Mary Read. She had expressed her joy this morning by heaping armfuls of roses and wild orchids on her friend's grave.

Matt took his bride into his arms and sealed his vow with a kiss.

The reality of their days joined the fantasy of their nights and within a month of Matt's tender lovemaking, Mary Elizabeth had conceived. With her he seemed wrapped in Eden where time beats only in the wings of birds and the earth spreads thick and green with broad leaves and thin floating in a sunlit sea. Their transparant bodies traced by golden light, they stood hand in hand with the universe.

At the tavern at Port Morant Bay, Sarah lay in the arms of a sleeping soldier and listened to the conversation between two men in the next room. She could not understand what they were saying, but she recognized the voice of William Thomas and that was why she listened.

"Guns. I can't get any more guns," William Thomas exclaimed in a hoarse but hushed voice. "I've wrung every last armament from my contacts at Rock Fort and Kingston and if any more stores are missed at the fort at Port Antonio, the commandant will become suspicious. What do they intend to do, anyway, blow up the entire island?"

Caleb Foote studied his young companion. Of one thing he could be sure, if more arms could have been obtained this greedy lad would have gotten his hands on them.

"It ain't easy for me, either, since Cap'n Stoddart died. The new commander is a stickler for inventories." He lowered his voice even more and said, "There's a new lieutenant at Fort Morant, come since you been away. Tonight he's here with that pretty nigger wench, Sarah. She's a real gypsy, that one. She wouldn't be much for a pretty pin like yourself. Persuade her to dally with you a while."

"What good would that do?"

"Well now, there's a shipment of arms due at Fort Morant within the month. You get that wench under your girdle, then coax her to pry information out of the lieutenant. She finds out the route of the shipment, the day and the time, then a few of Nanny's boys take it from there."

A sudden weariness came over William. "Get out now, Caleb."

"Well, will you do it?"

"I've had a long ride today. Tomorrow we'll talk." His left hand reached up and clutched his right shoulder.

"You ain't gone soft on me, have ye, lad?"

William grabbed Caleb's grimy collar and gave it a choking twist. "Get out of here, Caleb. I'm weary of your talk."

"All right, all right, tomorrow."

William opened the windows and rain splashed in on the sill. God, I wish these rains would quit. He looked around the room, his home for a year and a half now, and he was weary of it too, weary of looking at the same bed, table, chair, wardrobe and washstand. He sat on the window seat and let the night rain cool his burning forehead. Sarah. Her pretty face appeared in his mind's eye, her large firm breasts heaved on her small frame, inviting hips flared under the soft fall of her muslin dress. Sarah, Esther's sister. Suddenly he was more weary than before. She is no match for me. I have heard her appetite for love-making is insatiable. What if she hates me? She ought to. That wildhearted creature will tear me to pieces. I am no match for her there either. William poured himself a brandy and drank it down in one long gulp. Seduce Sarah? Never. She'd eat me alive.

The door opened and closed softly. William turned and looked at Sarah, more alluring in the dim candlelight than in the firelight of his mind. He could not move. Dropping her shift to the floor, she approached him like a tiger stalking an enemy. Her hands circled his neck, sending a prickling sensation down his spine. She drew his head to hers and wiping the brandy from his lips with her tongue, probed his mouth for more. She nipped his eyelids and running her nails down the sides of his face bit one ear and inserted her tongue in the other.

Driven to a frenzy William moved with her to the bed. She had no intention of waiting for his one-handed fumblings; she ripped off his clothes. As she took him in her mouth, he writhed on his back like a dying insect. Bringing him to the brink several times, Sarah allowed him release only after what seemed to William a painful eternity. When she did, she spit him out of her mouth and let him splash into the empty air.

In October 1741, heavy rains battered Hill Haven and showed little sign of letting up. All the shutters were secured. Very near her time, Mary Elizabeth was made as comfortable as possible in the storage cellar under the house. The large room contained a fireplace at one end, complete with baking ovens and cooking pots. Baldwin recalled once when he was a boy, the family had used it as a hurricane shelter. Bertha busied herself laying in provisions for the family.

Servants brought down straw mats for sleeping, plates, cups and other utensils for eating, and buckets of water.

Ruth and Anne fixed up a private corner for Mary Elizabeth, stocking it with every necessity in the event she should give birth during the storm. Mary sank her heavy body into a mound of counterpanes: pillows fluffed around her. She thought about complaining but there was no one to complain to. Everyone was moving in and out too quickly, trying to make a suitable home out of the cellar room.

The last thing she had wanted to do today was leave her comfortable upstairs bed. Mary Elizabeth had occupied John Sommerwood's room since the night Esther had died in her bed. It was spacious and airy and commanded a majestic view of the mountains. The sturdiness of her grandfather's furnishings lent a warmth and stability to her life with Matt. Her child had been conceived in John's oversized four poster. She had hoped the baby would be born in it.

Mary's hand slid off the pillow onto a small, smooth, round object resting on the floor. It was cold to her touch. She picked it up to look at it. Her thumb rubbed the greasy dirt away to reveal the blue-black glass of a marble, one she and Esther used to play with as children. She felt along the floor for others, but there were none within her reach. She and Esther had come here as children to escape Sarah. She thought it odd that this particular agate should have been left behind. It was one of Esther's favorites. Polishing the stone on the comforter, Mary held it up to the candlelight. The black glass threw a tiny spot of the most brilliant blue onto her hand. The blue dot seemed to hide under the curved edge of the ball and was encircled by the dark shadow cast by the marble. Following the blue dot into the shadow, she drifted off to sleep.

Sang discharged his men to look after their own houses and supervised the boarding up of Sommerwood Settlement. The inhabitants were removed to a provision cellar in one of the larger outbuildings. Firewood, food and other supplies were laid in. Lusen was nowhere in sight. Sang dismissed his concern, thinking Lusen might be helping Baldwin and Matt in the fields as they worked a crew in the rain to secure the cattle in pens.

"We'll lose all our young plants if these winds don't let up," Baldwin shouted through the rain at Matt.

"Old Sam told me two days ago a hurricane was coming," Matt replied.

"Now, how does he know that? The skies were clear two days ago."

"Said he could smell it. Also said the sky had a yellow look to it."

"A yellow look?"

"That's what he said."

"Well, come on then. Let's see that the horses have enough food and water." Although Baldwin had been raising his voice louder and louder, his words died in a rushing of rain and wind. The weather worsened. There was nothing to do but ride it out.

Lusen dragged a piece of canvas and a length of rope up the mountain. He fashioned a makeshift tent out of the sailcloth in the shelter of a large banyan and huddled with his family inside it. The wind howled and tore through the trees. Large pieces of brush flew past them, heavy limbs crashed down about them. The sailcloth flapped and shredded until the pieces finally blew away. The bamboo slapped and creaked and whipped about.

Lusen spotted the hollowed out stump of a cottonwood

tree, dragged a reluctant Afiba toward it, and put her inside where she crouched gripping the baby in her arms. Shaking his head and waving his arms Lusen tried to tell the frightened woman that the spirits had left this tree. "Gone! Gone!" he screamed above the wind. She read his lips and smiled, partly believing him, but mostly because he looked so ridiculous flapping his arms about. He kissed her hands which clutched the baby, and tied the rope around the stump to hold it together in case part of it should crack off. What they would do should the stump be uprooted or if a heavy branch should fall on it, he did not know.

With the baby sandwiched between them, Lusen and Afiba crouched in the hollow of the tree and waited. A tree crashed nearby. From time to time Lusen pitched into the wind a bush which had been swept into their shelter. Then came a stillness even more frightening in contrast to the thundering wind.

"It ober?" she whispered.

Little Quaco whimpered his discomfort at being squeezed between them.

"No. Ole Sam tol' me dis quiet cum, it las' only few minutes, den da win' start 'gain. I can't let you go back ta da village alone, an' I can't go wid you, but you can cum wid me. House strong. Baby be safe dere. Please. It da only way I know you be safe—wid me."

He cut away the rope, stood up, moved the twigs away, and stretched out his hand to her. She hesitated. "Quaco tree mus' stay wid him. We take?"

"No time now. I cum back."

Afiba realized that if she was going to put her old life behind to take up a new, she must do it now. The baby reached out his tiny hand and grasped his father's outstretched finger. Afiba stood up and followed them down the mountain.

It was because of the silence that Mary Elizabeth's scream startled everyone in the cellar room. Matt stood up shaken. Baldwin reached up and took his hand, and the boy sat back down again. The baby was coming and his assistance was not needed now. Ruth and Anne rushed to the makeshift bed.

"She's here! She's here!" Mary screamed.

"Try calm yo'se'f, Mary."

Anne lifted off the coverlet to receive the baby.

"No. Not the baby, Esther. I felt her hand on my arm."

Ruth slid her hand off Mary's shoulder and sat back on her heels amazed.

"Her touch was not cold but warm and reassuring. I think she was trying to tell me that everything ... everything would be ... all right ... oh ... it begins."

"Mary, do you have pain now?"

"I think so, Mama."

"It's okay, lie back."

"Don't worry Mama, I will do fine."

"I know you will, dearest." Anne unclenched her daughter's fist and found a black marble in it. Taking it, Anne noticed that the object was cold. She thought that odd because it had been clenched in Mary's warm hand for such a long time. Anne set the marble on the box they were using for a night stand, took up one of the oriental screens, opened it, and placed it near the head of the bed. Matt came to help.

"Is she all right?"

"Yes, she's fine, said so herself. That's a good sign."

"I'm scared to death."

"I know."

"Matt, you heard her just now?" He nodded. "Tell me, has she felt Esther's presence before?"

"Not often, but sometimes, she would wake in the night thinking she felt Esther's cold hand on her arm. She told me she had been awakened the night of Esther's suicide because she felt something cold on her arm. It was Esther's hand holding her forearm." Mary Elizabeth groaned. "Can I do anything to help?"

"Just put up these screens. I'll see to the fire."

"Aye."

Anne went to Baldwin, who was stoking the fire.

"The wind howled the night you delivered Mary Elizabeth." Baldwin took Anne's hand in his and kissed it tenderly. "We're going to have a grandchild soon. How does that make you feel, old woman?"

"More in love with you than ever, if that is possible." She kissed each of his fingertips before placing his hand to her cheek.

Lingering before placing the last screen, Matt watched Mary Elizabeth. Ruth pressed cold cloths to her forehead. She looked so pale and fragile lying there. He wondered how she would ever endure the rigors of childbirth. A pain struck her and he clutched the screen, almost cracking it in his powerful hands. Ruth pushed the blankets aside. Mary's body heaved, she gasped for air. Ruth lifted Mary's gown and applied a gentle rhythmic stroke to the girl's distended belly, softly urging her not to fight the pain.

"I love you," he whispered. He must have spoken out loud, for Ruth gasped and looked up at him. She sprang to her feet and took the screen from his hands.

"Go on, git. Dis no place fo' you. Fetch Miz Anne, her I need, you I don'."

He knew she was not angry. That was just the way Ruth spoke to all her children. Anne kissed Baldwin and touched Matt's arm reassuringly as she passed by him.

The storm grew violent once again. Baldwin checked for flooding. Everything seemed secure. Mary's screams tore in and out of the roaring wind. Matt listened to the sounds. He was an observer at nature's contest, one physical, the other elemental. It seemed to him that the wind matched Mary stroke for stroke. She'd gasp, the wind would halt; she'd moan, it would wail. This contention went on for hours.

Matt bared his raw nerves. "How long can she keep this up?"

"All night,' replied Baldwin. He had some knowledge of this kind of waiting. "It took eighteen hours with Will . . ." This had been the first time he had spoken his son's name in over a year and it startled him. Matt endeavored to change the subject, both for his sake and Baldwin's.

"And the storm? How long before it passes?"

"Hours, days. There is no telling with storms or women."

The incessant howling of the wind fell into intermittent gusts about midnight. Mary kept on. Anne came out to allay all fears. Yes, the baby was still alive. It was taking its own time, that's all. Then she immediately went back to her daughter's side.

"Mama."

"I'm here, Mary." Anne took Mary's hand in her own.

"God, it's taking so long. I don't think I can keep this up much longer."

"You can, Mary, I know you can."

"Help me, Mama." Anne squeezed Mary's hand as another pain came, lingered for a moment and went away. "I'm afraid, Mama. I'm such a coward."

"You're no coward, Mary Elizabeth. The rigors of childbirth would tax the endurance of an Amazon."

In and out of a sea of stabbing pains, Ruth's soft voice calmed Mary and Anne's gave her strength.

Around three o'clock, a tiny hand appeared. Anne held her daughter while Ruth began to guide the baby's arms and head through the passage. The earth began to rumble and shake beneath them. Jars and bottles rattled from the table. The screens fell. Matt and Baldwin caught them and laid them on the floor.

Anne, holding a fallen screen with one arm, issued further orders to the two men. "It's an earthquake! Matt, Baldwin, douse those lamps before the glass breaks and fires start up. Light candles and bring them here. Ruth can't see what she's doing. Hurry!"

Standing at the foot of the bed, holding one candle in each hand, Matt saw his daughter come into the world.

When the earth stopped shaking, Ruth took the child to bathe it. Anne ministered to Mary Elizabeth. Needed no more, the two men holding the candles were dismissed by the busy women. Baldwin lit the lanterns again and stoked the fire.

Matt sat in dazed wonder. He had a child, a daughter, and he had seen her being born. How lucky he was. How happy he was.

Anne called him to his wife. He planted exuberant, grateful kisses all over her wet face and hair. "You're wonderful, you know that. Wonderful! And I love you. I love you, you hear me, I love you!" Mary was too weak to respond.

Sang came to the door. "Safe ta cum out now, Massa Baldwin. I open da house. You all can go back." After a moment's silence he asked, "Eb'ryting all right here?"

"Everything is wonderful here!" shouted Matt. And as if suddenly imbued with the strength of ten men, he lifted Mary Elizabeth into his arms and carried her up to their room. Baldwin folded his arms around Anne holding the baby. He kissed Anne's forehead and they went into the house.

Ruth began to gather up the bed linen.

Sang finally spoke. "Ruth, you all right?"

"Jus' tired is all."

"She's here, Ruth."

"What?"

"She's here. The girl from da mountain."

"You mean Lusen . . ."

"Yes, dey both here . . . an' day hab a boy baby."

Ruth did not know what to think about these new events, but the joy she felt at the news pumped new energy into her weary body.

"What we do now, Ruth?"

She took her husband's hand. "We go home. I want see our grannie."

"Den what?"

"I don' know. We tink o' someting. We all safe. dat what matter now."

A thought crept uninvited into his mind. Safe. For how

long? He wondered.

The earthquake destroyed Port Royal as it had on June 7, 1692, the night Mary Read was born in London. Mary had told Anne that she thought it strange that she should hang at the very place destroyed the night she was born. She prayed the ground would roll beneath the scaffold and the earth would open up to swallow it and her shame. Anne wondered if there was any special portent in the fact that Mary's granddaughter was born during an earthquake. What did fate intend for little Maura? Anne prayed their granddaughter would not share the ignominious destiny of Mary Read. Anne would have to secure the best possible future for the girl.

The Sommerwood plantation had suffered damage to its crops and outbuildings. Only a week had passed since the hurricane and it would be some time before the plantation would settle back into its easy routine. Meanwhile carpenters busily repaired shutters on Hill Haven, and penkeepers mended their fences.

One day, by mutual decision, Lusen and Matt traded jobs. Lusen went with Baldwin to work with the field gangs. Matt learned the complexities of supervising the cattleboys, the mulemen and the hogmeat gangs. Now that he had a family to work for, his energy seemed inexhaustible.

He galloped after a stray calf. "I have a family," he shouted. He could hardly believe it. "A beautiful baby girl." Matt drove the calf back to the herd.

"Ho, boy!" Sang reined in his horse. "Matt, rest a minute."

Matt fell in alongside him. "What is it, Sang? Am I doing something wrong?"

"No, Matt. I'm gettin' too ole to dribe dese cattle so hard. Some o' dem ole too prob'ly. Boy, how yo' work so hard an' keep a smile on yo' face?"

"I have a daughter." His tanned face beamed and his smile broadened.

"What you all decide ta call dat girl?"

"Maura."

"Is she pretty like her mama?"

"Not yet, but she will be. She looks like a wrinkled old man now."

Sang thought about his new grandson, and for the first time he smiled.

The hurricane had beaten down several houses in New Nanny Town and the earthquake shook the mountain, damaging crops. Nanny and Yamou had braved the storm in search of Afiba. During the worst part of it, Nanny had to lash Yamou to a tree to prevent his being swept off the mountain. The earth felt like surging waves beneath her feet and she feared that it would open up and swallow them both. Then the howling wind blasted a message into her ears. "Afiba an' baby Quaco safe. Win' no carry dem off mountain, plantation boy carry dem off." And like a stab, more hurtful than any knife, Nanny realized that Afiba had gone of her own will. Her eyes clouded and the winds and rains subsided.

Once order had been restored in her village, Nanny raised the abeng to her lips and summoned a war council. Ryna, a welcome guest at the village since the birth of Afiba's baby, was to be privy to her plans. But, she was too despondent to leave the small grave of her baby and did not come at the first sounding of the abeng. Her little girl had been injured in the storm and had died this very day. Nanny came to her.

"Womon, what you do fo' dis chil' now? You no bring her back."

"She firs' baby, Nanny, sweet baby. I sad. Ryna no he'p dat."

"You cry here all day? Nanny need you at war council. You strong womon. You hab mo' babies. You soldier now. Time cum you be womon 'gain."

Reluctantly, but at Nanny's insistence, Ryna attended the council. Yamou sat at Nanny's right. Her need to organize infiltrators on the plantations to stir up rebellion was the major part of her plan. This would take months. They would need many more guns. Caleb Foote and the boy with the withered arm would provide for them one last time. Then she would kill them both. She addressed her warriors, inspiring them with her confidence.

"Dis time Windward Maroons win war. Strike all plantation in de East an' burn dem out. No mo' planters in Jamaica. Soon Maroons rule dis island!"

Great shouts rose up.

Nanny thrust her hand into the air, palm front, fingers spread. "Yamou, I make colonel, here, now. He lead you. He hab great cause. Plantation people steal he sister, our princess. Eb'ry white mon, womon an' chil' pay fo' dat!"

Cries of war turned to chanting and dancing. Nanny watched with approving eyes. "I be revenged on you debil womon. I be revenged on you datter fo' datter." As the drums beat faster and faster, Nanny's eyes directed the frenzy into the mind of her enemy.

Anne woke with a start, sat upright and clasped her hands over her ears to stop the drumming riot in her head. Maroons? As she moved to get out of bed her hand touched cold metal. She removed the sheet to see what it was. Win's wedding ring. Why is it here? Where is he? A sudden foreboding struck her. She shook out her fears with the shaking of her dressing gown. It must be late and he's gone out. Why did he leave this behind? Anne put the ring on her forefinger and quickly dressed. His ring must have slipped off. Yes, he has lost weight since his heart attack. That's it. More at ease now and her dream forgotten, Anne went to check on Mary Elizabeth and the baby. Then she would go out in search of her husband.

It had been two weeks since the hurricane and Anne and Ruth decided it was time to tend to some gardening. The grasscutters had cleared away much of the debris left in the wake of the storm. They had also pruned the fruit and flowering trees. The grounds flourished. Only one place required their caring hands, and it was the last place either one of them wanted to go. No one had been to the garden house since that dreadful night. It had been padlocked.

"Ruth, have you the key to the garden house?"

"No, Miz Anne, it on da head grasscutter's ring."

"Shall we go find him, then?" Anne put the question to Ruth and waited.

Ruth searched Anne's eyes for the answer. Esther had been her loss. Anne had lost her son. Although he lived, he was as good as dead to her. Almost two years had passed, and these two women who worked side by side each day and had so often shared their thoughts, had never once spoken of what grieved them the most.

Ruth pondered. Anne had supervised the cleaning of Mary Elizabeth's old room because she would not go near it. The least she could do was to help Anne clear out the garden house since the lady seemed determined to do it.

Finally Ruth spoke. "I tink da grasscutters in da bamboo walk today."

Anne reached out her hand to Ruth who took it. "Let's go there then, shall we?"

After securing the key, Anne stopped by a clump of dead bamboo. "Ruth did you see this when it was in bloom?"

"Aye, Missus. I neber see bamboo flower before. Grasscutter say dat take t'irty year or mo' an' happen only once. Den bamboo bear fruit, den it die."

"Flowers once and dies?"

"Dese young shoots hab grown big dis pas' year."

"Aye."

The rusty padlock finally opened after both women, in turn, attacked it. Cobwebs blocked the entrance. Flailing arms cut through the sticky, stringy mess.

Looking about, Anne determined that parts of the thatch had fallen in long before the hurricane, but the rest of the roof had been carried away by the storm. Ferns had taken over, but the plants looked green and healthy from the recent rains. The wild orchids were thriving; they had rooted even in the floor.

"Dese cushions no good." The material on the wicker chairs and lounges had rotted in several places. The vengeance with which Ruth tossed them out of the garden house did not escape Anne's notice.

First Anne carried out the larger pieces of fallen thatch, then she began to rake up the small debris. Leaves, bits of broken lattice, a rum bottle, odd-shaped pieces of candle wax covered the dirt floor.

The trash pile outside grew. Ruth saw that several limbs of the banyan had broken off in the storm. Any one of them could have crashed through the house but none had. She would get the grasscutters over here tomorrow to clear the limbs away.

Something caught her eye as she swept a few stray objects onto the pile of trash. Kneeling, she rummaged under the leaves and dirt and pulled a remnant of crochet work, soiled now, but once multicolored and delicately stitched. Brushing a tear away, Ruth buried it deep within the pile and with quick, strong movements raked more and more leaves onto the heap. She did not stop until her aching arms refused to move. When she went inside again, Anne was resting on the bench.

"Come, Ruth. Sit a minute."

Ruth picked up the small water jug she had brought along, sat down and handed it to Anne.

"No, you first, please. I need to catch my breath a minute. You know the place is looking better already and we haven't worked an hour yet. She looked around the room. Why it almost looks . . ."

The tears came at last and, although she tried, Ruth could not stop them. Finally she buried her head in one hand as Anne took her other hand. For a long time she could not speak. She had never sobbed this way before. "I sorry. I t'ought I could do dis."

"Do you hate my son, Ruth? You have every right."

"I did fo' long time. Me an' Sang we fight almos' like we hate each odder. Fo' long time we no talk. Den we talk

an' say 'dis no good, way we act hurt only each odder
—drive Sarah out da house and make Lusen go into hisse'f.
We better now. No mo' angry, but I still hurt when I tink
o' Esther."

Anne dropped her head. "How is it . . . why is it,
children bring the most intense grief we can ever know."

"Some joy too, I 'spect." Ruth dried her eyes with her
apron and retied her kerchief around her head.

"Of course, yes. One mustn't forget the joy, but the
sorrow one can never forget. The joys are intermittent and
fleeting at best. The sorrows freshen with every passing
day."

"And yesterday, Missus? When you see Lusen's baby,
dat fresh grief?"

"Aye. I didn't mean to frighten the little boy. I should
have realized the baby had never seen a white face before,
let alone . . ."

"I never see you cry like dat, Miz Anne. You hug dat
baby and sob yo' heart out. I wonner, Missus. What is it?
Who you see in dat boy? Mebbe you tell Ruth. Him sweet
baby. No cry when you pick him up. He only cry when
you cry. He watch yo' face, like he want ta stop tears . . .
like he say someting ta you wid his touch."

"Long ago, I had a son who died, when he was about the
same age as Little Quaco. He looked very much like him."

"His doddy dat African you tell me 'bout?"

"Yes."

"We lived on an island with his family. One day
Spanish raiders came, and . . . murdered my boy, and his
father. They killed everyone, except me. I was working in a
field far from the settlement."

"What you do den, Missus?"

"I . . . killed them all."

Ruth gasped. "I sorry, Miz Anne. It hard fo' me ta tink
you kill anybody—you kind loving womon. Dis not easy
fo' Ruth ta believe, eben dough . . ."

"It's easy to kill, if you have cause. What's hard is to
live with the hurt."

A tall, striking, Ashanti woman appeared in the doorway of the garden house. She carried a large basket on her bejeweled arm and she waited for the women to look her way. Ruth recognized her as the woman she had seen in the Kingston market that day, long ago.

"Goodday, my ladies."

"Goodday," said Ruth.

Anne was drawn out of her grim reverie by the melodious quality of the woman's voice. "Goodday."

"My name is Ryna. I work da markets o' Kingston, sell all pretty tings. Only market gone now. Big win' cum an' carry 'way quay. Shaking eart', many buildin's crumble. Ole Harbour, she swept 'way. Many people hurt, my datter, too. She die las' night."

Anne started to interrupt the woman, but Ryna ran on ahead of her.

"I be tol' you hab need o' wet nurse. I be bery good midwife, too."

Ruth looked at Anne's startled expression. As far as she knew, Mary's milk was good.

Anne stood up, but didn't speak. She was too stunned. Just this morning Mary had complained that she felt her breasts drying. Anne had thought to wait until the baby's noon feeding, and observe the situation herself, before telling Ruth to look for a wet nurse in the settlement. No one knew of this, other than herself and Mary Elizabeth; and Mary was still confined to her room.

"Who told you this?" Anne demanded.

"De girl on de road. One o' de slabe girls, I 'spect. De same lovely girl who tol' me I fine you here."

Ruth stood up beside her mistress. No one besides the grasscutter knew they were at this place.

"And this girl's name?" asked Anne, hoping to solve this mystery once and for all.

"Why, she don' gibe me her name, Missus, but she 'bout your height an' color," she said indicating Ruth. "An' she wear a lovely blue dress wid green at da hem and trim wid white lace."

CHAPTER ELEVEN

"Imparadised in One Another's Arms, The Happier Eden . . ."
—*Paradise Lost* IV. 506-7

The year turned.

Ryna had been employed five months as wet nurse for Maura. Anne admired the woman's quiet dignity, and the gentle loving way she cared for her granddaughter. Above all Maura liked her. The baby was fascinated by the woman's jewelry. She loved to bite on her bracelets, pull her neck chains, and tug on her earrings. Ryna talked and played with the baby for hours. Mary Elizabeth, again with child, was grateful, not only for Ryna's help with Maura, but for saving the life of the baby growing within her.

Several weeks past, Mary had begun to bleed. In the dead of night Anne had sent Matt to fetch Ryna who had taken residence in Ruth's old hut in the settlement.

After propping up Mary's legs on several bolsters, Anne concentrated her efforts on quieting her frightened daughter.

"You must stop crying, Mary."

"Mama, I'm so scared. I don't want to lose this baby."

"Crying won't help. It only makes matters worse. You must try and calm yourself."

"I wish I had your courage."

"You overemphasize my courage, Mary. You have your own kind of bravery. You'll find it. Courage comes when you need it."

"I try to be brave like you."

"My courage has yet to be tested, yours too. Here, lie back in my arms, that should help."

Anne talked softly and soon Mary relaxed the wrenching grip she had on Anne's hand. "Put out all thoughts of losing the baby. Ryna is coming. She is on her way right now. She will know what to do."

The woman answered her door, dressed in a long full robe.

"Ryna, you must come to Mary Elizabeth, quickly!"

"What hoppen to de girl?"

Although distraught Matt was too embarrassed to speak. "She . . . she . . ."

"Well, tell me, boy. I mus' know what ta bring. Dis no time fo' foolishness."

"She . . . bleeds."

Ryna carefully brought down certain bottles and jars from the shelf. She was particularly selective about the leaves she would take along.

"Hurry, please!"

"Boy, calm you'se'f," she said sharply. "You no want Ryna make mistake, bring wrong ting?"

Matt took a deep breath. "Forgive me."

Ryna placed all the medicines along with a small bowl and grinding stone in a basket. She quickly wrapped a cloth around her head and closed the door behind her.

Once she was in the carriage, Matt had control. He flicked his whip and the horses raced to the house. He took the stairs three at a time and was standing in the bedroom a full minute before Ryna appeared in the doorway. Maura began to cry. Anne started to get up.

"No, stay, I'll get her," Matt said.

"An' please ta stay in da nex' room wid de baby." Ryna said softly but firmly.

"Yes, of course. I will." Matt was gone in a flash.

Ryna selected several leaves from her basket and began to grind them. "Miz Anne, can you bring me boilin' water in a cup please?"

"Aye."

Since it was February and Mary Elizabeth had felt a

chill earlier in the evening, Matt had built a fire. Anne filled the kettle and hung it in the fireplace over the dwindling log. She poked the log.

By the time the water boiled, Ryna had finished preparing the mixture of herbs. She placed three spoonfuls in the cup of boiling water and stirred for a long time. "Drink dis down, all o' it."

Mary sat up and choking on the first swallow of the bitter-tasting tea, she stretched the cup toward Ryna who pushed it back.

"All o' it. Eb'ry drop I say."

Anne held the cup and Mary forced down the brew.

"Good girl, an' keep it down too."

"Do you think she'll be all right now?" asked Anne.

"Soon. We know bery soon. You hab fresh rags?"

"Aye." Anne brought the rags. Leaving Mary Elizabeth in Ryna's capable hands, she went to see how Matt was doing with the baby. He was bouncing around in one spot, holding the baby next to his chest.

"Funny little dance you're doing."

"Maura likes it. Don't you, little girl?"

The baby gurgled and grabbed one of his fingers to chew.

Anne settled wearily into the rocking chair.

"How's Mary? Is she better now?"

"We'll know soon." Anne pressed two fingers to her closed eyelids.

"I knew she'd be all right once I got Ryna to the house."

"Her confidence disturbs you, does it?"

"I should say so. Damned infuriating sometimes." He bounced closer to Anne and said. "That robe Ryna is wearing, striped and tentlike, does it look familiar to you?"

"I really hadn't noticed."

"That night in Nanny Town, I took one like it off a dead Maroon woman and wrapped you in it. Are they African, do you think?"

"I've seen women in the village wearing similar

garments. Does that worry you?"

"Somewhat. I can't place my fear. She is so good and loving with our daughter. And Mary Elizabeth has grown quite attached to the woman. I guess it's nothing really."

Anne lifted herself from the chair. "I'll go see how Mary is doing." She gave the baby's fat little leg a squeeze and kissed Matt on the cheek. "Don't worry, Papa."

"Tell me when I can come in and see her?"

"I will."

The bleeding had stopped. Matt thanked Ryna profusely. She received his thanks graciously as she did all things. Rather than have Matt take her home, Ryna decided to sleep in the next room with Maura. It was getting close to her feeding time anyway. As she closed the door of the bedroom, she instructed Matt to call her if Mary experienced any discomfort.

He thanked her again. Matt decided to sleep in his clothes, just in case there was an emergency. Lying down, he kissed the hand of his sleeping wife. She smiled and woke.

"Sleep, Mary. I didn't mean to wake you."

"You didn't wake me; I've been waiting for you. You know I can't sleep without you by my side."

"You frightened me tonight."

"I frightened myself."

"I don't know how I could live without you."

"Nor I you. I saw you tonight in my mind's eye. My black knight riding out into the night to fetch help for his princess. You raised your whip, didn't you? A thing you rarely do."

"Am I so transparent?"

"No. I love you. I can't love you unless I know you."

"You know me too well already, and we have a lifetime of discoveries to make."

"Then you'll have to create dark mysteries for me to uncover."

"But you, no more surprises like tonight. I don't need that kind of excitement in my life."

"Some black knight, you are."

Mary whispered drowsily and fell asleep in Matt's arms.

Baldwin was standing on the gallery when Anne returned to their room.

"It's cold out here, Win. You'll catch your death."

Taking her hand, he closed the louvers and crawled under the counterpane. "Is Mary all right now?"

"Yes, Ryna gave her something."

"I had to leave. The blood frightened me, Annie. I don't know why."

"It doesn't matter, Win."

"I wasn't afraid for Mary, I knew she would be all right somehow. I was afraid for myself."

Anne took him in her arms and held his head against her bosom. Soothed by the rhythm of her breathing, Baldwin fell asleep.

Lying in Sarah's arms the young lieutenant at Fort Morant revealed the place and time of the arms' shipment as easily as a young boy runs to tell his mother his latest accomplishment. With this information, Caleb and William made arrangements with unscrupulous officers to buy arms. Cannon and muskets would be safely lodged at New Nanny Town within a fortnight and the Windward Maroons would be ready to launch an attack of staggering proportions. Had Sarah known that the lives of the white inhabitants of eastern Jamaica lay in her hands, she might have kept the information to herself, but she did not know about the evil plan afoot. Her revenge centered on one man. She did not, and would not, think or see beyond her personal plot for vengeance.

The thought had entered her mind as she watched William and Caleb bend close in consultation that having now given William the information he wanted, his interest in her would fade. At that moment he looked up at her and smiled almost softly. Oh, no, she thought. He mine, all mine now. I must wait for da right time, and da proper place. And so, like a cunning warrior, Sarah beguiled her enemy, maneuvered him, confounded him, and waited.

She returned his smile, and he rose to join her. Arm in arm they climbed the tavern stairs as they had done every night during the past months. And every night William had pushed himself beyond the point of endurance to enjoy her. She did not love him, he knew that. Sarah could love no man. And it was not love he felt for her but a trust which gave him a kind of comfort he had never known.

Caleb Foote, leading a band of Maroon warriors, hauled the armaments up the mountain. Although he carried no guns, he huffed and groaned with each step. He occupied himself by turning over in his mind a plan to cheat his partner. William was to meet him later that night, after the celebrations, at a place where the path to the village veered off from the Negro River. There, at midnight, they would divide the prize.

Sarah had been promised a small share in the spoils. Caleb had a vessel ready at Port Royal. It would be an easy matter to leave the haunt an hour or two early, lure the girl away with gold and gems, board his vessel, and leave the island forever. 'Tis no great loss to leave this place, he thought to himself. After these Maroons initiate their plan, not one white man, woman or child will escape. I'd like to carry that sweet brown wench with me. The very thought heats my prick. Oh, to enjoy that Sarah. Money might do it, for she's a greedy wench. There's time yet to snatch her from him. The bastard itches for more of the profits with each new exploit. I trust these black devils more than him.

The conspiracy spread wide throughout the east, from St. Ann's and St. Mary's and Portland in the north, around Port Antonio, along the eastern shore, on in to the southern districts of St. Thomas and St. Andrew's.

Although Afiba and her baby were safe on the Sommerwood plantation, Ryna did not know it. Lusen had taken her directly to his father's house in the woods, where they had ridden out the remainder of the storm. Sam's hut had been leveled. Now he and Bertha lived there with Ruth and Sang. Lusen was building a house for his family nearby; as soon as it was completed, he would build one for his grandparents. Anne had been their only visitor, and Afiba soon learned that all secrets were safe with Mistress Anne.

Sitting at Nanny's council Ryna listened to the final details of the plot designed to kill every white man, woman, and child in the Windward districts of Jamaica. Infiltrators from other plantations were also in attendance. Ryna was glad when another woman asked the question burning in her mind, but one she could not put in words. "I be nurse ta white baby. Kill him too? Kill all babies?"

As leader of the raiding party, Yamou answered in a commanding voice. "Kill eb'ryone, eben babies."

Ryna waited for Nanny to contradict him. Surely Nanny, who loved little children, would not murder hundreds of innocent babies because they were not of her color.

Nanny remained silent.

Ryna kissed the earth, binding herself with the other conspirators, and drank gunpowder rum, a mixture containing human blood and grave dirt, the final seal to her lips and the brew to steel all hearts against the dangerous mission.

The council broke and moved to one of the dance pavilions located at the northwest end of the village. Caleb Foote joined the spectators. He had finished instructing Yamou's select corps in the use of the armaments. After the entertainment and celebrations Nanny would pay him a handsome reward for his labors.

Caleb swilled rum, watched the mock fights, and waited. Naked men brandishing sharp spears and shields of plaited palm rolled on the ground as if on fire. Deftly they shifted positions, leaped, and twisted in the air to dodge the thrusting spears. At first the fury in their looks startled him, but then the force and sweep of their antic gestures began to blur in front of his eyes. Jumping dances followed the mock fights. Indefatigable athletes flipped and tumbled in the air.

Yamou tied a goat to a stake in the center of the dance pavilion. He danced alone, around the goat, to the steady rhythm of the drums. Obeah men from among the conspirators on the neighboring plantations spat raw rum into the ring. Yamou danced, rattles clattered as his feet pounded the earth. His sharp knife flashed in and out of the moon's brilliance. The crowd chanted.

Standing very near Caleb Foote, Yamou let out a bloodcurdling shriek, flew past Caleb and shot to the top of a coconut tree. Sober now, Caleb moved to the outer edges of the crowd. Singers encircled him. The drums beat louder and faster as Yamou slid back down the tree and danced back into the circle. Caleb tried to laugh and break into the ring of people to dance with them. Each time they spun him back into the middle and left him there alone with Yamou. They locked hands and danced around him. In his panic Caleb whirled about looking for a weak link in the circle, a means of escape. The goat ran around the pole, twisting his rope shorter and shorter. Yamou danced closer to the animal. Drums beat wildly. Yamou's feet stopped moving; he rose into the air. The cries of the people surrounding Caleb, the goat and Yamou swelled. Drums ceased. Knives flashed.

Silence prevailed while obeah men studied the two sets of entrails, looking for a sign which might spell the success of their raid.

William Thomas had no difficulty finding the path. Except for a few clouds, the night was clear, the moon full and bright. With Sarah, he waited at the designated spot till long past midnight. He didn't wonder when Caleb was late. Double-dealing was second nature to Caleb Foote.

"Wait here, Sarah." William drew out his pistol and started up the path to the Maroon village.

"You no 'fraid ta go up dere?"

"I fear I've been cheated, that's all I fear."

Pushing branches aside with his pistol, William made his way up the narrow mountain access to New Nanny Town. He had gone only a few yards when he tripped over what seemed to be a man's booted foot. Just then a cloud passed over the moon shielding its light. The moon emerged and William was drawn into the gaping eyes of Caleb Foote. The man's head was entwined in his bowels.

Momentarily transfixed by horror, William's feet seemed rooted where he stood. Suddenly he found himself beating down the path; branches whipped at his face and arm.

Rushing past Sarah, he called out to her to follow him down the slope and out across an open field until they collapsed on a bed of leaves in the woods beyond. Gasping for air, William looked around. He had no idea where he was.

Sarah pulled him to her. Although she did not know this place she felt secluded. Now was the time. Wrapping her arms around him she would hide him from the world. The butt of his weapon dug into her chest. Once his breathing slowed he allowed her to take the gun from his hand. She laid it and his dagger beside her within reach of her right hand. She wiped his brow and carressed his hair as her tongue probed his mouth distracting his mind from fearful thoughts.

The feel of her soft breasts reassured him, and the touch of her hand on his face wiped the lingering horror of what he had just seen from his mind. Nothing remained but this shrouded place, this quiet moment, and Sarah, his lovely Sarah.

He never thought of love. But now this moment holding her a feeling never before experienced swelled in his breast and warmed him. Safe in her arms he was a boy again and wished he had two arms to love her better. Would that this ecstasy could last forever.

He slipped inside her.

His gentleness disarmed her. Sarah whipped herself into

a passion, hoping lust would drive out any shred of love. As their excitement mounted, Sarah bit her hand. Her cry was swallowed up in the sounds of love. The taste of blood steeled her resolve. She felt him approach his height. In that instant of oblivion, she put the gun to his side and pulled the trigger.

His release flooded her belly.

William fought for consciousness as his groping hand found the knife. He lifted his body enough to plunge it into her breast. A surprised gasp escaped her. Sarah's chest heaved and her arms reached around him, coupling him to her bosom. Their spirits mingled and departed.

At four o'clock the morning of the uprising, Ryna gave Maura her breast. The baby sucked hungrily as Ryna wiped the tears from Maura's face. I no let dis sweet baby die hungry, she thought. How Ryna watch dem put knife in dis baby? I no can. Dis baby be like my own—I lose mine; now get Maura. An' dese people so kind to Ryna, treat all dere people good. Ryna no kill dese white folk.

Maura bellowed when Ryna pulled herself away and put her in her cradle. Closing her dress, she pounded on the door of the adjoining room. Matt answered.

"What is it? The baby sick? Why is she crying?"

Mary Elizabeth staggered in sleepily, picked up Maura and rocked her. "What is it, little one? You sick? Is she ill, Ryna?"

"No, baby fine for now, not for long."

"What do you mean?" Matt grabbed her shoulder. "Woman, what are you talking about?"

"We bes' fetch Miz Anne and Massa Baldwin. Den Ryna tell—Ryna tell eb'ryting."

The Maroons were to attack at dawn—less than two hours. Anne watched Baldwin's left thumb turning his gold wedding band around his finger as he formulated a plan. His main concern was for Mary Elizabeth and the baby.

"The old step-down well is the best hiding place," said

Matt.

"Take them there, then. Ryna, can you shoot?"

"I can if I mus'."

"Take this musket and cutlass."

"Anne, ride out to Sang." Baldwin looked at the baby, then at Matt. "I'll ride out to warn the other planters."

"No, Baldwin, I'll go." Matt slung the baldric with his mother's sword over his shoulder and collected three pistols from various places in the room.

"You will not. You and Lusen will position our men and defend this place."

There was a moment of silence in which Mary prayed Matt would not insist. The mission was much too dangerous. Matt stuck the three pistols in the brace across his chest, looked at Anne and nodded his consent to Baldwin.

"Anne, tell Lusen to meet Matt at the settlement. Sang should go with all speed to the fort, then warn the village. Ruth will be safer at home. You can warn Peter and the colonel. I'll ride toward Morant Point."

Anne rushed to embrace him; she did not want to let him go. The memory of a hundred foreboding dreams flared in her mind.

"We must hurry, Annie." They kissed again. When they pulled apart, Baldwin's ring slipped off into Anne's hand. She put it back on his finger. In turn they embraced Matt, Mary Elizabeth, and baby Maura, and were gone.

Matt took the women to the well, loaded a musket and placed it in Ryna's hands and gave a pistol to Mary. His hand touched the cold damp stone and a memory of a night twelve years past flashed through him. He embraced his wife, holding her as he did that night. "I'll be back."

"Please, soon."

"Soon, Mary. I won't come here, but I'll be outside, nearby where I can watch this place. Keep the baby quiet. I love you." He turned to Ryna. "Use that gun if you have to."

"I watch out for dem. You no worry."

Matt loaded a wagon with muskets, pistols, and cutlasses, and rode out to the settlement. Lusen arrived shortly after. Armed men were stationed at the settlement, around Hill Haven, near the stables, and outbuildings. Women loaded buckets of water onto carts and drove them out to these locations. If the Maroons burned the cane fields nothing could be done, but Matt hoped the buildings could be saved.

A little before dawn Sang rode with all haste to Fort Morant. Anne had some difficulty convincing Ruth to stay at home.

"Mary and little Maura will be safe."

"Safe wid dat womon!"

"She warned us, didn't she? She didn't have to do that, Ruth. She could have let us all be murdered in our beds."

"Oh, dear Lord!"

"Ruth, listen. I must go. Sang has weapons here. Assemble in one house, and arm yourselves. Please, I love you. Stay here and protect your family. I must warn the others."

"Miz Anne, be careful out dere. Cum back ta us."

"I will. Don't worry."

Anne warned the colonel, then rode under the lip of the mountain across to White Hall. As she approached Peter's plantation she rode past rows and rows of coffee plants whose berries hung bright red from the limbs of the shrubs. She had encountered no one on the way and hoped Baldwin had been as fortunate.

The first orange-red threads of dawn broke through the fog. It would be too dangerous to return to Hill Haven now. Peter insisted she wait with him until a detail of soldiers arrived to escort her back.

"Baldwin will do the same," he said. "He'll stop with Paterson or Winter or one of the other planters near the Point."

"Oh, God, I hope so. I'm scared, Peter."

"I know, so am I. God knows who among my slaves I can trust. Come. Let's remove to a safer place."

Baldwin left Paterson's and was in the vicinity of Point Morant heading for home. The general alarm had been sounded and through a network of planters word would eventually reach Portland. Too late, he thought. News would come too late to save those people.

His bay hesitated to gallop along the narrow road in the fog. Baldwin urged him on. Nearing Winter's plantation, a thought to stop there struck him, but he dismissed it and rode on. He wanted to go home.

Two Maroon men dropped out of a tree on top of him, knocking him off his horse. Baldwin managed to get off a shot, killing one man. He drew his sword and killed the other, but there were others. He fought desperately but was finally overtaken by plantation slaves, men abused to the point of revolt by Robert Winter and his sadistic overseer. A shirtless man, his chest a mass of thick scars, took his only weapon, a giant meat hook, and drove it into the soft flesh of Baldwin's stomach and hooked him by the ribs like a slab of beef, then hung him in a tree. His limp body swung on the hook for a time. His eyes arced past men, some of whom he recognized, had even spoken a friendly word to in the past. Finally the smoke from the fire they had built around the tree clouded his eyes. Life ebbed slowly. He thought of Anne. He saw her wrestling for the emerald ring and lying bespectacled on his chest reading the *Gazette*. She was smiling at him. Would he see his father? he wondered. He tried to remember what his mother looked like. Was that she coming toward him now, and who was that with her . . . ?

After alerting the fort and watching the details of soldiers ride out in every direction, Sang went to the village. He warned the town, then looked everywhere for Sarah. The seamstress had not seen her since yesterday morning. The tavern keeper told him he had seen her leave with William Thomas sometime before midnight. Young Sommerwood had not returned to his room all night. The man thought Sang might like to know that.

He waited at the tavern till well past midday. His daughter never returned. He wondered if she had gone willingly with William. The innkeeper spoke as though they were seen regularly in each other's company. How dat be? he argued with himself. How she keep company wid da mon who rape her sister? He'd just say Sarah ran off, left the island.

He walked outside. A sudden shower hit him. Through the driving rain he saw soldiers approach. They had a gang of prisoners, black men and women chained together, stumbling along the road in front of the cavalry. Townspeople followed them down to the wharf where ten of the ringleaders of the conspiracy were to be hanged. The uprising in St. Thomas had been put down. Sang tried to find out the extent of damage but could find no one who had been to the Sommerwood estate. One officer told him that the heaviest fighting in St. Thomas had been at the Winter plantation. Many people had been killed. Some of the Maroons had escaped. They had not received reports from Portland, Port Antonio and St. Ann's but expected wholesale slaughter in those places.

Sang followed the group to the wharf. The captives not ordered to be hanged were herded into a sloop and would be dispatched from the island as soon as sails could be set and anchor weighed. Ten were condemned to be executed. Sang's eyes went to a young Maroon with a scar running the length of his left thigh. He resembled Afiba.

A giant fig tree served as a gallows. Nine bodies dangled from the limbs at varying heights and cast ghastly shadows across the people gathered at the site. The last to hang was the young Maroon with the long scar on his leg. The instant he was hanged, it appeared to Sang, from the movement of the boy's legs, that he was climbing a tree. His legs continued to move in this manner even after his bloated and twisted face announced his death.

Robert Winter arrived at Hill Haven only moments after Sang. As she prepared tea, Ruth smiled at her husband, indicating that all was well at their home. Mary Elizabeth came down after helping Ryna put Maura to bed. Matt chatted excitedly with Mr. Winter about how lucky they all had been.

"Those bastards did not expect a show of arms. We fixed them. Only a few returned our fire. Where'd they get guns anyway?"

"I couldn't say, lad."

Anne knew by the distraction in his voice that Robert Winter had not come to Hill Haven for idle conversation.

The distressed man continued. "We are indebted to Mr. Sommerwood for saving our lives . . . I . . . Mistress . . ."

It was not until this moment that Sang noticed that Baldwin was not in the room. He was always quiet when the family gathered, watching from some corner and smiling. Sang searched Ruth's eyes for an explanation. None came.

Anne placed her teacup on the table and stood up. "You know why my husband hasn't returned, don't you, Robert?"

Mary Elizabeth took Matt's arm for support.

Sang looked at Winter's dark face and realized the secret about Sarah and William he had locked away could in no way compare with the news Winter was obliged to tell Anne at this moment.

Anne interrupted his stammering attempts to deliver his message. "The kindest thing would be to tell me quickly."

How could he tell her that her husband had been brutally murdered near his plantation by his people? Words failing him, Robert Winter reached into his pocket and pulled out a small object which he placed in Anne's outstretched hand. For a long time she stared at Baldwin's wedding ring glittering in the afternoon sun.

"That is your husband's ring?"

"Yes."

"I had to be certain." Robert Winter turned to go.

Anne stopped him. "Where is my husband's body?"

"Please, Mistress Anne, the magistrate will come here soon. I am an old man, please forgive me."

He left the house and met Colonel Hargrave on the veranda.

"Did you tell her?" asked the colonel.

"I could not, I gave her the ring is all."

"The murderers have been caught and taken to the gaol. The man who informed on the others will be given thirty-nine lashes, with your permission, of course, and sent off the island."

"Aye. That is agreeeable to me."

"Go now. I must tell Anne what happened."

When the colonel entered the room he found Anne pacing the floor with long agitated strides.

"Mistress Anne, I've come . . ."

Anne stopped, looked straight up into Colonel Hargrave's eyes. He fell silent.

"Colonel, my husband is dead. I've guessed that much. What I want to learn from you is where his body is kept."

"There is no body, Mistress. I think . . ."

"I don't care what you think—I demand to know. It is my right to know."

"His body was burned."

"How? Why?" Anne's voice was so harsh, so desperate, no one in the room dared move.

"We might never have known, Mistress, but for one eyewitness. It seems two Maroon men and a gang of Winter's rebellious slaves attacked Mr. Sommerwood on the road near Winter's place. He fought bravely, killing the two Maroons and one or two of the slaves before they . . ."

"They what?"

The colonel glanced at Mary Elizabeth clutching her mother's hand. Anne realized the colonel's concern. "Ruth, take Mary Elizabeth up to her room, please."

"No, I'm staying here. I will hear this."

"You see, Anne, they hooked him in a tree, then set fire to him."

Matt was on his feet. "Hooked? You don't mean a meat

hook, do you?"

"Aye."

"Jesus God!" Matt did not see Anne fall into Mary Elizabeth's arms or Ruth rush to help them both to the sofa. That day working with Sang he had seen the hogmeat gang using hooks which resembled the prong of an anchor. Matt turned to Sang for confirmation of the hideous picture forming in his mind. The black man stood rigid, his hat crushed in his two hands, tears streaming down his face.

Anne revived somewhat, held upright between Mary Elizabeth and Ruth. The colonel continued. "One of the men who knew your husband ran to the plantation house to get help, but it was too late. The tree was blazing by the time they got back to the place."

"Baldwin is buried there, then?"

"After Winter found the ring, he ordered mounds of dirt and covered the area. We caught the men who did it. They will hang at dawn." Unable to stop himself, he launched into a full report of the day's events. "The uprising is put down. The Regulars caught the conspirators, and the leaders were hanged. Others are to be shipped off the island. The Maroon chief, a woman, if you can believe it, one Nanny, has escaped. When they find her she will be forced to sign a treaty. The governor will offer generous terms in order to prevent another incident like this one. He intends to grant her five hundred acres in Portland. At any rate, the captain thinks those will be the terms. If she offers any resistance, however, she will hang."

"Birds fighting over branches."

"Mistress?"

"Nothing, Colonel. Thank you for your trouble." Anne rose and went to the window. Concern for her mother had stopped Mary's tears but now she fell sobbing into Ruth's arms.

Colonel Hargrave cleared his throat once or twice. "I'll take my leave now, Mistress?" She had not heard him. Her mind was miles away; he could see that. Likewise, Matt and Sang dwelt on their own feelings. "Well, yes, I think

I'll go." The colonel thought it best to slip quietly out of the house.

"Anne?" Matt's intention was to offer her some word of comfort, but when he looked into her eyes, tears welled up in his own. Anne took him into her arms. He cried much the same way he had as a boy. Only this hurt went deeper than a bruised knee, and his tears were those of manly grief. "I'm sorry. I didn't mean to do this. Are you all right?"

"I will be. Go to Mary Elizabeth. She needs you now. She has just lost her father."

"I too."

"Indeed yes; he was a generous, loving man to all of us." She felt tears choke her words.

Ruth hesitated only a moment before coming to Anne to gather her into her arms. Anne's strength seemed to leave her and she gave herself up to Ruth's trust and friendship, needing, accepting her comforting touch. Having absorbed Ruth's physical warmth and love, Anne now needed to share the thoughts which had been gathering in her mind, feelings which she could not express.

Ruth sensed what Anne was thinking. "Where you go now?"

"To Mary."

"You want Ruth, or you want go 'lone?"

"I'll go alone. Please don't worry." She squeezed Ruth's hand reassuringly and left. Ruth looked at her husband. He stood in the same spot, head bowed, face wet with tears. She went to him and folded her arms around him. How very lucky she was, she thought, to be able to hold him once again.

Anne heard a parrot screech and lifted Mary's sword into the air to follow its flight across the sky into the mountains. She would follow it. As she turned, her hip struck hard against stone, her sword arm fell and the blade clattered onto Mary's tomb. Anne felt the scrape of Baldwin's ring against the stone as her body sank to the ground. Sobs tore through the marble as if to shake into life the bones interred there.

"You're not here. You've never really been here," she murmured as her lips met cold stone. "Mary!" Her cry of abandonment echoed in the mountains.

A purple flower fell into her hand. Anne stared at the delicate petals fluttering in her palm until their color absorbed her consciousness. "There you are," she said to Mary Read who stood smiling at her, dressed all in white, a glittering white. Suddenly a streak of violet shot forward as Mary held a small flower out to Anne. Slowly Mary's other arm rose as she pointed into the distance. "No, no, I can't." Anne shook her head. "I can't go there." Mary did not move. "No!" Anne's eyes flashed. After a moment she looked long and hard at the flower in her hand. "This is not the same . . ." Anne pulled herself to her feet. The odor of scorched wet leaves filled her nostrils, and the acrid taste of fear rose in her throat. Her hand gripped the hilt of Mary's sword, crushing the flower into her palm.

While Ryna prepared the baby's bath, Mary Elizabeth rocked Maura in her arms and Matt held them both in his. They had expressed their gratitude to the Ashanti woman as best they could, but Matt found no words to describe the feelings he experienced as he held his family secure in his arms. Ruth's frantic knocking broke into his dream.

"I sorry. No want trubble you, but I fine dis, like dis." She placed Matt's baldric and empty scabbard in his hands. "Why she take it?"

"Who? Anne? Where is she now?"

"Wid yo' mudder. I'spect."

"Ruth, get Sang and come with me. Mary, stay here."

"No, I'm coming with you. Ryna, take Maura."

Matt put on his brace of pistols and took up his musket and ammunition. "Ryna, keep this pistol. There may be more trouble."

Anne found the abeng on the moist ledge in the mountain wall where she had left it twelve years before.

Without laying down her sword, Anne took up the horn and swished it in the pool until it gleamed in the late afternoon sun. Then placing her finger over the hole at the tip of the horn, she put her lips to the opening on its concave side and blew. An eerie blast sounded up the mountain. Laying the abeng aside, Anne held Mary's sword in both hands and waited.

Nanny heard both calls, first what sounded like her name echoing in the valley and now what she knew to be her name voiced by the abeng.

"Who call Nanny?" Closing her eyes and clamping her hands over her ears the words roared up from the depths of her and reverberated in her body. "I bring da mountain down on her. Now I do dat." Nanny opened her eyes to fix a piercing stab at the ledge above the waterfall but a black shield dropped in front of her eyes and blocked her vision of falling rock. A strange feeling of fear rumbled her bowels. She considered the unfamiliar sensation and recounted her losses. Many my people die dis day an' many mo' sent 'way in ships. Yamou hanged. "Afiba, why you leave Nanny alone!" Anguish clouded her eyes, rendering her powerless once more. She groped for her machete. Raging against destiny, Nanny approached the precipice above the fall.

Anne tossed the abeng into the water. She wanted to jump in after it and slip into death, but that would not secure the plantation for her children and grandchildren. Only a final confrontation with Nanny would accomplish that. What if I fail, she thought; the old fear like a slow poison dissipated her resolve. She tightened her grip on the sword hilt and at once her body flooded with warmth.

After what seemed an eternity Nanny appeared on the ledge above her. Dropping down a rope she descended the mountainside and stood before Anne. She was clothed in a striped robe just as she had been the first time Anne had seen her.

It seemed another eternity before Nanny took her eyes from Anne's and advanced towards her, machete in hand.

Blocking Nanny's thrusts, Anne retreated around the rim of the pool. Nanny advanced steadily and Anne's skill seemed useless against the power of the Maroon woman's assault. As Anne's foot tangled in the undergrowth bringing her to her knees, Nanny slipped in the slime at the water's edge. Both women recovered their footing and the fighting continued.

Anne could find no advantage until they came into the darkened narrow passage under the falls. Her vision dimmed by the change in light, Nanny hesitated for an instant. Anne's sword lashed across Nanny's eyes, blinding her. At the same moment Nanny thrust at Anne a mortal wound. The sound of approaching horses thundered in her ears as Nanny beat the air with her machete, trying to find her enemy. Through darkening eyes Anne saw Matt level his pistol and fire. The ball struck Nanny's right shoulder and the machete dropped from her hand.

On her knees now, clutching her side, Anne grabbed Nanny's weapon and tossed it into the pool. The clatter of more horses alarmed the Ashanti; Nanny reached for the wall and used it to guide her way out of the falls. Just as the soldiers arrived Matt fired again, this time hitting Nanny's left shoulder. Neither bullet seemed to bother the woman. As the detail of soldiers advanced on her, Nanny continued to grope her way along the wall toward the rope she had dropped.

Once the Maroon chief had moved out of the falls, Matt ran to Anne and caught her as she was about to slide into the pool. He placed her in Mary's arms, then moved out of the way as Ruth tried to stem Anne's bleeding.

The soldiers had been ordered by their captain to capture Nanny alive. If there was to be lasting peace in the East, someone had to enforce it. Only Nanny could do that. She must surrender. Sensing the nearness of the soldiers, Nanny bellowed like a wild beast and swung her giant arms in every direction. The captain ordered his men to point their rifles towards the sky and fire.

Nanny forced her consciousness to become aware of her

physical body. If she had been mortally wounded, she would not linger but would will her soul heavenward. Nanny did not need eyesight to work that magic. She felt no new pains, but a stiff breeze pulled the cloth of her garment tight against her thighs and Nanny felt her warrior self desert her. She thrust both fists forward and waited for the soldiers to bind her wrists.

Mary rocked Anne in her arms, pleading with her mother not to leave them. Although she knew the action was useless, Ruth continued to press her napkin to Anne's side. Matt held Anne's hand to his wet cheek.

"Bury me next to your mother, Matt. Leave Baldwin's ring on my finger."

"Yes, don't talk now. We'll get you home soon. Ruth?"

Ruth put her hand to her lips and shook her head. Rinsing her napkin in the cool water, she bathed Anne's forehead, stroking it gently.

"Don't go, Mama. We need you. How will Maura grow up without you? Who will teach her to be strong?"

"You will . . . your courage will . . ." Anne felt herself slipping into darkness and clutched at Ruth to pull herself out of the horizon. "Those shots. Ruth, is she dead? I must know before . . ."

Anne gasped as pain seized her. She clutched Ruth's hand.

Ruth watched the soldiers lead the Ashanti woman away. Although dignity clung to her every move, defeat enveloped her bearing.

"She gone, Miz Anne. Nanny no hurt us anymore. You . . . you go . . ."

Mary kissed her mother's lips and felt Anne's body go limp in her arms. The drumming of the water was the only sound heard as colors streaked the sky silhouetting the figures at the waterfall in the Blue Mountains.